'TIL DEBT DO US PART

MICHELLE LARKS

URBAN CHRISTIAN

www.urbanchristianonline.net

Urban Books
1199 Straight Path
West Babylon, NY 11704

ISBN- 13: 978-1-60162-994-4
ISBN- 10: 1-60162-994-X

First Printing July 2009
Printed in the United States of America

10   9   8   7   6   5   4   3   2   1

This is a work of fiction. Any references or similarities to actual events, real people, living, or dead, or to real locales are intended to give the novel a sense of reality. Any similarity in other names, characters, places, and incidents is entirely coincidental.

Distributed by Kensington Corp.
Submit Wholesale Orders to:
Kensington Publishing Corp.
C/O Penguin Group (USA) Inc.
Attention: Order Processing
405 Murray Hill Parkway
East Rutherford, NJ 07073-2316
Phone: 1-800-526-0275
Fax: 1-800-227-9604

'TIL DEBT DO US PART

Dedication

This book is dedicated to all my angels who helped me in my time of need, beginning November 2008: Mr. and Mrs. Akkman Sage, Mr. Jackie Anderson, Mr. and Mrs. Gregory Evans, Amania Drane, Kelly Manges, Mrs. Bertha Larks, and Sabrina Harris. I will always appreciate your outpouring of love and kindness! May God bless you, as you have blessed me!

Acknowledgments

First and foremost, I'd like to give thanks to God from whom all blessings flow. Where would any of us be without His grace and mercy? I'd like to especially thank those who've supported me from day one and continue to do so today. You have no idea how much incentive and encouragement you give me to continue writing. Thanks for those of you who email me and offer feedback. Keep it coming.

I'd like to thank my reading committee: Eveline, Angie, and Keisha. Your comments and criticism have been duly noted. Thanks for reading fast for me, and you know why. I owe you.

I'd like to thank my family: my mothers, Mary, Jean, and Bertha; thanks for loving me and always being in my corner. To all of my sisters and brothers: know that I love you with all my heart. It is an honor and privilege to be your sibling. To all my nieces and nephews: I love you, and I am so proud of the young men and women you have become. And to the younger ones, I know you will make me just as proud! Families are a blessing.

To my daughters: what can I say except I'm so proud of you and love you so much. . . .

To the many book clubs that selected my books to read: thank you! To the ones that invited me to participate in your meetings: what an honor, and I had such a great time. You made me feel right at home.

Special thanks to Joylynn. You are a treasure. I can't stop singing your praises. Tee, thank you for always having my back.

To all the online book clubs and reviewers: thank you for your gracious support!

I would be remiss if I didn't send a special shout-out to a great group of people, whom I've never had the pleasure to meet in person. They are my MySpace friends. These people send me comments everyday or weekly and are such a source of inspiration. They make me laugh and cheer me when I'm feeling low. Thank you for being there, Heavenly, Jazzy Diva, Patty, SisterNCharge, Rhonda, Peaches, VanillaLatte, Lady E, Elvita, Bobbi, Maggs, Bea, Rhonnie, Kathy Rolanda, Karen, Melinda, Work In Progress, God's Angel, Prophetess Sabrina Brown, Reverend Charlotte Brooks, Len, Destined for Greatness, Slim, Liz, Dee, Southern Hospitality, Dusti, Sensual Sounds, All For The Glory of God, CJ, Mizz Dee, Dr. Annette, Lady Deborah, Hot Caramel, It's All About Me and My Babies, Shanki, Pastor Gary Martin, DIU, DelWilngVesl, Mrs. G., Tylene, Sherry, Christella, Ms. Sexy T., Cleo, Shelli, Shawnique, Meserette, Lady G., Joe-Will Productions, Pastor Sheila, Tiffany, Blessed, Bea, Curthena, Karen, NardsBaby, Women Of Greatness Virtual Book Store, Angel, Minister Jak, and Bea! Keep the comments coming . . .

I'd like to send special kudos to my sister, Patrice. She untiringly promotes and sells my books as if they are her own. Love you, sis.

Last, I'd like to thank my husband, Fredrick, my #1 fan and promoter.

Michelle

Chapter 1

Harrah's Casino, located in Joliet, Illinois, is also known as "the boat" by the local population. After Chicago, Joliet is the second largest city in Illinois and is located about forty miles south of the Windy City. Joliet is nicknamed the *City of Champions*, and gamblers pay homage to the moniker daily as they try to excel and beat the gambling odds.

The floating venue was jam-packed, as it always tends to be on Friday evenings as people try to become the next millionaire. The weather outdoors was unseasonably warm. The temperatures tend to be fickle in Chicago, and residents hoped spring weather was waiting just around the corner.

It was the first Friday of March 2001. It was payday for many of the casino customers, so the pickings were sweet for the wealthy owners.

Men and women of all ethnic backgrounds were mostly dressed casually in jeans and colorful tops. They stood or sat, waiting for their turn to dance with Lady Luck.

Good fortune comes in the guise of the roulette, blackjack, and crap tables; as well as the coveted piece-de-resistance ... the slot machine.

The atmosphere crackled with excitement as bells sounded or red and blue bulbs flashed ... announcing winners.

A firm tug on the handle of a slot machine could change a person's financial status magically, or as usually was the case, create new ones.

With bated breath, the patrons awaited the outcome of the flip of a card, roll of the dice, or display on the slot machine. Hoping and praying the gambling gods would shine upon them.

Waitresses flitted in and out of crowds, carrying black trays filled with cups of soft drinks and alcoholic beverages. The clientele gratefully gulped down the cold liquids as they continued their quest for financial freedom.

Exclamations of joy and relief shone on the winners' faces when they hit the jackpot. Those not as fortunate sat tensely with worried expressions on their wrinkled brows as they chewed their fingernails to the quick with anxiety, wondering how they were going to pay their bills since they used that money to gamble.

A ring of perspiration stained the armpits of Nichole 'Nikki' Singleton's mandarin orange silk blouse. She had removed the matching brown tweed jacket of her pantsuit hours ago. It was slung half off the back of her seat.

Nikki's round dark brown eyes glinted with anticipation. She unconsciously stroked her chin as she mentally calculated the odds of her winning the roll of the dice. Nikki looked down at her stack of chips on the craps table; coming up was the all-important make or break bet.

She clutched the dice tightly in her shaking, damp left hand. Her honey brown face was drawn with tension. And Nikki's perfectly coifed, bone straight, shoulder length, relaxed, dark hair stood spiked on end from her continually running her hands through it.

Before the tiny white and black cubes left her hand, Nikki looked upward and said a quick prayer. "Lord, please let the dice fall in my favor." Her eyes widened in disbelief, and her shoulders slumped forward dejectedly after seeing how the dice landed. She hadn't been able to catch a break the entire evening.

The croupier raked Nikki's former chips to his side of the table. He shook his head at her apologetically as she picked up her purse and jacket and stepped away from the table. Her stomach cramped spasmodically from the sizeable amount of money she'd just lost.

An older white woman, clad in faded stonewashed blue jeans and an old faded Northwestern sweatshirt with big, brassy blond hair and dark shades, shot Nikki a sympathetic look. She shrugged her shoulders as she slipped into Nikki's vacated place.

Nikki and her best friend, Maya Nelson, had arrived three hours ago, around seven o'clock that evening. As soon as they entered the vessel, Maya made a beeline to the ladies' room while Nikki sped to the cashier cage and plunked down a cashier's check for fifteen hundred dollars. She wanted the amount credited to her Harrah's gambling card.

Nikki had counted on winning big that evening, emphatically sure that Lady Luck would hover over her. Instead, as the evening progressed, the capricious woman deserted her unmercifully.

As Nikki stood in silent shock a few steps away from the table, she massaged her temples, pondering the latest dent in her finances. Meanwhile Maya punched the spin button on the slot machine that she had been playing on for most of the evening. Like Nikki's, Maya's stash had dwindled, but not as drastically. She looked across the room and noted the panicky expression on Nikki's face; frozen in place like a doe caught in headlights.

Cutting her eyes at the machine morosely one more time, Maya decided to call it a night. She strolled across the room to see how badly her friend was faring. A woman darted into Maya's warmed seat and pulled her Harrah's card out of her purse.

"How's it going, girl?" Maya sighed audibly, pushing a thin micro braid away from her face. "You look like you lost your best friend. And we know that's not the case because I'm right here. So what's up?"

"This just isn't my night," Nikki said. Her voice trembled with frustration. Like a raging brush fire, her mind was consumed with getting her hands on more cash.

"You know the first rule of winning is quitting while you're ahead," Maya said, scolding her friend. She yawned and covered her mouth. Her fingernails were painted a cocoa brown shade, which nearly matched her even skin tone. She was dressed in a black rayon pantsuit and a frilly white chiffon blouse that flattered her full-sized figure. Minus a few strategically placed strands, her micro braids were pulled off her forehead into a thick ponytail. "It's getting late, Nik. And since I have to work in the morning, I'm gonna head home now. How much longer do you plan on staying here?"

"I need to at least try to win back some of the money I lost; so probably another hour," Nikki replied. She tried not to look too eagerly at the ATM machines located near the cashier's cage. She wished Maya would just leave so she could handle her business.

"Okay, I'm out. Call me when you get home to let me know you made it safely." Maya looked at Nikki with concern. "Remember . . . gambling is just a recreational activity just like a ballgame. It's just something to do to pass the time. Don't make the mistake of taking this stuff too seriously."

"I know." Nikki sighed as she patted down a lock of her unruly hair. "I don't plan on staying here much longer either. Unlike you, I have a long ride home."

The friends lived in different parts of the city. Nikki resided on the far north side of Chicago, and Maya lived closer to Joliet in a southern suburb. When they traveled to the boat, they usually didn't ride together. The two young women bade each other farewell.

As Maya stood before the double exit doors, her full cheeks morphed from a smile into a frown. She pulled the black leather strap of her shoulder bag onto her shoulder as she watched her friend walk over to what her six-year-old son, TJ, called the money machine.

Nikki's manicured pearl-tipped fingers shook as she entered her pin number on the keypad and pressed enter. A slip of paper listing her account balance, spewed from the tiny slot. The paper informed her that she had already reached her maximum withdrawal limit for the day.

As Nikki held the paper away from her face, her eyes nearly bulged out of their sockets. The account balance of the household account she shared with her husband, Jeff, was dangerously low. And Nikki had overdrawn her own personal checking account about a week ago.

Miniscule watery pinpricks of fear stung Nikki's eyeballs. Her heart began palpitating rapidly as she realized the balloon payment for the home equality credit line that she and Jeff had borrowed from the bank for remodeling the apartment building they owned, was due in a couple of weeks.

Wiping her eyes and squaring her shoulders, a million reasons justifying her actions seeped through Nikki's mind. She cocked her head to the side and mathematically calculated how she could continue to play and win since her luck had been so rotten. She told herself not to panic and to write the casino another check for five hundred dollars. Realistically, doing so should be okay since payday was Tuesday, and her account was sheltered by overdraft protection. The action could possibly extend her credit. After all she was a VIP customer. At least that's what Harrah's told her in the letters that came to her house monthly with free comps.

An hour later, following futile stints on the roulette table and slot machine, Nikki still hadn't managed to recoup her losses. She groaned as she half-heartedly pulled the handle of the slot machine one last time. Nikki glanced at her wristwatch and shuttered. It was already eleven o'clock. She only had an hour to get home before Jeff did.

The night had been a total bust for Nikki. She'd lost the entire fifteen hundred dollars, plus the five hundred dollar check she'd written to the casino and her fifty dollars seed money that had been folded up inside the depths of her wallet.

As she put on her jacket and headed for the exit, Nikki suddenly remembered the monthly bank statement would probably be delivered tomorrow. She broke out in a cold sweat, and her breathing became shallow as her thoughts darted to the possibility of Jeff opening the mail before she did. There was no doubt in her mind that her husband's anger would blow the roof off the house if he discovered her extracurricular activities. Nikki had been positive that she was going to win tonight and be able to deposit the monies in their joint checking account that was precariously low at that moment.

She burned rubber as she departed the parking lot and drove perilously close to eighty miles per hour on Interstate 55. Upon reaching the outskirts of the downtown area, she exited onto Interstate 94 and made it home with fifteen minutes to spare. She hurriedly backed her custom tinted baby blue colored Chrysler 300 inside the garage at the rear of the three-flat apartment building.

Jeffrey and Nichole Singleton resided on the north side of Chicago in Wicker Park. And the distance was not a hop, skip, or jump from Joliet.

As soon as Nikki shut and locked the front door, she unbuttoned her blouse, unzipped her pants, and hopped down the hallway into the bathroom. She quickly shucked off her clothing and dropped it into an untidy pile next to the clothes hamper. Then she slipped into a red and black teddy hanging on the peg of the bathroom door. When she finished, Nikki heard the lock turn on the back door, and she dove into the bed like an Olympic swimmer diving into a pool.

She shifted her body to her left side, away from the door, hoping her rapidly thudding heart would slow down. Nikki burrowed her body under the brown and beige striped comforter.

As Jeff walked into the darkened bedroom, he turned on and dimmed the overhead light. He glanced at the bed, and then walked into the blue and white striped wall-papered bathroom. He scooped Nikki's clothing from the floor and dropped it into the white rattan clothes hamper. Then he opened the shower stall door and turned on the faucets. A deluge of warm water from the showerhead soaked his five foot eleven inch, lanky, dark teak brown frame.

After he finished showering, Jeff draped a towel around his midsection and returned to the bedroom. He sat on the side of the bed, and with another towel, dried his close-cropped hair. His eyes were small and beady, and he had long lashes and thick eyebrows. A thin moustache covered his thick upper lip. His left cheek bared the remnants of a fading scar that he received during a brawl at school in eighth grade. Jeff was employed as the second shift supervisor in the Information Technology Department for the City of Chicago.

He glanced over at Nikki again, surprised she was already in bed. Usually after he arrived home from work on Fridays, they would go out to one of the local cafés for a bite to eat.

Jeff leaned over and kissed his wife's shoulder. Nikki shrugged her shoulders, feigning sleep. She opened one eye, then the other. Nikki looked up and returned her husband's smile.

"Hey, honey. You're home already? I guess I lost track of time." She sat up in the bed and stretched her arms over her head. "How was your day? I didn't hear from you all evening."

"I was busy," Jeff admitted. He picked up the bottle of lotion from his nightstand and smeared the white liquid over his body. "We had a major system outage tonight and couldn't get a hold of the primary or backup on-call programmers. So that made for a tense night. Finally, I ended up calling one of the team leaders." He waved his hand impatiently. "Needless to say, Mr. McDonald wasn't happy about his weekend being disturbed."

Nikki smoothed her hair back. "Give me the lotion so I can do your back." Jeff handed her the bottle and she poured drops of the pear-scented lotion into her hand, then massaged the thick liquid onto Jeff's shoulders and upper back. "That's terrible. I don't understand how you can work in the IT field. I couldn't do it. The job would be too stressful for me."

"It's not too bad most of the time." Jeff nodded his head. "Ahh, that feels good." When Nikki finished, he slithered into the bed and pulled her into his arms. His breath felt velvety soft on Nikki's neck. "I thought we'd try the new sushi bar that opened down the street when I came home tonight. What's wrong? Why are you in bed so early? Don't you feel well?" he asked.

"I had premenstrual cramps earlier," Nikki lied. She shifted her body in the bed to get comfortable. "After I came home from work, I took some painkillers and laid down for a while. I feel much better now."

Jeff turned on the television, and they lay entwined in each other's arms, watching the news.

"How was your day?" Jeff asked during a commercial break. He stroked the top of Nikki's head, which rested on his shoulder.

"It wasn't too bad. Victor assigned me a new project today, even though my plate is already full." Her dainty nose wrinkled in exasperation. "I have the dubious honor of creating print ads for a new retail, startup dot-com company. The concept is for the client to have an enterprise like a virtual shopping mall." She regaled him with tales about her day, deliberately omitting her clandestine trip to Joliet.

Jeffrey Singleton was an intelligent, methodical man with his eyes on the prize. His firm desire was that he and Nikki attain financial freedom and be able to retire from their jobs before the age of fifty.

When Nikki and Jeff announced their engagement six years ago, they solicited advice from several friends employed in the finance field. They eventually selected Jeff's college buddy, Ronald Sheldon, along with Nikki's friend, Lindsay Mason, to develop a financial plan for them.

After further discussion, Nikki and Jeff mutually decided Ron was best suited to oversee their financial investments. Jeff handled the household finances the first two years of their four-year marriage. Then last year, Nikki decided that she wanted a shot at the task. Their finances had been on a downward slope for the past seven months. And to make matters worse, Jeff was left in the dark regarding his wife's costly new hobby that would wreak havoc over their lives.

Chapter 2

On a sultry July afternoon, shortly after Nikki and Jeff's third anniversary, Nikki and her friends, Arial, Lindsay, Pearl, and Maya had met at an Italian bistro located in Old Town for their monthly book club discussion and dinner.

All of the women, except Maya, were married. She had been divorced for two years. The friends had just finished their meals and were still discussing the book of the month, *PG County*, by Connie Briscoe.

The waitress had just departed from the table after delivering dinner beverages to the women. Arial steered the conversation to finances, and how the heroine in the book, Barbara Bentley, was totally dependent on her husband.

"I think we're all in agreement that whoever makes the most money and pays the bills is the breadwinner, and by rights, head of the household," Arial observed. "Let's talk about who pays the bills in our households. I'll start." She giggled. Her green and black, polka dot sleeveless sundress fit Arial like a glove. "I tried writing the checks for a while, but I forgot to include some of Charles's bills . . . like his student loans. And like Marvin sang, I had to give it up. We were almost headed to Judge Mablean's court behind my snafus." She snickered at the memory.

Maya shook her head from side to side and interjected. "When I was married," she pointed to her chest, "I had no choice except to handle the finances. Money slipped through Tony's hands like running water from a faucet. That's part of the reason we're not together today," she joked, though the experience still stung.

"I'm not good at managing money either," Pearl confessed. Her pretty ivory face reddened. She reared her head back, and her long black hair cascaded over her shoulders. "Money isn't my or Lemont's strong suit. He tossed a coin and unfortunately, I won the call." She chuckled as the women stared at her with undivided attention, like they were watching a movie. "The first month I was late paying the rent, and then two months after that, I totally forgot to pay the rent. We were almost evicted before Lemont took over paying the bills."

Nikki laughed along with her friends. This was the first time the women shared any type of financial woes with each other. She debated whether she should say anything about her and Jeff's arrangements. She looked up to find Arial's eyes boring into hers. Nikki's body tensed up, and she nervously twirled the straw in her virgin daiquiri.

Instead of being merely pretty, Arial was the beautiful one of the group. Her features oozed sex. Her heavily lidded bedroom eyes, with light brown irises, and her high cheekbones, screamed model. Arial had an hourglass shape, which she showed off by wearing tight, revealing clothing.

"Well, we know who pays the bills in my house," Lindsay said smugly, folding her arms across her ample chest. "I didn't major in finance at DePaul and get an MBA for nothing." She turned and stared at Nikki. "Aron has no problem with me handling the finances." She sipped her Apple Martini and patted her bobbed coif of red frosted colored locks. "What about you and Jeff? Who wears the pants in your household? I mean besides your husband," she said to Nikki.

"Well," Nikki answered slowly, "I'm sure everyone here has probably figured out Jeff manages the money in our household." She smiled brightly. "Now me, personally I just like to spend it. The more we make for me to spend, the better." She guffawed, and she and Maya shared high fives.

Lindsay tsked and raised her perfectly arched left eyebrow. Her family had migrated from Haiti in the early sixties. Lindsay was short in stature, dark in complexion, and thick in build.

"Nikki, Nikki, Nikki." Lindsay looked at her friend contemptuously. "I don't understand your reasoning at all. Didn't you do a double major in Accounting and Art at CSU? I think that accounting degree says you're just as capable as Jeff at handling the family finances. And why is it you always seem to defer to your husband, and let him call the shots? It seems to me," Lindsay nodded, looking at Arial for confirmation of her statements, "that Jeff definitely has the upper hand in your marriage."

Nikki's friends were an ethnicly mixed group of women. Pearl was of Asian descent, while Lindsay was Haitian. Arial, Maya, and Nikki were all African-Americans. They named the group the League of Nations Book Club and hoped at some point to attract other women of varied cultural backgrounds.

Maya picked up a breadstick and slathered butter over it. She paused, then held the knife out toward Lindsay and drawled, "You know what? You ain't right, Lindsay Mason. You're just trying to start trouble. Now I look at it like this. If Nik doesn't have a problem with Jeff paying their bills, then neither should you. Let's keep it real. I wish I had a man to pay my bills. I'm with Nikki; finances are just a thankless task. But someone has to do it."

"Humph," Lindsay snorted as her head swiveled on her neck. She stared at the women around the table. "This is the new millennium. Hello! The last time I checked, women are just as capable as men at doing anything, and that includes making the money and paying the bills."

"I'm not representing womanhood, Lindsay. Jeff is just better at handling finances than I am." Nikki tried feebly to defend herself. *Arial probably set me up so Lindsay could go in for the kill.* "Is there any possibility we could have a book club meeting without you dissing my husband?"

"I didn't know you were keeping count," Lindsay answered coldly. "We all know how controlling Jeff is," she proclaimed, cutting her eyes sharply back at Nikki. "We just don't want you to end up like Barbara Bentley in the book. She was a prime example of a woman not being in control. Don't you remember reading how her husband walked all over her? We're too strong to put up with that kind of antiquated mess."

Nikki looked to Maya for back up. "The last time I checked our bank balance, it didn't say Jeff and I were multi-millionaires. So I don't see a comparison between me and my husband and the couple in the book," Nikki stated vehemently. Her hands trembled slightly as she clutched her drink. The atmosphere was becoming heated at the table.

"And it's not like you two are hurting for money . . . y'all own property," Lindsay interjected quickly. "Your mama gave you an apartment building for a wedding gift. That's a lot more than the rest of us can say we received from our parents." She looked at the ladies. Arial had a smirk on her face, Pearl looked uncomfortable, and Maya wore an angry scowl.

Lindsay continued with her tirade. "Aron and I were

paying a thirty-year mortgage until I convinced him to see the light. We refinanced and procured a fifteen-year mortgage. Shoot, you own the building you live in free and clear, and you have tenants occupying apartments as well. It's not like Jeff brought anything as substantial to the table."

"Now, Lindsay, that was just foul," Pearl lisped, as she held her hand out. "It sounds like you have a grudge against Nikki because she and Jeff passed on the financial plan you put together for them."

Lindsay shook her head vigorously from side to side, denying Pearl's accusations. Her plump brown face, surrounded by a pair of dimples, segued into a frown. She leaned forward and rapped on the table.

"Now let's just keep it real, ladies. Jeff vetoed my proposition, not Nikki. And you're right, I'm still a little hurt that *our girl* didn't stand up for a sister," Lindsay admitted.

Maya dropped the half-eaten breadstick on her plate and rubbed her hands together. "What you need to do is let that old mess go. Nik and Jeff have been married for how long . . . a little over three years now? You need to drop it." She quickly changed the subject and looked around the table at the other women. "What book are we reading next month?" she asked.

Lindsay's mouth snapped shut. She clinched her lips tightly together, feeling if she opened her mouth, she'd end up saying something she might later regret. She stood up abruptly and took a few steps away from the table. She paused, then glanced at Arial and said, "I'm going to the ladies' room, and when I return, I'll be ready to go. I'll send the waitress over with the check."

Maya telegraphed vibrations of annoyance at the two women. Pearl's face reddened with embarrassment at

Lindsay's snide antics. Arial reached inside her burgundy Coach bag and removed the matching wallet.

The waitress brought the check to the table. "Can I get you ladies anything else?" The women shook their heads. She laid the leather money holder on the table next to Arial. "The young lady told me to give this to you," she said.

Arial picked up the bill and quickly scanned it. Then she reached into her bag and pulled out a miniature calculator.

Nikki's lower lip trembled. She blinked rapidly as her eyes became awash in tears. She had never felt so humiliated in her life. Through bleary orbs, she removed a twenty-dollar bill and five ones from her purse. She laid them on the table next to the white and red-checkered napkin to the left of her plate.

"I'm going outside. It's a little bit too stuffy in here." Nikki stood and snapped her handbag shut. "I'll see you at church tomorrow," she said to Arial. "Pearl, I'll talk to you next week." She stumbled through the sea of white linen topped tables, and out the front entrance.

Lindsay arrived at the table wearing an *I-don't-give-a-darn* expression pasted on her face. "Where's Nikki? Did she leave already?" she asked innocently, as she sat in her seat.

Maya stood and threw her napkin that had been resting on her lap on the top of the table. "You know what your problem is, Lindsay?" She pointed a quivering finger in Lindsay's direction. Her chest was heaving with righteous indignation. "You're jealous of Nikki. You've been acting this way since we were in high school. Guess what, sister? School is over, and that's what you need to do . . . get over whatever issues you have with Nik. Heck, I wouldn't trust you with my money either. Jeff and Nikki are doing just fine. Keep your opinions to yourself and leave them alone."

"You know what?" Lindsay folded her arms across her shaking chest and glared at Maya. "I didn't ask your opinion, which means you should keep it to yourself like you just advised me. You're still fighting Nikki's battles for her like you did when we were in school. How much do we owe for the bill, Ari?"

"Um, hold on." Arial looked down and quickly divided the total and tip by five. She looked up at the women. "Twenty-two dollars each . . . that should do it," she answered. She returned a card, which listed tip amounts in increments of fifteen and twenty percent, back inside her wallet.

Lindsay stood, walked around the table, and gave Arial her portion of the bill. She then returned to her seat.

"Ladies, I wish I could say this evening has been a pleasure, but I'd just be lying." With that said, Maya sashayed out of the restaurant after dropping a twenty-dollar bill and eight quarters on the table in front of Arial.

"I'm going home too," Pearl said as she rose from her seat. She looked at Arial disapprovingly. "Sometimes you and Lindsay go too far," she said, before making her exit.

Arial put the money in the holder. "Perhaps you were a little hard on Nik. You know she's sensitive," she said to Lindsay.

Lindsay opened a tube of lipstick and lined her lips, as she looked at the mirror inside her silver compact. She snapped it shut and peered at Arial. "Maybe I overdid it a little bit, but sometimes I get tired of Nikki simpering over how wonderful Jeff is. Just listening to her makes me want to vomit. And yes, I still feel hurt that she decided to go with her husband's recommendation for their financial planning over mine. We've been friends for too many years for Nikki to pick a white boy over me."

Arial stood and picked her book up off the table. "But

as you just said, Jeff is her husband. Her first loyalty should be to him."

"Not then he wasn't." Lindsay tossed her locks over her shoulder. "Technically, he was just her fiancé then. Don't you remember us telling you how Nikki, Maya and I took a vow never to put a man before our friendship when we attended high school?" She stood and smoothed down the front of her tight black skirt. A ribbed tube top encased by a wide red belt, black stiletto heels, and dark hosiery completed the ensemble. "Let's go. I want to check out that new club uptown before it gets too late," she said to Arial, glancing down at her watch.

"Okay, but I can't stay long. I told Chas I wouldn't be out too late. He's watching the baby." Arial and Lindsay exited the building together and walked across the street to Arial's black Nissan Maxima.

As Nikki drove home, her face was flushed from anger. She turned on the radio and listened to an oldie station. "Mama Said" was playing. How appropriate. When she walked inside the apartment, her footsteps were heavy on the waxed, glossy hardwood floor.

She found Jeff lying on his back atop the black and white striped couch in the den. One of his legs was thrown casually across the arm of the sofa. He was barefoot and dressed in an old, worn football jersey and cut off dark denim shorts. The threads on the neckline of the top were unraveling.

He was watching a bootleg copy of the new Bruce Willis movie that a friend had loaned him. The action sounds on the big screen television were equal to that of movie screen quality. Jeff didn't miss the consternation on his wife's face when she plopped down wearily on the chair across from the sofa. He sat upright, glanced at the television, and then back at Nikki.

"How was dinner? What did you have to eat, and did you bring a doggy bag home with you?" He smacked his lips and rubbed his hands together.

"We had Italian cuisine," Nikki answered absent-mindedly, clenching and unclenching her fists. "The food was quite good. We went to a restaurant that one of Lindsay's clients recommended."

Jeff lifted his chin a notch defensively when Nikki said Lindsay's name. Of all his wife's friends, Lindsay was his least favorite. He turned his attention back to the television and pressed the pause button on the remote control before dropping it on the sofa. As Jeff stood, he noticed Nikki was still staring into space. "I'm going to the kitchen for a Corona. Do you want anything?"

"No," Nikki sighed. "I do want to talk to you though."

After he returned from the kitchen, Jeff sat back down on the sofa. He gave Nikki his undivided attention after he twisted open the bottle. "What's up?" He sensed that Lindsay had been needling his wife again. Jeff knew what a drama queen Lindsay was and he hated when Nikki went out with her friends, especially when Ms. Mason was in attendance.

Nikki nervously twirled the ends of her hair and moistened her lips. "What do you think about me handling the household finances?"

"Why would you want to do that? I thought we had decided that I would do that task," Jeff took a sip of his beer.

"I know that's what we decided before we got married," she corrected her husband. "But what's wrong with me doing them now?" Nikki had a plaintive, defensive whine in her voice.

Jeff opened his mouth. He tried to rein in the impatient feelings that coursed through his veins. Nikki was in a snit, and he didn't want to upset her more. "You know something; I really hate when you go out to dinner with your girls." He held up his left hand. "Don't get me wrong. It just seems like something always comes up afterward that directly affects our relationship."

Nikki stood up and draped her arms across her chest. She walked to the maple fireplace, then turned and faced her husband; choosing her words carefully. "What if something were to happen to you, Jeff? I wouldn't have a clue as to how you have things set up. Plus my doing the finances will give you a break for a while. I'm not saying that I want to do them forever, but long enough to know I can handle the bills if you were out of commission."

Jeff slumped against the back of the sofa. He laced his hands together and placed them behind his head. "I don't understand why you let Lindsay get to you the way that you do. She knows which buttons to push to get you going. You never liked arithmetic, accounting, or anything relating to mathematics."

"True." She nodded. "I just majored in accounting in college to appease my parents. Anyway that's beside the point," Nikki added entreatingly. "Aren't we supposed to be a team? You know I came straight from my parents' house after we got married. I never had the opportunity to live alone, or with a roommate, other than in college, and my parents took care of my bills then. All I'm asking for is a chance to see if I can cut the mustard." She leaned forward in the chair and clasped her hands around her knees.

Jeff nodded and whispered, "You know we're a team, baby. I just don't see why you feel you need validation from your friends about what we do or don't do in our own house."

Nikki noticed his gruff demeanor. She decided to see if she could erase the frustration lines that bit deeply into his forehead. She walked over to him and sat down on his lap. Nikki held his face tenderly between her hands and sprinkled tiny kisses on his forehead and cheeks.

"Come on, Jeff. You know I don't like it when we argue. All I'm asking for is a shot at overseeing our finances, and if I screw things up, I'll gladly hand the checkbook back to you." She stroked the side of his face.

Jeff set the bottle on the end table and leaned forward. His arms encircled his wife's waist. "I guess your paying the bills is fine with me, but under one condition." He waggled his finger at her. "I don't want us to deviate too far from Ron's plan; especially the savings. Doing so will affect our other investments. How about we go over the checkbook on a weekly basis, and then eventually to a monthly basis? We'll check out the finances on Saturday mornings, and if the plan appears to be in jeopardy," he took Nikki's hands from his face, "then we're gonna have to start over. Because the significant dates we have planned for the future will fall behind . . . like having a baby."

Nikki smiled winningly and took Jeff's hand in her own. "I can live with us going over the numbers on Saturday mornings. But you know I'm not going to do anything to put our plan at risk." She rolled her eyes upward. "I want a baby just as much as you do." Gently tugging the frayed collar of Jeff's tee shirt, she added, "Did you miss me while I was gone?"

"What do you think?" He leaned over and kissed her lips.

The couple stood and walked hand in hand into the bedroom. Jeff embraced Nikki as they stood in the doorway. He kissed her deeply, devouring her lips. "Did I tell you how fine you looked this evening?" he asked.

Nikki shook her head, indicating he hadn't. Then she did a little pirouette in front of her husband. Jeff closed the bedroom door behind them.

Having dinner with her girls, and her having her way with Jeff later that night, led to Nikki being in charge of the family's finances. Access to all that money would also enabled her to succumb to a fierce gambling addiction.

Chapter 3

Following her severe loss at the casino, Nikki didn't get much rest the remainder of Friday night. She tossed and turned all night long. Her mind was consumed with thoughts of how she could keep the truth from Jeff about her debt; at least until she could win back the money.

Around seven o'clock the next morning, she fell into an exhausted sleep and didn't wake up until noon. Jeff, barefoot and wearing an old navy blue cotton robe, walked into the bedroom bearing breakfast delights.

Nikki sat upright in the bed and patted her tangled tresses of hair. She smiled at Jeff and kicked the sheet off her legs. She made a motion to rise from the bed to retrieve the coffee she could smell brewing from the kitchen.

"Whoa. Stay where you are," Jeff instructed her, gesturing his head toward the bed. He set a tray on a round, gray and purple striped clothed table positioned in a corner of the bedroom. He moved it next to the bed. "I'm in charge of breakfast this morning."

Nikki sat back against the headboard and crossed her legs. "That was sweet of you, honey. To what do I owe this pleasure?" she asked Jeff when he returned to the room carrying another tray for himself.

"Why does there have to be a reason or occasion? Can't a brother just spoil his woman sometimes?" He handed Nikki one of the trays that had a single white rose inside a crystal vase atop it.

Nikki's stomach grumbled at the sight of waffles smothered in maple syrup, with a dollop of butter running in the crevices, two sausage links, and a mug of coffee. Jeff had also prepared a bowl full of sweet blueberries with a sprinkling of sugar. He passed the bowl to Nikki, who immediately picked up a berry and ate it.

Jeff returned to the bed and retrieved his tray from the table minus the newspaper, which he left lying on the table.

"You can spoil your wife anytime you want," Nikki announced, popping another berry into her mouth. The fruit was sweet on her tongue. "Um, that tastes good," she moaned. She put one in Jeff's mouth, and he chewed it, smiling at her appreciatively while savoring the taste.

When they finished breakfast, Jeff took the trays into the kitchen. Then he returned to the bedroom and turned on the television to *CNN Headline News*. He lay back, and fifteen minutes into the program, he had dozed off.

Watching the rise and fall of Jeff's bare chest and the sated expression on his face, Nikki felt torn with indecision thinking maybe she should tell Jeff about her forays to Harrah's. What was the worst he could do to her? Sue her for divorce? She knew that she'd have to listen to him moan for the rest of their lives about how she messed up the financial plan. The losses were just that—*money*. There were more important aspects of life, like one's health. They were a young couple and could rebound from the trouncing of their finances since they had good jobs. And with God's help they could overcome the crisis.

Nikki nestled closer to her husband's body. She knew that she was the one who created the mess, and it was up to her to fix it. There was no doubt in her mind that the law of averages was on her side, and that her luck would change for the better at the casino. She just had to ride out the storm. Nikki finally drifted off to sleep.

The couple awakened a few hours later, feeling relaxed and energetic. Nikki reluctantly got out of bed and walked into the bathroom to shower. After she was done, she hunted through her side of the walk-in closet for an outfit to wear while Jeff went into the bathroom to shower.

After Nikki dressed in a cotton tee shirt and jeans, she lay across the bed on her stomach. Then, as if a light bulb switch had been turned on in her head, Nikki remembered the mailman should have made his postal rounds by now. She hopped off the bed and ran downstairs to the vestibule to check the mailbox.

She rifled through the envelopes and spotted an ominous looking piece of mail from Harrah's. An apprehensive feeling toyed with her stomach muscles as she plodded slowly back upstairs.

Nikki glanced guiltily toward the bathroom attached to their bedroom, where Jeff stood before the mirror over the sink, brushing his hair. Their eyes met.

"Where did you go?" he asked, pausing from his grooming for a few seconds.

"To the mailbox," she replied, trying to sound unconcerned.

He set the brush down on the counter and picked up his toothbrush. "Did anything come for me?"

"No. There was just a lot of junk mail." Nikki had stuffed the letter from Harrah's inside her jean pocket and deposited the rest of the mail on the kitchen table. "I'm going to clean up the kitchen." She walked back to the kitchen and placed a stack of dishes in the dishwasher.

After Jeff was dressed, he walked into the kitchen and picked up his keys from the counter. "Hey, I'm going to take my SUV to the car wash. Do you need anything while I'm out?" he asked.

"Nope," Nikki replied as she wiped down the stove.

Jeff strolled over to his wife and gave her a peck on the cheek. "Did the bank statement come today?"

Nikki nodded that it had as she washed the counters.

"The car wash is probably crowded by now." Jeff glanced at his wristwatch. "Why don't we go over the statement after I come back? Is that okay?"

Nikki's throat felt dry as a desert. She nodded her head. "Sure, no problem."

Jeff winked at her before he closed the back door.

A few hours later, Nikki had completed her household chores. She sat down in a chair at the kitchen table, reached into her pocket, and pulled out the envelope from Harrah's. Her body sagged, and she almost tumbled out of the chair when she read that she owed the casino close to sixty thousand dollars. The letter informed Nikki that she needed to call, or come to the casino immediately to discuss repayment or they would repossess her house. Nikki had conveniently forgotten while she was gambling that she had put the couple's nearly half-million dollar apartment building up for collateral if she ever defaulted on her debt.

Nikki's legs began to shake violently. She grabbed the edge of the table to steady her balance. She knew there was no way she could tell Jeff about her dilemma. More importantly, she didn't have a clue how she was she going to pay Harrah's back. Nikki chided herself for being so careless. She could hardly believe she owed the casino that much money. The debt had skyrocketed in a matter of months. She looked upward. "Oh Lord, what am I going to do? Obviously Harrah's has made a mistake."

Her mind sped a mile a minute as she tried to think of various ways to cover her losses. All of the household bills were set up in both of their names, and Nikki had come perilously close to maxing out their joint credit cards. Her face reddened as she thought of the five new credit cards she had opened in her name, in addition to the Harrah's card. The new cards were at their credit limit, and she had only been making minimum payments.

Nikki's head ached as she felt the beginning of another migraine coming on. She couldn't think of a way to cover her losses. The black wall-mounted telephone rang, shattering her trancelike state.

"Hey, baby," Jeff greeted her cheerfully. "I ran into Justin and Craig at the car wash. They're on their way to the gym to shoot hoops. If you don't have anything planned for us to do other than to go over the bank statement, then I'm going to hang with them for a while. Oh, I also told them we'd meet them and their ladies at Heaven On Seven for dinner this evening."

"That's fine. Go ahead and play ball." She pushed her bangs off her forehead. "I'll see you later."

"And you don't have a problem with me changing our dinner plans?" Jeff sounded as if he were holding his breath in anticipation of her answer.

"No, that's fine. Having dinner with the gang is okay with me."

Nikki sighed after she hung up the phone. She felt she had been given a small reprieve. Justin and Craig, whom she normally didn't care to go out with, had given her a little breathing room. Now all she had to do was come up with a sure-fire plan to cover her bets. And more importantly, keep Jeff in the dark while doing so.

In reality Nikki was fooling no one, not even herself. There wasn't any way she could adequately explain what

had happened to her without someone thinking she had
lost her mind. She felt edgy knowing there was a real possibility that Jeff might even leave her.

The couple had about five thousand dollars that was
liquid. The rest was tied up in investments, and the penalties for tapping into their portfolio were astronomical.

Initially Nikki stayed on top of the money situation. She
showed more acumen than Jeff as far as saving money.
She wanted to fast-forward their plans and have a baby
next year instead of in two years.

But Nikki hit a bad spell from which she hadn't yet re-
bounded. No matter how hard she tried to win back the
money she wasn't able to. And her losing streak had continued. Like most people, Nikki won big when she began
gambling upwards of hundreds, even thousands of dollars.

Maya called Nikki one Friday evening about nine months
ago before the conclusion of their work day, and asked her
friend, "What are you doing when you get off work?"

"I don't know; I don't have anything planned," Nikki
had answered, clicking the save icon on her computer
screen. "Why? What do you have in mind?"

"I haven't been to the boat in a while, and you've never
been. Why don't you come to my house after you get off
work, and then we can ride out to Joliet together? We can
have dinner and play a couple of games. You'll have plenty
of time to get home before Jeff gets there."

"I don't know. Southbound traffic is horrendous on Friday evenings." Nikki had powered off her computer. Then
she took her purse out of her bottom drawer.

"Come on, Nik. It's not like you have anything better to
do," Maya had cajoled her friend. "We haven't had dinner—just the two of us—in a long while. The restaurant

serves an excellent buffet dinner. I promise I'll have you home before the stroke of midnight, Miss Cinderella."

"Okay, I'll go with you," Nikki replied guiltily. "You're right; we haven't had time to catch up on the happenings in a long time. I'm leaving work now. I'll see you later."

Traffic was as bad as Nikki had expected that evening. It seemed like months had elapsed before she finally turned onto Maya's block. Nikki had tooted her horn to announce her arrival as she pulled into the black-topped tar driveway.

When Maya exited her tan bricked, ranch-style house, she walked to Nikki's side of the car. "Hop out. Let's go in my car. I know some shortcuts, which will get us to the casino faster, since you don't know the way."

The two friends had entered Maya's teal green Pontiac Grand Am, and as Maya drove to Joliet, they gossiped about the latest events. An hour later, Maya made a right turn into Harrah's parking lot. Nikki was surprised to see so many vehicles.

"If I didn't know better, I'd think we were at a concert or something. It's really packed here." Nikki looked around, taking in her surroundings.

"Wait until we get inside," Maya cautioned her friend with a laugh. "You ain't seen nothing yet."

Once she and Maya entered the casino, the rambunctious crowd and energetic atmosphere fascinated Nikki. She had beginner's luck and won big, and Maya's invitation for her friend to spend time at a casino became the impetus that drove the Singletons' financial plan in dire jeopardy.

After Nikki's third visit to the casino without Maya, she became hooked on gambling, like a junkie looking for her next fix. Her favorite activities were the craps table and slot machines. Nikki applied for a Harrah's credit card.

Because of the couples' healthy savings account and good credit, the casino extended to Nikki a ten thousand dollar credit line, much to her surprise and delight.

A few months later, Maya was with Nikki one evening during one of her gambling jaunts. She told Nikki, "You need to put at least half the money back into your account. Think of it as saving for a rainy day because luck doesn't last always."

But Nikki didn't heed Maya's advice. Feeling heady with her good gambling fortune, she returned to the boat again and again, like a moth drawn to a flame.

Nikki stood and walked over to the kitchen cabinet like a zombie. An envelope from the County Assessor's Office, and other unpaid bills were crammed haphazardly in the back of the drawer. She gathered the pieces of paper and stacked them on the kitchen table. She removed a knife from the dish rack and slit open the letter from the County. Nikki read that the May taxes on the apartment building were overdue, and she needed to contact the office immediately to make arrangements to satisfy the arrears amount, or the note could be sold.

"I thought the bill was due in September," she said aloud.

Nikki stood up jerkily, as hot tears scolded the sides of her face. She removed a box of matches from the kitchen drawer, took the pile of unpaid bills to the stove, opened the window over the sink, turned on the faucet, and burned the papers. An ungodly stench filled the room. She turned on the blower over the stove to mask the odor, and removed a can of air freshener from the bottom of the sink.

She walked through the house, spraying the rooms. When Nikki was done, she went back into the bedroom and sat on the bed. She tried desperately to think of something plausible to tell Jeff.

Later that evening, around five o'clock, Jeff walked into the bedroom and found Nikki in bed. Though she was fast asleep, he noted she looked worried and was grinding her teeth. He went into the bathroom, removed his damp clothing, and took another shower. When he returned to the bedroom, Nikki was sitting up in the bed. Her face was cupped inside her hands.

"What's wrong, sweetie?" Jeff asked with a concerned look on his face.

"I can't believe what I did. I forgot and left the checkbook at work yesterday. Can we go over the bills next weekend? I've balanced the figures, and everything looks fine," she informed Jeff soberly.

"I don't have a problem with that. Why don't you go and get ready for dinner? The fellas and I made dinner reservations for seven o'clock. You have exactly an hour to turn yourself into a ravishing, beautiful creature. Craig also said there's a decent jazz band playing at a club in Old Town tonight. He and Cynthia have tickets to see them. I told him we might join them if that's okay with you?"

"Sure, that's fine," Nikki answered woodenly. She rose from the bed and walked toward the bathroom, like she was sleepwalking.

"Hey, Nik, don't beat yourself up." Jeff rubbed her arm as she walked past him. "Forgetting the checkbook isn't the end of the world. I know that you usually balance the checkbook while you're at work, so I can understand you leaving it there. Get that sad look off your face. We're going to have a good time tonight."

Nikki felt guilty as sin. "Thanks, Jeff. You're so good to me."

When they departed the house, the sun was beginning to set. It resembled a fiery orange orb in the sky, and the wind stirred anemically in the air. The pair made an attractive couple. Jeff wore black pleated pants with a black and white jacket and a white button down shirt. Nikki was wearing a black and silver sleeveless maxi length cocktail dress with black sandals and a white shawl over her shoulders. Her hair was piled high in curls atop her head.

When the Singletons arrived at the restaurant, Craig and his wife, Cynthia, and Justin and his girlfriend, Tiffany, were all seated at the bar.

When Craig noticed his friends exiting the elevator, he stood up. A shrill whistle pierced the air. "Hey, Jeff and Nikki, we're over here!"

By the time the bartender brought Jeff and Nikki glasses of wine, the hostess informed them their table was ready.

"What are you going to eat?" Jeff leaned over and whispered in Nikki's ear.

"The blackened catfish looks good. I think I'll have that," Nikki responded. She pushed a drooping curl off her face.

"I think I'll have the gumbo," Jeff said, scanning the menu.

The waitress brought a basket of warm bread to the table. Craig broke off a piece and passed it to Cynthia.

During dinner, the group discussed current events and other topics. The women discussed television programs and which stores—Carson's or Marshall Field's—had the best sales. The men talked about sports. Jeff noticed Nikki seemed to be preoccupied. She kept her part of the conversation to a minimum.

After dinner, Jeff ordered a snifter of cognac, and Nikki a cup of tea. The waiter presented Jeff with the dinner check, since he had informed the group that the meal was his treat. He pulled his Visa Gold card from his wallet and put it into the leather credit cardholder.

The waiter returned to the table five minutes later. He walked over to Jeff, licked his lips and announced nervously, "I'm sorry, sir; your card was declined."

"That's strange," Jeff said, shrugging his shoulders. "I only carry one card. Did you try it more than once?"

The waiter informed him that the cashier had run the card through twice.

"Nikki, do you have your card with you?" Jeff asked. She looked at him and shook her head.

Jeff reached in his pocket for his wallet. He pulled out two one hundred dollar bills . . . his emergency stash. He handed it to the waiter.

"I wonder why the card was declined?" Jeff commented to his wife.

"Maybe the system is down?" Nikki gulped and her hands shook uncontrollably. She wished she could disappear. She'd forgotten she had maxed out their joint card a couple of weeks ago.

The waiter returned with the change, and Jeff set aside a portion of it for the tip.

"We may have a problem going to the club," Jeff whispered to Nikki. Their friends pretended nothing was amiss. "Do you have any money on you? If not, then we won't have enough to go to the club."

Nikki set her doggy bag on the table and checked her purse. "I only have twenty dollars. Is that enough?"

"Not really. I guess we'll have to call it an early night."

"I'll call the bank on Monday and find out what happened," Nikki promised, knowing full well what the problem was.

After biding their friends farewell, the couple walked under the starry night back to the parking garage. The valet drove Jeff's black Range Rover down the circular ramp. When they entered the vehicle and put on their seatbelts, Jeff turned on the CD player, and the jazzy sounds of Miles Davis filled the car.

Jeff stopped at the first ATM machine they passed and

tried using the card. The printout read insufficient funds. He walked back to the car looking dejected.

When he entered the car, he told Nikki, "I don't understand what happened. The printout says the account has insufficient funds. Maybe we should try calling the bank when we get home."

"Hmmm, maybe you're right," Nikki answered. "I'm sure there's a logical explanation. But I think the customer service department is closed until Monday."

"We can at least check the balance by phone when we get home." He entered the ramp for the Kennedy Expressway, I-90, and drove home.

As soon as they walked inside the apartment, Nikki decided the only way she would be able to distract Jeff from the snafu at the ATM would be to put the moves on him.

She didn't initiate lovemaking often, but when she made the effort, Jeff considered it a treat. She wound her arms around his neck and kissed him passionately, and Jeff got the message. He removed Nikki's arms from around his neck and pulled off his tie. Then he took Nikki's hand inside his and said in a thick emotion filled voice, "Let's take this party to the bedroom."

Chapter 4

When Jeff awakened Sunday morning, he peeped at the clock. It was almost nine. He reached out for Nikki, but she wasn't in the bed. He called her name aloud, but he didn't receive an answer. Getting up and walking through the house, Jeff found his wife curled up on the sofa in the den. The television was tuned to a religious program, and Nikki nearly jumped off the sofa when she noticed him in the room.

"I didn't mean to scare you," Jeff apologized. "We're going to church, aren't we?" he asked, as he sat down beside her.

"Yes, I'm supposed to sing a solo today. What time is it?" She pulled the belt of her robe tighter around her body.

"It's time for us to get dressed if we're going to make it to church on time." He pulled her off the couch and kissed her forehead.

An hour later, Jeff was dressed in a black suit, and Nikki wore a canary yellow linen two-pieced suit complemented by a lemon colored blouse. Traffic was light on the I-90 expressway. Jeff and Nikki arrived at their church, located on the south side of the city, well before the eleven o'clock service was to begin.

After Jeff parked the car in the lot, which was filling up rapidly, they entered the church. Jeff bid Nikki farewell and walked to the Trustee's room, while she strolled to the choir room to change into her choir robe.

Bianca, the plump musical director of the senior choir, stood in front of a full length-mirror and put a red collar over her neck. She patted her hair down, smoothed out an imaginary wrinkle from her robe, and then turned to look at Nikki. "Good morning, Nichole. How are you feeling this glorious day the Lord has seen fit to bless us with? How is your voice?"

"Hi, Bianca." Nikki zipped the front of her white robe. "I'm fine. And yes, I'm ready to give praises to God through song."

Before long, the other choir members arrived, and the choir room became crowded. When everyone was clad in their robes, they joined hands and Bianca led the group in prayer.

"Gracious God, we thank you for waking us up this morning clothed in our right minds. You brought us safely to church from all corners of the city this morning and bestowed upon us another opportunity to worship in your house."

Nikki, along with several choir members, murmured, "Amen."

Bianca continued. "Lord, make our voices strong as we give praises to you, and our Father above, in song. Lord, bless Pastor Dudley as he delivers our Sunday meal . . . your Word. Shower down your blessings on us and everyone gathered here today. These blessings we ask in your son's name and for His sake. Amen." Bianca opened her eyes and in an energized voice said, "Let's do this, people."

The fifty-plus men and women walked two-by-two to the outer doors of the sanctuary. They marched in cadence, from left to right, inside the middle door of the vast auditorium as the church organist, Latrell, played "Blessed Assurance."

After the choir took their seats, the assistant minister, Reverend Evans, walked to the microphone and led the congregation in prayer. When he was finished, he instructed the congregation to stand and sing "The Lord's Prayer."

After the church clerk read the weekly announcements, Bianca rose from her seat in the front row and stood in front of the choir. She held out her arms and raised her hands, motioning the group to stand. Then she nodded to Nikki, indicating she should leave her seat and walk to the podium. Nikki adjusted the microphone as the organist began playing the opening strands of "Amazing Grace."

Still feeling overwhelmed by her financial woes, Nikki missed her cue to begin singing. Latrell frowned at her and re-played the melody, but the debacle had just begun. Not only could Nikki not hit the notes, but her timing was off. When the song finally ended, feeling completely mortified, Nikki returned rapidly to her seat in the choir stand. She felt like everyone was staring at her, and fled from the choir stand in the middle of the choir's second selection.

Jeff had known something was wrong as soon as Nikki had stepped to the podium. As he sat in his seat, he had tried to catch his wife's attention, to help steady her nerves. When she made her escape, he rose from his seat near the middle of the sanctuary and followed her. He found her crying uncontrollably in the choir room. It took him ten minutes to calm her down.

"I want to go home. I made a total fool of myself this morning," Nikki cried desperately. She raised her tear-streaked face and glared at Jeff.

"Everyone has off days, Nikki. You're no different from anyone else. Why don't you calm down, and then we can go back to the service?"

"No." Nikki's voice rose hysterically. "I just want to go home. I can't face anyone right now. I let everyone down." She snagged the material as she unzipped her robe.

"I think you're overreacting." Jeff chastened his wife as he helped her out of her robe.

They walked silently to the car. Overcome with humiliation, Nikki was still sniffling when they got inside the vehicle.

Eveline left the sanctuary and ran as fast as she could to the parking lot, after checking the choir room for her daughter. "Jeff! Nikki!" she yelled at the top of her lungs, as she used both hands to clutch her green and yellow straw hat atop her head. Her white purse swung back and forth on her arm. "Stop! Wait a minute!" Eveline ran up to the car. "What's wrong, Nikki? Why are you leaving so soon? Church isn't over yet," she said, out of breath.

"Isn't it obvious why I'm leaving Mom? I made a fool of myself in there," Nikki replied. Her voice trembled with rancor. "I let Pastor and the choir down. Today just isn't my day."

Jeff shifted the car into park and said, "I told her she was being overly sensitive; that she had an off singing day, and that it happens to everyone."

"Well, not to me," Nikki sniffed. She rubbed her eyes. "I just want to go home. Mom, I'll call you later."

Eveline looked at her daughter, then at Jeff. "Make sure you do, Nikki. This isn't like you to leave church so abruptly. Jeff is right . . ." Her voice faltered.

"Mom, can we have this discussion when I call you this evening?" Nikki's lower lip quivered.

"Sure," Eveline said. Then she stood back and watched their car exit the church parking lot.

Nikki slumped in the passenger seat of Jeff's SUV. Her eyes were closed. During the ride home, Jeff tried to coax her into telling him what was wrong with her, but he made little headway. Nikki had shut down emotionally. When they arrived home, he tossed his keys on the table in the foyer. Nikki walked into the den and stood peering out the window with her hands folded over her chest. Jeff followed her into the room and turned her body toward him.

"What's wrong, Nik? You haven't been yourself lately. Don't think I haven't noticed. You know whatever is wrong, we can talk about it." Jeff gently pulled her chin up so he could see her face. His brow wrinkled, an indication he was clearly disturbed about his wife's mental state.

Nikki looked up into Jeff's eyes; her own were moist. "I just don't feel well," she complained.

"Do you need me to call your doctor?" Jeff's arm encircled Nikki's waist. "Babe, I'm really worried about you. What hurts?"

Nikki leaned against his body. She then pulled away from him, and said in a shaky voice, "No, I don't need to see a doctor. I just need to rest." Her footsteps were heavy as she plodded out of the room, down the hallway, and into the bedroom. Nikki closed the door softly behind her.

She paused at the door and stuffed her fists in her mouth, to stifle the screams that threatened to rip from inside it. Tears scalded her eyes as she sank onto the bed.

Jeff stood indecisively inside the den. He couldn't figure out what was wrong with his wife. He loosened his tie, then sat on the edge of the sofa and covered his face with his hands.

Half an hour later, Jeff tiptoed into the bedroom and changed his clothes. He peered at Nikki's inert figure on the bed. Her back was turned toward him.

When the telephone rang, Jeff walked quickly from the bedroom into the kitchen and answered. "Hello."

"Hey, Jeff. Where's my girl?" Maya asked. She sat at her kitchen table, stirring sugar into a glass of iced tea.

"Um, she's sleep. She's a little under the weather," Jeff lied. The phone was cradled in his neck as he removed a whole chicken from the freezer. He pushed the door closed with his elbow.

"I was surprised to see you guys leave church before the service ended today. What's wrong? Does she have a virus or something?" Maya asked, sipping her tea.

"She's been tripping since we left church, about how she let everyone down. I told her she was being too hard on herself," Jeff informed Maya. He set the frozen chicken in the sink.

"Nik has always taken singing seriously. She's been that way since we were kids. And you're right; she's her own worst critic."

"That she is." Jeff sat down at the kitchen table and rubbed the top of his head. "Say, Maya; do you think there's anything bothering Nikki? She hasn't been herself for a couple of months. You think she's seriously ill or something and just hasn't told me?" His voice cracked.

Maya laughed out loud. "No, she doesn't have a terminal disease or anything like that." Then her voice became serious. "But I agree with you that she's been preoccupied about something. But I don't think it's anything serious. Give her time; she'll come around."

Upon ending the conversation, Jeff went back to the bedroom to check on Nikki. She had pulled the comforter over her shoulders. He walked out of the room and into the den where he turned on the television to watch a basketball game. The Chicago Bulls were playing the Miami Heat. The score was 25 to 20, with Miami in the lead.

Jeff stretched out on the leather sofa and eventually fell asleep. When he awakened, Jeff got up and went to check on his wife again. She was still breathing. *I might as well fix dinner.* He decided on roasted chicken, green beans and mashed potatoes.

From the bedroom, Nikki could hear pots and pans clattering from the kitchen. She assumed that Jeff was preparing dinner. She pulled the comforter over her head, and became lost in thought. *Lord, how did I get myself into such a mess? I should have known better. My life is in utter chaos. Jeff is going to pitch a fit when he finds out what I did. There's no way I can fix this situation without his finding out.* Nikki clasped her hands together and closed her eyes. *Our Pastor said if you call on Jesus in your hour of need, He'll answer your prayers. I'm calling on you, Lord. This is an emergency 911 call.*

Please, Lord, I need you to help me out here. I'm begging you. If you help me, Father, I promise I'll never gamble again. Nikki's eyes were saturated with tears. She brushed them away.

With swollen eyes and a runny nose, she walked into the bathroom and removed a bottle of Vicodin from the medicine chest. She popped two pills in her mouth, turned on the cold water, and used a few handfuls of water to wash down the medication. Then Nikki went back to the bedroom and reclaimed her place under her comforter. Within minutes, the powerful painkillers took control of her body, and she was fast asleep again.

After Jeff finished preparing dinner, he went to the bedroom and shook Nikki's shoulder, awakening her. "Dinner's ready. Are you hungry? I can bring a tray in here, and you can eat in bed," he informed her.

Nikki replied listlessly, "I'm not hungry. Thanks anyway." Her eyes were red and bleary. She felt a wave of shame at the bewildered look on Jeff's face. "I'll get something later. I'm still sleepy. I promise when I wake up that I'll eat."

Jeff sat down on the side of the bed. He gathered his

wife in his arms. "Nikki, I love you. I'm your partner. Don't you know that whatever affects you, affects me too? Please, baby; talk to me. Tell me what's wrong."

"Everything is fine." Nikki was so ashamed that she couldn't meet Jeff's eyes. She clasped her hands together nervously. "I admit I was upset about messing up the song in church today, but I feel better now." She caressed Jeff's cheek. "Don't worry about me, love."

"Prove it to me, Nikki. Let's have dinner together right now." Jeff looked at his wife.

"Come on, Jeff. I don't have anything to prove," she answered defensively. She waved her hand in dismissal. "Don't you remember me telling you last week that I've been a little stressed out from work? That's the only thing bothering me."

Jeff's heart sank to his midsection. He knew Nikki was lying because she was chewing her lower lip . . . a sure sign of deception.

"I'm going into the den to eat and finish watching the game. Call me when you're ready to eat." He looked at Nikki one more time, and then walked out of the room.

Nikki sighed audibly and relaxed against the mattress. A few minutes later, she had fallen asleep again.

Jeff stood in the kitchen at the stove and loaded up a plate with food. He then went into the den and half-heartedly watched the rest of the basketball game. Stabbing a piece of chicken with his fork, Jeff vowed within himself that he would call Dr. Rollins tomorrow if Nikki didn't snap out of her funk.

The telephone rang. Jeff didn't pick up the receiver. Instead, he waited to see if Nikki would answer it. When she didn't, he peered at the caller ID, and upon seeing his mother-in-law's name, Jeff clicked on the cordless telephone.

"Hello, Mother Baldwin."

"Hi, Jeff. Is Nik up?"

"No, she's not." He shook his head. "Something is definitely wrong, but she won't open up."

"Tell her to get on the phone." Eveline's order came with a no-nonsense tone.

"Hold on." Jeff laid the phone on the end table and walked into the bedroom. "Hey, Nik; your mother is on the phone. Do you want to talk to her?"

Nikki lay motionless in the bed. He repeated his question louder.

"Huh?" Nikki opened her eyes. "No, tell Mom I'll call her back in the morning." She closed her eyes and turned over in the bed.

Jeff padded back to the den. "Mother Baldwin, she doesn't want to talk. She says she'll call you in the morning," he informed his mother-in-law tersely.

Eveline sucked her teeth. "Tell Nichole that she'd better call me first thing in the morning. I'm getting ready to eat dinner now. I'll talk to you later, Jeff."

"Have a good evening." Jeff clicked the telephone off and resumed eating his meal. As he chewed the chicken slowly he vowed to get to the bottom of what was troubling Nikki. Jeff didn't have a clue of the storm clouds that were gathering steam like Hurricane Katrina and making a beeline to his family's front door.

Chapter 5

The following morning, the alarm blared loudly, awakening Nikki. She tried to swallow, but her mouth felt dry as cotton. She pressed the snooze button twice before rising and going into the bathroom to shower. When she was done, Nikki returned to the bedroom and dressed for work lackadaisically.

Jeff watched her movements somberly from the bed. "Do you feel up to going to work today?" He didn't begin his workday until the afternoon, but would usually arrive an hour before his starting time.

"I feel okay," Nikki answered as she stood at the dresser and brushed her hair. She had picked out a long sleeved, cerise and teal colored two-piece skirt suit to wear to work. "I'll call you later," she promised Jeff after kissing his forehead.

After locking the door and walking outside, Nikki got into her car and headed south instead of north. She dialed her job and placed the phone to her ear. Dead silence greeted her. The cell phone had been shut off. Crying aloud, Nikki drove to the nearest gas station. She prayed her credit card would allow her to purchase gas and breathed a sigh of relief when the sale was approved.

Nikki spied a telephone booth near the tire air machine and walked inside to call her boss, Victor. She left a message on his voicemail, stating she wouldn't be at work due to illness. She thoughtfully put the receiver back on the hook, then returned to the car and sat passively inside it for a few minutes. Her arms were outstretched, and her hands clasped the sides of the steering wheel tightly. She laid her head on top of her arms.

Nikki felt hopeless, like her world was crashing into small pieces. She was plagued with uncertainly, still torn between telling Jeff what she had done and simultaneously rejecting the notion. Nikki's gambling luck, like that of so many gamblers, had deserted her like she'd broken a mirror or walked under a ladder. Lady Luck had said goodbye and sayonara, and she didn't plan on returning anytime soon.

The attendant, who had been watching Nikki from inside, walked outside the station and deposited a bag of trash into the dumpster. He walked over to Nikki's car and taped on the window.

"Miss, are you all right?" He looked at her curiously. His blue uniform was slightly soiled.

The sounds at the window startled Nikki, and she jumped in her seat. "Yes, I'm fine. I was just leaving," she said, blinking her eyes rapidly. Nikki put the car in drive and pulled out of the station. With nowhere to go, she repeatedly drove around the block. Looking at the clock on the dashboard, she thought of going to Maya's house. Her friend should be on her way to work by now. From Maya's house, Nikki could call Harrah's.

After sitting in rush hour traffic for nearly an hour and a half, Nikki parked her car in Maya's driveway. She then used her spare key to enter the house and walked into her friend's immaculate kitchen. Nikki laid her purse on the beige counter top, and when Maya suddenly walked into the kitchen, both women screamed in fright.

"Nichole Deidre Singleton, what are you doing here?" Maya asked, after she'd calmed herself. She was clad in her underwear and an opened Japanese red and white silk robe.

"I thought you had gone to work already. I'm so used to you parking your car in the driveway. You must have parked it in the garage last night. I needed to come some-where quiet to think," Nikki said, her thudding heart rate decreasing. She sat down on a kitchen chair.

Maya's eyebrow rose. "And you couldn't do that at home?" She sat at the kitchen table. "What's up, Nikki? What's bothering you? Jeff and I agreed when we talked last night that you haven't been yourself in a while."

"Nothing's up." Nikki denied the allegations. "I just need some space away from Jeff. A neutral ground to think over some things."

"Well, all you had to do was call. You know that you're my girl, and I've got your back. Is there anything I can do?" Maya paused at the doorway, as she was walking back to her bedroom.

"Just keep being my friend." Nikki sighed, and a tear trickled down her cheek.

Maya looked alarmed and rushed to her friend's side. "Do you want me to stay with you?"

Nikki brushed the tear away. "No, go on to work. I need some time alone."

A half hour later, Maya was fully clothed and ready to depart for work. She squeezed Nikki's shoulder before she walked out the back door.

After Maya left, Nikki pulled her palm pilot out of her bag and accessed her telephone book. She walked to the cabinet, rummaged through the drawer, and found a slip of paper and a pencil. After sitting back down on the white and red peppermint candy striped cushion, Nikki jotted down the telephone numbers on the paper from her palm pilot and prepared to make her calls.

Her hands shook as if she had palsy when she picked up Maya's cordless phone and dialed the first number. Calling the Cook County Assessor's office, Nikki was greeted with an automated menu and pressed the zero key to talk to an operator. Elevator music played until a woman came on the line.

"This is Mrs. Rinaldi of the Cook County Assessor's office. How may I help you?"

Nikki took a deep breath and blurted out, "My name is Nichole Singleton. I live at 4336 West Armitage Avenue. I received a letter from your office, stating the taxes are behind on the three-story building that I own. I'd like to know what I can do to get out of arrears and get my tax bill current."

In a nasal tone, Mrs. Rinaldi replied, "What's your tax ID number?" Nikki gave her the information. "Please hold while I look up your information on the computer." Mrs. Rinaldi's hands flew across the keyboard. "The property is registered to Nichole Singleton. Is that you?"

The deed to the building was in Nikki's name alone. She had meant to add Jeff to the document but had never gotten around to doing so. Jeff hadn't pressed the issue because Nikki's father had deeded the property to his daughter before he passed eight years ago. Nikki knew if she had followed through on her intentions and added Jeff to the deed, then he probably would have visited the County Assessors Office by now to verify Nikki was up to date in her tax payments.

Nikki replied, "Yes, that's correct."

"As you know, property taxes are due in June and September. According to my records, you didn't pay anything on either date. I suggest you come in as soon as possible and take care of this matter," Mrs. Rinaldi informed Nikki, in an imperviously manner.

"Does your office offer a payment plan?" Nikki was hopeful, making the sign of the cross across her chest, and then crossing her fingers.

"No, Mrs. Singleton; we don't. Payment must be made in full, along with any accrued interest."

Nikki's hand began shaking. "I know property can be sold for unpaid taxes. Is there a time limit before that happens?" *Lord, please don't let me lose the building. It's my home. God, Daddy would be so ashamed of me if he were still alive. I can't bear the thought of losing everything Jeff and I have worked for.*

"You have approximately a year to make good on the taxes. Otherwise, you're correct, the property can be sold." Mrs. Rinaldi closed the file. "Would you like me to send you a letter with your current charges, Mrs. Singleton?"

"Yes, please do that. Can you send the letter to my work address instead of my home?" Nikki tried to keep a panicky whine out of her voice.

Mrs. Rinaldi said, "I don't see why not." Nikki gave the woman her work address. "Will that be all, Mrs. Singleton?" She sounded bored with the conversation.

Nikki answered, "Yes."

"You can expect that document in three to five business days. Have a good day."

"Thank you, Ms. Rinaldi. You too." Nikki clicked off the telephone, wrote $7,000 on the piece of paper, and scribbled circular doodles under the amount. She glanced at her watch. Today was payday, and her check was normally deposited into her checking account at midnight. She quickly called the bank to verify the funds were available, then telephoned her wireless provider and remitted a payment.

The letter from Harrah's was folded inside the zippered

section of Nikki's purse. She reached inside and pulled it out. The letter was from Richard Stanhope, the collection manager at Harrah's. Her stomach seized with convulsions as she read the folded piece of paper. She felt light-headed. *I can't believe I owe the casino this much money. They must have made a mistake.* Her eyes scanned the letter again.

Nikki picked up the receiver and dialed the number slowly. "Extension 204," she croaked out to the telephone operator.

After being put on hold a few minutes, a voice came on the line. "This is Richard Stanhope. How may I help you?"

"Good morning, Mr. Stanhope. My name is Nichole Singleton. I'm calling you in response to a letter that you sent me . . ." Nikki's voice trailed off.

Mr. Stanhope picked up a file from his desk. "Hello, Ms. Singleton. Thank you for calling me so promptly. What can I do for you today?"

"In the letter, you asked that I call you about my debt." Nikki refused to call it a gambling debt. Her grip on the telephone receiver displayed every line on her fingers. "Truthfully," Nikki's voice deepened emotionally, "I think there must be a mistake with that figure, Mr. Stanhope. There's no way I can owe your casino that much money."

Mr. Stanhope opened the file and thumbed through the pages. He quickly read the figure on the last page, and then cleared his throat. "I'm sorry, Mrs. Singleton; the figure is correct."

"But I made a payment last week," Nikki protested. "Has that amount been credited to my account?" The conversation wasn't going as she planned.

"Yes, the payment was received and credited to your account last week. But my records show you visited the casino two days later and lost the same amount," he stated curtly.

Alarm mushroomed through Nikki's body. She had completely forgotten she'd gone back to the casino in hopes of winning back the money. "So, where does that leave me?"

"Well, we need you to make good on your debt as soon as possible, of course. We aren't overly concerned about payback, because you used your apartment building for collateral."

Nikki almost fell out of the chair. "What do you mean my apartment building is collateral? I don't remember signing a document to that effect."

"My records show you signed a collateral agreement three months ago," Mr. Stanhope said. "The document appears to be legal and binding. The signature is the same as the one on your application. Your collateral was the reason the casino increased your credit line."

"But sixty thousand dollars? That's ridiculous," Nikki protested hysterically. "I would've had to be gambling all the time and lost consistently. I did win occasionally." Her head began pounding, and a twinge of pain indicated a monster headache was on the way. She closed her eyes as tears trickled from them.

"That's true, Ms. Singleton. But when was the last time you used real old fashioned money? My records show you always used funds from your Harrah's account. That's the reason you have such a high outstanding balance." Mr. Stanhope didn't feel sorry for her, since he had heard it all before. He personally felt it was just too bad some people let their addictions get out of control before they tried to rectify the situation.

"I don't know where you expect me to come up with sixty thousand dollars. It's not like I have that kind of money just lying around." Nikki's eyes were still closed, and white ghostlike shapes danced behind her eyelids.

Mr. Stanhope looked at her application again. "When

you filled out your application, you stated you had monies in investment accounts. I would suggest you get the money from there or get a loan. I don't know what else to tell you, Ms. Singleton, except the money is due. We can work with you, of course. But if you can't come up with the monies owed, then we have no choice but to make good on the collateral."

"So, just like that, you would take my home?" Nikki moaned. She felt the conversation was taking on a bizarre quality. This couldn't really be happening to her.

Her cell phone sounded. She looked at the caller ID and saw that Jeff was calling her. She pushed the ignore call button so he would be routed to voicemail.

"We only take our patrons' homes as a last resort." Mr. Stanhope's voice deepened, sounding ominous. "I suggest you call me back within a week, and we can discuss arrangements then. Good day, Ms. Singleton."

Nikki was rendered mute. The telephone tone bonged rapidly in her ear. She set the receiver inside the cradle and rubbed her temples rapidly.

"God, what a mess I'm in. Lord, why didn't you stop me from going to the casino? What am I going to tell Jeff?" Nikki said aloud as she sat at Maya's table. Her head felt heavy, and her shoulders slumped as if they were weighed with blocks of cement.

She had no idea what her next move would be, but she knew she had to make one. And soon.

Chapter 6

Jeff stood facing the bathroom mirror, tying his navy paisley tie under the collar of the yellow shirt that he wore with navy khaki slacks. It was nearly time for him to leave for work. He ran his hand over his head after brushing his hair, then smoothed aftershave lotion on his face. Jeff's face was sunken with worry lines, leaving him looking haggard, like he hadn't gotten enough sleep.

When he completed his grooming, Jeff strolled rapidly to the telephone to call Nikki's job. As before, he was immediately routed to her voicemail. He slammed the phone down into the cradle, so aggravated that he felt like throwing the white telephone against the wall. A moment later, Jeff picked up the receiver again. The idea of calling Nikki's job's main number ricocheted across his brain. He hurriedly dialed the telephone number.

"Hello. May I speak to Nichole Singleton? This is her husband," he said when the receptionist answered the phone.

"This is Fatima Mayhew, Mr. Singleton. Your wife called in sick this morning," she said.

Fatima's eyes sparkled like diamonds with glee. A smirk filled her face as she contemplated the fact that her co-worker didn't bother to inform her hubby that she wasn't coming to work today. Fatima speculated there was trouble in paradise. The young woman's lips curved into a gossipy smile.

After Jeff stammered a lame excuse, stating he'd forgotten, Fatima pressed a button and disconnected the call.

Jeff gulped as he realized that he had committed a major faux pas. Now Nikki's office would be aware of their personal business. Jeff's face was drawn as he picked up the telephone again and called his wife's cell phone. The phone rang five times before he was routed to voicemail. He was relieved to discover her cell phone service was restored, but his mind spun scenarios of how Nikki could be lying hurt somewhere. Maybe in the hospital. He wondered why she hadn't called him back. Jeff's wristwatch beeped, reminding him it was time to depart for work.

He stood in the middle of the room debating if he should go to work or not. "Something is up. I'm not leaving this house until I talk to my wife," he vowed aloud.

He unfastened his tie pin and pulled the material forcibly from his neck. He then picked up the telephone to call his job. Luckily for Jeff, his manager, Reese Ogilvy, had no problem with him taking the day off. "I'll be in tomorrow," Jeff promised. "An emergency came up at home, and I need to take care of it. I'll call Ernesto when I finish talking to you to tell him I won't be in today. He can reach me on my cell phone if he needs to. Thank you for being so understanding, Mr. Ogilvy."

Jeff disconnected the call, then tried calling Nikki again, without luck. He slammed the receiver down so hard into the cradle that the plastic cracked. He paced the room like a caged tiger. Before the call to Nikki's office, he was genuinely worried about his wife's welfare, but now he was quickly becoming angry. Jeff was incensed that Nikki had put him through unnecessary drama and was put out that she wasn't answering his calls. He couldn't understand what she could possibly be doing that as so important that she couldn't call him back. He wondered if she was with another man.

The vein in his forehead throbbed portentously. *Naw, Nikki wouldn't play me like that. Or would she?* The thoughts converged in his mind and took root like a potted plant. Jeff walked out of the bedroom and into the den.

He rushed to the bar and toyed with the idea of pouring himself a shot of Tangeray, and then dismissed the idea. He knew he had been hitting the bottle too heavily lately trying to escape his worries about Nikki. Jeff walked over to the reclining chair and sat down. Jeff bowed his head. "Lord, I know my wife is struggling mightily with a problem. Whatever it is has been eating at her for a while. Father, show me the way to get her to open her heart and talk to me. Maybe I should have pressed her harder yesterday as to what's going on. Her behavior is a mystery to me, Lord, because we've always been able to talk to each other about anything. Lord, please help me."

Further words deserted Jeff, and a little voice crept into the recesses of his mind. It taunted him unmercifully, playing devil's advocate with his head. *Whoa, brother, now you know that's a lie. Nikki ain't been telling you much lately. Sure the sex has been great, but she's holding out on you. Something ain't right in the Singleton household. That's what you need to be thinking about.* Losing the battle with the bottle, Jeff poured himself a shot of gin and sat in the chair sulking.

When the telephone blared, Jeff stumbled as he jumped up from the chair. Before he could greet the caller, he heard a woman say, "Hey, Nik, I was checking to see if you'd made it back home yet."

Jeff removed the base from his ear and looked at the caller ID. His eyes swarmed in and out of focus. He put the phone back to his ear. "Maya, is that you?" His voice broke in disappointment.

Maya felt a plummeting sensation in the pit of her stomach. "Uh, hi, Jeff. I thought you were at work by now." Her voice trailed off. It was obvious Nikki wasn't home from Jeff's tone of voice.

"What's up, Maya?" Jeff replied through clenched teeth. His voice rose aggressively. "Well, it's apparent that you've talked to Nikki today. Where's my wife, Maya?"

"I don't know," Maya answered weakly. Her face was seared with embarrassment. She wished Nikki had just stayed home and handled her business instead of coming to her house that morning.

"You sounded like you expected her to be at home. Well, she isn't, and I haven't talked to her all day," Jeff said. "What's wrong with Nikki? How come she couldn't stay home and talk to me?"

"I, uh, talked to her earlier at work and she told me she might go home," Maya lied, trying to cover for her friend. "She told me she didn't feel well and that she was going to leave work early. That's why I called your house."

"Don't insult my intelligence by lying for Nikki." He punched the side of the chair he was sitting in. "She didn't go to work," Jeff growled. "I called her job earlier. Have you seen her? Is she all right?" He jumped up and paced the floor, clearly agitated.

"I'm sorry, Jeff," Maya apologized. "I didn't mean to lie to you. I did talk to Nikki earlier. I just don't want to get in the middle of your and Nikki's issues. She was upset when I talked to her, but she didn't say what was bothering her."

Jeff's feelings were hurt. It cut him to the core that his wife had chosen to confide in her best friend instead of him during her time of crisis. "You mean to tell me that you talked to her and she didn't tell you what was bothering her?" Disbelief dripped from his voice.

"I . . . I . . . tried to talk to her, Jeff, but she wouldn't confide in me what the problem was." Maya felt miserable. The pencil she held in her hand trembled along with her legs. "If she calls me, I'll tell her to call you immediately. In fact, I'm going to get off the phone now and call her cell phone."

"She isn't seeing another man, is she?" Jeff regretted the words as soon as they left his mouth. He wearily rubbed his forehead.

"Good Lord, no." Maya's mouth dropped open. She grasped the phone tightly. "Even though she didn't say what was bothering her, I know another man isn't the case. Nikki's a Christian, and she wouldn't do something like that." She tried to assuage Jeff's feelings. "I'm going to call her now. If she's doesn't call you back within an hour, then call me back."

"Okay, Maya. Forgive me for going off on you. I'm just worried about Nikki. It isn't like her to just disappear without saying a word or calling me." Jeff sank back into the chair.

"She just isn't thinking clearly, Jeff. I can tell you that much. Let me see what I can find out and we'll talk in an hour," Maya said, trying to be helpful.

Jeff thanked her, and then hung up the phone reluctantly. He felt like Maya was his sole link to his wife. He snapped his fingers. Maybe Nikki was at her mother's house. His hand hovered over the telephone. Then just as quickly, he discarded the idea, surmising there was no need in getting his mother-in-law upset if Nikki wasn't there.

Deciding to wait for Nikki or Maya to call him back, Jeff walked to the computer desk, sat down on the chair, and booted up the PC. "I might as well do something to take my mind off this stuff," he said aloud. He picked up the glass, sipped the gin, and set the glass on top of the desk.

Ten minutes later, he was busy checking his emails. When he was done with that chore, he called Ernesto, the lead operator at work, to get a status on the evening activity.

"It's quiet here, boss. I got a handle on everything," Ernesto assured.

After hanging up the telephone, Jeff checked his AOL account, hoping Nikki had emailed him. But she hadn't. In an attempt to put his mind on less stressful matters, he decided to login and check their bank statement. But the screen informed him that the password he used was invalid.

With his mouth open, Jeff glanced at the flat screen monitor and retyped the password. The same message appeared. His body mushroomed with righteous indignation that Nikki would change the password without telling him. Jeff's head tilted to the left as he considered the fact that maybe Nikki did tell him about changing the password and he'd forgotten that she had. He scratched the side of his head.

Scrolling down his *favorites* list until he reached the utility companies, he arbitrarily attempted to access those accounts too, only to find out that all of the passwords had been altered. Something was definitely wrong. Jeff immediately thought to call the bank to find out their account balances, but the phone rang, interrupting his plan.

Jeff glanced at the caller ID; it was his stockbroker. "Hey, Ron, what's up?" he said, greeting his friend.

"You got it, man," Ron said chuckling. He peered at his computer screen, and shifted the telephone to his other ear.

"So, what's happening?" Jeff asked, as he looked out the window, hoping to see Nikki's car coming down the street.

"I meant to call you earlier today, but I got busy," Ron replied. He popped a mint inside his mouth. "Remember when we talked last week about you investing in the pharmaceutical company?"

"Sure. Why? Is something wrong?"

"Well, the stock has dropped a bit, and you're down about $5,000. I'm monitoring the company activity closely. But I wanted you to be aware of what's going on."

"What do you suggest?" Jeff asked as he leaned against the back of the chair.

"If your money situation isn't tight, then I think you should ride out the storm for now. I'm hearing from a lot of reliable sources, and the word on the street is that the stock is going to rebound. I'll keep a close eye on things. I just wanted to give you a heads up because I know you're trying to raise the funds for your professional endeavor."

"Five thousand isn't bad. I went into this venture knowing you win some and lose some. Let's ride it out," Jeff said to his friend.

"Okay, I'll email you tomorrow or call with an update. Peace out," Ron said.

"Yeah, I'll talk to you later." Jeff hung up the telephone.

Dusk was beginning to fall. Giant shadows were being cast around the darkening room, like clothes hanging on a clothesline. Jeff powered off the computer. He went back to the living room, walked to the bar, and took the bottle of Tangeray back with him to his lounging chair. Then Jeff unceremoniously sat down and waited for his wife to return home.

Chapter 7

Nikki sat at Maya's table with her head hanging disconsolately between her hands. Self-inflicted scratches covered her arms. Her financial situation was far worse then she ever could have imagined. *Lord, why didn't you stop me from making the biggest mistake of my life? Why didn't you just smite me down?*

As if by rote, Nikki picked up her cell phone and checked her voicemail messages. Jeff had left so many messages that her log was full. She debated calling him back, but decided she wasn't ready to face the inquisition in store for her. After clicking her cell phone off, Nikki's eyes dropped to the piece of paper that lay on the table in front of her. It contained circular doodles and the total amount of debt she owed. The figure was astronomical.

When Maya's wall phone rang, Nikki looked at it until the answering machine on the kitchen counter kicked in.

"Nikki, if you're still there, pick up. Jeff has called me twice. He called your job, and they told him you were off today. He's going crazy. You need to call him or me." Maya sounded tense.

Nikki walked over to the wall and removed the olive-colored phone. "Hi, Maya. I was just getting ready to go home. I'll see Jeff when I get there."

"What's going on?" Maya asked uncomfortably. "It isn't like you to just up and disappear and not talk to your husband."

"You're right. I should've talked to Jeff when he called earlier, but I wasn't quite ready to. I still had some things I needed to clear up in my mind."

Maya sighed dramatically. "Don't wait too long, Nikki. "It's not fair to Jeff. He's a good man, and he just wants to help you. Heck, I'll help you too, if you would just tell me what's going on."

Nikki squeezed her eyes shut. "Sometimes a person has to handle issues in her own way. Right now I don't need any help. I just need you to be my friend and give me the space I need to work through my problems."

"I hear you. But would you just call Jeff? He's upset with me, and I don't want to be in the middle of what's going on between you two."

"I said I'm going home right now," Nikki retorted impatiently. She bit her bottom lip. "I'm sorry. I'm leaving your house now. I'll call you later." She hung up the telephone, walked to the table, and began gathering her belongings. Nikki stuffed the papers inside her tote bag before turning off the light and walking out the back door.

Yolanda Adams' voice flooded the interior of Nikki's automobile as she powered up the engine. Nikki's thoughts turned to the conversations she had with her creditors. She had bought a little time with the County regarding the taxes on their home, though Nikki didn't have a clue as to how she was going to pay the amount.

Her dilemma with Harrah's was a totally different matter. The casino could seize her home. The idea of talking to a lawyer came to her mind. She still couldn't believe that she had racked up that huge a debt; no matter what Harrah said. Nikki scolded herself about letting down her husband and family. Her eyes brimmed with tears.

She opened her mouth and wailed like a crazed woman. The headache that she thought had dissipated began to signal its return. Jeff was not going to be happy when he learned what she had done. Morbid thoughts slithered in and out of her head as she weighed her options. Maybe she could leave town, or even put herself out of her misery. At least with the lump sum from her insurance policies, Jeff could keep the house.

Nikki glanced down at her watch. It was five forty-five in the evening. Rush hour had traffic backed up in every direction. It took Nikki ninety minutes to travel from the south suburbs to the north side. Opening the garage door with the remote control, she parked and walked to the front entrance. Her stomach careened wildly out of control at the thought of facing Jeff when he got off from work.

Before going up to their apartment, she checked the mailbox, which was empty. When she entered the apartment, Nikki dropped the tote bag heavily on the floor near the front door. She walked into the living room and closed the green mini-blinds at the window.

Nikki was surprised when she walked into the kitchen to find the day's mail scattered on the kitchen table. They were mostly utility bills, which she had managed to keep current. *God, I feel so overwhelmed by life.* She walked into the darkened den, and flipped the light on. Jeff sat on his lounger, giving her a menacing stare.

Nikki's hand fluttered to her throat. "You scared me. Why are you sitting here in the dark?"

"Haven't you been keeping me in the dark?" Jeff replied somberly.

Nikki swallowed before she replied. "Jeff, I'm sorry

about not calling you back today, but that doesn't give you the right to jump on my case as soon as I walk in the door," she said taking a step backward. She wanted to flee the room.

"Who are you to tell me what does any good or not? At least I don't run away when the going gets rough," Jeff said in a tight voice. His arm shot out and knocked an empty crystal brandy snifter off the end table. Shards of glass glistened from the hardwood floor.

Nikki looked at her husband in disapproval. "You need to clean that up so the stain doesn't set in the flooring."

Jeff rose from his seat. "I must be in the twilight zone or something. You've been gone all day doing God knows what, and now you have the nerve to come in here and give me orders. I don't think so, Nichole. Not today; not ever."

"I'm sorry for not returning your calls today. But I haven't done anything wrong, Jeff. I just needed a little time to myself. Is that too much to ask?" Nikki stood facing him. Her face was bright red and her hands were stuck on her hips.

"See, what you fail to remember is that there isn't any you anymore. We're a team, Nikki. What affects you, also affects me."

"Is it too much to ask that I just be me . . . imperfect Nichole Baldwin-Singleton? Darn it, Jeff, I have a problem! Can't you give me a little space to work it out?" Nikki's eyes filled with tears as her shoulders slumped forward in defeat.

"Yes, Nikki, it's too much for you to ask." Jeff jumped up from his chair and stood in front of his wife with his finger in her face. "We're a team. You could've at least given me the courtesy of returning my calls. Instead, you slinked out of here this morning like you were going to work." Spittle flew from his mouth.

Nikki flinched and stepped away from her husband. She threw her hands in the air in resignation. "Look, we can stand here and argue the rest of the night. I said I was wrong and apologized. I don't care if I'm your wife or not; if I have a problem, I'm going to deal with it the best way I see fit. I made a mistake. Forgive me. If you're just going to yell at me, then you can do it alone because I'm going to bed." She walked away from Jeff, leaving him standing in a daze, looking at her back.

He rushed behind her and pulled her by the arm. "Don't walk away from me. I'm not done talking to you."

Nikki squirmed away from him. "Let's not get physical. I have a headache and I don't feel up to fighting with you tonight. We'll discuss it tomorrow," she said firmly.

Jeff looked at Nikki, loathe sparking from his eyes. "Like you called your mother back today? Come on, you're just trying to get out of telling me where you've been." His voice dropped to a petulant whine. "Where were you? Were you with another man?"

Nikki rubbed the area between her eyes. "Of course not. I was at a quiet place, thinking. I would never cheat on you. Although you can't tell at this very minute, I do love you very much. I just have a lot on my mind right now. I promise we'll talk about it soon." She refused to meet Jeff's eyes as she walked away.

Jeff felt his blood pressure careen wildly out of control. He was livid. How dare Nikki leave for the day, and then return home and not say a word about where she'd been? He punched the wall, then flung open the closet door, grabbed his jacket and slammed the front door as he exited the apartment.

When Nikki heard the door close, it sounded like a bomb had gone off. She knew her husband was angry, and rightfully so. But she couldn't cope with his feelings at the moment. Nikki knew it was a bad idea for Jeff to drive as upset as he was and also because he had been drinking. She shrugged her shoulder and shook her head, unsympathetic to his plight. Nikki had too much on her plate to cope with Jeff's feelings. Knowing her husband well, Nikki assumed he wasn't going too far; perhaps to Justin's house where he would complain to his friend about her behavior. Nikki hadn't eaten anything all day, and as she yawned, her stomach rumbled. The hunger pangs only amplified her throbbing headache.

Nikki walked into the kitchen and turned on the teapot. While the water heated, she went into the bathroom and swallowed down two Extra Strength Tylenol caplets; all the while, ignoring her ringing telephone. Entering the bedroom, she stripped off her clothes and tied her mauve terry cloth robe around her body before walking back to the kitchen. She removed a Lipton teabag from one cabinet and a mug and spoon from another. Sitting at the table, she dipped the teabag into the hot water and stirred in two teaspoons of sugar.

Nikki bowed her head and prayed that the medicine would hurry up and kick in. Shooting pains made her head feel weighty. "Lord, please help me. I don't know what to do. I know I should have talked to Jeff about what's going on with me, but I know he won't understand how I could let this happen. I don't quite understand how this happened myself. Why would I sign away my house? I must be crazy."

Nikki rocked back and forth in the seat and finished drinking the tea. Then she walked back into the bedroom, turned off the light, and curled her body in a fetal position.

Jeff sat in his Range Rover for a few minutes. He was still dazed from what he perceived as Nikki's cavalier explanation as to what she'd done that day. She acted like she wasn't accountable to anyone. Using his remote, he raised the garage door and turned on the vehicle. Jeff wasn't sure where he was going; he just knew that his house didn't feel like home and his wife had gone loco.

He pondered driving to Justin's house, a few miles south of where he and Nikki lived. But instead he drove toward I-90. When Jeff merged onto the Dan Ryan Expressway, he decided to swing by his old neighborhood. He fiddled with the dials on the dashboard, trying to keep his mind off of Nikki and rolled the window down so the cool air could help him sober up faster. Before long, he was exiting the expressway onto 47th Street.

As Jeff surveyed where he had come from, he knew he'd been blessed by God's mercy. The area had deteriorated dismally. Jeff's eyes met those of a man who looked to be around his age. The man shot him a pleading look and held out his hands. Jeff shook his head no, and the man held up his middle finger. Jeff drove away thinking, *but for the grace of God, that could be me standing on the corner in a ragged coat, begging for a handout.*

His vehicle passed boarded up businesses and apartment buildings as he steered the car east on 47th Street. The neighborhood was nothing like when he lived there as a child. He had come to the hood regularly until his mother passed away a few years ago.

He felt ashamed because he had tried to get his mother to move north with him and Nikki. But Carmen Singleton was born and bred on the south side of Chicago, and she had no plans of leaving the area. With a quiet dignity that embodied Carmen's spirit, she thanked her son and daughter-in-law for thinking of her, but politely declined the offer. Jeff improvised by giving his mother a monthly stipend.

A lump rose up in Jeff's throat, and tears oozed from his eyes. He quickly brushed them away. He still felt pangs of remorse that he didn't get his mother away from the neighborhood before tragedy struck. A crack addict broke into her apartment, and though she wasn't injured, Carmen died of a fright-inflicted heart attack during the theft.

Jeff turned down Evans Street and drove slowly. He felt so far removed from the place, but it was still where he was born and raised. His eyes traveled to the second floor of the three-story gray stone apartment building. A torn window shade was flapping from a gaping hole in the pane. He debated parking his vehicle until he noticed a group of teenaged boys walking down the street. He quickly pulled away from the curb and gunned the motor as he drove down the street.

Jeff was haunted by feelings of being remiss and felt he should have been more persuasive in urging his mother to leave the neighborhood, even if he had had to pick her up and physically remove her from this place. He berated himself for allowing the situation to happen, although Reverend Dudley had often told him that it wasn't his fault.

Carmen had never asked for anything, and most of the time, Jeff had had to beg her to accept his checks. A part of him realized he had been a good son. He hoped that Carmen had forgiven him for not being there for her when she most needed him most.

Jeff remembered the turbulent time he experienced when the police came to his door to tell him his mother was dead. Nikki had been a rock for him and had had his back during his most vulnerable state. It took days of wheedling from his wife for Jeff not to return to his old neighborhood to try to avenge his mother's death.

After driving aimlessly for a few minutes, Jeff decided to go home. There was nothing to be gained by going to Justin's at this time of night. His problem was on the north side . . . at home. He was going to have to try to be more patient with Nikki. At least she had admitted there was something wrong. Now his dilemma was to coax from her the details of the problem. He didn't buy her story that she was stressed out from work.

As Jeff drove back toward Dan Ryan Expressway, he felt calmer. Looking at the road ahead of him, he cried aloud. "Lord, no one said life was going to be easy. The church teaches us how couples have ups and downs, but as Christians, we're supposed to deal with our issues in a more God-like way than non-believers. Lord, I know I drink a little too much when I'm upset, and I need you to help me stop that vicious cycle. You've brought me from a mighty long way, and I've been so blessed. I realize that I'm supposed to be a helpmate to my wife, not a hindrance. So Lord, fill my heart with love and understanding so that I might help Nikki. Amen."

Several hours later, Nikki heard the back door open then close. She whispered, "Thank you, Lord, for bringing Jeff home safely," then she closed her eyes. Nikki was grateful he made it back home in one piece. She hoped Jeff hadn't been drinking wherever he'd been, and that he wouldn't start nagging her when he came inside the room. She could hear him walking down the hallway. His gait seemed steady, so she began to think that maybe he was all right.

She faced the wall and held her breath when he walked into the bedroom. She could feel Jeff staring at her, trying to gauge if she was asleep or not.

"Nikki, are you awake?" Jeff whispered as he walked to the closet. He turned on the light and began removing his clothes. "If you are, I just want to say I'm sorry. I should've been more understanding of your feelings. I just get frustrated because I love you and want to help you."

Nikki didn't reply. She lay motionless on her side of the bed.

"I'll try to do better. Be patient with me," Jeff said, glancing at the bed. He went into the bathroom, brushed his teeth, and splashed water on his face. He took a deep breath and walked back to the bedroom and got in the bed.

Though Nikki's back faced Jeff, he wanted to reach out and gather her in his arms. But he decided not to act on his longings, knowing she needed her space. Tomorrow was another day, and maybe she would feel like talking to him about whatever had taken her to such a dismal place. Jeff just wished his wife would return to him so they could resume the relationship they'd enjoyed for so long. He closed his eyes and said a silent prayer before he finally drifted off to sleep.

Chapter 8

Nikki awakened a little after six o'clock and peered at the clock. She had ten minutes to spare before it was time for her to rise and shine to face a new day. She turned to look at Jeff. Though he was asleep, he looked miserable, and Nikki knew why. But until she figured out a way to fix her problems, she couldn't share with him what was going on with her. Turning off the alarm clock before it sounded, Nikki rose from the bed and walked into the bathroom where she prepared herself for work.

She was in the kitchen, debating if she should rouse Jeff, when he walked into the space. He looked at her cautiously as he stood at the counter with his arms folded across his bare chest.

"How are you feeling this morning?" he asked.

"Since I took a couple of Tylenols last night, my headache has been reduced to a dull throb," Nikki answered. She rubbed the side of her head. "But it doesn't matter. I have to go to work to meet my deadlines; one of which is Friday. I'll probably have to work late every day this week to make up for yesterday." She opened her purse and removed her car keys.

"Look, I'm sorry about what happened yesterday," Jeff said.

"I am too," Nikki apologized. "But I don't have time to get into that now. We'll talk another time." She didn't meet Jeff's eyes. The keys jangled nervously in her hands. "I'm going in a little early to get a jumpstart. I'll call you later." She looked up at Jeff and held up her palm. "I promise."

"Okay, babe. Have a good day." If today had been any other day, he would have kissed her goodbye; back when their lives were normal. Instead, he stood frozen in place like a sentry guard at a military base.

As Nikki walked downstairs, Jeff walked over to the window and watched her enter the garage. After she departed, he returned to bed to get some sleep before he had to leave for work.

Nikki's efforts to make it to work early were jeopardized. An eight-car pileup on the Eisenhower Expressway slowed traffic to a crawl in both directions. As she sat in traffic, she wished she had brought a thermos of coffee with her to irrigate her dry mouth.

An hour later, and already feeling stressed out, she rushed inside the glass door of the advertising firm where she worked.

"Good morning, Nichole," Fatima said with a fake smile on her face as she laid the phone in the cradle. She sat inside a green, white, and chrome modular cubicle. "That was Mr. Prescott, and he wants to see you this morning as soon as you get settled."

"Would you call Vic and tell him I'll see him in about ten minutes?" Nikki asked. Victor Prescott was one of the owners of the advertising agency.

Fatima's appearance was always immaculate. Her long,

tawny colored hair was parted on the left side, and her mane fell so naturally on her shoulders that it looked as if it had been spray painted on her head. Her white teeth were capped, and her café au lait face was flawlessly made-up. The petite young woman wore a navy blue double-breasted suit with a white button down cotton blouse and matching pumps and accessories. Fatima was fresh out of college, and Nikki felt the younger woman was overly am-bitious. She and Nikki had never clicked because Nikki felt Fatima was gunning for her job.

"I sure will," Fatima answered, as she picked up the tele-phone to answer an incoming call. "Good morning, Sloan, Greene and Prescott Advertising Agency. How may I direct your call?"

As Nikki walked to her cubicle, she could feel stares from curious co-workers. Troy Bennett, who sat in the cu-bicle across the aisle from Nikki, leaned out of the opening of his workspace, and said laconically, "Good morning, Nichole. I hope you're feeling better today. Victor was on a rampage yesterday. He ran around here ranting about how you had a customer presentation scheduled yester-day, and then you called in sick."

The tote bag Nikki was carrying crashed to the floor, along with her stomach. "Oops, I forgot." Her hands flew to her mouth. Then she picked up the bag and set it and her purse on her desk. She powered on her PC and walked over to Troy's cubicle.

"Was Vic very upset?" Nikki asked, wringing her hands together. She sat down in the chair next to Troy's desk.

"He was mad as a wet hen. The clients were onsite." Troy's bass voice dropped. "I tell you, it wasn't a pretty sight. If I were you, I'd watch my back and the person up front."

Fatima walked up the aisle and stopped at Troy's cubicle. "Oh, there you are, Nikki. Mr. Prescott wants to see you now. That is, if you're available." Her eyebrows arched upward.

"Sure, I'm on my way," Nikki said and then looked at Troy. "I'll talk to you later." Nikki rose from the seat and followed Fatima out of the office. She was surprised when she noticed Fatima following her to Victor's office. "Where are you going?" Nikki turned and asked Fatima.

"Mr. Prescott wants to see us together," Fatima answered with an edge of mystery. "That's why I have a pad of paper with me. You're welcome to borrow a sheet," she informed Nikki sweetly as she dipped her head backward, her hair cascading over her shoulders.

Fatima knocked lightly on the door of Victor's office. "Come in," he said in a gruff voice, looking up at the women as they entered. "Have a seat," he added.

Nikki sat stiffly in one of the chairs across from Victor's desk. She wished she had brought a pad and pencil with her.

Victor peered at Nikki over the top of his silver-framed half moon glasses. His face was red, a sure sign that he was seething. The sleeves of his blue denim cotton shirt were pushed over his elbows. His gray hair shimmered from the sunlight streaming through his office window.

"Are you feeling better today?" he asked.

"Yes, Vic, I am. I think I had one of those twenty-four-hour bugs yesterday. In fact, I tried to get to work early today and there was a bad accident on the Eisenhower Expressway, so I was a little later coming in than I planned." Nikki folded her shaking hands together on her lap.

Victor picked up a pen and twisted it through his fingers. "I was surprised you called in yesterday. Did you forget we had the appointment with Swift Patisserie?" His eyes pierced her.

Nikki kept her eyes averted from her boss. "Uh, no, I didn't forget; I just wasn't in any shape to come in to work yesterday. I spent most of the day in the bathroom heaving." She coughed weakly and prayed Fatima hadn't said anything to Victor about Jeff's call yesterday. Fatima looked at her in amusement.

Victor's aquiline nose flared like a stallion's. "Luckily, I was able to talk Tim into rescheduling for a week from today. That brings me to the other reason I called you two into my office."

Oh Lord, I'm about to get fired. Nikki's stomach muscles clenched and unclenched as she held her breath.

"Nikki, you have quite a few projects due for completion within the next month. And right now, I'm not feeling very confident in your ability to make the deadlines. I'm assigning Fatima to assist you. I hired a temp to assume her duties for a month. After this meeting, I want you to bring Fatima up to date on where you stand. I'm warning you, I expect all of your projects to be completed on time." Victor's mouth snapped shut, like he'd bitten a sour lemon.

Nikki felt humiliated and her cheeks burned. Of all the people in the office, Victor had to choose Fatima to assist her. His edict fueled her fears that Fatima was trying to steal her job. Nikki resolved not to trust Fatima as far as she could see her.

"Did you hear me, Nikki?" Victor scolded when she didn't reply

Fatima looked at Nikki with false concern. She quickly threw in, "Victor, I'll do . . . I mean, we'll do whatever it takes to complete the projects on time. Nikki and I would hate for the company to lose money over a mere virus. Right, Nikki?"

"Yes, I heard and understand everything you said, Vic." Nikki looked from him to Fatima. "May I speak to you alone?" Her eyes pleaded with Victor.

"I'll start moving my stuff into the empty cubicle next to Nikki's," Fatima said as she stood up. Thank you, Vic. I won't . . . I mean, we won't let you down."

Victor smiled up at Fatima gratefully as she walked out of his office.

Nikki looked at Victor and all the hurt she'd felt the past few days was telegraphed to her boss by the dour expression on her face. Her lips drooped and her eyes were watery. Small red blotches dotted her cheeks like blush.

"Did you have to chastise me like I was child in front of Fatima, Vic? I've been working for you, for what, six years counting my internship. You've never had a problem with my work before, and for you to embarrass me in front of a receptionist . . . that wasn't fair." She leaned forward in her seat.

Vic's eyebrows rose in disbelief. "I don't know what's been happening with you, Nikki. But I do know that you haven't been yourself lately. If you have a problem, you know my door is always open." He flipped open a pad of paper lying on his desk. "You've missed ten deadlines over the past three months. Your creativity output is fine, but you're not translating it in your presentations. You know how I feel about missing deadlines. I don't tolerate it. Also, you've taken what, five unscheduled days over the past few months." He looked at her inquiringly. "What's going on with you? Are you having marital problems?"

"No," Nikki said timidly. Her voice choked up, and tears threatened to burst from her eyes.

Upon seeing the tears about to flow from Nikki's eyes, some of the sting went out of Victor's voice. "Then what is it?"

"I'm . . . I'm . . . I . . ." Nikki took a breath, and then managed to say, "Nothing is bothering me."

"You know my door is open if you need to talk," Victor said. "But you can't miss any more deadlines, young lady.

You know my policy is three misses and then you're written up. After four, you're terminated. So if anything is bothering you, now is the time to talk about it."

"I'm okay, Vic." Nikki stood up. "I'll make the deadlines; I promise. I just wish you had told me about Fatima working with me ahead of time, instead of telling me in front of her," she said with a pinch of hurt in her voice.

"Truthfully, I wish things hadn't come to this. But you left me with no choice but to write you up citing your performance. We're a business, and productivity equaling dollars is the bottom line. See that you make your deadlines, Nikki. I'd hate to have to let you go." Victor looked at her regretfully, and then his eyes dropped to his desk. He picked up a piece of paper and scanned it.

Nikki turned on one heel abruptly, and her foot slid on the plush beige carpeting. She nearly fell on her face. With all the dignity she could muster, she walked out of the office, suppressing a moan. She ignored the nosy stares from co-workers and walked straight into the ladies room.

Thankfully, she was able to find solitude there. Nikki angrily pulled open a gray stall door and locked it. She pulled down the cover of the toilet, sat on it, and allowed the tears to spill down her cheeks. Nikki wanted to scream at what she perceived as injustice, but work was not the place to totally lose control of her emotions.

"Jesus, help me." As she dried her eyes with toilet paper, it wasn't lost on Nikki how she'd brought all of the misfortune on herself. She knew it was a no-no to miss work and go to the boat as she had in the past. She rued the first time Maya had invited her. Nikki knew how strict Victor was about following rules at the office. Her shoulders slumped as if the Lord was putting more on than she could bear. She knew from the many sermons she'd heard at church that the Lord didn't overburden His children, but with her world falling apart, she had doubts. She closed her eyes and prayed for the Lord to work with her and help her overcome the huge obstacle she faced.

When Nikki heard the door to the restroom open, she rubbed her eyes with tissue, waiting for the person to leave. She inhaled deeply and prayed she could weather the storm. All things are possible through the Father. Nikki surmised that she just needed to chill out and think logically about everything that had happened and focus on resolving her problems. She needed to find her faith . . . faith the size of a mustard seed and remember that the Lord would see her through her dilemma.

When she heard whoever was in the restroom leave, she walked out of the stall, over to the sink, turned on the faucet, and towel wisped her face.

Ten minutes later, she had managed to get her emotions under control. When she returned to her desk, she heard Fatima bustling about in the cubicle next to hers.

Troy rolled his chair to the opening of his space. He gestured toward Fatima and mouthed, "What's up?"

Nikki shrugged her shoulders helplessly, and shook her head in regret. She sat at her desk and logged on to the system. Fifty emails awaited her attention.

Fatima peeped in the opening of Nikki's workspace. "Would you like to have lunch together? I figure we can go over our duties for the projects." Her face seemed to glow in triumph as she looked at Nikki.

Nikki continued looking at her monitor. "I already have lunch plans," she lied. She actually planned on working through lunch. "Come back to my cubicle in fifteen minutes and we can get started."

Fatima opened her mouth as if to reply. Then she nodded her head and returned to her own workspace.

Nikki responded to a few emails before her telephone sounded. "Nichole Singleton."

"Hey, baby. How's your day going?" Jeff asked. He was

sitting on the side of the bed reading the newspaper and sipping a cup of coffee.

"I've had better ones. I'm really swamped with work." Nikki looked up and saw Fatima standing outside her cubicle. "Someone's here to see me. I'll call you later." She hung up the telephone. "Fatima, come in. Let's get started."

By noon, Nikki had given Fatima a list of tasks to work on. "I guess we can break for lunch now," Nikki murmured.

"That's fine with me." Fatima stood and smoothed down the hem of her jacket. "After I come back from lunch, do you want me to start on the list of tasks, or do we need to talk more?"

"Why don't you go ahead and get started. We'll meet a half hour before quitting time and see where we are," Nikki answered.

"Okay, I'll see you this afternoon." Fatima glanced at her watch and departed.

Troy almost tripped over his feet as he rushed into Nikki's office. "What gives with Fatima?" he whispered.

"She's assisting me," Nikki answered, looking unconcerned. Then she dropped her eyes. "If you're going out to lunch now, would you mind picking up a sandwich for me? I need to catch up on my work." Her hand swept over her desk. "I'm going to work through lunch."

"Sure; no problem. You know if you needed help with anything, all you had to do was ask me." Troy's voice dropped as they watched Fatima saunter from her cubicle.

"Well, I'm asking for help now. Would you bring me a tuna salad on a croissant with lettuce and mayo?" Nikki said, smiling.

"What do you want to drink?" Troy seemed eager to please.

"A Diet Coke will be fine."

"I'll be back in a jiffy," Troy promised.

Nikki picked up the telephone and dialed Jeff. "Hi," she said when he answered the phone. "I just wanted to let you know that I'll probably have to work late all week. So if I don't answer the phone here at work, that means I'm busy."

"You must be working under a tight deadline," Jeff said. He reached over on his nightstand, picked up his watch, and slid it over his wrist.

"Yes, I am. I'll try to call you later, hon. I'm really sorry about what happened yesterday. Chalk it up to stress."

"Apology accepted. I'll see you tonight if I don't catch up with you later," Jeff replied soberly. He knew Nikki was making an attempt to make amends, but his feelings were still hurt.

Nikki hung up the telephone, and then lifted it from the cradle again; quickly dialing a number. "Hi, Roslyn. Is Reverend Dudley available?"

"Hello, Nikki. How are you this blessed morning?" the church secretary asked cheerfully.

"Good. And you?"

"Girl, I'm happy the Lord woke me up this morning clothed in my right mind. He allowed me to see another day. Pastor is busy right now. Would you like to leave a message for him?"

"I'd like to see him if he has time open this evening. I know this is short notice." The last part of Nikki's statement sounded like an apology.

Roslyn flipped the pages of the leather bound calendar. "Hmmm, let's see. You're in luck, Nichole. Deacon and Mrs. Lowry were supposed to meet Pastor tonight, and they canceled. Their appointment was at eight o'clock. Can you make it then?"

Yes, that will be perfect. Thank you, Roslyn," Nikki said gratefully.

"My pleasure, sister. I hope you're feeling better," Roslyn inquired solicitously.

"Yes, I am. I've got to go; duty calls," Nikki said.

"Okay, have a wonderful day."

After hanging up, Nikki looked at her PC and printed out the specs for the Swift account. Then she clicked on the Adobe icon, and looked down at her watch. It was time to get to back to work. Maybe help was on the way later in the guise of Reverend Dudley. He might be Nikki's last resort. She needed help, and she needed it badly.

Chapter 9

Jeff arrived at work forty-five minutes before his three o'clock start time. He stopped in the computer room and checked on the operators. After discussing the night's rerun jobs with his crew, he walked over to the activity board and checked the work schedule before he went to his office. He quickly booted his PC and replied to his many emails.

An hour later, he walked out of his office and to the bank of elevators. His hands were folded inside his pockets as he waited for the elevator to arrive. Finally, the bell sounded and the doors parted allowing him entry. He pressed the button for the fifth floor.

Jeff and Maya worked for the City of Chicago. He worked the evening shift, and Maya the day shift. She was employed as a System Analyst.

As Maya sat at her desk entering data on the keyboard, she sensed a presence behind her. She rolled her chair around.

"Hi, Jeff," she said, flashing him a weak smile. "What

brings you to my neck of the woods? I hope it wasn't because one of my jobs failed."

Jeff stood awkwardly near her desk. "Hey, can't a brother just stop by and speak to one of his favorite people?" He tried to joke, but came off sounding flat.

"Sure you can. Why don't you have a seat?" She gestured to the empty chair in front of her desk.

"I'm just going to come straight to the point and not beat around the bush," Jeff said. "I'm really worried about Nikki. She hasn't been herself lately." More worry lines seemed to have accumulated on his furrowed forehead since last night.

"Hmmm," Maya said. Her hands were folded atop her desk. "I agree with you that something is bothering her. But she still hasn't confided in me about what it is, if that's what you're asking."

Jeff's voice choked. "She won't talk to me, Maya. She's shut me out, and that's not like her. Nikki has been very distracted these past few weeks. We had a terrible argument when she came home last night. Normally, I try not to involve other people in our business, but I'm at my wit's end. I don't know what to do." He twisted his wedding band on his finger.

Maya winced, seeing the misery in his eyes. She leaned toward Jeff. "Normally I try to stay out of other people's business. But in this case, I'm going to make an exception. Nikki was at my house yesterday, so you can set your mind at ease as to where she was."

"And she couldn't tell me that!" Jeff's voice rose incredulously. Then he lowered it. "So, when I talked to you yesterday, you knew where she was, and you didn't say a word?"

"Whoa," Maya said, holding up her left hand. "Let's not get sidetracked here. Nikki was distraught when she showed up at my house, and she thought I had gone to work. We didn't pre-arrange her coming over there."

"She's become so secretive," Jeff muttered, smacking his left fist into his right hand. "You saw how abruptly she left church on Sunday. And when we got home, she just slept most of the day." He ran his hand over his head. "What can I do?"

Maya patted Jeff's arm. "You're going to have to be patient and wait for Nikki to open up. Give her time; I know she'll come around."

Jeff's eyes narrowed to slits. He cocked his head to the side. "What if she doesn't, Maya? That's what I'm worried about. Would you please talk to her and see what's going on?"

Maya sighed. She flipped a braid over her shoulder. "You know I love you like a brother, and Nikki is my sister in everything but blood. But I don't feel comfortable doing that. You know Nikki values her privacy. What if me and my girl's relationship is compromised in the process?"

"I'll take the blame, I swear." Jeff put his hand over his heart.

Maya expelled loudly. "I'm not making any promises, Jeff. But I'll see what I can do." She glanced at her desktop screen. A pop-up message indicated she had new mail.

"That's fair." Jeff stood up as his beeper went off. "I've got to get back to work. I'll talk to you at the end of the week."

"Okay." Maya smiled at Jeff as he left her office, though her heart felt overburdened. Generally when Nikki got like this, Maya waited for her to open up. Trying to coax her best friend for information was like pulling teeth. Despite Jeff's urgings, Maya knew Nikki wouldn't disclose her problem until she was ready.

* * *

Jeff walked briskly from the elevator to the computer room. He walked to a console and read the messages scrolling across the bottom.

Ernesto, his second in command, was on the telephone. He cupped his palm over the telephone receiver and said to Jeff, "One of the production CICS regions abended about five minutes ago. We're getting many calls about the failure. I assume you got a page?"

Jeff nodded and pulled out a chair from the long work area. "Give me the second page of the notification list, and I'll start making calls," he instructed.

Twenty minutes later, the crisis was averted.

Ernesto looked over at Jeff and said, "I can handle it from here, boss."

"Thanks, Ernesto," Jeff said, standing up. "I'll be in my office if you need me for anything else."

"I'm sure it'll be quiet from here on out," Ernesto joked. When the telephone immediately rang, he added, "Maybe I spoke too soon."

Leaving him to answer the call, Jeff walked back to his office. He sat down heavily in his ergonomic chair. The Microsoft Windows logo floated across his PC monitor. He picked up his and Nikki's wedding picture that sat on the left side of his desk and peered at Nikki's face. Jeff marveled at how happy she looked and wondered what could have happened to wipe that smile off her face. How had things gotten so bad between them? Jeff closed his eyes and leaned back in his chair. A pain shot through his heart at the realization that he could only speculate what was wrong with his wife. She had shut him out so completely. It was normal for Nikki to become quiet when she was upset, but not to this degree.

"Lord, show me the way. Help me find the words I need to say to ease Nikki's burdens," Jeff prayed.

* * *

Nikki worked nearly non-stop until five o'clock. She had managed to make a decent dent in her projects. She rolled the mouse across the pad and clicked the save button on the computer screen. Pleased with the first draft she had prepared for Swift, she reached up and massaged the back of her neck.

Fatima walked inside Nikki's cubicle. Her coat was tucked neatly across one of her arms. She handed Nikki a stack of papers. "Do you need anything else done?" she asked.

Nikki shook her head from side to side, indicating that she didn't.

"Okay then; I'm done for the day. Are you sure you don't need me to do something else before I leave?"

"No, I'm good," Nikki answered, setting the papers on her desk. "I'm going to be heading out shortly too. I just need to print out a copy of my first draft of the ad so I can look at it on paper."

"Okay, I'll see you in the morning." Fatima slipped on her coat and waved goodbye.

"Have a good evening," Nikki responded.

"You too," Fatima answered. She quickened her pace and rushed toward the elevators.

Nikki rose from her seat and walked to the color copier located around the corner from her office. When she returned to her desk, she critically scanned the photo and scrawled ideas on the margins of the paper. Then she picked up Fatima's notes. After reading them, she grudgingly had to admit that Fatima was talented and had come up with some good suggestions that would enhance the project.

Nikki glanced at the telephone and felt guilty for not calling Jeff back. She was tired and didn't feel like listening to him ask her for the umpteenth time what was wrong. Nikki knew Jeff like the back out her hand and figured he had probably gone to see Maya while he was at work today and asked Maya to talk to her. She knew it was a matter of time before her friend would phone her.

On cue, Nikki's cell phone chirped. She smiled and shook her head when she saw Maya's cell number on the caller ID. "What's up, girl? I thought you would've called before now." Nikki laughed as she greeted her friend.

"Ain't nothing up." Maya laughed too. "I was just calling to see how you were doing since you didn't return my calls yesterday. You know you ain't right."

"You mean to say that you aren't calling me because Jeff asked you to?" Nikki responded mockingly.

"All right, you got me there. You know your husband," Maya admitted. She was driving home from work. In accordance with the state law, she wore a device in her ear for hands free driving while talking on the cell phone. "But that doesn't mean I'm not worried about you myself. What's up with you, Nikki?" she asked.

"I'm okay. I just have a few issues on my plate, and I'm dealing with them as best as I can." Nikki heaved a heavy sigh.

"I beg to differ," Maya said pointedly. "You showed up at my house yesterday morning looking like someone had just told you that you had a month to live. Your husband goes on a rampage looking for you. And who's caught in the middle? Yours truly."

"I know, and I'm sorry. Jeff overreacts sometimes, and yesterday was one of those times," Nikki replied.

"You know I'm not criticizing or judging you, Nik. And you know I'd never put Jeff's feelings over yours, but personally, I feel your husband had a right to be a little upset yesterday. You lied to him, be it through omission or whatever, about going to work. I know he must've been humiliated when he called your job, and they told him you were out. I hope whoever took his call was a close friend of yours."

"Murphy was on the case yesterday," Nikki admitted. "The person who took the call was our receptionist, Fatima. I'll call you when I get home and give you the 411 on that," she said.

"Are you off work yet?" Maya asked. She accelerated slightly. Traffic had started to pick up after she passed 95th Street on the Dan Ryan Expressway.

"No, I worked late. I plan on leaving within the next half hour," Nikki said.

"Why don't you drive out my way, and then we can talk?" Maya suggested helpfully. She focused on the traffic ahead of her.

"I don't feel like driving that far," Nikki complained. She opened her desk drawer and pulled out her purse. "Anyway, I have an appointment, so we'll have to postpone that talk for another day."

"What does your schedule look like for the rest of the week?" Maya asked.

"I'm a little behind on my projects, so I'm going to have to work late all week and probably over the weekend."

"I know you said they were keeping you busy, but that's ridiculous," Maya said, feeling sorry for her friend.

"Tell me about it. Anyway, we'll talk over the weekend. Maybe we can meet for breakfast on Sunday morning. Dolton is so far from the north side. You need to move back in the city," Nikki joked.

"You're right, but Tony lives out here, so I stay here because of TJ. Otherwise, I'd get stuck bringing him back and forth to see his father," Maya said.

"Okay, then. I'll call you when I get home if it's not too late," Nikki replied.

"Take care, girl. And please think about what I said,"

Maya advised. "Jeff is really just worried about you. We both love you and have your best interest at heart."

"I know," Nikki said contritely. "I promise to give your comments some thought, and hopefully we'll get together on Sunday."

"Okay," Maya replied before hanging up.

Nikki was seated at an Italian Bistro off Rush Street an hour later. She felt tired and almost rescheduled her appointment with Reverend Dudley. But she knew she needed someone to help her find her way back to sanity. She cut a piece of lasagna and put it in her mouth while she thumbed through the latest edition of *Essence* magazine.

"Nikki Singleton, is that you?"

Nikki looked up and watched Lindsay walk over to the table.

"Hi, Lindsay. What are you doing here?" *Of all the million people in Chicago to run into tonight, why did I have to see her?* Nikki gritted her teeth and smiled up at her feebly.

"Well, I just finished having dinner with a potential client. What brings you out on a weeknight?" Lindsay slid into the booth opposite Nikki.

"I had to work late, and I have another appointment, so I decided to have dinner to kill time. How have you been?"

"Just fine. Business is picking up," she answered. She was dressed in a purple pantsuit with fox fur trimming the collar of the jacket. She wore purple pumps and gold accessories. Her locks looked shiny, like she'd just gotten them tightened.

"That's good. Work has been busy for me too. The agency has picked up a lot of new business, and luckily, I've been assigned to some of the projects," Nikki said.

"Well, good for you," Lindsay replied. "How's Jeff doing?" Her nose crinkled distastefully.

"He's doing fine. He's still working in the IT Department for the city."

"Well, I've got to run," Lindsay said. "It was nice running into you. I guess I'll see you at the next book club meeting. What are we reading?"

"I believe we're reading *Church Folks*, by Michele Andrea Bowen. I suggested we read a Christian fiction book for a change of pace." Nikki couldn't help but see the look of revulsion on Lindsay's face.

"Personally, I prefer mainstream fiction, or even nonfiction. But to each his own, I guess. Have you started reading the book yet?" Lindsay rose from the seat and put the strap of her purse on her shoulder.

"You know me; I like to wait and read the book as the meeting time draws near," Nikki said. "Well, take care of yourself, Lin."

"Yes, you do the same. Be sure and tell your husband I said hello," she said, heading for the rear of the restaurant balancing her to-go meal in her hands.

As Nikki watched Lindsay leave, a bead of perspiration rose on her forehead. Using her trembling right hand, she wiped it away. She felt uneasy as she watched Lindsay depart the restaurant. There was something about Lindsay that threw Nikki off kilter. She was never sure what was going to come out of her friend's mouth. Nikki glanced at her watch. It was time for her to head to the south side to church. She knew her financial situation was spiraling out of control, and she hoped that her pastor could help her. She needed someone neutral to talk to, and prayer couldn't hurt the situation.

With a raised hand, Nikki gestured to the waitress to bring her check. If Reverend Dudley couldn't help her, then she was at an impasse. Even with all that had happened, the urge to go to the casino hit her strongly; feeling it was time for her luck to change. Nikki quickly nixed the idea. It was that kind of thinking that got her into her predicament in the first place. She breathed deeply and commanded herself to stay focused.

By the time she paid the check and returned to her car, traffic had eased on the Dan Ryan Expressway. She arrived at the church with minutes to spare. Nikki was surprised to see a good number of people inside the church. She walked into the foyer surrounding Reverend Dudley's office, and he opened his door upon her approach, welcoming her with a warm smile.

"Why don't you come on in, my dear?" Reverend Dudley said. He closed the door softly behind her entrance.

Nikki laid her coat across the back of the chair opposite the one she planned to sit in, and set her tote bag at her feet. She chewed on her bottom lip, feeling flustered. *I hope I didn't make a mistake coming here; I don't want Pastor to think badly of me.*

Reverend Dudley relaxed his body against the back of the burgundy leather chair and rested his arms on the edge of his desk.

He looked up at Nikki and said, "What can I do to help you, Nichole?"

Chapter 10

Nikki's eyes roamed around the office as she tried to think of the correct way to describe to her Pastor what was happening in her life. She opened her mouth to speak, and then closed it suddenly becoming tongue-tied.

Reverend Dudley didn't miss the look of despondency on Nikki's face and tried to put her at ease. "How is your family doing, Nikki? Jeff and I have had conversations about his joining the Finance Committee. Your husband is a real go-getter. He has some good ideas; you must be proud of him."

Nikki scowled though she tried to smile. Her stomach muscles danced rhythmically. She exhaled a deep breath, trying to relieve the building tension. "Everyone is doing fine, Pastor."

"That's great."

The pastor noticed Nikki's watery eyes and rose from his chair to walk to the credenza opposite his desk. He turned on the CD player that lay on top of the cabinet and lowered the volume. He was stalling to give Nikki time to compose herself. As Father Hayes and the Cosmopolitan Choir belted out the lyrics of "Jesus Can Work It Out," Reverend Dudley peeped over at Nikki and noticed that her body was hunched over, and she was quietly sniffling. Her suffering was apparent.

Reverend Dudley returned to his seat, clasped his hands together, and said, "Nikki, I hope you know that you can share with me whatever is troubling you. Your father was a close personal friend of mine. I'm your godfather, and I've tried to step up to the plate and take Lincoln's place when needed. You're like a daughter to me, as well as a part of the church family." He took a handkerchief from his jacket pocket and passed it to Nikki.

"Thank you, Pastor." Nikki dabbed at her eyes, and replied in a shaky voice, "What I really need is for you to pray for and with me. For the past few months, I've been going through a tough time, and done some things I'm not proud of. And these acts that I've done threaten to destroy the very fabric of my life." She coughed and cleared her throat.

"Perhaps you're being too hard on yourself." Reverend Dudley looked at Nikki with a benevolent expression on his face. "It seems that when we're facing trials and tribulations, they grab a hold of us like a rabid dog and just won't let go. And it feels like we can't resolve the issue no matter how hard we try. But remember that you don't have to face your troubles alone. Our Father in heaven is watching over you and directing your path. And don't forget you have your husband to lean on, as well as Eveline and Linc."

"I can't talk to them about my problem, Pastor," Nikki whispered. Her face became scarlet from embarrassment. She dropped her head toward her lap. Her eyes filled with tears again.

"Surely it can't be that bad, Nichole." Reverend Dudley leaned forward in his chair. "Give me your hands," he instructed.

Nikki's hands trembled as Reverend Dudley took them in his. He closed his eyes and bowed his head. "Father, I give you thanks for allowing your faithful servants to meet in your house tonight. Lord, I ask that you help Nichole. Please lift her up, buoy her spirit during this tribulation she's facing. Lord, we are so grateful that you supply our every need again and again. And I know you'll supply Nichole's.

"Lord, I ask that you help Nichole remember that she's not alone. Her husband, mother, along with you and I, will help our daughter defeat Satan and make him out the liar that he is. Shower your blessings down on your daughter, Lord. Guide her and give her peace. These blessings I ask in your name. Amen."

"Amen," Nikki uttered. She quickly wiped her eyes with the backs of her hands, then noticed Reverend Dudley glancing at his watch. She knew he had to be tired. Some days he was at the church or the hospital as early as six in the morning.

"You know I'm available for you whenever you need me, Nichole," he reminded her. "Are you sure you don't want to talk to me about whatever's bothering you?" Reverend Dudley folded his hands together in a triangle, as his elbows relaxed atop his desk.

"I don't think I'm quite ready yet, Pastor. I know you're here for me and I want you to know I appreciate it. I've just really gotten myself into a jam, and it's up to me to fix it."

"Now see, that's where you're wrong," Reverend Dudley interjected, shaking his head from side to side. "Letting go of your problems and putting your trust in God is what will help you overcome all obstacles. God never leaves us alone; we just have to be still and let the Holy Spirit guide us."

Nikki sighed and reached down on the floor for her purse. "I know what you're saying is right, Pastor. But I feel I have to resolve my problem on my own. It's my fault I'm in this predicament. I brought all of this upon myself."

"I hear you, but as you continue your walk of Christian faith, you'll see firsthand what I'm talking about. Now I want you to do something for me, Nichole." Reverend Dudley stared in her eyes.

"What's that?" Nikki's hand fluttered to her chest. She was taken aback by the intensity of his gaze.

"Actually there are two things," he said earnestly. "First, I want you to stop being so hard on yourself. Until you can forgive yourself, you won't be in a position to accept help from others. Which leads to my next request. Don't be too proud to ask for help. Jeff adores the ground you walk on, and your mother and brother are extremely proud of you."

Nikki stood and put on her coat. "I hear you, Pastor. And I'll certainly give what you said some thought. I have to go now. I have a long ride home, and I need to go into work early tomorrow." Her cell phone started chirping. She pulled the phone out of her pocket and looked at the caller ID. "That's Jeff," she told Reverend Dudley. "I'll call him back when I leave here."

He walked around the desk and picked up Nikki's bag; handing it to her after she finished buttoning her coat.

"Thank you," Nikki said, trying to sound stronger than she felt. She hugged Reverend Dudley and added, "I'll be fine, Pastor. I don't want you worrying about me."

Reverend Dudley released her. "Don't forget, I'm here if you need me. Sometimes when we keep problems inside, they eat at us and magnify the issues, making them seem even larger."

"Thanks for giving me a little of your time." Nikki smiled solemnly. "I'll be back on Thursday for choir rehearsal."

"I'll see you then, my dear. Be careful driving home. I'll be praying for you, Nichole," Reverend Dudley said as he walked her out of his office.

A few minutes later, Nikki sat in her cranked car pondering her talk with Reverend Dudley; trying to decide if he had helped or not. As Nikki pulled out of the parking lot, she found herself heading toward an Off Track Betting facility in Crestwood, Illinois, a southern suburb of Chicago. She was sure her luck had changed. After all, the house could only win so many times. Excitement raced through Nikki's veins as she glanced down at her watch. It was only eight-thirty, and Nikki had traveled that route before. It would only take her half an hour to get to the facility, and she could be home by nine. Desperation had taken hold of her mind and refused to let it go. It was imperative she win back some money to try to save the house. Nikki still had one credit card that she hadn't maxed out yet. The card only had a three hundred dollar limit, and Nikki swore to herself that she wouldn't spend any more than one hundred dollars unless she won.

As Nikki entered the ramp for the Dan Ryan Expressway, a little voice in her head berated her. *You're pushing it, sister. You need to take your butt home, and make sure you're prepared for work tomorrow.*

Jeff hung up the telephone. He had just finished talking to a customer service rep at ComEd, the utility company that supplied electricity to the Chicago land area. To his relief, the utilities were paid and up to date. After thinking about Nikki's erratic behavior lately and his maxed out credit card, Jeff suspected Nikki was having trouble paying the bills, but that didn't seem to be the case. *So now I know the bills aren't behind, but I wish to God I knew what's bothering Nikki.* He rubbed his eyes.

The evening at work for Jeff had proceeded without a hitch. None of the batch jobs or online files had experienced any problems. The application systems were the bread and butter of the city. Jeff logged onto his E-Trade account. He hadn't bothered to enlighten Nikki when he opened the account. He had invested a couple thousand dollars with the online brokerage company after Nikki took over the bills. Just in case she ran short of money.

On the one hand, Jeff was proud that Nikki was able to handle the household finances, but he felt unappreciated and at loose ends. As the head of the household, he felt that he should be the one paying the bills. His eyes glimmered as another thought occurred to him. He was aware that Nikki wanted a baby now instead of when they planned to start on the family within the next couple of years. He hit the side of the desk in glee as the idea marinated in his brain that maybe Nikki was pregnant and she didn't know how to tell him. Jeff nodded as he thought how her condition could justify her actions.

A big grin broke out across his face and then disappeared. Jeff supposed that Nikki would tell him if she were with child. His lips pursed thoughtfully as he considered maybe she didn't know how to break the news to him. He'd never told her how much he wanted a daughter. The idea of a little mirror image of his wife running around their house filled his being with joy. Jeff's eyes crinkled with glee.

The telephone rang, shattering his ecstatic mood. "Jeffrey Singleton. How may I help you?"

"Hey, man. What's up?" Ron greeted his friend and client.

"Hey, Ron. What's up with you? Don't tell me that you're calling to inform me that I've lost more money?" Jeff chuckled as he leaned back in his chair and placed his feet up on the edge of his desk.

"Well, aren't you the psychic? Actually, that's why I'm calling. The stock dipped about two percent since the close of today's trading. But it's nothing for you to be concerned with. If it falls any further tomorrow, then you'll be close to your limit. I want to find out what you want me to do? Ride out the drop, or give it another couple of days?" Ron picked up a pencil to make notes.

"Well, I can't afford to go far below my limit. You know we cushioned my limitation amount somewhat. So I'm not in bad shape right now," Jeff replied. His voice lowered to a whisper. "Man, between me and you, I think Nikki's having a baby."

"Congratulations, man. I'm happy for both of you. So I guess that means you can't afford to keep investing like you have been?" Ron asked.

"Hmmm, maybe. We'll have to wait and see. We just need to be more cautious about the stock you pick," Jeff said.

Ron laughed aloud. "No problem, man. We can do that. So do you prefer a boy or girl?" he asked Jeff.

"Secretly, I prefer a girl. But you know me; I'll just deny that if you ever try to go public with that bit of news. The truth is, I just want a healthy baby." Jeff couldn't stop smiling.

"So what do you want me to do?" Ron noticed the light flashing on his phone, indicating he had another call coming in.

"Let's give it one more day." Jeff pursed his lips, then added, "Then you can drop or sell the stock if the price continues to fall. Why don't you give me a call around this time tomorrow?"

"Will do. Tell Nikki I said hello, and I'll holla at you tomorrow."

"Okay, man," Jeff said before hanging up.

He leaned back in his chair and began to take stock of his life. Even if Nikki were in a snit, life was good. He and Nikki were morally good people and followed God's teachings . . . most of the time. Sometimes he tended to drink when he felt stressed, but his imbibing hadn't gotten out of hand.

He and Nikki had completed college, were engaged for two years, and their children would be born in wedlock. Additionally, they owned an expensive piece of real estate located in a prime area of the city. To Jeff's way of thinking, they had followed God's commandments, and nothing but good things lay in store for them.

Jeff had a mental ruler in his hands, measuring the dimensions of a third bedroom in their apartment. He could picture the room painted yellow with light wood furniture and a rainbow mural drawn on the ceiling. He and Nikki would have to bite the bullet and share the fourth bedroom as their joint office, leaving the second bedroom as the guestroom.

They'd had discussions about having more than one child, and agreed to expand their living quarters by knocking down the walls of the apartment next door if necessary. Taking it all in, Jeff whispered, "God is good all the time. Thank you, Lord, for blessing me and my wife."

He shook his head, as if to clear the cobwebs from his mind. It was time for Jeff to get back to work. He had a gut feeling that Nikki was pregnant, and he vowed to give her the space she needed to confirm his supposition in her own way.

Nikki sat at a table, glancing up at the monitor in the Off Track Betting location in Crestwood, entranced by a trifecta horserace in progress. She glanced at her watch. Time had drifted away from her. She was pleased with herself because she'd keep her composure and only lost fifty dollars. Considering her track record, the outcome could have been worse. She giggled out loud. Nikki didn't have a clue as to how to pick the horses at the OTB, and she actually thought there was a possibility that she might win. It was time for her to head north since tomorrow was a workday, and she had told her boss that she'd be at work early.

She hurriedly donned her coat and flew out the building like a stream of angry bees were on her heels and walked rapidly to the parking lot.

Nikki had a habit of speeding as she drove, usually adding ten to fifteen miles per hour to whatever the speed limit was. Traffic was light, and she arrived home in less than thirty minutes.

Chapter 11

The following morning, when Nikki awakened and glanced at the clock, she did a double-take. "I can't believe I overslept!" she screamed, jumping out of the bed. Her eyes roamed the room, looking for Jeff. "Jeffrey, why didn't you wake me up?" Nikki wailed.

Jeff walked into the room, carrying a tray of food. "Oh, you're up. I decided to let . . ." His voice trailed off at the sight of his wife rushing around the room. He set the tray on the table. "What's wrong?" he asked.

"What's wrong is that I was supposed to be at work early this morning." Nikki flew to the closet and pulled out a couple of wrinkled outfits. "God, I don't need this; not this morning." She took a camel brown pantsuit off the hanger and threw it toward Jeff. "Would you please press this for me?" Jeff caught the outfit as Nikki ran into the bathroom.

"Sure. I'm sorry I didn't wake you up. You were just sleeping so peacefully, that I hated to wake you," Jeff said. *Plus you need your rest.*

He was finishing his task when Nikki rushed into the

kitchen, clad in peach panties with a matching bra and flesh colored panty hose. Jeff's eyes swept over Nikki's body intently. She hadn't gained any weight yet. By the same time next month, he imagined that her tummy would be slightly rounded, her breasts fuller, and how his baby might even have some back.

"What are you looking at?" Nikki screeched. "Give me my clothes so I can get out of here."

"What's the rush? Are you late already?" Jeff asked as he handed her the pants. Nikki hopped on one foot as she pulled them up.

"I told you I had to be at work early all this week. I wish you had checked to make sure that I had set the alarm before you went to bed as you usually do. You know how I forget to do it sometimes." She looked at Jeff accusingly as she zipped the top of the pantsuit.

"I thought you needed your rest," Jeff stammered. "Is there anything else I can do for you?"

"No, you've done quite enough. If I'm lucky and don't run into traffic, I might only be ten minutes later than my normal starting time."

Nikki ran into the bedroom and slipped her feet into chocolate brown, ankle length boots. Then she rushed to her dresser and put earrings in her earlobes, a gold bracelet on one wrist, and a watch on the other. She walked to the closet and pulled out a hat that matched the pantsuit and shoved it on her head. She would style her hair after she arrived at work.

When she went back into the kitchen, Jeff had placed her tote bag and purse on the kitchen counter. She pulled her keys out of her purse. "I've got to run. I'll call you later," she said impatiently as she walked to the door.

"Okay. Again, I'm sorry." Jeff pecked Nikki on the check. She galloped out of the apartment like she was a filly running a race.

She decided to take side streets during her morning commute and made it to the office building within twenty minutes. When the elevator arrived, it was crowded and all the buttons were lit up. Nikki beat up on herself silently as the car rose upward. She wondered if she had a death wish or something. As much as she knew her job was in jeopardy, she had the audacity to arrive late today. *Lord, I can't afford to lose my job. Please don't let Victor be in yet. If he isn't, I promise I'll never gamble again.*

Finally, the elevator stopped on the 30th floor . . . Nikki's floor. She tore a path to her cubicle, quickly took off her coat, and threw it on the back of her chair. Then she powered up her PC.

Fatima walked into the cubicle. "I wondered what had happened to you. I expected you at least half an hour ago. Do you have anything for me to do this morning?" She looked at Nikki as if she expected her to say no.

Nikki reached inside her bag and handed Fatima a sheaf of papers. "Take a look at my suggestions, and we'll discuss them later."

"Okay." Fatima looked at her co-worker dubiously and walked out of the cubicle.

Nikki pulled her hat off her head and smoothed a few stray curls. She reached inside her bottom drawer and pulled out a black handled curling iron. Her eyes sneaked a peek at the telephone on her desk. The red light, which indicated whether she had messages, wasn't lit. A sigh of relief escaped her lips.

"Now, if I don't have any emails, then I'm home free," she muttered.

Her PC had finished booting. Nikki set the curling iron on the side of her desk, and logged onto her corporate email account. Her body sagged with relief. She didn't have any messages from Victor.

"Thank you, Lord. Today, at least, I still have a job." Her

mind shied away from the possibility that she was at Victor's mercy and could be terminated at any moment.

Nikki scrolled through and replied to emails from co-workers. She pulled the revised draft of the Swift Patisserie ad out of her tote bag, logged onto the software, and made the revisions she had notated the night before.

A few hours later, she clicked on the save icon and closed the program. Nikki looked up when Fatima walked into her office.

"Do you have a minute, Nikki? There are some things I'd like to go over with you," Fatima asked, hesitating at the entrance to the cubicle.

"Sure, come on in." Nikki waved her over. "I just finished my revisions on the Swift Patisserie ad."

Fatima sat in the chair and flipped open a page of the notepad she'd brought with her. The two women discussed the amendments and half an hour later, came to a meeting of the minds regarding the progress of the project.

Fatima closed her pad. She leaned close to Nikki's desk and looked behind her. After seeing the coast was clear, she whispered, "Uh, Nikki, I wanted to put your mind at ease. I'm not going to say anything to Victor about what happened the other day."

Nikki gulped a mouthful of air. She narrowed her eyes at Fatima. "What do you mean?"

"About you taking the day off. You obviously weren't at home sick, because your husband called here looking for you. It's a good thing I answered the phone." She looked at Nikki smugly, like the cat that swallowed the canary.

Nikki felt like an imaginary noose was tightening around her neck. Her eyes widened dramatically then narrowed to slits. "You're right, I wasn't home. But you really don't know why I wasn't. I could've been at the doctor, or picking up a prescription." Her voice turned frosty.

"Yes, you're right. But somehow I doubt that's the case. Wouldn't your husband have known that? Your home phone came up on caller ID, so he was at home," Fatima answered smugly. She sat erect in the chair.

"First, it's none of your business. And second, it's my personal business, and I won't discuss it with you. If you feel like you need to go to Victor, then be my guest." Nikki's body began shaking and she tried unsuccessfully to keep an annoyed trembling out of her voice.

Fatima's hand fluttered to her chest, accidentally knocking the notepad off her lap in the process. She scooped it off the floor. "Look, Nikki, I didn't mean to come off sounding threatening or anything like that. Victor wants us to work together on these projects, and I can do that. I was trying to put your mind at ease and clear the air between us." Her voice twanged, like her feelings were hurt.

Nikki gritted her teeth. "If that was the case, why bring it up at all? You shouldn't have mentioned it. Everyone here knows that you're ambitious. And when people are overachievers like you are, they don't stop at anything to attain their goals," she accused.

Fatima looked at Nikki with incredulity on her face. She waved her hand impatiently. "Look, I just wanted to lay my cards on the table so you wouldn't think I was backstabbing you or something like that. It's no secret that I'd like to be where you and the other designers are. I went to an accredited art school, and it's only a matter of time before my turn will come. I certainly would like to make more money, but I don't have to resort to petty tactics to attain my goals. I know my stuff, and I believe how well I perform on this project will be a boost my career."

Fatima stood up and looked down at Nikki. "I don't know what's going on in your life, but something is wrong. I was hoping you could mentor me. I've been asking Victor for months to let me assist you with some of your projects. But if you don't feel comfortable with that, then I'll ask him to assign me to another designer."

Nikki stood up and said to Fatima's receding back, "Fatima, I'm sorry. I didn't mean what I said. I'm just under a little strain right now."

Fatima turned around and looked at Nikki with a serious expression on her face.

Nikki spoke again. "Can we move beyond this? I was up late last night working on revisions, and forgot to set the alarm clock. I'm just a little stressed from trying to meet my deadlines. Other than that, there's nothing else bothering me."

Fatima hesitated and then nodded her head. "I guess so. But I need you to stay on track. Our futures are linked together. If you need me to do something, all you have to do is ask. You're good at what you do. We're both African-American women, and I'd like to think we can work together."

Nikki held up her hands. "Truce?" Her eyes pleaded with her co-worker.

Fatima said, "Yes." She walked over to Nikki's desk, and they shook hands. She said, "I'm going to get back to work on the revisions for the Swift account and then we can meet after lunch if you're available."

"I'll make the time. I'm going to finish up and move on to the next project. Let's meet at two o'clock this afternoon," Nikki said.

"Fine, I'll be back then." Fatima walked out of Nikki's cubicle.

It seemed like every time Nikki turned around there was another fire to douse. She wasn't quite sure if she could trust the seemingly perfect Fatima and was wary of the so-called truce. Nikki knew she would just have to be on guard until she could determine Fatima's motives. Nikki sifted through a stack of files on her desk and found her notes for the next project. After reading them, she emailed Victor and copied Fatima on the email, attaching the proposal for Swift that she had finished that morning.

An hour later, Nikki sat at her desk, trying to decide what she was going to do for lunch when her telephone rang. "Hello, this is Nichole Singleton."

"Hi, Nikki. How are you doing?" Eveline asked her daughter.

"Hello, Mom. I'm okay, just extremely busy with projects at work," Nikki said as she looked upward trying to calculate how soon she could get her mother off the telephone.

"Is that why you haven't called me back? I know Jeff told you that I called you on Sunday evening," Eveline said. Her voice held a hint of betrayal.

"Yes, he did. Mom, I'm sorry, I meant to call you back. I have deadlines for work, and I just hadn't gotten around to it."

"Well, I was worried about you. The truth is, I still am. You left church so abruptly on Sunday, and I didn't know what happened."

"I know. I guess I was stressed out, and after I botched the song, I just wanted to get out of there as quickly as I could," Nikki said.

"Are you sure you're all right? I had a dream about you last night. I don't remember the details, but I know when I awakened, I felt apprehensive."

"Of course I am." Nikki fidgeted in her seat, smoothing the bottom of her jacket, as she tried to calm her mother's fears. "Mom, you're being paranoid. I promise you, nothing is wrong with me other than a little work related stress. I've been staying late at work all week and bringing work home with me. The company has signed on new clients, and I've been assigned to work on quite a few projects."

"Well, when I called the church this morning to order

flowers for the altar on Sunday to commemorate your father's birthday, Roslyn told me that you had made an appointment to see Reverend Dudley earlier this week." Eveline's brows wrinkled with worry. "I don't want you to think I'm checking up on you or anything, but I'm concerned about you."

Nikki felt like a small child caught in a lie. Her face turned bright red and the corners of her mouth turned downward. In all the drama that had taken a firm hold of her life, Nikki had forgotten her father's birthday. "I had something I wanted to discuss with Pastor; that's all."

Eveline knew her daughter wasn't being totally truthful. Roslyn hadn't revealed why Nikki was at church, and Eveline knew she wouldn't. "Okay, if you don't choose to confide in me about what's bothering you, that's fine. I just want you to know I'm here for you if you need me." Her slender fingers nervously untwisted the bunched up phone cord.

Nikki's throat felt like a chicken bone was lodged inside it. She blinked rapidly, as she tried to choke back a sob. "Mom, I'm . . ." Nikki held her forehead in her left hand.

"Nichole Deidre Singleton, I suggest you make time to stop by and visit me today when you get off work," Eveline said in a strict tone of voice.

"But I have to work late this evening," Nikki protested. She closed her eyes.

"I'm not going to take no for an answer," Eveline insisted, as she stood and paced around her immaculate kitchen. "If you don't come here, then I'll come to your job. It's your choice."

"Okay, I'll be there. I'm not sure what time though," she said before ending the call and hanging up.

Nikki clutched the pencil she held in her left hand so tightly, that it snapped into two pieces. The sound startled her, and she slumped forward in her seat. She wasn't quite ready to see her mother until she got a handle on her emotions and finances. Nikki's mother had an uncanny way of seeing through her. Eveline could always sense when Nikki had a problem and would nag her daughter until she fessed up.

Nikki stood up and stretched her body for a few seconds before picking up her coffee mug from the corner of her desk and going to the ladies room. After she wiped her eyes and used the washroom, she strolled to the kitchenette and poured herself some coffee.

Though her day had started off shaky, Nikki was able to make great headway on the Swift project. Fatima's assistance proved to be invaluable. They had put their heads together and made a couple more minor improvements. Later that afternoon, Nikki emailed Victor a copy of the newly revised proposal, and scheduled a meeting with herself, Fatima, and Victor for in the morning to discuss the presentation of their latest brain-storm.

A notification email message from Victor popped up on Nikki's monitor an hour later. She opened it.

Nik,

The rough drafts look great. Kudos to you and Fatima for a job well done. I knew you ladies would make a good team. I've attached just a few corrections that I know you'll have done by our meeting tomorrow. If all looks well, then I'll submit them to Swift and schedule a meeting for next week.

Nikki chortled with glee as she forwarded the email to Fatima. She pumped her fist in the air. *I still got it.*

Another email popped in her inbox, it was from Merrill Lynch and was a summary detailing her 401K plan. Nikki absently scanned the email and then an idea bloomed in her head. Merrill Lynch might be her savior. Nikki asked herself why she hadn't thought of borrowing from the investment house sooner. Her retirement fund could serve a dual purpose of saving her life and her marriage. She remembered Pastor Dudley saying during one of his Sunday sermons, "Ask and ye shall receive." Nikki wasn't sure exactly how much she could borrow from the fund, but hoped it would be enough to pay off her casino debt and the property taxes. Though she didn't agree with Ron at the time when he suggested she and Jeff take the maximum contribution amount for retirement plans, now she was grateful, Jeff had pushed her into doing so. Nikki made a pledge to herself that if she could extract herself from her debt that she would never gamble again.

Nikki's hand flew across the keyboard as she typed rapidly. She logged onto her company's human resources site and looked up the email address for Merrill Lynch. She composed an email, asking for her account balance. Afterward, she logged off the computer. It was now time for her to prepare an impermeable defense to deal with her mother.

Chapter 12

Jeff had been at work for two hours and had attended a meeting with the other shift managers to discuss the weekend activities. A big file conversion was planned for the weekend, and he wanted to make sure his team and the one on the other shifts were aware of the importance of being fully staffed. The conversion would last the entire weekend, and Jeff picked up the attendance chart to make sure they had adequate coverage. He would probably come in just to check on things during the day Saturday.

He walked back to his office, obsessed with thoughts of Nikki. Jeff had talked to his wife an hour ago, and she informed him that she was going to visit her mother after work. He was hoping that Nikki would confide in her mother about the pregnancy. By now, Jeff was 99.9% sure that was this wife's problem. What else could it be?

Jeff sat on his chair and pulled a letter out of his briefcase. The letter was from Chase Bank, reminding him and Nikki that the balloon payment was due on the first of the month—two weeks away—for the repairs done on the apartment building. Twenty thousand dollars seemed like a large sum, and Ron had advised Jeff against that kind of credit.

Jeff claimed the amount was just a drop in the bucket. Nikki didn't know it, mostly because she was never interested, but they had nearly $75,000 in tangible assets. The figure deviated, depending on the market. Still it was a healthy bottom line for a couple in their late twenties.

They had received nearly $10,000, in lieu of wedding gifts. Though Nikki initially balked at the idea, Jeff had suggested they invest the money. Ron was a genius when it came to investments. Jeff was glad he had decided to retain his frat brother's services instead of Lindsay's. Jeff had also been dabbling in the stock market, setting up his own e-trade account, unbeknownst to both Ron and Nikki.

Taking his cell phone off the holder attached to his belt, Jeff dialed Ron's number. The line was busy. Jeff clicked off the phone and frowned. A busy signal was unusual. He figured he'd be routed to voicemail. *Oh well, I'll try later.* He decided to start on the performance reviews due after the first of the year.

There was a knock on his closed door. "Come in," Jeff said, looking up at the door. Walter, the first shift supervisor, walked into the room. The tall, full-bearded, dark-skinned man sat down on one of the padded chairs in front of Jeff's desk. "What's up, man? I didn't expect you to still be here."

"It's all good, man." Walter's voice lowered. "I don't know if you heard or not that Mike Nichols is leaving the city. He's moving on to greener pastures in the private sector."

"Shut your mouth. Really?" Jeff asked, surprised. He leaned back in his chair.

Mike Nichols was the Operations Manager, and Jeff coveted his job as a future steppingstone to upper management. Mike was only a few years older than Jeff, so the odds seemed stacked against him attaining the position unless Mike quit working for the city. But most city employees never left their jobs.

"That's the buzz coming from the fifth floor," Walter confided.

"Do you know if the powers-that-be are going to replace him with someone in-house?" Jeff could already picture himself, possessions and all, in the spacious corner office on the 5th floor.

Walter stood up and quietly closed Jeff's office door. He sat back down in the seat. "It's not written in stone or anything, but I heard Mr. Esposito is going to give all the shift managers a shot at it."

Jeff couldn't stop a smile from appearing on his face. He rubbed his hands together. "That's cool. So, my competition is you and Lance then?"

"No, it's just between you and Lance. I don't have any aspirations of moving up the corporate ladder here in the city; it's too political. I prefer the corporate route at a privately-owned company. I've put out a few feelers. I just thought I'd give you a heads up because you know Lance isn't going to take any prisoners when he guns for the position," Walter said.

"Thank you, my brother," Jeff answered with a twinkle in his eye. "I plan to continue working here for maybe another five or ten years, if I can move up. The extra income from a promotion certainly wouldn't hurt right about now." He thought about the new addition to his and Nikki's family.

"You do what you gotta do then. Lucas Halprin is supposed to make a formal announcement later this week."

"How did you find out about it?" Jeff looked puzzled.

"You know me. I got my sources." Walter stood up and smiled. "I'ma holla at you later."

"Thanks for the heads up, Walt."

Alone once more, Jeff tried calling Ron for the second time, but still got a busy signal. Giving up, he realigned his thoughts and concentrated on the performance review he had been working on earlier.

With traffic backed up horrendously on Lake Shore Drive, the journey to Eveline's house was slow. Nikki and a hundred other drivers were creeping along at ten miles an hour. A light mist of rain had turned into a steady downpour, and her windshield wipers made a squishy noise as the blades flipped back and forth.

The sky was gray and gloomy. The weather forecast predicted the rain would turn into snow later that evening. *I should have called Mama and begged my way out of meeting her this afternoon. That would have given me time to think of a plausible excuse for the twenty questions she's prepared for me.* Nikki peeped at the car speeding up behind her with soaring alarm and sighed with relief as it slowed down before hitting her bumper. Nikki planned to keep her visit short with her mother. She would use the weather as an excuse. Chicago was due for a snowstorm tonight; though most of the time the meteorologists got it wrong

Thirty-five minutes later, Nikki exited at Jeffrey Boulevard and headed east toward Pill Hill, where her mother resided. Twenty minutes after that, she was parking in front of her mother's pristine two-story Georgian home. The light over the storm door lessened the darkness. Before Nikki could put her spare key in the door, her mother opened it. Nikki leaned over and kissed her mother's cheek as she stepped inside the door.

Eveline looked comfortable in a loose fitting aqua caftan. She was a few inches shorter than her daughter, and her hair modeled a blunt cut. Although she would turn fifty on her next birthday, her face looked youthful; free of wrinkles. Lincoln Sr. had left her financially stable, so she retired from teaching and volunteered at the church a couple days a week, tutoring students. Eveline and Nikki shared the same honey brown complexions and medium build physiques.

Eveline took her daughter's coat and hung it in the cedar paneled closet. "Let's go into the den."

A fire crackled in the fireplace, making the room warm and cozy. After her husband passed away and to keep herself busy, Eveline had redecorated the house. The room was paneled with maple wood. A chocolate brown and beige striped sofa and matching lounge chair made up the furniture. Two maple end tables sat on each end of the sofa, and a cocktail table was placed in front of it.

A glass and chrome desk, with a matching bookcase, was positioned on one wall in the room and a plasma television on another. A floor-to-ceiling bookcase was built on another wall, and it was crammed full of books. *Jet* and *Ebony* magazines graced the cocktail table.

"Are you hungry? I made a pot of beef stew," Eveline said, watching her daughter closely, trying to discern what was bothering her.

"Stew sounds good. I only had a salad for lunch, and my stomach is growling." Nikki rubbed it. "I can smell the soup from here and it smells heavenly." She followed her mother into the kitchen.

"I like that suit you're wearing; it's flattering on you. Have a seat," Eveline instructed. "I'll fix us both a bowl."

"Thank you. I bought it at a boutique on the north side. Mom, you don't have to wait on me," Nikki protested. "Why don't you have a seat and let me wait on you?"

Eveline had already reached inside a dark cherry wood cabinet and removed two bowls. "Why don't you pour the iced tea? It's in the refrigerator."

"Okay, I can do that." Nikki walked over to the refrigerator.

Her mother was a neat freak, and her kitchen, as well as the rest of her house reflected that. Like the other rooms in the ten-room house, the kitchen had experienced a major makeover. The walls were painted eggshell white, and the floor was a red and white ceramic tile. The curtains at the window matched the floor. And a dark cherry wood table that could seat ten, stood in the middle of the room. The kitchen counters were topped with white marble, tinged with red, and all the appliances were white.

Knowing her mother was a stickler for proper etiquette, Nikki quickly set the table for two. She pulled silver utensils out of the cabinet drawer. They sat at the table and bowed their heads.

"Heavenly Father," Eveline prayed, "we thank you for the meal prepared for the nourishment of our physical bodies. Lord, I ask that you stop by here tonight and help us take care of our spiritual bodies. Lord, please take care and guide us as you promised. Amen."

Thinking that her mother was laying it on a bit thick, Nikki made a great effort not to roll her eyes. She cut a piece of buttery cornbread with her spoon. It was so good that it seemed to melt in her mouth. She followed it up with a spoonful of stew. When she finished chewing, Nikki said, "Um, that's good. Mom, you put your foot in the soup."

Eveline preened at the compliment. "Thank you, Nikki. How was your day at work?"

"Not too bad. As I said, I've been very busy working on assignments. I just haven't had much free time." She averted her eyes from her mother's brown probing ones, and put another spoonful of stew into her mouth.

"I know you've been busy. It seems like everyone is busy these days." Eveline pointed her spoon at Nikki.

"But you still have to take care of yourself and slow down. Stress kills."

"I know, but the advertising field gets crazy sometimes. I just have to ride out the storm."

"Are you sure that's all that's bothering you?" Eveline asked. Her eyes were awash with concern. She picked up her glass of iced tea and sipped.

"Of course that's all that's bothering me." Nikki cut another piece of cornbread. Beads of sweat broke out on her forehead. She knew her mother was staring at her through eagle sharp eyes. Eveline was shrewd, and didn't miss a thing.

Eveline opened her mouth to speak, but instead, spooned stew into it. She decided to give Nikki time to relax and not inundate her with questions just yet. If Eveline kept picking, Nikki would just get defensive and clam up.

"How's Jeff doing?" she asked, changing the subject. And she didn't miss the relief that emitted from Nikki's face.

"He's fine." Nikki crumpled her nose and wiped her mouth with a napkin. "I think I'll get a little more stew. Would you like me to get you some more?"

Eveline waved her hand and shook her head. "I know that you two are working hard, climbing the corporate ladder. I just hope you don't lose sight of your marriage, which is more important than anything else in your life after God."

Nikki sucked her breath and said impatiently, "We haven't, Mom. We spend time together. We've just both been busy with work, that's all." She put the lid back on the top of the big pot and sat back down.

Eveline picked up the remote from the table and turned on the radio, setting the volume low. "I usually listen to Donnie McClurkin while I'm having dinner," she remarked.

"I bought his latest CD a few weeks ago. It's good; very

inspirational," Nikki said. She finished eating the remainder of her cornbread and leaned back contently in her seat. "Mom, dinner was scrumptious."

"Why don't we finish our tea in the den, unless you want me to fix a pot of coffee?" Eveline asked.

"Sure, the den is fine with me. No coffee for me. It's too late, and I'll be wired the rest of the night. I have to go to work in the morning, unlike you," Nikki teased.

Eveline took a plastic container out of the cabinet and poured the remainder of stew into it. She snapped the lid shut while Nikki gathered the bowls and spoons and put them inside the dishwasher. Eveline dimmed the light in the kitchen and turned off the CD player. Mother and daughter walked into the den, and Eveline turned on the television and sat beside Nikki on the couch.

Nikki's eyes traveled around the room. "The house sure looks different from when I lived here. When Linc and I were growing up, the walls were always painted white. I can't believe you now have blue, green, and red walls. That blows my mind."

Eveline smiled. "That just goes to show we can change our ways and tastes as we grow older."

"I know it's the house I grew up in, but sometimes it doesn't feel like home. When Linc and I were kids, you had French provincial furniture in the living room, and now you have modern furnishings," Nikki remarked, her eyes wandering to the television.

"Re-doing the house was just a project to keep me busy. I felt at loose ends when your father passed," Eveline explained.

"A lot of people don't stay married five years these days. I'm impressed by the number of years you and Dad were together." Nikki told her mother.

"You and Jeff aren't having any problems, are you?"

Eveline asked her daughter bluntly. Her brown eyes stared at Nikki intently.

"No, we're fine. Jeff can be a little controlling at times, but I know how to handle him," Nikki commented smugly. "I guess Daddy was the same way at times."

"Yes, he could be. But times were different when we were married. Men were supposed to be that way. Luckily, I didn't take it personally and did what I wanted most of the time." Eveline swung her legs on the couch and tucked them under her body.

"Did you two ever fight or argue about money?" Nikki asked, holding her breath.

"No, not really," Eveline answered, surprised by the question. "Why? Are you and Jeff having financial problems?"

"No. Jeff is still obsessed with his five-year plan." Nikki laughed. "We made some improvements on the building. We had the roof replaced, some tuck pointing done, and the windows replaced. We took out a loan for it, and the payment is due next month, I think. It's high, but we felt we needed to do the repairs so the property value wouldn't decrease."

"That makes sense. You know when your father and I struggled financially, we didn't have anyone to turn to. That's why we wanted to make sure you and Linc wouldn't have to face some of the obstacles we did." Eveline picked up the remote and changed the channel to *Fox News*.

"Believe me, Jeff and I are grateful." Nikki cut her eyes to her mother, then back to the television. "So Mom, if Jeff and I were having financial problems, would you help us out? Or do you feel like you've done enough by giving us the apartment building?"

Eveline laughed. "I couldn't help you if I wanted to."

Nikki tried not to panic. "Why not?"

"I have just enough money to live on comfortably for the next twenty or so years. The rest I donated to charities and set up a couple of scholarships at me and your father's alma maters."

Nikki sat in stunned silence for a moment. She knew her worst case scenario wasn't an option anymore. Now she had to borrow as much as she could from her 401K plan. "I can't believe you gave away that much money," she finally said.

"I don't see where I did anything wrong. I didn't want to be bothered with the upkeep of the buildings. That's why you and your brother received apartment buildings, and the other two buildings I sold. And I own this house free and clear."

"I didn't know that. I just assumed you still owned the other buildings. Why didn't you ask Linc and me if we wanted to buy the buildings before you sold them?"

"I guess I didn't think about it at the time," Eveline admitted. She glanced at the television and laughed at the antics of a sitcom family. "We had low mortgages on a few of those properties. I didn't want the financial burden, and it was always my dream to set up the scholarships. I wanted something lasting . . . a legacy to leave to my grandchildren."

"That was your right, I guess," Nikki said, backing down a little. The wind had been taken out of her sail.

"You and Linc are adults now. Your father and I raised y'all, put y'all through college, and gave y'all property. I felt like I was in a position to do something for myself, and that's what I wanted to do."

"You're right, Mom." Nikki sighed. Her face blanched from fear for an instant, and Eveline didn't miss it. Nikki glanced at her watch. "I really need to head home, Mom. I had a great time with you tonight. Can I take some stew home for Jeff?"

"Of course you can." Eveline rose from the couch and padded to the kitchen.

Nikki retrieved her coat from the closet and put it on. She fished her car keys out of her pocket and walked to the kitchen.

Eveline handed her a brown paper bag. "I put some cornbread in there too. You know Jeff loves my cornbread."

"That he does." Nikki smiled. "Come and walk me to the door."

"Nikki, if you need help with anything, all you have to do is ask. You're coming to church on Sunday, aren't you?" Eveline asked, as she unlocked the door.

"Yes, I am. And unless I have to work late, I plan on attending choir rehearsal on Thursday also. I'm fine, Mom. I don't want you worrying about me." Nikki leaned over and kissed Eveline's cheek.

"Call me when you get home," her mother said, hugging her.

"I will," Nikki promised.

Light snow was falling as she walked to the car. She started the engine and shifted into drive. Nikki was despondent. She had thought about asking her mother to loan her the money. That idea went out the window when Eveline told her that she had sold her properties. Nikki decided to stop at White Hen Pantry and buy some scratch lottery tickets. She figured it wouldn't hurt. As she drove home, she prayed that there was enough money in her Merrill Lynch account to correct her world.

Chapter 13

By eight o'clock that evening, Jeff still hadn't been able to catch up with Ron, and he was beginning to worry. It wasn't like his man not to answer his work or cell phones. All of Jeff's calls had been forwarded to voicemail. Ron must have been tied up in meetings. Jeff had just returned from lunch when his cell phone sounded. He nearly ripped it off the carrier on his belt and checked the caller ID. Answering, he said, "Ron, where you been, man? I've been trying to catch you all day?"

"I'm sorry, Jeff. I've been tied up all day. This wasn't one of the best days here at the CBOT," Ron said regretfully.

"What do you mean?" Jeff's face whitened apprehensively. His grip tightened on the phone. *I can take anything, but Lord, I don't ever want to be broke again in this lifetime.*

"Chill out, man. I meant in general, not just for you. Although you did suffer some minor losses, it was nothing substantial. What happened is nothing for you to get bent out of shape over." Ron tried to set Jeff's mind at ease.

Jeff sighed and mopped his moist brow with his free

hand. "I told you that Nikki's having a baby, and she's going to have to take off from work once the baby is born. We can't afford any upheavals in our finances right now." Jeff couldn't stop a smile from approaching his face at the thought of fatherhood.

"You're okay for now. The market experienced an aberration today, and you lost a couple thousand. But on a positive note, the pharmaceutical stock finally rose a bit. Don't get your hopes up too much though," Ron cautioned. "You know how fickle the market can be."

"And you know how I feel about losing money," Jeff countered. "This isn't the time for me to have money issues. Maybe you should invest in mutual funds," he suggested. One of the operators paced outside his office door. Jeff finally looked up and noticed his employee. "Ron, I'll call you back. I have a visitor."

"Do that. I'm leaving work in a few minutes, so hit me on my cell," Ron said. He shook his head and thought briefly about his next call.

"Okay, man. I'll holla at you later," Jeff said before hanging up. He waved Oscar Lomax into his office. "Have a seat," he said to him.

Oscar was a tall fair-skinned, barrel-chested man, and his friends called him Big O. He was in his middle twenties and wore his hair styled in cornrow braids. Oscar sat tensely on the edge of the seat. He wore blue denim jeans and a green and white checkered oversized shirt with gold Timberland boots.

To most people, Oscar looked like a straight up thug. Jeff had sensed something feasible in the young man during his job interview, and had hired him against the wishes of his boss and the other shift supervisors.

"What can I do for you?" Jeff asked.

"How you doing, Mr. Singleton?" The man fidgeted in his chair.

Jeff sensed something troubling was on Oscar's mind and nodded his head in response to his query.

"I'ma just get to the point. Ernesto told me and the guys about the weekend work . . . the conversion, and I have a problem." Oscar looked down at the floor.

"What is it?" Jeff felt like a dentist pulling teeth. Oscar jiggled his leg as he sat in the chair. "Well, I don't know if you know this or not, but my girlfriend, Shari, is expecting a baby. Her doctor says it's a high risk pregnancy. I always thought of her as high maintenance," Oscar quipped, trying to joke and failing miserably. "Anyway, her doctor is inducing labor, and it's scheduled for this Friday, the same day as the conversion."

"Hmm. Hold on a minute." Jeff's fingers flew on his keyboard. "You've been off quite a bit over the past six months, haven't you?" He peered at the screen, and then at Oscar.

"I know, Mr. Singleton, but Shari has been really sick during the pregnancy." He leaned closer to Jeff's desk. "This is our first baby, and I'm trying to be supportive to my girl."

"I understand, but you're close to being maxed out as far as your days off are concerned. Did you apply for paternity leave?"

"I meant to, but I didn't get around to it yet."

Jeff began typing again and accessed another menu on his screen. He clicked on an icon and printed the form, handing it to Oscar.

"Before you leave here tonight, I want you to fill this out and return it to me. I'll try and push it through. Go ahead and take the time off; we'll work something out. You may need to come in on your off days after the baby is born," Jeff advised the young man.

"Thanks, Mr. Singleton. I appreciate it." Oscar's expression brightened, and then dimmed like a flickering light bulb. "Will you talk to Ernesto for me? He said it was mandatory that we not take any time off this weekend."

"Didn't you talk to him about your conflict?" Jeff asked, clasping his hands behind his neck, and leaning back in his chair. He was a believer in following the chain of command.

"No, I didn't. I was so worried about Shari that I thought I should talk to you first. After all, you call the shots around here," Oscar said. He knew Jeff was a stickler for proper protocol, but he also knew if he worked this weekend, Shari would never forgive him. She might not even let him see the baby. He frowned at the thought.

"Don't worry about work at this time. Family comes first, but in the future, please try to follow the chain of command," Jeff said, taking a load off Oscar's mind.

Oscar stood and thrust his hand out to Jeff. "Thanks, Mr. Singleton. Shari and I appreciate it . . . especially me."

Jeff grasped his employee's clammy hand. "Handle your business. Make sure you bring that form back to me. If not, I might have to rethink my position," Jeff joked, with a deadpan expression on his face.

Oscar's head bobbled up and down. "I will. I promise, Mr. Singleton. You've been a lifesaver."

"Okay, I'll see you later."

"Yeah, for sure." Oscar held up the paper and whistled as he strode quickly out of the office.

Jeff mused that he could be in Oscar's shoes down the road. He hadn't planned to come to work over the weekend, but now he would and fill in for Oscar. He knew everyone needed help sometimes; even employees. Jeff was still concerned about his stock so he called Ron to get an update. When Ron answered the call, Jeff asked, "Is this a good time?"

"It is. Anyway, to put your mind at ease, as I said, you lost about two thousand dollars today. I don't consider it a setback. Your account is still healthy. Don't worry about Jeffrey Junior. By the time he's eighteen, we'll have college tuition accumulated for him and his sister." Ron leaned down and tugged at the handle of his bottom drawer, to make sure he'd remembered to lock it. Then he sat back upright in the chair.

"I guess. But I don't want any surprises. I'd like you to be a little conservative as far as the investments are concerned," Jeff admonished.

"Have I ever steered you wrong?" he asked as he snapped open the locks on his brown leather briefcase.

"By and large, our relationship has been profitable," Jeff admitted grudgingly. In the past, he had allowed Ron to do his thing, and just went along for the ride. But times had changed.

"So how is Nikki doing? Did she finally get around to telling you about the baby?" Ron placed his desk calculator in his briefcase. He picked up his keys off his desk and locked the briefcase. Then he turned off the overhead lamp on his desk.

"No, not yet," Jeff said, stroking his chin. "I expect her to tell me over the weekend."

"Hey, weren't you guys holding off until next year before having a baby?" Ron pulled his coat off the rack.

"Yeah, but I guess she must have forgotten to take her pill or something. Look, Ron, I've got to go; duty calls. I'll talk to you in a few days."

"Okay, enjoy the rest of your evening," Ron said, hanging up.

As Jeff was putting his cell phone back in the holder, his work phone rang. Jeff picked it up. "What's up, Ernesto?"

"I think we got a hardware problem," the operator responded. Ringing telephones sounded in the background. "Do you think you could come down here?" he asked.

"Okay, Ernesto, I'm on my way." He set his calls to voicemail and left the office.

Nikki stood in line at a White Hen convenience store, located a few miles from her house. She covered her mouth, hiding a yawn. The day had been a long one. She knew she wouldn't be getting anymore work done when she arrived home as she had planned.

Finally, she was the next person in line at the register. The salesclerk, a bored looking young woman, stood with her arms folded across her chest and golden braids down to her waist. She looked at Nikki like she wished she were anywhere but in the store working.

"Can I help you?" she asked, her jaws puffed up like a chipmunk, as she chewed a wad of gum.

"Yes, give me ten, five dollar scratch off instant lottery tickets, please," Nikki said as her eyes strayed to a point beyond the clerk.

The clerk's eyes seemed to perk up when she heard Nikki's request. Nikki, on the other hand, avoided meeting the clerk's eyes. The young woman cracked her gum. She leaned toward Nikki and whispered, "Do you ever win?"

"I beg your pardon?" Nikki's hand flickered to her chest. The strap of her purse slid from her shoulder, down her arm.

"I asked do you ever win any money? I don't remember you ever coming back to the store to claim any winnings."

"I don't think that's any of your business." Nikki looked at the clerk's nametag. *Khadijah Jones.* "Your comments are out of line."

The clerk removed the tickets with long manicured, gold tipped fingernails, from a stand on a shelf behind her. She punched in the total on the cash register. "That will be fifty dollars."

Nikki fumbled in her purse, trying to find her debit

card. Her hand shook as she handed it to the young woman.

The clerk ran the card through the scanner in a fluid motion. She blew a bubble and handed the card back to Nikki. "Miss, your card was declined," she informed loud enough for the people in line behind Nikki to hear.

Their stares made Nikki wish she could melt into the floor and disappear. She pulled her wallet out of her purse and laid it on the counter in front of her. She felt along the fraying leather and pulled out six ten dollar bills. Then she spied her Chase One debit card inside one of the plastic card protectors, pulled it out, and handed it to the impatient clerk, who smirked insolently at her.

Nikki held her breath until she read the total owed was zero on the register LED readout. She sighed in relief. Nikki's heels made a disjointed sound on the pavement, as she walked hurriedly to her car. She felt humiliated by the scene in the store.

Ten minutes later, Nikki opened her apartment door. Her nerves were raw as she took off her chocolate brown colored trench coat and let it fall to the floor near the closet. She dropped her purse and tote bag next to the olive green Japanese-styled table in the foyer. Nibbling her lip with frustration, Nikki walked into the living room and sat on the sofa. A tiny part of her mind was aware that she had a serious addiction while another part of her psyche screamed its denial. The voices seemed so real that Nikki covered her ears with quivering hands.

She dropped her head in her hands, then fell to the floor. Nikki clasped her hands together and prayed aloud, "Lord, please help me. I feel like I'm losing my way. You said all I had to do was ask in your Son's name, and it would be given. Well, Lord, I come to you on bended knees. I don't know what's wrong with me. Why am I willing to give up everything I worked so hard for and disap-

point people who believe in me . . . like Jeff and Mom?"
Her voice soared in despair. "I don't want to gamble, God.
I promise I don't, but it's like an itch, a case of measles or
chicken pox gone awry. Like when you're a child, and
your mother tells you not to do something. And you want
to be so grown that you do it anyway.

"Please help me, Lord. Drive this demon from my body."
Nikki opened her eyes and sat down hard on the floor. Tears
welled up in her eyes, and she swallowed a few times. She
looked up toward the ceiling and said, "Lord, won't you
help me? Please, God; don't let Jeff and Momma hate me.
God, I hate myself for what I've become. Why am I doing
this?" Nikki's arms snaked around her body. She rocked
back and forth on the floor and babbled over and over,
"Lord, don't leave me."

Nikki knelt on the floor a couple more minutes before
she arose and went into the bedroom to prepare for the
workday.

Chapter 14

Nikki managed to arrive early to work on Wednesday and Thursday. With Fatima's help, she was closer to finishing her projects in a timely fashion. At the end of the following week, Victor had faxed over a working copy of the ad to the patisserie company, and they had requested a few minor revisions.

On Thursday, Nikki completed revisions for another client project and emailed the finished product to Victor and Fatima. The workday was officially over, and she had mixed emotions about attending choir rehearsal later that evening. She knew Bianca would be all up in her face, demanding to know what happened last Sunday.

As Nikki was getting ready to shut down her computer, she received an email pop-up notification message from Merrill Lynch. Her hands shook ever so slightly as she clicked on the message and opened it. Her stomach churned from tension.

Nikki raised her hand and said "Thank you Jesus," as she read the contents of the email. She gave thanks that the Lord had heard her prayer and answered it. After reading how much she could borrow from her pension fund, Nikki saw that she wouldn't be able to pay off her Harrah's debt, but she would be able to put a sizeable dent in it. She concluded that maybe everything that had happened was for the best. Nikki was also in denial about how seriously she was addicted to gambling. She still looked at her activities as a hobby, albeit an expensive one.

The email indicated her account balance was sixty thousand dollars, and that she could borrow up to fifty thousand. Nikki's smile turned to a frown when she read that her spouse's signature was required for the transaction. She knew that her only choice was to forge Jeff's signature on the loan application.

Nikki's loan from Merrill Lynch would cover the taxes and arrear amount, but not the total debt she owed to Harrah's. A thought ricocheted through her mind as to whether she could continue to gamble while she owed money. Nikki shook her head and lightly swatted her hand. She chided herself to stop thinking along those lines and waved her hands in the air and said, "Thank You Jesus."

Fatima walked inside the cubicle and looked at her co-worker strangely. "Uh, are you busy or something?" she asked Nikki, waving a copy of the ad Nikki had just emailed to her.

"No." Nikki sheepishly looked over at Fatima. "I plan on leaving shortly. What's up? Do you see anything wrong with the copy?"

Fatima shook her head and stood near the cubicle entrance. "I just wanted to tell you that you did a good job," she congratulated.

"Thank you." Nikki smiled. She stood and put on her coat, then slipped her keys in her pocket. "It was a team effort. I appreciate your assistance."

"Believe me, I enjoy working with you. Are you just

about caught up on your other projects? I wanted to know how much longer you think we'll be working together?" Fatima asked coyly.

"Well, I can stretch things out a bit. So let's say I'll be fully caught up in a couple of weeks or so." Nikki popped a peppermint inside her mouth that she removed from her coat pocket. She dropped the wrapper in the trashcan.

"Thanks, Nikki." Fatima blushed. "I know we got off to a rocky start. But I've learned some new techniques by working with you. You're quite good at what you do."

Nikki walked over to Fatima and shook her hand. "Thank you. I'll do whatever I can to help you . . . like putting in a good word with Victor."

"Would you really do that?" Fatima's eyes glittered with happiness. "I'd appreciate it. Well, I better get out of here so you can continue with what you were doing."

"I'm headed to choir rehearsal," Nikki said, as her eyes scanned her desk once more to make sure she hadn't forgotten anything.

Fatima turned and waved at Nikki. "Have a good evening."

"You too," Nikki murmured as she shut off her PC and removed her purse from the bottom drawer.

An hour later, Nikki backed her car into a parking space in the church parking lot. She picked up her purse and tote bag, and as she was getting out of her car, a car horn tooted behind her. Maya waved and then parked her car in a spot behind Nikki.

"Hey, girl. How you doing?" Maya asked breathlessly as she rushed over to where Nikki was standing.

"My soul is at peace. I'm sanctified and blessed by the Lord," Nikki answered serenely.

"Well, good for you. I had to work late for the conversion scheduled for the weekend," Maya said.

"I think Jeff mentioned something about that," Nikki

said, as the two of them walked toward the rear entrance of the church. "You know Bianca's going to lay into me tonight, don't you?"

"You can handle it," Maya replied. "You're positively glowing tonight. You must have had a good day."

"Actually, it wasn't bad. I need to talk to you about something that happened at work this week." Nikki pulled the heavy wooden door open.

The friends walked quietly to the sanctuary where Bianca was sitting at the organ with Latrell. He was playing a couple of riffs. Nikki and Maya greeted the other choir members before taking their seats in the choir stand.

Ten minutes later, Bianca stood. "Ladies and gentlemen, let's get started."

Over the next ninety minutes, Bianca and Latrell went over two new songs with the sopranos, altos, tenors, and basses, and then the entire group practiced the selections for the Sunday service.

At the conclusion of rehearsal, Bianca's eyes swept the choir loft. She said, "Jessica, Cedric and Nikki, I'd like for you three to stay a little longer. I'll see the rest of you on Sunday morning."

Nikki squirmed in her seat when she heard Bianca call her name.

Maya stood up and put on her coat. "I'll wait for you outside," she whispered.

"Okay. Hopefully this won't take long," Nikki replied.

Bianca asked Jessica first, and then Cedric, to come to the organ. Each went through the solo parts of the songs quickly. Jessica was slated to sing the lead to "Magnify the Lord," and Cedric would lend his deep bass melodious voice to a rendition of "Pass Me Not, O Gentle Savior."

After the two finished singing, Bianca gazed at Nikki intently, and gestured for her to come to the choir stand. She said, with a displeased expression on her face, "Nikki, if you didn't feel up to singing last Sunday, why didn't you say something to me? I don't know what was going on with you, but it didn't look good for the church, Pastor, or the choir, but most of all, you."

Nikki felt like she was on the hot seat. "You're right. I didn't feel well on Sunday, but I honestly thought I'd feel better as the morning went on. I should've apologized to the choir before they left. I'm sorry," she choked out as her hands shook slightly.

Latrell's hands flew across the keyboard. "Pastor called me this week. He put in a request for Sunday morning. He wants you to sing "His Eye Is On The Sparrow." Are you up to it?" he asked, playing the opening notes.

Nikki looked at him incredulously, like he'd asked her if she could walk. Then she closed her eyes, opened her mouth, and the purest sounds emanated from within her throat. Latrell matched her note for note.

When Nikki finished singing, she looked at Latrell and Bianca and smiled. "What do you think?" she asked.

"I think Pastor has his request for Sunday." Latrell smiled. He played another note and looked at the choir director. "Bianca, what do you think?"

Bianca stared at Nikki sharply through her rose tinted glasses. "Don't let us down on Sunday. That's all I ask. If you aren't up for it, then tell me before we look incompetent in front of the church."

"I'm okay, and I'll be here. See you on Sunday. May the rest of your week be blessed." Nikki turned and walked out of the church. She strolled to Maya's car and got inside. "Well, Bianca wasn't too bad. Sometimes I have to remember I'm a Christian when I deal with her," Nikki laughed.

"You know she's just extremely anal. I think her life is centered on the church, and she doesn't have a life outside of this place," Maya replied. "Anyway, what were you going to tell me? I don't have too much time because my mother is babysitting TJ at my house, and I have to take her home."

"I was written up at work," Nikki admitted as she looked out the windshield, refusing to meet Maya's eyes.

"Why? What happened?" Maya's eyes conveyed concern.

"I fell behind on my projects, and one was a big one. When I was at your house the other day, I forgot I was doing a client presentation, and to put it mildly, Victor wasn't pleased."

Maya rubbed Nikki's arm. "I'm sorry to hear that. Whatever you're going through, Nik, you know I'm here for you. And don't tell me it's nothing, because I know something is happening with you."

"You're right. Most of it was due to being stressed out at work. Last Tuesday, Victor assigned the receptionist to work with me. I'm sure he did that so she could check up on me," Nikki said bitterly.

Maya felt worried. Her brow wrinkled with anxiety. Things were much worse with Nikki than she had suspected. "You know these companies, and how they aren't concerned about anything but the bottom line. Maybe Victor's looking at it from that perspective."

"I don't know, Maya. Sometimes I feel like my life is spinning like a kite out of control on a windy day. I try to use the string to rein it in, but it keeps drifting away from me," Nikki said sadly.

"How has the receptionist been acting toward you? Do you feel like she's on your side or pursuing her own agenda?" Maya asked.

"I was upset when Victor assigned her to work with me. But she's actually been very helpful," Nikki admitted reluctantly. "Fatima has made no bones about the fact that she wants to be a designer. You know I try to do my work and not participate in office gossip. But I must admit I'm a little concerned, just in case Victor has decided she's going to be my replacement."

"Is that all that's bothering you? Jeff stopped by to see me earlier this week, and he wasn't a happy camper. Not by a long shot," Maya said.

"I've probably unconsciously been taking my frustrations out on him," Nikki acknowledged. "But it's been a crazy time for me. My mother called me yesterday and demanded I stop by and see her. If I refused, she threatened to come to my job."

Maya clucked sympathetically. "Ms. Eveline had a bee in her bonnet, and wanted to make sure you were okay. Hmmm, that analogy can also be used to describe Jeff's actions too." She held her hands out. "We're just worried about you, Nik, that's all."

"I know." Nikki swallowed a big lump that rose in her throat. "But you all need to give me space to work out my issues. I know that Jeff, you and Mom love me. But love has nothing to do with what I'm going through."

"Okay." Maya took a tissue out of her purse, and waved it in the air. Nikki laughed heartily at her friend's antics. "I surrender," Maya proclaimed. "But if your issue becomes a burden too heavy for you to bear alone, remember you have all of us to lean on."

"I will," Nikki murmured. Because she knew she would be receiving a check from Merrill Lynch, she felt like her problems were over. She assumed all she had to do was pay the taxes and Harrah's, and her life would return to normal, and it would if she followed that plan. But would the gambling monkey on her back allow her to resume her old life that easily?

* * *

Saturday morning, Nikki sat on the lowered toilet seat inside the bathroom attached to their bedroom. When she came out of the bathroom, Jeff was still asleep. They had gone to dinner the previous night at a Mexican cuisine restaurant.

Nikki took Maya's words to heart and after she and Jeff arrived home, they shared a glass of wine. She deflected Jeff's questions about what had been bothering her like a pro. She went into their bedroom and heated oil, and massaged Jeff's body, leaving him feeling weak as a kitten when she was done. Before he went to sleep, Jeff instructed Nikki to wake him up at seven o'clock, so he could get to work on time.

It was six forty-five. Nikki remembered a representative from Merrill Lynch was supposed to call her yesterday and hadn't before she left work. She slid out the lilac colored sheet, picked up the cordless telephone, and went into the bathroom to call her voicemail at work.

A few minutes later, she clicked off the phone after listening to the message the representative had left. The woman notified Nikki that she had emailed a loan application to her employer email account, and she should fill it out and mail it back to Merrill Lynch at her earliest convenience.

Nikki smiled to herself. She would print off the application and take it to the post office after Jeff left for work. She returned to the bedroom to rouse her husband.

She stood near the doorway of the room for a minute, watching the rise and fall of Jeff's hairy chest. Then she slid in the bed beside him and gently poked him in the side. Jeff didn't stir. Nikki kissed the side of his neck, and his eyes fluttered open. He stretched his muscular arms and wiped his eyes with the heels of his hands.

"Good morning, beautiful. How are you feeling this morning?" He smiled at Nikki.

"Just fine, baby. I just wish you could spend the day with me, but I know how intense conversions are for you."

"I'd love nothing better than to spend the day with you." Jeff glanced at the clock. "But with one of my guys out today," he stole a look at Nikki, "it's best that I go in."

Nikki nodded. "I know." She rolled over and snuggled into Jeff's side. His arm slid possessively around her waist.

"If all goes well, I should be home no later than six this evening. Do you want to do something when I come back? Go to the movies, or out to dinner?" He sat up on the side of the bed.

"We just went out to dinner last night, and there's nothing new at the movies I want to see. How about if we just stay home and I cook dinner?" Nikki was actually more than a decent cook. She just didn't do it very often.

"For real?" Jeff rubbed his hands together in anticipation of a home cooked meal. "That sounds like a winner to me. You haven't cooked in how long?" He put his hand on the side of his head, and looked upward like he was thinking. "Maybe last year this time?"

Nikki sat up and playfully punched Jeff in the shoulder. "Quit exaggerating. Just call me some time during the day, and I'll have dinner ready when you come home."

Jeff leaned over and kissed Nikki. His lips clung to hers for a few moments. "I love you, Nikki, with all my soul. If I've done anything to upset you, then I'm sorry. I know I can be a bit insensitive sometimes, but you're my world, and when you hurt, so do I."

"Apology accepted, and I second what you said." Nikki smiled. "Now get up and go to work so you can hurry up and come back home to me. I'll put on some coffee for you."

"Okay, I'm going." Jeff kissed her again. Then he stood and went into the bathroom.

Nikki could hear water cascading from the shower. She stood up, grinned, and walked into the kitchen.

A half an hour later, Jeff had departed for work. Nikki went to the bedroom and pulled out a pair of jeans, a melon colored angora sweater, and underwear. Then she headed to the shower.

When she was done, she powered on the PC and quickly logged into her job's website. When she accessed the email from Merrill Lynch, she sent it to the printer and sat at the desk and filled it out. Using quick strokes, she untidily scrawled Jeff's name on the application, then rummaged in one of the desk drawers, found an envelope, and addressed it to Merrill Lynch. An hour later, she locked the back door and decided to walk to the currency exchange, post office, and grocery store.

There was a crisp chill in the air and Nikki was glad she had worn her brown bomber leather jacket, and matching suede ankle boots. She walked jauntily down the street. Nikki felt blessed to be alive, loved by her man, and happy to put an end to the nightmare that dogged her.

After she finished with her errands, Nikki stopped at *McDonald's* and purchased a fruit salad for lunch. Then she returned home and unpacked the grocery bags. *I need to call Maya.* She removed the telephone receiver from the wall unit, sat at the kitchen table, and dialed Maya's telephone number.

Maya answered on the second ring. "Hello."

"Hey, girlfriend. How are you feeling this morning?" Nikki asked.

"I can't complain. Tony just picked up TJ, so I have a little free time on my hand."

Nikki quickly caught the hint behind her friend's words.

"No, Maya. I know your ways. You want me to come out to Dolton, and I'm not driving out that far. I have plans."

"Oh, now you got plans. You can't spare any time for your girl? Is that what you're saying?" Maya injected a pseudo hurtful tone in her voice.

"I just finished running some errands, and Jeff's at work. I promised I'd fix him a home cooked meal when he gets off work."

"Well, good for you," Maya replied. "I guess my feelings aren't hurt too badly then. What else do you have planned for today?"

"Not a thing. I'll probably start reading our book for the meeting this month. Have you started it yet?"

"No. I'll probably still be reading it the day of the meeting. It's at Pearl's house this month, isn't it?" Maya asked.

"Yeah. The reviews I read of the book are great. At least Lindsay can't draw any parallels to my life when we discuss that book." The two friends laughed aloud.

"Ain't that the truth," Maya said. "How was work yesterday? Are you still on track with meeting your deadlines?"

"Girl, I'm handling my business like Mike Tyson in the ring back in the day," Nikki bragged. "I'm on top of things. Yesterday, Victor called me into his office and told me my performance had improved one hundred percent."

"That's good. I know his comments help you feel a little bit more at ease. There's nothing worse than getting written up at work."

"Yeah, you're right about that. Victor also asked me how Fatima was doing, and if I thought she was ready to start designing without supervision."

"Wow. What did you say?" Maya held her breath, waiting for Nikki to answer.

"Well, I was honest. I told him she was close, but probably needed a little more training."

"What did he say?"

"He asked me if I'd mentor her." Nikki sighed.

"I know you said yes." Maya's hand tightened on the telephone receiver.

"I'm still not sure about her, but I said yes. I felt like Victor was telling me. Asking me was more of a formality than anything else."

"Truthfully, the writing was on the wall when he asked her to assist you." Maya nodded sagely.

"Yeah, you're probably right. Well, let me get up from here." Nikki stretched out her legs. "I'm going to finish cleaning my house, take a nap, maybe do some reading, or work on a project before I start dinner."

"Okay, girl," Maya said. "I plan to relax since I have a free weekend. If I don't talk to you later, I'll see you at church tomorrow."

"Okay, enjoy your day," Nikki said before ending the call and heading to her bedroom to change clothes. Weekends seemed to fly by so quickly, and before she knew it, the two-day reprieve from work would be over. She glanced at the clock on the nightstand. Jeff would be home in five more hours.

A couple of hours later, the house shone from Nikki's tender loving care. She had mopped and waxed the light-colored hardwood floors, and she had dusted and polished the glass tabletops until she could see her reflection. Her last chore was lighting jasmine potpourri throughout the apartment.

After enjoying a nice relaxing soak in the bathtub, and a short nap, Nikki went to the kitchen where she seasoned the T-bone steaks she'd bought for dinner. Then she set them on a plate inside the refrigerator to marinate. She washed two baking potatoes and put them in a pan, then prepared a tossed salad.

Nikki wiped her hands on a dishtowel and glanced at the clock over the stove. She had another hour before Jeff arrived home from work. She opened a cabinet to see if she had ingredients to make a sweet potato pie for dessert since that was Jeff's favorite. She didn't so she had to improvise.

When Nikki was at the grocery store, she had purchased a half gallon of French vanilla ice cream and chocolate syrup. That would be a perfect substitute. She also snuck to the 7-Eleven to buy lottery tickets for the million dollar jackpot drawing scheduled for the evening. She wanted to avoid the obnoxious gum popping store clerk who waited on her the last time she went to White Hen.

When Jeff arrived home a little after seven o'clock, he was exhausted. But when he noticed how immaculate the house looked, and heard WBEZ, his favorite radio station playing on the Bose stereo, he got a second wind. His grumbling stomach led him into the kitchen where he found Nikki removing delectable looking steaks that had been broiling in the oven. She looked up at him standing in the doorway and grinned.

"Wow," Jeff said enthusiastically as he admired his wife's rear end. He wished he had stopped at the florist and bought her a bouquet of roses. "I can tell you've been busy since I've been gone. The house looks great." His nose twitched as he inhaled the tantalizing aroma of beef. He walked over to Nikki and kissed her cheek.

Nikki set the pan with the steaks inside of it on top of the stove. She wrapped her arms around Jeff's neck and kissed him deeply. The two stood hugged together for a few minutes.

"While you finish in here, I'm going to take a shower," Jeff said. "I'll meet you back in here in fifteen minutes." He reluctantly pushed Nikki away from him.

She held up her arm and looked at her watch. "You have fourteen minutes and forty seconds." When he turned to go into the bedroom, she smacked him lightly on the behind with a kitchen towel. "Hurry back, Jeff; you're on the clock."

Chapter 15

Sunday morning, Nikki awakened feeling positively elated. She stretched her arms over her head and smiled contently, knowing her gambling problems would soon become a thing of the past. Merrill Lynch had informed her in the email she received from them yesterday, that upon review of her account, the funds she requested would be transferred into her bank account by the end of the following week. Nikki had plenty of good fortune to thank the Lord for.

He had brought her out of the darkness, and into the marvelous light. She looked over at Jeff. One of his legs peeked from under the covers, and he was on his stomach, snoring softly.

I've treated Jeff abominably for a while. I'll make it up to him; I promise. She leaned over and kissed his cheek, then smiled when his eyes slowly fluttered open.

He looked over at Nikki, and a broad grin curved along his lips. "Good morning. I don't have to ask how you're doing. I can see that." He pulled her into his arms.

"I'm blessed, Jeff; simply blessed. God has been so

good to me," Nikki said as she snuggled next to his warm body.

"No, we're both blessed," Jeff said, correcting his wife.

They lay together quietly for a few minutes, each lost in their own thoughts.

"Is there something you want to tell me?" Jeff turned Nikki's face toward his own.

Her body tensed, and her heart did a two-step. "No. Everything is fine. I know I haven't been in a good mood lately, but that's over. Please accept my apologies. I love you. I was just going through a bad time, but the storm has passed."

"That's good, Nik. Next time, please don't shut me out. As a couple, we have to support each other through good and bad times, as Pastor has taught us."

"Pastor is right." Nikki nodded. "I'll try to do better. Why don't I fix breakfast this morning?"

"That'll be fine," Jeff answered morosely, his mood becoming deflated. "I'ma go take a shower." He had expected Nikki to tell him she was pregnant. He consoled himself with the thought that maybe she'd make her announcement after church or next week. Jeff decided to be patient.

Nikki smiled gratefully at Jeff as she rose from the bed and walked into the bathroom. Jeff lay comfortably in the bed and eventually went back to sleep.

When Nikki came out of the bathroom, she slipped on her robe and shook Jeff awake. "I'm going to go start breakfast. Bring your appetite to the table with you."

Though Jeff still felt tired, he got out of bed and went into the bathroom.

Nikki disappeared into the kitchen and opened the refrigerator. She removed a carton of eggs, a package of turkey bacon, cheese, and milk. A loaf of bread out of the breadbox joined the ingredients on the counter.

Twenty minutes later, she was finishing as Jeff walked into the kitchen. Nikki prepared a plate for him and set it on the table.

"It smells good in here. I'm going downstairs to get today's paper," he remarked.

"Great," Nikki said. She put two cups of hot coffee on the table. By the time Jeff returned with the paper, she had fixed her plate and was seated at the table.

Jeff and Nikki bowed their heads as Jeff said the prayer. "Lord, thank you for the food we're about to eat. Most of all, bless the cook. Lord, we look forward to partaking in your spiritual food this morning at church. Lord, we just ask that you continue to look over and bless us. Thank you for allowing us to see another day. Amen." Jeff opened his eyes and looked at Nikki. "Let's eat."

They arrived at church ninety minutes later. Before they exited the car, Jeff said to Nikki, "In case you're nervous about singing today, don't worry your pretty head. I know you'll be fine."

"I know. The Lord already told me," Nikki answered him serenely. "I'll see you after church." She blew Jeff a kiss as he walked to the finance office.

Nikki looked attractive in a camel-colored suit, chocolate brown blouse, and a gold chain belt that encircled her waist. She wore gold accessories with brown pumps. A few church members greeted her as she made her way to the choir room. She carried her choir robe encased in a plastic covering across her arm.

Bianca breathed a sigh of relief when Nikki walked inside the room. "I thought you were going to be late. I listened to the radio on the way to church and heard there was an accident on the Kennedy Expressway," she said gratefully.

"We must have missed it. We made it here with at least ten minutes to spare," Nikki answered, glancing at her gold watch.

"Go ahead and put on your robe. It's almost time for us to march in." Bianca ran her hand through her short bobbed hair.

"I'll be ready." Nikki walked to the clothing rack, slipped off her coat, and placed it on a hanger. Five minutes later, she held hands with another soprano, with her eyes closed, listening to Simone, the president of the choir, pray.

When the choir left the room and took their place in front of the double doors leading to the sanctuary, Latrell played the opening bars to the song "We Are Climbing Higher and Higher." Two-by-two, the choir marched to the choir stand.

The choir typically sang an A and B selection, and then one more selection after Pastor preached.

Cedric was up first. His bass voice soared as he sang, and the congregation waved their Bibles at him and hummed along. The congregation clapped enthusiastically when he finished the song and returned to his place in the choir stand.

Latrell played the opening bars to "Magnify the Lord." Jessica walked sedately to the podium. She adjusted the microphone stand to her shorter height and sang flawlessly.

When Reverend Dudley took the stand, clutching his Bible, he first greeted his members and commented on the fine singing they had been honored with that morning. "The Lord put a sermon on my heart regarding how we as Christians should weather the storms in our lives. It seems that we go through so many dilemmas and crises. But I'm here to tell you, no matter what you're going through, with the Lord's help and the power of prayer, Jesus can work it out. If you're feeling disheartened and can't see the light, I want you to know Jesus is able, and He'll supply our every need."

The church members appreciatively murmured, "Amen."

"Please open your Bibles to First John, chapter five, verses one through fifteen. Please read along with me."

The church was quiet. You could hear the members flipping the pages of their Bible. Along with Reverend Dudley, the congregation read the verses.

After everyone recited the scripture, the pastor began his sermon in earnest. Nikki's mind wandered. She closed her eyes and prayed, *Lord, please don't let me mess up my song this morning.* Then she opened her eyes and sighed. She knew she was going to be just fine. As she listened to Reverend Dudley, her mind went around the fifteenth verse like a carousel.

And if we know that if he hears us, whatever we ask, we know that we have the petitions that we have asked of him.

Pastor was in the thick of his sermon. Sisters stood and waved handkerchiefs at him. The Mother's Board stared adoringly at their minister like he was their son. Eveline sat in her seat, rocking back and forth. Reverend Dudley was sweating profusely. When he finally took his seat, the pastor mopped his brow with a white handkerchief.

On cue, Nikki walked to the microphone. She closed her eyes, which was her usual habit before she began singing a song. She swallowed and moistened her lips. Her beautiful first soprano voice rang resounding when she opened her mouth. The sound was pure and clear. Nikki's voice rose majestically when she sang, *his eye is on the sparrow, and I know he watches me.*

If anyone thought she would stumble that morning, they were mistaken. Nikki took the microphone out of its stand atop the podium and walked the length of the choir stand. She waved her hand in the air as she nailed the high notes. Pastor even stood up and waved his sodden handkerchief in her direction.

Eveline thanked God. *Please keep my child on track. Strengthen her, Lord.* She stood on her feet along with other members of the congregation and clapped her hands wildly.

Jeff felt humble, like he was in the presence of royalty. He was never prouder to be Nikki's husband. His baby had a gift, and she was using it to praise the Lord.

When Nikki finished the song, the church members gave her a standing ovation. Her robe was dampened with sweat when she returned to her seat. Bianca nodded approvingly at the star soprano. Nikki felt exhausted. She wiped her brow, leaned back in her seat, and closed her eyes. *Lord, I know I'm not worthy. I hate letting Jeff and my mother down. I know by prayer and your grace, that gambling is a thing of the past. I'm not addicted, I just like to gamble. I promise, Lord, never to let myself become caught up in that mess again. I promise, Lord. Amen.*

The choir marched out of the choir stand and to the choir room after the benediction was given. As Nikki took her coat off the hanger and put it on, she smiled when she saw Bianca heading toward her.

"Well done, sister," Bianca commented.

"Thank you, Bianca. I told you I'd be fine. I'll see you on Thursday," Nikki said.

Bianca nodded, and walked away to talk to the other choir members.

"You tore it up, girlfriend," Maya said as she approached. "You were in rare form."

"Thanks, Maya. You didn't do too bad yourself. 'The Lord's Prayer' isn't an easy song to sing."

"What are you doing after church?" Maya asked, as she pulled her coat on.

"I'm not sure," Nikki replied.

"There you are," Eveline exclaimed to her daughter, while walking toward the two women. "I was looking for you. Would you and Jeff like to join me and your brother and his family for dinner? Of course, you're invited too, Maya. And bring TJ with you. I haven't seen him in a while."

Nikki said, "Let me check with Jeff first. I'm sure he won't mind. We'll be here for another hour or so. I'll call you when he's finished."

Eveline leaned over and kissed her daughter. Then she reached up and wiped her lipstick off Nikki's cheek. "You sounded so good, baby. I was so proud of you. God has given you a beautiful gift."

"Yes, and I praise Him in song whenever I can." Nikki nodded her head.

"I'm going home to warm up the food that I stayed up all night preparing. Hopefully I'll see all of you later." Eveline's glance swept over Maya.

"Sure, Mrs. Baldwin. I need to stop by my mother's house and pick up TJ. Both of them have colds. Otherwise my mother would have been at church today," Maya replied.

When her mother and friend left, Nikki sat on a wooden bench outside the finance committee office. She was lost in thought about receiving the check from Merrill Lynch, but looked up as Reverend Dudley called her name.

"Hello, Pastor." She stood hurriedly and thrust out her hand. "That was a fine sermon you preached today. I was moved."

"I'm glad to hear that, Nichole. I try my best to uplift the congregation. Everyone needs to know that even when it seems they're alone, God cares. You did a splendid job today as well. It always touches my heart when you sing "His Eye Is On The Sparrow.""

"Thank you, Pastor. When I'm singing, I try to give it my all."

Reverend Dudley looked probingly into Nikki's eyes. "You look like you're feeling better, Nichole. I hope your crisis is behind you."

"It is, Pastor. God truly answers prayers." Nikki nodded her head.

"Have a blessed week, child. I'll send Jeff out in a minute." Reverend Dudley knocked on the closed door, then opened it and went inside.

Nikki sat back down on the bench and pulled her Blackberry out of her purse to check her emails. She had just deleted the last one when the door swung open. Jeff walked out of the room with his coat slung over his arm.

Nikki stood up. "Mom invited us over for dinner. Linc, Shonell, and Lincoln III are going to be there; maybe Maya too. Do you feel like going over there to eat?"

"Sure," Jeff replied, putting on his coat, "that's fine with me."

Nikki turned off her Blackberry and dropped it inside her purse. She donned her coat, grabbed Jeff's arm, and they walked outside the church. Each one's heart swelled with joy. Jeff assumed she was going to announce the pregnancy while they were at her mother's house. Nikki was just grateful that her financial woes were about to come to an end.

Chapter 16

Linc pushed his chair away from the cherry wood dining room table at Eveline's house. The family had just finished having dinner. "Mom, you're one of the best cooks I know." He glanced at his wife and smiled sheepishly. "I'm not leaving you out either babe. But I think I've gained ten pounds, just from this meal alone." Linc groaned and rubbed his rotund stomach. He stood up and removed his suit jacket, which strained against his stomach.

"I guess that means this old lady still has the touch when it comes to cooking." Eveline smiled coyly at her son, picked up a glass of iced tea, and drained the contents. After she set her glass on the table, she looked at her family members. "Is anyone still hungry? I made plenty."

Groans sounded from around the table, assuring her they were full.

Six-year-old Lincoln perked up and said, "Can I have some ice cream, Nana? I'm still hungry."

"Sure, baby. Nana will get her little man some ice

cream." Eveline stood up. "Are you sure I can't get anyone something else?"

"Well, maybe I'll have a little more banana pudding," Linc said, sitting up erect in his chair.

Nikki popped up out of her seat and walked toward the kitchen. "I'll help you, Mom. I think I'll take some of that pudding home for me and Jeff to eat later." She looked down at her watch. "We really need to be heading home soon."

Eveline and her daughter walked inside the kitchen. "I made plenty of everything. Take some food home with you for tomorrow. That way, you don't have to cook when you get home from work."

"Thanks, Mom. I appreciate it. I'm still putting in long hours at work." Nikki reached inside a cabinet and removed a stack of plastic containers.

Eveline walked to the pantry, removed a brown paper bag, and set it on the table. "It appears that you and Jeff have managed to resolve your differences. I'm happy because I hate it when members of my family are at odds with each other."

"I wouldn't say what we went through was all that," Nikki said. She reached inside a drawer and removed a box of aluminum foil. Then she put a half dozen of Eveline's homemade rolls inside the foil and folded it. She slid the foil inside the bag.

"It's too bad Maya couldn't make it. I hope her mother feels better soon," Eveline remarked. She walked to the stove and put the lids back on the pots as Nikki put the rest of the containers inside the bag.

"Me too," Nikki said.

"Oops, I forgot to fix the ice cream." Eveline rushed to the freezer and hurriedly put generous helpings in two bowls. "Make sure you get some for you and Jeff," she instructed her daughter.

When Nikki and Eveline walked back into the dining room, Jeff and Linc were discussing politics, while Shonell gathered up the dishes. Shonell looked shyly at her mother and sister-in-law. "Lincoln and I want to host the Thanksgiving holiday." She looked at Nikki. "That is, if you and Jeff don't mind."

"You and Junior usually host the Christmas holiday," Eveline remarked. She stared at her daughter-in-law. "Have your plans changed this year?"

"Yes, Mother Baldwin. My father has been ill, and I'd like to spend time with him and my mother during the Christmas holiday. So we're planning on going to Dallas during that time."

"I understand, dear. You should spend time with your family." Eveline looked at Nikki. "Do you want to host Christmas? If not, you and Jeff can join me for dinner."

"We'll host it, Mom. We always have dinner here, so I'll do Christmas," Nikki responded.

"You know I don't mind," Eveline asserted. "It's no bother for me since I don't work."

"I'm sure I'll be caught up with my projects by then. I'll take a few days off from work. I think I have some vacation time left. We'll do turkey day with Junior and Shonell and Christmas at our house. I'll invite Maya and her family for Christmas," Nikki said.

Shonell glanced at her husband and cleared her throat. "We have an announcement to make," she said enigmatically.

Linc stood and walked across the room to where his wife was standing. Then he caressed her abdomen. "Shoney and I are having another baby."

Eveline's face radiated with joy. She strode over to the couple and hugged them. "That's great news. I can hardly wait. When is the baby due?"

"In approximately seven months," Shonell answered. She was positively glowing.

The women chatted about the new family member, while Jeff and Linc shook hands.

Ten minutes later, Jeff walked over to the women. "Are you ready, Nikki?" he asked.

"Yes. That's great news about Linc and Shonell. Hopefully, we'll have a niece this time," Nikki said.

The family exchanged hugs and kisses. Then Jeff and Nikki departed.

Once they were inside the Range Rover and had entered the Expressway, Jeff turned on the stereo and played a BeBe Winans CD. "This was one of the most enjoyable days of my life." He spoke over the music. "Church was uplifting, and you sang like the angel you are. To top it off, your mother cooked one appetizing meal."

Nikki nodded her head. "You're right; today was a blessed day." She hummed along to the tune of the song. "What's your work schedule like this week?" She turned and looked at Jeff.

"My workload should be easy. We don't have another conversion until next year. The Vice President of Information Technology scheduled a disaster recovery test for next month, but I don't think I'll have to travel to the site. Why? How do you think your week is going to be?"

Nikki sighed. "I have a client presentation on Thursday, so I'll probably have to work late a couple of evenings to prepare for that."

"Are you still working with Fatima? How is that going?" Jeff looked up at his rearview mirror and changed lanes.

"Not bad. Victor's going to assign her to a client in January, so I'm sort of mentoring her."

"That's good," Jeff remarked. He glanced at Nikki and back at the windshield. "Is there something you want to tell me, baby?" He stole another expectant look at his wife.

Nikki's heart rate accelerated. Did he know about her gambling? "Uh, no there isn't." She turned to Jeff with a puzzled look on her face. "What made you ask me that?"

"Well, I thought . . . never mind." With their exit coming up, he steered the car to the right lane.

Nikki sat in her seat feeling petrified that her husband would question her again about what had been bothering her. Thankfully, he didn't.

Once at home, they walked quietly up the stairs of the back entrance. When they entered the apartment, Jeff turned on the kitchen light, and Nikki put the food in the refrigerator. Jeff walked to the foyer and hung his coat in the closet. He looked toward the kitchen with disappointment shading his face. Jeff was baffled as to why Nikki hadn't told him about the baby yet. He thought for sure his wife would say something about it tonight. Jeff cautioned himself to be patient. It was just a matter of time. His wife wouldn't be able to hide her condition for long.

Nikki slipped off her coat, then laid it on the couch and headed to the kitchen where she checked the answering machine for messages. Bianca had called again to compliment her on her singing at church today. Nikki smiled to herself, and then walked back to the foyer to hang up her coat.

When she walked into the room, he was sprawled out on the bed watching television. He sat up and began undressing. Nikki opened the closet door, removed her clothes and slipped into a silk robe. She grabbed a brush from her vanity table, sat on her side of the bed, and began brushing her hair.

Jeff took the brush out of her hand. "Let me do that for you," he said.

Nikki moved toward him so he could situate his body behind hers. With tender strokes, Jeff brushed her hair.

Nikki moaned. "That feels good. You have a gentle touch."

Jeff spied her silk scarf lying on the top of the vanity. He rose from the bed, retrieved it, and wrapped the material around Nikki's head. Then he softly kissed her forehead. She snuggled under the comforter. Jeff walked in the closet and returned to the bed wearing pajama bottoms.

Nikki leaned over and kissed his lips. "Thank you, honey."

"My pleasure." Jeff lay back on the pillow, picked up the remote, and changed the channel to ESPN so he could catch the highlights of the day's football games.

Nikki fell asleep with visions of how she was going to fix her financial problems dancing through her head. When Jeff finished watching *Sportscenter*, he turned off the television and snuggled next to Nikki's warm body. Soon he too was in dreamland where visions of a baby girl danced in his head.

Chapter 17

Friday morning, Nikki's eyes fluttered open half an hour before the alarm went off. She looked at Jeff who lay deep in slumber by her side. She pushed the comforter off her shoulders and walked to her home office. She quickly booted up the PC and logged onto her bank's website.

Her body quivered when the screen, showing her balance appeared. The money from Merrill Lynch had been deposited into her account. She looked upward and said, "Thank you, Lord." Then she quickly logged off the system.

She walked into the living room on shaky legs to the bookshelf and removed the Bible Maya had given her and Jeff for a wedding present. An old copy of the pamphlet, *The Daily Word*, lay inside the book. The pamphlet was folded to a day of the previous year, and the scripture lesson was from the book of First John, chapter five, verses one through five. Nikki read them and sighed.

How true those words are. I asked, and the Lord provided. By tonight, all the agony I experienced regarding my debts will become a memory. One day I'll look back on this day and laugh. She clasped the Bible to her bosom as she smiled.

Nikki stood up and put the book back on the shelf. Today had become one of reckoning for her. It was time for her to get the day started. She had written Jeff a note explaining what had happened to the money. Nikki apologized to him and detailed her plan to fix the situation. She planned to leave the note in an open space where Jeff could see it. Then Nikki left the room and went to the bedroom to prepare for work.

During her workday, Nikki repeatedly logged on to Chase Bank's website to verify her account balance. It was as if she couldn't believe the money, which she termed her savior, was actually deposited into her account. During her lunch break, two voices took up residence in her head. One encouraged her to gamble, and the other gave her reasons why she shouldn't.

At two-thirty, she looked up to see Fatima standing in the doorway to her cubicle. "Did you forget Victor wants to see us in his office?" Fatima asked. She clicked the pen she held in her hand.

Nikki stood up and pushed her chair under her desk. She grabbed a pen and pad off her desk and followed Fatima to Victor's office.

Victor looked up at them over his glasses, which were perched precariously on the edge of his nose. Using his middle finger, he slid them back into place. He gestured for the two women to have a seat. Once they were settled comfortably in the seats, he said, "Ladies, I have some good news I'd like to share with you."

Nikki and Fatima exchanged optimistic looks. "Don't keep us in suspense. Share the news," Nikki urged.

Victor's face was flushed, and he couldn't stop a grin from bursting on his face. He leaned back in his burgundy leather chair and clasped his hands around the back of his neck. "As Nikki knows, I've always wanted a shot at an account with Coca Cola. I talked to their head PR person yesterday. They're looking for new ads . . . print and television. They're in the process of screening new agencies, and we have a very good shot at submitting a layout," he said.

"Wow." Nikki's eyes danced merrily. "That's great news, Victor. You mean you're going to let me—"

"I'm offering the project to three teams," Victor said in a conspiring tone, "and whoever comes up with the best ad will get the assignment."

"What do you mean by teams?" Nikki asked. Fatima sat serenely by her side. She hadn't asked Victor a single question.

Victor pulled a sheet of paper out of the folder on his desk. "I'm pairing Trey with Victoria, Michael with Tina, and the third team is you and Fatima." He paused to let the news sink into their brains.

"But why are you dividing us into teams?" Nikki asked with a baffled look on her face. She gripped the arms of the chair.

"Because the magnitude of work involved will require team effort," Victor explained. "You're better at executing designs, and Fatima's forte is literary composition; that's why I'm teaming the two of you up. You two have done magnificently on the other jobs you collaborated on. I thought this would be the perfect opportunity for you to combine your talents and come to a meeting of the minds."

"Victor, I don't know what to say," Fatima gushed. "Thank you for the opportunity."

"Make no bones about it. You two are going to work like you've never worked before. I plan to submit three proposals to Coca Cola's marketing director. The winning team will receive a substantial bonus. This account could put us on the map; right up there with the big boys in New York City. We're the only Midwest agency Coke is accepting submissions from."

Nikki smiled along with Victor and Fatima, but doubts began to creep in her mind. Why would Victor pair her with Fatima? Nikki thought collaboration with a rookie was a recipe for failure. The other teams consisted of veteran designers with experience totaling five years or more. Nikki couldn't follow Victor's logic.

Victor noticed Nikki's expression and said, "You're probably wondering why I selected the two of you and didn't team you with a more seasoned designer. I think you two mesh well together, and my money is on your team to take the prize."

"Thank you for having confidence in us," Fatima said graciously. She exhaled, relaxing her body.

"That's it for now. I'll schedule meetings individually with each team and give you each some guidelines for the Coca Cola presentation, which is tentatively scheduled for early next year."

Fatima rose from her seat, and then Nikki did the same. "Thanks, Victor," they parroted in unison and walked out of his office. Fatima followed Nikki back to her cubicle.

"That's something, isn't it? Who'd have thought we'd have a shot at even submitting our work?" Fatima remarked, after she sat in the chair in front of Nikki's desk.

"Yes, it certainly is an honor. We'll have to put on our thinking caps and come up with something new and fresh," Nikki commented.

"Well, I'm up for the challenge," Fatima remarked, as she stood up.

"Me too. We'll talk later. I'm leaving work early today. I have some business I need to take care of."

"Have a good weekend. I'll see you on Monday." Fatima departed.

As soon as Fatima left, Trey rushed inside Nikki's cubicle. Nikki began powering down her PC. "What's up, Trey?"

"Nothing but the real thing," Trey quipped, as he sank his lanky body in the chair Fatima had just vacated. "I take it you and Fatima talked to Victor. Wasn't that great news?" he asked, already knowing what Victor wanted to talk to them about.

"Yes, it was." Nikki put a batch of papers inside her desk. She reached for her purse, removed her desk key, and locked her desk.

"I wish Victor had paired you and me up. But he makes the calls," Trey said bluntly. "I guess he teamed you up with Fatima because you're both African-American women."

"According to Victor, it was because we work well together," Nikki replied tartly. "I'm leaving for the day, so we'll have to continue this conversation on Monday."

"Sorry." Trey drew out the word. He stood up awkwardly and held his hands up. "I didn't mean to offend you. Have a good weekend," he said, walking out of her cubicle.

"You too." Nikki stood and put on her coat. When she was done, she leaned over and picked up her purse and tote bag. She walked out of her cubicle and to the elevator.

Nikki was on her way to perform an errand that would save her life, career, and most of all her marriage. But was she strong enough to resist all the temptation of gambling away the blessing she was about to receive?

Chapter 18

"Man, I don't know what else to tell you," Ron, the bearer of bad news, told Jeff over the phone. "The market took a dive this morning, and you're down about twenty thousand dollars. Everything happened so quickly, and this is the first opportunity I've had to call you. I moved your money as soon as I could."

"Ron, I specifically told you that I couldn't afford any big losses this week," Jeff enunciated in a staccato tone of voice, clearly annoyed. His hand began sweating as he gripped the telephone receiver tightly. "The house repair payment is due next week. I didn't want to have to dip into our IRA accounts due to the penalties. But you're not leaving me with any options."

The red light on Ron's other extension phone began flashing. "Look, I've got to take another call. This may just be a bump in the road. The market could bounce back soon." He tried to raise Jeff's spirits.

Jeff glanced down at his watch. "It's already three o'clock. There's not a lot of time left in the trading day.

Salvage what you can, and call me back later," he instructed.

"If it's any consolation to you, you're not the only one who took a beating on Wall Street today. Hey, I've got to go, I'll ring you later," Ron said, before switching over to the other line.

Jeff hung up the phone and rubbed his brow and exhaled audibly. Maybe he should go to the bank and withdraw the money for the repairs and take care of the bill now. If the stock in his portfolio kept dropping, then he might not have the money to repay the loan. An uneasy feeling clawed at his stomach. He sat in his seat, debating with himself.

Jeff lifted the phone receiver and dialed a number. "Ernesto, it's me. I'm going to run an errand. If you need me, hit me on my cell. I shouldn't be gone more than a few hours." He disconnected the call and called his manager, relaying the same information.

Jeff opened his briefcase and removed the checkbook of his and Nikki's secondary account, which was strictly for emergencies and non-household accounts and strolled out of his office.

Twenty minutes later, he was seated at the desk of a personal banker at Chase Bank. Her nametag read Ms. COOPER. Jeff tore the check from the checkbook and presented it to the banker.

Ms. Cooper stood up and said, "I'll be back in a moment with a receipt for you."

Jeff nodded and sat back against the back of the hard chair. He couldn't shake the uneasiness that surged through his mind and body.

When Ms. Cooper returned, and with a reddened face, she said, "I'm sorry, Mr. Singleton. We couldn't honor the check. You don't have sufficient funds in your account."

"What do you mean there aren't sufficient funds in the account? I know for a fact the account has at least fifty thousand dollars in it. That should cover the check and then some." Jeff couldn't believe what he was hearing.

"Well, your wife has been making substantial withdrawals during the past few months. She came here yesterday and withdrew the bulk of the balance." The banker's words stunned Jeff.

"Say what?" he uttered. He felt like someone had knocked the wind from his body. His left knee began twitching. "There must be a mistake, or maybe a case of identify fraud." He looked at Ms. Cooper helplessly.

"It was definitely your wife. We validated her proof of identity. The payment on the home equity loan for the house repairs isn't due until next week, so you still have time before the payment is due and interest on it begins to accrue on the account."

Jeff felt so ashamed he couldn't look Ms. Cooper in her eyes. He focused his sight on a painting that hung on the wall behind her. "How much is left in the account?" he managed to ask.

"About fifteen thousand dollars," Ms. Cooper responded. She squirmed slightly in her chair.

"Thank you, Ms. Cooper. I'll be back next week with the payment." Jeff rose from his seat, and with as much dignity as he could muster, he left the office seething with anger.

Almost blindly, he walked outside the bank and clicked on his cell phone. He punched Nikki's office number and was routed to voicemail. He then tried her cell phone, with the same results. *How could she do something like that and not mention it to me? God, this could ruin us. What would Nikki need with that much money?*

Jeff called his boss and lied. "I just received a call from

my wife's job. She's ill and I need to go there. I'll try to come in later. If I don't make it back today, I'll be in tomorrow."

"Don't worry about the job. See about your wife," his boss said.

"Thank you. I'll check in later." Jeff closed the cell phone, and thought about his next move. He stood on the sidewalk, lost in thought. When he looked up, he saw Nikki on the other side of the street. She was walking rapidly, holding her purse close to her body.

Jeff opened his mouth to get her attention, and then shut it. He sprinted across the street and inconspicuously tailed Nikki as she walked inside the County Assessors Office.

Why was she going there? He was aware the taxes were due last month, and he reminded her at least twice to pay them. Nikki informed him that she had. Jeff's lips tightened in concentration. After further thought, he wasn't completely sure that she'd said that she paid the bill. Jeff slapped his forehead when he realized just how long it had been since he and Nikki had discussed finances. Perhaps it was time for him to put on his detective hat. He watched her take an elevator up to the third floor. He stayed on the ground floor, around the corner from the bank of elevators.

Nikki walked into the County Assessors Office and stood in line. When she got to the counter, she presented her check to the clerk.

A few minutes later, the clerk said, "Okay, Mrs. Singleton, your taxes are current. Here's your receipt."

"Thank you. I promise this won't ever happen again." She stepped away from the counter, and had to stop herself from doing a little jig. *Thank you, Lord. Now I have to go out to Joliet, the city of my downfall, then to Har-*

rah's, and I'll be set. I hate that I had to take money out of our IRA and secondary accounts, but this was truly an emergency. Jeff will understand once I explain to him what happened. Lord, I'm never going to gamble again.

She departed the building with a bounce in her step, unaware that Jeff was a few feet away from her as she walked to the parking lot to get her car.

As Jeff trailed his wife, he figured out she was headed to her car. He cursed silently. *Now I'm going to lose her. Where could she be going?* He wished his car was nearby. He'd parked in a garage in his usual spot, two blocks away from the garage where Nikki regularly parked her car. Jeff quickly spied a taxi.

He frantically thrust out his hand, flagging the vehicle. The yellow and green Checker Cab made a screeching noise as the driver halted the vehicle.

Jeff hurried inside of it and barked out, "Take me to the Madison Street Garage, and step on it."

The taxi driver put down the flag, and said, "Yes, sir."

Jeff assumed since he was riding and Nikki was on foot, he could be at her garage by the time she left for her next destination. He pulled out his cell phone and punched in the number to the garage where he parked. Jeff informed the attendant he was on his way to the lot and asked him to have his car ready.

Luck was with Jeff since he parked at a garage where he left the keys with an attendant. Ten minutes later, he was in route to Nikki's parking garage. Jeff put the SUV in park down the block from the garage. He sat and waited for his wife to make an appearance.

After the attendant retrieved Nikki's car, she got in, set her briefcase in the backseat, and pulled her cell phone out of her purse. Nikki turned up the volume. She had set the phone to vibrate when she attended a meeting at work earlier. She scrolled through a couple of calls and noticed that Jeff had called her about an hour ago. She dialed his work number and was routed to voicemail.

"Hey, baby, I noticed you called. Call me back," she said before closing the phone and began her journey to Joliet.

She drove westbound on Eighteen Street before entering the Dan Ryan Expressway. Jeff was in the left lane, four car lengths behind her.

He was perplexed. Jeff couldn't imagine who Nikki could possibly be going to meet. He hoped against hope that she was planning to visit her mother. Then his feelings of hope transcended to anger that Nikki, the minute his back was turned, was up to her old tricks; disappearing and not telling him where she was going.

As they traveled farther south, Nikki didn't exit on Lake Shore Drive as Jeff expected her to. That meant she wasn't going to Eveline's house. To his dismay, they continued on the Dan Ryan Expressway.

Jeff's spirits plummeted like a runaway elevator as he quickly assumed Nikki was going to meet another man. He regretted his decision to follow her sensing it was a bad one, and wherever Nikki was going spelled bad news for him. Jeff couldn't shake the feeling that his marriage was in jeopardy.

Nikki, on the other hand, was happy as a lark. She turned on the radio and listened to the news. The volume was turned up high to keep the voice in her head that taunted her as to whether she could keep her gambling addiction at bay.

Forty-five minutes later, she exited the Dan Ryan Expressway to I-55, and later made her final exit to I-80 . . . with Jeff still hot on her trail. When Nikki pulled into the parking lot, Jeff followed her, but he went in the opposite direction. He couldn't believe his eyes. His wife was at the boat. *What on God's green earth is she doing here?*

Chapter 19

When Nikki exited her car, a giddy feeling invaded her body. Once she walked inside Harrah's, she had to make a concerted effort not to run into the casino. Despite all the anguish she'd endured, Nikki really missed being there. The handles of the slot machines seemed to beckon to her to come over and play. Every table, be it craps or roulette, that had an empty spot, pleaded with her to come and sit down. Nikki closed her eyes. She had to be strong. Her body experienced a pure adrenalin rush.

The restaurant was located to the left side of the casino. Nikki looked back at the casino before rushing inside the eatery. She sat down at a table and dropped her head into her hands. She tried hard to battle the gambling demons that had taken possession of her soul. Her soul struggled as she argued with herself about trying to win back the money. No one would be the wiser. She debated about what to do.

She clasped her legs tightly together to keep her body from running inside the casino. With her head bowed, Nikki put her hands together as if in prayer. She knew she should be trying to find Mr. Stanhope's office to pay her debt and race straight back to her car. Nikki didn't factor into her thought process how much money she'd lost the last time she had been there. She almost convinced herself that she could win back the money and justified her actions by thinking the Lord wouldn't lead her to the casino to lose money again. She had been a good Christian, a faithful servant of the Lord. It didn't hurt that she was the lead singer of the choir, and that she and Jeff tithed each Sunday. No, the Lord wouldn't steer her in the wrong direction. After all, she was His child. All Nikki could see at that minute was how winning money would put her marriage and finances back on track.

Nikki opened her eyes, looking left and right. She sensed someone was watching her. She stood up, fetched herself a cup of coffee, and sat back down. Nikki listlessly stirred in a pack of sugar. Her chin was propped up on the heel of her left hand.

Nikki remembered how her pastor had prayed for her when she went to see him, and he assured her that, through Christ, all things are possible. She had prayed so hard after that meeting to overcome the demon that had overtaken her will. Nikki realized that if she lost the money she borrowed that there was a real possibility that Jeff might leave her. And Nikki couldn't imagine her life without her husband. Though Jeff didn't talk about it much, Nikki knew that Jeff's poverty stricken childhood led to his over aggression when it came to their finances. Nikki truly didn't want to let her mother down. She didn't know how she'd face Jeff and her mother if she lost the house. She prayed for help; a sign from God.

Nikki closed her eyes and began reciting the Twenty-Third Psalm softly. "The Lord is my shepherd; I shall not want. He maketh me to lie down in green pastures; he leadeth me beside the still waters. He restoreth my soul:

he leadeth me in the paths of righteousness for his name's sake. Yea, though I walk through the valley of the shadow of death, I will fear no evil: for thou art with me; thy rod and thy staff they comfort me. Thou preparest a table before me in the presence of mine enemies: thou anointest my head with oil; my cup runneth over. Surely goodness and mercy shall follow me all the days of my life: and I will dwell in the house of the Lord forever. Amen."

Nikki sat quietly inside the restaurant and continued to wait for a sign from the Lord. "Help me, Lord," she repeated over and over, like a chant.

Jeff sat inside his car dumbfounded. His mouth hung open. If anyone had told him that he'd find his wife at a casino, he never would have believed it. *So much for the other man theory. Boy, was I wrong.*

The reasons for Nikki's behavior over the past few months fell into place. A gush of sadness ejected across his heart when he realized there wasn't going to be a baby. With his shoulders hunched forward, Jeff got out of the car and walked the length of the parking lot, until he found Nikki's car. He peeped inside. The interior was immaculate.

With a plunging sensation in the middle of his stomach, Jeff used the spare key to Nikki's automobile, which he kept on his key ring, and unlocked the trunk to see if anything inside would give him a clue as to what his wife would be doing with the huge sum of money she'd withdrawn. When he looked inside, he was so horrified to see crumpled envelopes containing household bills that he nearly fell to his knees. Jeff's hands shook. His eyes widened in understanding. It was obvious Nikki had forced them into a precarious financial predicament.

Jeff gingerly picked up the utility bills that Nikki had paid, and the tax bill from the State. There was a sea of lottery tickets, and tickets from the Off Track Betting locations. His hand trembled as he picked up the letters from Harrah's. His legs could barely support his weight as he walked back to his vehicle.

He opened his car door and sat down heavily on the driver's side of the car. A tear streaked down his face. He snorted and quickly brushed the tear away.

Jeff put the letters from Harrah's in chronological order. He opened the flap of the first envelope and pulled the letter out. When he saw the total due to the casino, he dropped the letter like it was a live ember. He angrily hit the steering wheel, not believing how much money his wife owed the casino. A few thousand here and there he may have been able to force himself to understand; over fifty thousand dollars was inconceivable. She owed the casino enough for a down payment on a house. Jeff couldn't comprehend how Nikki could do that to them. He was further outraged that she had come back to the casino and couldn't understand how she could, considering their precarious financial situation.

A wave of dizziness struck Jeff's head as his blood pressure soared. He glanced at the building, irate that Nikki could be gambling away more of their future. Everything that he'd worked for had been for him and Nikki. Jeff couldn't fathom what his wife was thinking.

He picked the letter up off the floor and continued reading it. When he saw she had used the apartment building for collateral, and sixty thousand dollars was due immediately, he balled up his fists. Jeff's stomach churned like he was going to vomit. He couldn't finish reading the letter. The words had become blurred from the tears that washed his eyes.

His breathing became strained. His nostrils flared as he breathed loudly out of his mouth. He turned his head and stared desolately out the window. The words on the paper had signaled his worst nightmare had come true. Jeff couldn't bear it. He questioned the Lord as to why that misfortune had to befall him. In a matter of days, he and Nikki could be homeless like he was when he was a child. To his mother's credit, she tried her best to take care of him and didn't fritter away the little they had. Jeff decided that Nikki was *trifling*. That was the first word that came to his mind to describe her behavior.

Jeff's hand shook as he tried to insert the key in the ignition of the car. Finally, after several unsuccessful tries, he threw the key in frustration at the windshield. The impact left a tiny hairline crack. Still fuming, Jeff got back out of the car and headed inside the casino.

Chapter 20

Nikki still sat stoically inside a red cushioned booth at the back of the casino café. She leaned over and pulled a tissue out of her purse; using it to wipe her eyes and blow her nose. She balled up the tissue, and was about to stuff it back inside her purse, when she looked up and saw Jeff.

Jeff scowled at his wife. Nikki cringed from the hurt and disappointment oozing from his eyes. The tissue fell from her hand onto the floor. Nikki had hoped that she would never have to see that expression on his face directed toward her. But reality had become truth. Her legs felt heavy as she stood and walked toward him.

Flustered, Nikki held out her hands beseechingly and said, "Jeff, I know my being here looks bad, but I can explain everything."

He grabbed her arm roughly and steered her back to the booth. Nikki's legs were so shaky that she nearly fell into the seat. Jeff sat down across from his wife and threw the letters from Harrah's on the table. "Why don't you do that, Nikki? Explain these!" he said angrily.

Nikki opened her mouth and then shut it. She was busted.

Everything she had done was now out in the open. She looked down at the table. Her lips twitched. "Jeff . . . I . . . um . . . had a little problem, but it's under control now. I'm on my way to pay off my debt." She peeked up at Jeff's face. A lump rose in her throat at the rage that she knew that he was trying to suppress.

"And where would you have sixty thousand dollars stashed away? As far as I know, we have joint accounts. Sure you have your own account, but you never keep any more than a couple hundred dollars in it. I saw your bank statement in the car, and you're broke." Jeff's voice spewed venom.

Nikki cowered, she felt like her husband hated her. Jeff continued speaking. His tone of voice dripped with poison.

"You know what's even worse about this mess? It's how you had the audacity to take money out of our portfolio. That money was our backup; savings for a rainy day in case we ever lost our jobs or something like that. But you took it out of the bank without my knowledge for something as frivolous as this." His hand angrily swept the air.

Nikki nodded as tears gushed from her eyes. "You're right, Jeff. Everything that you've said is true. I wish I could go back in time and relive that part of my life. I won't ever step foot inside a casino again; I promise. I messed up, and as bad as I wish I could take back what I've done, I can't. I didn't want you to find out what happened because I knew you would react like this." Nikki tried to reach for Jeff's hands, but he pulled away.

"How did you expect me to react to what you've done, Nichole? You've put our house on sinking sand. The taxes hadn't been paid until today. You've opened up numerous credit card accounts. Yeah, that's right; I went through your mail. Sue me," he said nastily. "I called the utility companies, and they informed me that the payments are up to date, but then I find out you owe this frigging casino sixty thousand dollars, and they have a lien against the house. How did you expect me to feel and react?"

Nikki shook her head morosely. "I hoped you'd understand, and at least try to be supportive. This hasn't been a picnic for me either . . . robbing Peter to pay Paul. I realize for me to do what I did, something isn't right or is missing from my life."

"Oh, so now you're going to try and blame your gambling addiction on me? I don't think so." Jeff's left eyebrow rose, and the vein in his neck began throbbing.

Nikki clasped her hands together to stop them from shaking. "I'm not blaming you, Jeff. I take full responsibility for my actions." She picked up her purse and dropped it on the table. "I have the money for my debt; at least most of it. That's why I took money out of the account, so I could pay off most of it. I'm hoping Harrah's will let me pay the rest through a payment plan. I was just on my way to take care of my business when I saw you."

Jeff spoke through clenched teeth. "What you should've done was never stepped foot into this place." He put his finger in Nikki's face. "Do you realize that the payment for the repairs on the building is due next week? That's how I found out what you had done. Something, call it fate or whatever, told me to make the payment today. I felt like a fool when the banker told me we didn't have enough money in the account to cover the payment."

Nikki's hand flew up to cover her mouth. "I forgot about that. I know it sounds so inadequate, but I never meant to cause these problems. Please try and forgive me. I'm so sorry." Tears crawled down her face.

Usually Nikki's tears melted any ill will Jeff felt against her, but not this time. He stood up and slid out of the booth. "I've got to go. I can't stand to be around you right now. If I stay here, I may say something I'll regret."

Nikki rose from her seat on shaking legs. "Don't leave, Jeff." She pulled the arm of his jacket. "Please stay. Let's talk about this some more." She trailed behind him, aware that people were starting to stare.

"This isn't a good time for me. I begged you to talk to me weeks ago, but obviously it wasn't a good time for you. I'll talk to you another time," he retorted harshly.

"What do you mean by you'll talk to me another time?" Nikki's lower lip trembled uncontrollably. "Aren't you going home? As soon as I finish here, we can go home and finish talking."

"Not now, Nikki. Later." Jeff turned on his heels and walked briskly away from his wife.

Nikki's eyes were full of tears as she walked unsteadily back to the booth. She dropped her folded arms on the table, buried her face in them, and cried.

Jeff stormed out of the restaurant and rushed to his car. He searched his pockets for his keys, let himself in the vehicle, and slammed the door before speeding out of the parking lot. He wasn't sure where he was going, but he wanted to be as far away from Harrah's and his wife as possible. Jeff couldn't stop his mind from replaying repeatedly how Nikki had lied to him. He'd asked her over and over what was bothering her. Instead of coming clean, she shut him out. Trying to be a good husband, he gave her space instead of crowding her, and all he got for his efforts was money taken out of the account and a big fat lien on the house.

Jeff looked upward. "Lord, why me?"

Nikki was still seated at the table in the café, sniffing.

The hostess, an older woman in her sixties with a head of gray hair, walked over to the booth and asked, "Is there anything I can do for you, Miss?"

"No, I'm fine. I'll be leaving shortly." Nikki used the

back of her hand to wipe her eyes. She picked up her purse and pretended to look for something inside of it.

"My name is Doris. If you need anything, please let me know."

Nikki nodded. "I guess you and probably everyone else in the restaurant overheard me and my husband's discussion."

Doris sighed. "Yes, we did. But that's nothing new for Harrah's. I see situations like yours happening all the time. I feel sorry for anyone that has a gambling addiction."

"I don't know what you mean," Nikki said loudly. Then she lowered her voice. "I don't have an addiction. I just let the situation get out of hand. I have the money right here in my purse." She held up her purse. "I'm going to take care of my business."

Doris threw her hands up defensively. "I'm sorry if I offended you. I watched you when you came in, and I could tell you were battling monsters. If you have the money, then why haven't you taken care of your business already?"

"Because I was thinking, that's why," Nikki snapped. Her face burned. She knew what the older woman said was true.

Doris reached inside her pocket, pulled out a booklet, and handed it to Nikki. "When you're ready to do something about your addiction, I suggest you read this. I went through the same thing, except the bug bit my husband and not me. The disease is strong, and you can't fight it alone. This is a pamphlet about Gamblers Anonymous. They can help you."

Nikki pushed the pamphlet back to Doris. "I don't need this. I'm fine. Now if you'll leave me alone, I'll get myself together and do what I came here for."

"Okay," Doris said, leaving the pamphlet on the table.

"If you change your mind and want to talk, you know where to find me."

Nikki pulled her makeup kit out of her purse, and repaired her face. Her emotions bristled at the thought that Jeff would come into the casino and snap at her like he had lost his mind. After all, she contributed to their savings just as much as he did. Her mind flew back to what Lindsay said of how controlling Jeff was. Right now, Nikki totally agreed with her girlfriend. The showdown with Jeff had chipped away at Nikki's resolve not to gamble. At that moment, she didn't care if she won or lost.

Nikki shook her head and twisted her lips together as she thought how Jeff hadn't brought anything into their marriage. She couldn't believe how heavy-handed he was being, trying to run things. He had a lot of nerve. She was an adult and could do what she wanted with her money. And if she wanted to gamble, so be it!

Nikki's cell phone rang, crushing her thoughts. She searched through her purse, looking for it. She opened it without looking at the caller ID, and said, "Jeff?"

"No, this is your mother," Eveline said. "How are you doing, Nikki? I called your job a couple of times and got your voicemail. Then I called your house and got the answering machine."

"Oh, hi, Mom. I'm doing fine. I had some errands to run, so I left work a little early. How are you doing?" Nikki's voice sounded nasal from crying.

"I'm fine; or I was up until an hour ago when I started thinking about you. I fell asleep, and when I awakened, I had a terrible premonition that you were in trouble. Are you sure everything is all right?" Eveline anxiously twisted the phone cord.

"Mom, I'm . . . I'm . . . Mama, I'm in trouble." Nikki's voice broke. The phone shook unsteadily in her hand.

"What is it, Nikki? Are you hurt? Where are you? Do you need me to come where you are?" she asked, all in one breath.

"No, Mommy." Nikki's sounded like a child. She swayed back and forth in her seat. " I have to take care of this. I'm an adult. I can't run to you every time I have a problem. For real, Mommy, I'm okay."

"Nichole," Eveline said in her don't-you-disagree-with-me tone of voice, "I want you to come to my house right now. Don't make me leave my house and come looking for you. I knew something was wrong. A mother's intuition is never wrong. Tell me what's happening with you." Eveline's heart was beating so rapidly that it felt like it was going to burst from her chest.

"Mom, I messed up real bad. I think Jeff has left me," Nikki wailed. Her eyes filled with tears again, and she moaned. "He's never going to come back."

"Forget about Jeff. You're my baby. I'm worried about you. Please come to my house, Nikki. Let me try and help you," Eveline begged.

"I will. Just give me a little time. I have something I need to do." Nikki sniffed.

"Okay, baby. I'll be looking for you. You don't have to go through this alone. God is on your side." Eveline tried her best to comfort her daughter.

"Mom, I'll be there in a couple of hours." She clicked off her phone. After Nikki calmed down, she knew that the Lord had given her not one, but three signs—Jeff appearing out of the blue. Her mother calling her. And the waitress in the restaurant. Nikki was ashamed at how she had callously dismissed the woman, considering Doris was just trying to give her information that would be beneficial. Nikki knew the right thing to do was to get up from her seat and go pay her debt. But the desire was strong to go to the casino to gamble. Her first priority should have been to do whatever she could to make things right in her world. She hoped the Lord wouldn't desert her and that He'd give her strength for whatever lay ahead.

Nikki looked up to find Doris staring at her from across the restaurant with her hands folded across her chest. The older woman started walking toward Nikki's table. And Nikki was grateful that the Lord had sent someone to be with her during her time of need.

Chapter 21

Jeff steered his SUV onto the entrance ramp for I-55 and headed north. He had no desire to go to the house he shared with his wife just yet. His face was still ashen with fury. Jeff's mouth was shaped in a downward slash, and every time his mind wandered to Nikki's actions, he wanted to hit something. He leaned over and retrieved his ringing phone from the passenger seat. When he saw that it was Nikki calling, he dropped it like it was toxic. When he needed her to communicate to him what was happening in her world, she couldn't be bothered. Now the tables had turned, and he couldn't be bothered.

Jeff looked to his left and saw a stalled vehicle sitting on the side of the Expressway with the hood raised. Traffic had slowed to a snail's pace. He saw what looked like Reverend Dudley's Cadillac as he craned his neck, trying to get a better look at the vehicle. When he drove alongside the car, Jeff could tell from the license plate that the Cadillac belonged to his pastor.

Jeff put on his left turn signal and parked in front of the beige sedan. When he stepped out of the Range Rover, blustery winds buffeted his body, pushing him forward as he walked to the reverend's car.

"Reverend Dudley?" he called as he stuck his hands inside his jacket pockets.

"Hello, Jeffrey," Reverend Dudley replied after he rolled down the window.

"Do you need any help?"

"No, I'm fine, son. Triple A is on the way. They should be here soon. At least that's what I hope. What are you doing all the way out here? Playing hooky from work?" The grim look on Jeff's face cut into the pastor's tease. "What's wrong, son? Are Nichole and Eveline doing all right? Why don't you have a seat in my car and talk to me?"

Jeff obeyed, and the wind's force nearly slammed the door shut. "Man, I tell you it's getting cold out there." He rubbed his hands together and debated about lying to his pastor. They shared a reasonably close relationship, and since he had no desire to talk to his boys about what Nikki had done, he turned toward Reverend Dudley and said, "I was at the boat, Pastor. You do know what *the boat* is?"

Reverend Dudley laughed heartily. "Of course I know what the boat is. I'm not that out of touch with the secular world." His face sobered. "You don't have a gambling problem, do you, son?"

It was Jeff's turn to laugh, and his was a harsh one. "No, I don't. Your choir's lead soprano is the one with the problem. She's the one at Harrah's right now." He turned and looked out the window.

A tow truck pulled up behind the reverend's car. The driver got out of the truck and walked over to the Cadillac to talk to the minister. After a few exchanged words, the driver went back to the truck and began unloosening chains on the back of the vehicle.

Jeff asked Reverend Dudley, "How are you getting home? If you need a ride, I can drop you off."

"Thank you, son. I was going to catch a ride back to the church with the tow truck driver and have my wife pick me up later. But I think I'll take you up on your offer."

Jeff went back to his SUV to warm it up. By the time Reverend Dudley sat on the passenger side of the Range Rover, and Jeff steered the vehicle back into traffic, it had stopped snowing, and traffic had picked up a little.

Reverend Dudley held his Bible in his hands. "My father gave me this when I graduated from the seminary. He was a great minister and counselor. I've tried hard all my life to follow his lead and live up to his expectations."

Jeff glanced at Reverend Dudley, and then back out the windshield. "As I was saying, Nikki has a wicked gambling problem. She's into Harrah's for sixty g's."

"So why is Nikki there and you're here?" Reverend Dudley asked, obviously confused.

"Because I caught her at it red-handed," Jeff replied with still a tinge of anger in his voice. "She never bothered to confide in me how she spent her evenings there while I was at work."

"I knew something was wrong with her when she came to see me a few weeks ago," Reverend Dudley said pensively.

"She came to see you?" The SUV swerved a bit to the left.

"Now be careful; it's a little slick out here," the pastor advised. "Yes, she came to the church a couple of weeks ago, and I knew something was eating at her. She asked me to pray for her, but she didn't say why. I could see she was battling something mightily. That's why I requested she sing on Sunday. I hoped she would hear, as well as feel, the words to the song. And by doing so, it would bring her some measure of comfort."

Jeff was surprised to hear that Nikki had tried to seek help for her problem. He felt a dash of guilt. Then his heart hardened again. Prayer apparently hadn't been enough.

"I guess you're feeling betrayed right now?" Reverend Dudley reached out and patted Jeff's arm.

"Yeah, you got that right. I knew something was bothering her too. I kept asking her to tell me what was wrong, but she just blew me off. She was so moody that I thought she was pregnant," Jeff admitted, feeling abashed.

"I can understand that. But you know what? Whatever your wife does, no matter how bad it makes you feel, you have to support her. Nikki obviously has a problem, or she wouldn't have been in Joliet. Did you actually catch her gambling?"

"I don't think so. She was sitting in the café. She said she had the money to pay off her debt. But I don't see how, because she owes them so much. And our other bills have fallen behind. It was like my childhood had come back to haunt me in the worst way."

"What do you mean?" the Reverend asked.

"My mother and I were poor while I was growing up. I never knew who my pops was. There were times we went without a meal. No, let me correct that. My mother did whatever she had to do so I could eat. We kept an endless supply of candles because sometimes the electricity was shut off. For a time, we lived in the projects, then we were in and out of plenty of seedy apartments. I vowed never to let that happen to me or my family when I was grown."

"I hear you, son. But that's where you went wrong. You can't and don't control anything about your life or Nikki's. That's a job for our Father above."

"Are you saying God allowed this to happen?" Jeff looked up at the green sign, which spanned the width of the Expressway.

"God gives us free will to make our own decisions.

Sometimes we make the right ones and other times, we don't. That's what defines us as individuals . . . how well we cope with situations when times become hard."

"I know what you're saying is right." Jeff nodded his head. "But right now, I can't be around Nikki. I'm so furious, that I'm scared I might hurt her."

"I don't think that will happen. But maybe you do need a couple of days to cool off and consider what's more important to you. Is it your feelings of betrayal? Or being a husband and helping your wife, who is truly in need of love and understanding now. You took vows, saying you'd be there for each other for better or worse. It's the worse that seems to split up so many couples today," Reverend Dudley said.

"I knew you were going to say that. But I can't forgive Nikki; at least not yet."

Reverend Dudley thumped the Bible with his finger. "You know Jesus forgave His captors, even those who crucified Him. Try using Him as an example. I know it's tough for you, and I'm not condoning what Nichole did. I'm sure she's just as broken up as you are. This book," he waved it in the air, "says to judge not, lest ye be judged. We're all human and have our weaknesses, but to survive in this world until we get to our heavenly one, we must have forgiveness in our heart."

Jeff nodded silently. "I just need a little time, Pastor. Today feels like déjà vu."

"Pray and ask the Lord to help you. I have no doubt you'll do the right thing," Reverend Dudley replied. "You said the gambling really hurt you. But what's the worst that Nichole could do to you that would hurt you even more?"

"At this point, what she did seems like the worst, but I'm going to be honest. I don't know if I could ever forgive her if she were cheating on me. And it did cross my mind that she might be," Jeff admitted.

"If that's the worst, then you can count your blessings that she didn't do that. There's so much temptation in the world. What will save you and your marriage is your faith in God. Even though it doesn't seem possible at this minute, God is still at work. People always assume preachers are free from the hurts of the world. But that's not true. Me and my missus have experienced some hard times. We've never been able to conceive a child. The medical experts can't give us a reason why, and there's nothing medically wrong with either of us. For a short time, I was bitter. Then I had to accept that parenthood wasn't God's plan for me and Laura. Maybe the Lord wanted us to focus on the jobs of saving souls and counseling, and that's what we've done. Every day I count my blessings because without God, where would I be? Where would you or any of us be?"

Jeff nodded as he listened to the Reverend. "You're right. I guess I just hoped if I finished college, had a good job, and paid my tithes, that the Lord would exempt me from heartache and pain. But I guess that isn't so. I think I knew that in the back of my mind. Still the thought of losing everything we've worked for petrifies me."

"Son, with God on our side, we have nothing to fear. Surrender your burden to God, and let Him handle it. I suggest you give yourself a little time to calm down, think about the situation, and let God lead you. He's never failed us yet."

"Thanks, Pastor. I needed to hear that. I'm still not convinced we can overcome this, but I will try to let go and give it to God," Jeff promised.

"Now, you're cooking." Reverend Dudley nodded his head up and down. "When we get to the church, come inside and we'll pray together."

Chapter 22

After talking to Doris, Nikki felt a little better. She rose from the bench and picked up her coat and purse. She knew paying off her debt was the last chance to make things right. But while she sat alone, calling her husband repeatedly, Nikki felt angry and devastated that Jeff had left her so abruptly. She held the letter from the collections manager in her hand. All she had to do was take care of her debt.

She still had a powerful urge to gamble and win back her money. Her hands trembled from the need to go to the casino. How badly she wanted to pull the slot of a machine or toss the dice. She dropped her coat back on the booth. Perspiration coated her forehead and she brushed it off with the back of her hand. Her lips felt dry as sandpaper. Her mind kept urging her to play. Nikki couldn't gamble at Harrah's until her debt was paid. The Empress Casino wasn't far away just a few miles south of Harrah's. Her demon, it seemed wouldn't be denied.

Nikki chewed her bottom lip indecisively. Since Jeff didn't care, what difference did it make whether she gambled or not? He didn't even believe her when she told him that she had the money to pay toward her debt. Nikki sat back on the seat of the booth and moaned inaudibly. She didn't know what to do. Her hands itched to gamble. According to the song, trouble didn't last always, and besides, God wouldn't let her lose her home. Would He?

Eveline was beside herself with worry, not knowing what was happening with her child. She sat in the living room on the couch with her Bible in her hand, alternating between praying and peering out the window.

After an hour elapsed, she tried calling Nikki again. Her daughter didn't answer her cell phone. She tried Jeff's cell phone and was routed to voicemail. Eveline's next move was to try the couple's house phone. She half hoped that Nikki had gone home due to the weather. Eveline prayed that misfortune hadn't befallen her daughter. She walked to the window again. It was beginning to snow heavily.

The sound of chimes interrupted the stillness in the air. Eveline nearly tripped over the leg of the cocktail table as she ran to the door and flung it open. "Nichole!" Eveline looked down at the floor abashed. "Oh, Linc; I thought you were your sister."

Linc walked inside the house and brushed the snow off the arms of his jacket. "Hi, Mom. I was heading home and saw the lights on in the living room. I thought I'd stop by and shovel the snow for you." He leaned over and kissed Eveline's cheek. "What's wrong?" He stepped back and noticed the unhappy look on his mother's face.

"Nothing." Eveline sighed. She walked back to the living room and sat down on the couch. Linc followed her and sat in the wingback chair. He removed his pea coat and laid it on the arm of the chair.

"I know something is wrong, Mom. You look pale as a ghost, and your Bible is laying face down on the sofa."

"You're right," she said. "Your sister's in trouble, and I don't know what to do."

Linc held up a hand. "Whoa. What do you mean Nikki is in trouble? Are you sure?" Two worry lines creased his face between his eyes.

"I'm as sure as my name is Eveline Baldwin."

"Have you checked with Jeff?" he asked, sitting forward in the chair.

"I called his cell phone, but got no answer. I called their house with the same result. I've been so worried about her. I didn't tell you, but Nikki went to see Reverend Dudley last week. I feel like she's been off kilter for a while," Eveline confessed.

"Shonell said the same thing," Linc admitted. "I wish I had taken time to talk to her when we were here for dinner on Sunday. You don't think she and Jeff are having problems, do you?"

"If they are, she hasn't said anything to me," Eveline said. "It's something else. I just don't know what."

"Why don't I go shovel the snow outside, while you try calling Jeff again?" Linc suggested as he stood up and put on his jacket. He closed the door behind his exit.

Eveline looked at the cordless phone in fear. After dialing Jeff and Nikki's home number, she was disappointed when the answering machine kicked on. She waited for the beep and said, "Nikki or Jeff, would one of you call me when you get in? I'm feeling a little anxious. Nikki, you said you'd come by and you haven't, so I'm a little worried. I'm probably being silly." Eveline tried to laugh it off.

The machine stopped recording abruptly. "Mother Baldwin, this is Jeff. Nikki isn't home. We had a disagreement this afternoon, and she hasn't come home yet," he said.

"What do you mean she hasn't come home? What do

you mean you had an argument? Never mind that. Where is my baby, Jeff?"

"I left her at a casino in Joliet," he answered candidly.

"What did you say?" Eveline sat down on the sofa. All the blood in her body seemed to rush to her feet.

"I just found out today that Nikki has a gambling habit. She's in trouble."

"You found that out, and you just walked away from her?" Eveline shrieked incredulous. She shook her head as if she didn't quite believe what Jeff had just told her.

Jeff felt one foot tall. "I admit I might not have handled the situation in the best way, but I almost caught her red-handed. Apparently, she's been doing it for awhile."

"Good Lord, what are we going to do now?" Eveline sighed.

"I don't know about you, Mother Baldwin, but I don't plan to do anything right now. I need some time alone. Nikki didn't care about my feelings and I don't care about hers," Jeff said resignedly.

"Son, I know you need time to sort through all of this. But Nikki is your wife, and I can only imagine what's going through her head now. Is it possible for you to consider how she's feeling right now?"

"At this moment, I can't say I really care about how Nikki feels. She brought all of this on us. A huge gambling debt, and the taxes were behind on the house. And those are only the things I know about." Tension zigzagged through his body.

"I can't bear her being out there suffering alone like this. Linc is here; maybe he'll take me to Joliet to find her," Eveline moaned.

"I don't think you need to go through all that trouble, but you do what you have to, Mother. I'm done dealing with my wife for today."

Eveline heard her front door open and close. "Okay, Jeffrey. Needless to say, I'm disappointed in your position. We'll talk to you later." She hung up the telephone receiver and rushed to the foyer.

Nikki stood at the front door. Her eyes were like wet deadened orbs and her mouth twitched. "Mama, please help me," she said, collapsing into her mother's arms.

Chapter 23

Jeff turned off the light in the kitchen and walked through the dimly lit apartment to the den with the mail in hand. He sat on the sofa and riffled through junk mail and a credit card application for Nikki.

He laid the envelopes on the cocktail table and looked warily toward the bedroom. Then he closed and rubbed his eyes. Jeff laid his head against the back of the couch, feeling exhausted. Several minutes later, he clicked on his cell phone and called his job. Ernesto assured him that everything was under control.

Jeff scratched the top of his head, and then stood and walked to the bar. He poured himself a snifter of cognac, and then he set the snifter back on top of the bar. He needed to keep a clear head. Alcohol wouldn't solve his problems.

When the telephone rang, Jeff looked at the caller ID unit and snatched it up. "Hi, Ron. What news do you have for me?" he asked with a melancholy tone of voice.

"Good evening to you too. I called your job, and the lead operator told me that you had a family emergency. I hope everything is all right," Ron said in a concerned tone of voice.

Jeff sighed inaudibly. "Yeah, man. Things are fine."

"Anyway, I called to tell you the bleeding has stopped for now regarding the new stock. It's starting to rebound, so I'm going to hold onto it for you a couple more days, and then reassess the situation."

"There's been a change in me and Nikki's finances," Jeff said in a deadpan voice. "I . . . I . . . I think you need to just sell everything and send me a check."

"Whoa." Ron removed the phone from his ear and stared at it as if he could see Jeff through it. "Now don't be hasty. Are you sure you want to do that? I know the market has been down for a couple of days, but I think bailing out now would be premature," he said.

"Trust me, I don't have a choice. It's for an emergency." Jeff closed his eyes and leaned back against the sofa.

"I don't understand," Ron said confused. "Are we talking about a large sum of money? Is this something you need to decide right now? Maybe you need to sleep on it."

"I wish that was the case," Jeff said. "But I'm one hundred percent sure that closing the accounts is what I need to do. Hey, Ron, I've got to go. I'll call you tomorrow and send you something in writing." He clicked off the telephone and set it back on the base.

The telephone sounded again. Jeff glared at the Caller ID, clearly annoyed. "Reverend Dudley. How are you?" he said, answering the phone.

"I'm fine, son. After talking to you earlier, I couldn't help but feel concerned about you and Nikki. Did she make it home yet?" he asked.

"No, she didn't," Jeff replied through gritted teeth.

"Have you talked to her? Is she okay?" The Reverend sensed Jeff didn't want to talk to him.

"No, Pastor, I haven't. I'm sure she's still at the boat, or at her mother's or Maya's house. She's fine, trust me," he said.

"I don't mean to pester you or anything. But to resolve a problem, no matter how minor, you've got to talk. Keep the lines of communication open."

"Well, Pastor, you told me a little while ago that maybe I needed time to calm down. I'm still working on that. I just walked in the house." Jeff looked longingly at the snifter of cognac.

"Son, I know this situation is difficult for you, but it's not the end of the world. Sometimes God tests us to see if we have faith and believe in His Word. There's a reason I'm in the pulpit on Sundays to help my members understand the Word. Trust me, Jesus will work it out. One of my jobs is to counsel the church membership and compared to some of the stories I've heard, there's no doubt in my mind that your situation with Nikki can be fixed."

Jeff swallowed and then bobbed his head up and down. "I'm sure you've heard every story imaginable, Pastor. But this is my life, and I didn't expect this type of behavior from my wife. I grew up poor, dirt poor, and I vowed never to go back to that type of life, and here I am, back in the same situation that I vowed to escape from."

"That was your vow, Jeff, but our Heavenly Father has other plans in store for us. One day you'll look back and see what I'm talking about."

"I guess so," Jeff conceded. He knew there wasn't anything he could say to refute the Reverend's words.

"Well, I'm going to let you go. I hope Nichole makes it home safely. Both of you are in my prayers."

"Thank you, Pastor. I appreciate your call and concern," Jeff replied.

*   *   *

Reverend Dudley looked troubled as he walked out of his den. His wife was in the kitchen working on notes for a program scheduled for Sunday evening.

"What's wrong, dear?" she asked, noticing the concerned look on her husband's face.

The reverend sat in the chair across from Laura. "I didn't say anything earlier. I guess I was hoping the situation would resolve itself. Nichole's in trouble. He and Nichole are having problems."

Laura laid the pen on the table and shook her head. "That's a shame. I hope it's nothing serious."

"Well, it's serious enough." Reverend Dudley stood and removed a bottle of water from the refrigerator. "I just spoke to Jeff, and he's still very upset."

"Did he say what the problem was, or is it confidential?" Laura stared expectantly at her husband.

"Apparently Nichole has a gambling problem. I'm not sure why or what led to that habit. Jeff found out by accident and he isn't a happy camper right now."

Laura's mouth dropped open. "That's terrible. Poor Nikki and Jeff. My heart and prayers go out to them. Do you think Eveline knows?"

After draining the bottle of water, Reverend Dudley twisted the cap back on it. "I'm sure she does by now. I can't imagine she knew before today, because I know she would've said something about it."

"You're right," Laura agreed. "This is awful. Why don't you say a prayer for them, dear? I feel like they need a ton of blessings right now."

Reverend Dudley stretched his arms across the dark wood tabletop, grasping his wife's hands. "Father in heaven, we come to you with heavy hearts tonight, but secure in the knowledge that you know best, and all of our lives are in your hands. Lord, I ask that you send your blessings down to Sister Nichole and Brother Jeff tonight.

"They're hurting, Lord, and are in need of your comfort. You said we only have to ask to receive your blessings, and Lord, I ask in your Father's name to bring peace and resolution to these young people's lives as they work through their problems. Let them realize that we're never alone, and just have to listen to and heed your word. These blessings I ask in your Son's name and for His sake. Amen."

"Amen," Laura echoed. "I hope everything works out for Nikki and Jeff."

"Oh, trust me, the situation will work out," Reverend Dudley remarked. "God may not answer our prayers when we think He should, but He will eventually. Of that I have no doubt."

Laura closed the pad she'd been writing on before her husband came into the kitchen. She looked across the table at him and asked, "Did Jeff say whether Nikki was at home or not?"

"He said she wasn't at home. I don't think he knows where she is."

"That's not good. The weather is horrible tonight. Do you think we should call Eveline or go over there?" Laura asked.

"I was thinking the same thing myself," Reverend Dudley admitted as he shrugged his shoulders. "Maybe we should let Eveline handle the problem, especially if Nikki is at her house. Jeff thought she was either at Eveline's or Maya's."

"Nichole is close to her mother. If I had to venture a guess, I'd say she's at Evie's house," Laura said.

"I agree with you, hon. Maybe I should call Eveline and see if she needs us to come and assist her." He rubbed the top of his head.

"I can't even imagine what my friend must be going through," she added sadly.

Reverend Dudley stood and walked to the recycling bin near the trash receptacle and dropped the empty water bottle into it. "I don't think it would hurt to call."

"I think that's a good thing to do," Laura agreed.

Chapter 24

Nikki sat huddled on her mother's sofa. Her expression was lifeless. She hadn't uttered a word since her crying spell ended. She'd been at her mother's house for about half an hour. Eveline held her child in her arms, and endured the storm until Nikki pulled away from her grasp and sat on the end of the couch, where she still sniffled sporadically. Linc had come inside from shoveling snow. He sat in the chair across from his mother and sister, looking distressed.

Though Eveline was aware of the cause of her daughter's misery, she bided her time and decided to wait for her to tell her what was bothering her. "Can I get you a cup of tea? Are you hungry?" she asked Nikki, smoothing her hair. She wanted to just touch her daughter, to remind her that she wasn't alone.

Nikki didn't answer. She just shook her head.

"Come on, Nik," Linc said. "Just talk to us. We're on your side."

"Honey, I know you're hurting," Eveline interjected. "But I want you to know there's nothing you can tell me that I haven't heard before. I'm your mother, and I love you unconditionally, just like Christ loves us. Please talk to me, baby, and tell me what's on your mind."

Nikki's hands trembled, and she shook her head helplessly.

The ringing telephone brought Eveline to her feet. "I'll be right back."

Nikki's voice sounded hoarse. "If that's Jeff, I don't want to talk to him." Her lips quivered uncontrollably.

Eveline walked toward the kitchen. "I think you should speak to him. If you don't, you'll never get the situation resolved. But I'll abide by your wishes."

Linc rose from his seat, then he sat on the other side of his sister and patted her hand.

Nikki wiped a tear from her eye. *God, I've failed everyone . . . Mom, Jeff, and myself.* She rocked back and forth in her seat. *What am I going to do?*

Eveline padded silently back into the room and sat on the couch.

"Who was that on the telephone?" Nikki couldn't stop herself from asking.

"That was Pastor. He wanted to know if I wanted him to come over," her mother said.

Nikki covered her face with her hands and rocked faster in her seat. "Why would Pastor ask if you need him to come over here? He doesn't know what happened, does he?" she shrieked, almost out of control. "Please tell me you didn't tell him to come here, Mother? I couldn't bear him to see me like this." She uncovered her face and looked at Eveline with tear-stained eyes.

"I don't know exactly how, but Pastor knows you're going through a conflict. And I did ask him to come over. There's something I need to talk to you about, and it might be better if he were here while I do it."

Nikki looked at her mother with a mystified look on her

face. "What could you possibly tell me that Pastor needs to hear? You aren't going to tell me that I'm adopted or something like that, are you?"

"Of course not." Eveline tried to smile, but her lips stretched into a grimace instead. "I prefer not to discuss it until he gets here. But trust me, what we'll talk about may bring you comfort during your dilemma."

"I'm going home, unless you need me to stay, Mom. Shonell hasn't been feeling well, and I don't want to leave her alone with Lincoln too long," Linc said.

Eveline stood up. "No, you go on home, son. Pastor and I will handle this."

Linc kissed his sister's cheek. "Take heart, Nik. Everything will work out fine. Call me if you need me." Then he hugged his mother and left.

"Mom, Jeff has walked out on me. And I haven't even told you what I've done yet. I'm on probation at work. My life is in shambles." Nikki clenched and unclenched her hands and waved them weakly in the air.

Eveline scooted closer to her daughter. "When I ask you to trust me, baby, I mean just that. I know in my heart," she put her hand over her chest, "that what's going to transpire tonight isn't going to hurt you."

Nikki shrugged helplessly. She stood up weakly and swayed back and forth. "I'm going to the bathroom. I'll be back." She walked out of the room.

Eveline stood and went back into the kitchen, and after peeking toward the living room, dialed Nikki's home number. As she suspected, her call went to voicemail. She whispered into the receiver, "Jeff, I know you're upset, and you have every right to be. But there are some things you haven't been made privy to. I know it's a lot to ask of you, but could you please come to my house? Pastor is on his way over here, and I think it would be beneficial for your marriage if you joined us." She softly laid the telephone back on the cradle, then darted back into the living room.

Though her mother was sitting exactly where she left her, thumbing through her Bible, Nikki asked suspiciously, "You didn't call Jeff, did you?"

Eveline looked away from Nikki and shifted her weight. "I didn't talk to Jeff, but maybe you should call him."

"You're making whatever Pastor is coming here to talk about sound very mysterious. Now I'm even more worried." She shot her mother a look of desperation.

Eveline took Nikki's hands in her own. "You don't have to be, darling. I would never hurt you. I love you, Linc, Shonell, my grandbaby, and Jeff dearly. All of you are high on my love list, after our Lord and Savior. I would never willingly do anything to hurt any of you. And I promise you that you're not adopted. Now, why don't I fix you a cup of tea while we're waiting on Pastor?"

Nikki nodded. After Eveline went to the kitchen, she checked her cell phone to see if Jeff had called her. He hadn't, and her heart felt even heavier. Her face crumbled, and she stood and walked rapidly to the bathroom to get a Kleenex tissue.

She stood in the mirror and dabbed her eyes. Nikki thought her life couldn't get worse after she was put on probation on work, but it did. She still beat up on herself for getting herself into the situation. To make matters worse, despite everything that had happened, Nikki still wanted to go to the casino. The idea that she actually had an addiction flitted through her mind. Nikki sat on the lowered toilet seat and began weeping earnestly.

Eveline returned to the living room. Her hands shook slightly as she set the teacups on the cocktail table. She could hear Nikki's sobs. She rubbed her eyes and went to the bathroom. Eveline knocked on the closed door, then turned the knob and walked inside. Her body sagged at the sight of her daughter sitting on the toilet crying. She walked over to Nikki and hugged her tightly.

Jeff sat in the recliner, staring at the red blinking light of the answering machine as if he were in a trance. He had lost his battle with the bottle. When he saw Eveline's number appear on the caller ID, and an icon informing him that she'd left a message, Jeff turned up the snifter and guzzled another swig of cognac. A part of him wanted to hear the message she'd left and his fingers itched to enter the code and listen to voicemail. Instead, he exhaled a deep, weary breath.

The other part of his psyche just didn't want to be bothered or get caught up in Nikki's drama. Jeff still blamed his wife for all that had happened. Nikki wasn't his child, and he didn't need to clean up her messes. She could leave that to her mother and Reverend Baldwin. Maybe their prayers could drive the gambling demon out of her body. Maybe the church had an exorcism just for gamblers, and Reverend Baldwin could use the rite on Nikki. Jeff laughed out loud at the thought.

He stood abruptly, a little woozy from the alcohol he'd imbibed and strode into the kitchen, throwing the snifter into the sink. It dissolved into tiny glittering pieces. *How appropriate. They say a picture is worth a thousand words. And those tiny slivers of glass describe how my marriage is now . . . broken.*

Jeff groped the sides of the wall as he walked back to the living room. He picked up the telephone and entered the code to retrieve the message from voicemail. He stood with his arms across his chest and with his lips pursed tightly together as he listened to Eveline plead for him to come to her house and try to work things out with Nikki.

Jeff harrumphed. "I ain't going nowhere. Nikki made

her bed, let her lie in it." He staggered to the bedroom and lay down in the bed. His cell phone vibrated on his nightstand next to the bed. "Darn it, can't a man get some rest?" Jeff snatched up the cell phone. His fumbling fingers accidentally activated the call.

"Jeffrey Alvin Singleton, you'd better have answered my call," Maya scolded. "Where's Nikki? I went to see you before I left work, and Ernesto told me you'd left early because your wife was sick. I tried calling Nikki, but she isn't answering. What's going on?"

"Maya," Jeff grumbled, rubbing his head, "can we have this conversation in the morning? I'm really tired."

"No, we can't. Put Nikki on the phone."

"Um, she isn't here."

"What do you mean she isn't there? It's ten o'clock at night."

"I'm speaking English, ain't I? She ain't here. She's at her mom's," he said.

"Boy, you'd better watch yourself. Don't talk to me like that. What is Nikki doing at her mother's house?"

"I suggest you call Mother Baldwin's house and find out for yourself why your friend is there. I don't feel like talking now. We'll discuss this another time," Jeff said, closing his eyes.

"I'm sorry I bothered you," Maya replied sarcastically. Her voice rose. "My best friend is MIA, and you have the nerve to tell me that this isn't a good time for you to talk? Boy, have you lost your mind? Don't make me get my baby up out of bed and come over to your house. You know I have a key. I suggest you start jacking your jaws and tell me what's going on. Don't make me get ghetto on you," Maya spat.

A pang of agony shot through Jeff's head. He opened his eyes, moaned softly, and hissed through teeth clenched tightly together. "Where were you when Nikki was out gambling and lost our house? Tell me where you were then? She's been lying to me about where she's been and spending our money like it was flowing from a fountain."

"What do you mean where was I?" Maya responded. Her mouth drooped with astonishment. "Nikki is your wife, Jeff. Maybe you need to ask yourself where you were. How come you weren't there? Too busy working perhaps?" Maya's chest heaved uncontrollably. "Don't get up on that high horse with me."

"Now just a minute," Jeff began angrily. He sat upright in the bed, but the pounding in his head caused him to fall back on the white fluffy pillows.

"No, I won't wait a minute. You're acting all sanctimonious. Whatever happened to Nikki, you'd better believe you had a hand in it. Did you tell her about your little E-trade account that you maintain in addition to your portfolio with Ron? I'll bet all the money I have in the bank that you didn't. Yeah, I know you're wondering how I know, and it's because men like you can't hold water. One of my co-workers said he heard it through the grapevine how much money you're making on the stock market. I guess you think you're a trader now? Let me guess; it's your hobby.

"I'm sorry my girl was gambling and you may lose your house. But that type of behavior is symptomatic of a deeper problem. Something is obviously bothering Nikki. Did you ever stop to think it might be because of your controlling ways with the money? Did that thought ever cross your mind, Jeffrey?"

Jeff rubbed his head. Maya sounded strangely like his mother, when she was disappointed in something he did as a child. "Look, I didn't put a gun to Nikki's head and cause her to gamble. That was a choice she made on her own without consulting me."

"She's not your employee, Jeff, she's your wife. You dictated what you wanted as far as the marriage was concerned. Do you know how much she wanted a baby now, and not according to your plan? Jeff, you made decisions and just expected your wife to blindly obey you. You never stopped to get her input."

Jeff licked his bone-dry lips. "That's not true, Maya. Nikki and I make decisions together." But a seed of doubt was planted in his mind. Jeff mentally stepped out of the conversation with Maya for a few seconds and asked himself if his actions could have contributed to Nikki's gambling. He shook his head in dismissal of that idea. He reasoned that, no matter how he acted, his actions couldn't have caused Nikki to gamble. Maya was Nikki's best friend and of course, she would be on Nikki's side. Jeff's returned to the conversation.

"Jeff, you may think that you consulted her, but you really didn't. I'm not saying you're a bad husband, and you're right, Nikki's choice to gamble was her own." Maya felt an outpouring of guilt, because she was the one who took Nikki to the boat.

"Well, thank you for throwing me that bone." Jeff sat up on the side of the bed. He peeked at the clock.

"Everybody does wrong sometime. You had your little secret, and Nikki had hers. I'm not judging either of you. Marriage is hard, and no one knows that better than I do. Tony was on drugs, and there were times I didn't know if I was coming or going. He took my dignity, my money, but he couldn't touch the core of me . . . my inner self. I stayed on my knees, and cried like my tear ducts had a permanent leak in them. My hair fell out. The Bible teaches us that marriage is eternal, and to let no one tear asunder what God has joined together. To maintain my sanity, I talked to Pastor on a daily basis until I decided I couldn't take anymore," Maya admitted.

Jeff was aware of Tony's drug dependency, but he had

never ventured to talk about it to Maya. He continued listening to her speak.

"Little Tony is hyperactive, and it may be because of Tony's drug use. There were times I had to drag myself out of bed after trying to find a reason to go on. But one day, Pastor's talking took root inside my heart. I had to remember God is my refuge. I'd looked at my baby's scrunched up face when he was crying, asking me why his daddy doesn't come to see him. I'd try to comfort TJ as best I could. His sobs would remind me that one of the reasons I was put on this earth was to take care of him. My road in life hasn't been easy. I thank God that Tony has been clean for two years, and I'm pulling for him to stay that way."

"Would you ever take him back?" Jeff asked curiously.

"I don't pretend to know the future. I do know that I'll always have love for Tony, because he's the father of my child. As far as us resuming our marriage, only time will tell. But enough about me. If Nikki's at Mrs. Baldwin's house, then don't you think you need to be there too? Trust me; Nikki's probably hurting worse than you. She may not show it because I know how she is. Did you know that she's been having problems on the job?"

Jeff shook his head mournfully, despite the jolts of pain that screamed inside it. "No, I didn't know that. What kind of problems? She just told me that she's stressed out."

"She's having the kind that lands you on probation. I'm sure the gambling was a factor. I didn't know about her habit, but now that I know, it explains so many things."

"Wow, I don't know what to say . . ." Jeff's voice trailed off.

"Say that you'll step up to the plate, and go to Mrs. Baldwin's and help your wife," Maya ordered.

"I can't promise that, Maya. Obviously there are some things I need to work on regarding myself."

"Jeff, there's no *myself* anymore." Maya's voice rose in

frustration. The two of you are one; please try to keep that in mind. I'm going to hang up now and call Mrs. Baldwin to see if there's anything I can do to help Nikki. Thank God today is Friday, and I don't have to work in the morning. I'm going to pray for you and Nikki, my brother. God never fails," Maya said.

"I don't know what to say, except you've given me a lot to think about and I will consider what you've told me."

Ending the call, Jeff sat on the side of the bed with his head resting on his free hand. His stomach started rolling from drinking the cognac without eating. He ran to the bathroom and leaned over the toilet. As the contents erupted into the bowl, he broke out in a cold sweat. Jeff washed his face with a towel when he was done and looked at his reflection in the mirror. *I never could drink without consequences.* He folded the towel and put it back on the rack.

The floor creaked under his weight as he walked back to the bedroom. Jeff felt so conflicted. The threat of poverty was real to him every day. Maybe he was too controlling, and his actions were the catalyst that forced Nikki into gambling. Other than this lapse, their marriage had been strong. Jeff knew Nikki well enough to know that she was probably too ashamed to come to him and confess her addiction.

As he paced the length of the room, Jeff debated going to his mother-in-law's house. For the first time in a while, he wasn't sure what to do. He didn't know the proper protocol for dealing with a spouse who may be the cause of losing everything he held near and dear.

Chapter 25

Nikki had managed to rein in, though just barely, her tenacious emotions. When the women heard a car pull up outside the house, Eveline rushed to the drapes and peeped out. Reverend Dudley walked briskly to Eveline's door, and she opened it, embracing him upon entrance.

"Oh, Pastor, I don't know. I can't believe this is happening again," she whispered, wringing her hands together helplessly.

He slipped off his coat, and Eveline hung it inside the closet. They walked into the living room. Pastor Dudley sat in the chair while Nikki and Eveline sat on the sofa.

Nikki looked fearfully at Reverend Dudley and broke into a fit of tears. She lifted the sodden tissue to her eyes and wiped them. "Pastor, I'm so sorry. I messed up really bad," she said.

Reverend Dudley moved to the couch and pulled his goddaughter into his arms. "There, there, Nichole. You just be grateful that God is listening, and He's in the healing business. Whatever the problem is, He said, *'Take my yoke upon me, and learn of me, for my yoke is easy and my burdens are light.'"*

"I couldn't take anything else upon me at this time, Pastor. My shoulders are permanently bent." She looked wide-eyed, like a young child. "I don't understand why you're here. Why did you call Mom tonight?"

"Actually, I had car problems this afternoon, and when Jeff left Joliet, he saw me on the expressway and gave me a ride to the church."

"I call that divine intervention," Eveline commented. She held her Bible in her hand and lightly stroked it.

"I know what you're going to tell me . . . how wrong I was. I feel so repentant, but on the other hand, I want to go back to the boat and gamble. Does that make any sense to you?" Nikki asked, puzzled.

"It does," Reverend Dudley answered. "Being a minister of the church, and a chaplain of the penal system, I've heard so many tales of despair. And like I tell the women and men in prison that I counsel, even in your darkest hour, the Lord is by your side, just waiting for you to confess that you need Him."

"I have." Nikki's nose crinkled. "I have prayed many times a day, but He hasn't answered my prayer."

"Even though you feel He hasn't, I beg to differ because you've taken the first step. You're here." His hand swept the room. "Your mother and I can help you if you allow us to." Reverend Dudley smiled matter-of-factly. "Your mother and I have something we'd like to share with you. But before we do that, I'd like to read a scripture and pray first."

They stood and formed a small circle. Eveline took Nikki's hand in her own. The women closed their eyes and bowed their heads while the pastor prayed. Then Reverend Dudley opened his Bible and read Psalm, chapter twenty-one, verses one through five.

"I know you're wondering why I'm here." Reverend

Dudley said to Nikki once he closed his Bible. He glanced at Eveline, then continued. "The reason why is because of your father."

"My father?" Nikki said, looking at the pair with a befuddled expression. "What does he have to do with this?"

Eveline cleared her throat. "Your father had the same type of sickness that you do."

"What did you say?" Nikki was so taken back, that the blood rushed to her head. She grabbed the arm of the sofa and held on for dear life.

"I think what your mother is trying to say, is that your father indulged in gambling like you're doing," Reverend Dudley answered gently.

Nikki's eyes roamed first to her minister then Eveline. "Are you trying to say that my gambling is hereditary?"

"No, I think what we're trying to say is that someone else close to you has suffered from the disease. And my dear, believe me, it is a disease," the Reverend interjected quickly.

"Did he ever lose everything? That's what I did. I gambled and have lost so much." She said the words she had hoped never to utter to anyone. She expected to feel relief, but the grief she felt was too new, and her heart pounded as she closed her eyes, waiting for condemnation from her mother and the Reverend.

"Child, your daddy was a great gambler for the most part. Being an educator, he understood the law of averages." Eveline smiled. "But he lost as much as he won."

"But I bet he never lost the house we lived in like I did." Nikki's lower lip trembled.

"You're right; he didn't lose the house, but he did gamble away Linc's college fund. Before that happened, he felt invincible. His ego was enormous, and like you, he failed to take into account how the house always wins in the end. When he told me about Linc's college money being gone, I came very close to leaving him." Eveline's lips snapped shut, and a distant look came into her eyes, like she was reliving the memory.

"Mom, I'm so sorry you had to go through this again with me." Nikki took her mother's hand and kissed her knuckles.

"I know whatever you were doing you couldn't help it, and I think you need prayer and counseling to find out why you felt the need to gamble," Eveline said.

"Well, I know you and Daddy stayed together. So how did you cope with his problem? I don't think Jeff will ever forgive me. He really has a phobia about being poor, and I literally put us in the poor house." Nikki moaned.

"Your mother coped by letting go and surrendering her burdens to the Lord." Reverend Dudley stroked his gray beard. "Sometimes we experience situations that we can't control, and we just have to let go, and let God handle it."

"That's true. When your father and I talked to Pastor about your dad's gambling problem, he read us that same scripture. I had to believe God was my rock and fortress, otherwise I never would have weathered the storm," Eveline said.

"I don't know that I can easily overcome this." Nikki rocked as she spoke. "Despite everything that has happened, I still want to go to the casino and win back my money. I tried to slow down and play Lotto or something, but it's nothing like rolling those dice or pulling the handle of the slot machine."

Eveline and the pastor looked at each other and shook their heads. Then Eveline said, "That's the same thing your daddy said. He just knew he was *due to win*. When the suburbs opened those darn Off Track Betting places, I just knew he was gonna backslide, but he didn't. I think losing Linc's college fund was a wake-up call for him. He never gambled again; at least to my knowledge."

"I guess I got it bad then. But Linc still went to college, and you paid for me to go. How did that happen?" Nikki asked.

"Your father stopped gambling. He took up an interest in the stock market instead. He thought computer related stock was the way of the future, and he invested in a company called . . . I can't think of the name of it now, give me a minute." Eveline snapped her fingers.

"It was Cisco," Reverend Dudley supplied. "It was the one time I should've listened to my buddy. He made a bundle."

"We ended up taking out student loans for Linc to enroll in college. Then when he graduated, and the loans were due, your father paid them off with his investment from Cisco. That's how we were able to buy the buildings, and I was able to retire."

"Wow," Nikki exclaimed. "Even I know about Cisco. Neither you nor Daddy said a word about his windfall. Does Linc know what happened, and did Daddy keep any of the stock?"

"Linc knows what happened. And no, your father sold all his shares and set up trust funds for the grandchildren," Eveline murmured. "But let's not lose sight of what's going on here, Nikki. I don't want you to feel like what you did was okay. It's obvious you have a severe problem. We need to see what can be done about the house and getting you help."

"Maybe you should allow time for Jeff and Nikki to work it out, and see what they can come up with," Reverend Dudley suggested wisely. "After all, it's Nikki's and your son-in-law's house now, Evie. Give them a chance to see what they can do."

"If Jeff was that concerned, then he'd be here tonight with his wife," Eveline complained. Her eyes flashed repugnance. "I expected better from that young man."

"Mom, it's not his fault. He just can't stomach the thought of being poor. Jeff doesn't talk much about it, but I know his childhood was hideous from a financial standpoint. That's why I feel so awful," Nikki said.

"This family has been nothing but good to him, and at the first sign of trouble, he turns tail and runs. I thought he was made of more sturdy stuff," Eveline couldn't resist saying.

"Evie, I think you're being a bit harsh on the young man." Reverend Dudley shook his head and pointed his finger at her. "Do you remember how harshly you reacted when Lincoln confessed he'd lost Linc's college fund? Reacting negatively didn't accomplish a thing. Only after prayer and Lincoln assuring you that he would make things right, were you able to overcome your dilemma. And in time, Lincoln did make things right," Reverend Dudley reminded Eveline.

"I guess you're right. But I'm still disappointed by Jeff's behavior," Eveline conceded.

"All this time I thought my daddy was perfect," Nikki said, shaking her head in amazement.

Eveline opened her mouth to speak and closed it immediately.

"I know what you're going to say, Mom," Nikki interjected. "No one is perfect except for God, and maybe Reverend Dudley." She glanced shyly at him.

"Oh no; not me." Reverend Dudley placed his hand over his chest. "I'm just a man steeped in the Bible and God's teaching. I've also learned a great deal about human nature from counseling, so I'm doing what I can to help mankind. Lincoln was my best friend, and I prayed for him with all my might. I'm happy to say he eventually overcame his addiction. But it didn't happen overnight."

The doorbell chimed. Eveline looked at the gold numbered LED clock on the cable box. "I wonder who that could be this time of the night." She walked to the foyer and said a prayer of thanks when she opened the door and saw Jeff's face.

When he walked into the room, Nikki stared at her husband and swallowed back tears. Her breath became tangled inside her throat when she saw his face. He didn't look happy, but at least he had come.

"Can I take your jacket?" Eveline asked.

"No, that's okay, Mother Baldwin. I'll keep it with me." Jeff sat down in the chair diagonal from Reverend Dudley. He took off his jacket and laid it on the back of the sofa. Then he sat down a foot away from Nikki, not speaking to anyone else in the room.

"I think I'd like a cup of tea, Evie," Reverend Dudley said, nodding toward the kitchen.

"Sure, I'll fix all of us some," Eveline replied. She and the Reverend left the room.

Jeff and Nikki stared mutely at each other. Jeff's jaw was set with tension, and Nikki's eyes were full of sorrow.

"I am so sorry, Jeff," Nikki said, leaning forward on the couch. "I don't know what I was thinking when I spent the money. I know you're probably thinking the worst of me. But I'm going to do whatever I can to try and fix things regarding the house and our marriage."

"Nikki, I was so hurt when I found out what happened. I just can't believe you allowed the situation to spiral out of control the way you did. If only you had told me what was going on, I would have helped you."

"I know. But at first, I was winning." Nikki looked embarrassed. "And I thought I had the touch. But I found out in the worst way that I don't. I'm so ashamed of what I did and how I let everyone down. Mom, Pastor and I have been talking, and Mom told me that Daddy had a gambling problem that led to him lose Linc's college fund."

The room grew quiet for a moment and then Nikki said,

"Whatever made you come here tonight, I want you to know that I'm so glad you did."

"It was Maya," Jeff admitted, looking away from his wife's teary gaze. "She let me have it with both barrels. I guess since we're playing confessions, then I need to tell you about something that I've been doing."

"What's that?" Nikki looked mystified.

"I've been investing in the stock market," Jeff confessed.

Nikki's eyes nearly bulged out of her head. She couldn't suppress a chuckle and burst out laughing.

"What's so funny?" Jeff asked.

"According to my mother and Pastor, playing the stock market is what my dad did when he retired from gambling," she said, still laughing.

"Oh," Jeff said, looking down at the floor, failing to see any humor in the situation.

"Are you any good at it? Why didn't you tell me about it?" she asked.

Jeff was silent for a moment. He considered lying, but thought better of that idea. "I didn't want to hurt your feelings or want you to think I didn't have faith in your paying the bills. I've always been fascinated by the stock market and I decided to invest so we could have a nest egg, in case you fell behind in handling the bills. That way, we'd have a cushion to fall back on."

"I guess that was a smart thing to do, except you didn't factor in a huge gambling debt, did you?"

"No, not really," he replied, refusing to meet Nikki's eyes.

"Well, at least you didn't lose big bucks or a house. I can't say the same for myself."

"Well, I've lost and made money. I tend to rely on Ron's recommendations, and I do a little research on my own."

A blanket of silence enveloped the room. Then they both started to speak at the same time.

"You go first," Jeff said. A part of his mind still couldn't cope with how quickly their finances had changed.

"Do you think you can ever forgive me?" Nikki laced her shaking hands in her lap and held her breath, waiting for her husband to reply.

Jeff rubbed his chin. He looked miserable. "Nikki, I . . . I can't answer that question yet. I suppose in time I can, but right now I need more time," he said.

Nikki had never felt more hurt in her life. She wiped a tear from the corner of her eye. "That's fair, I guess. Do you want me to come home with you?"

"I honestly think we need to spend some time apart, to work on our issues. Something is missing in the relationship or we wouldn't be in this predicament. We've kept secrets from each other, and shut each other out. That's not how a marriage is supposed to be. Perhaps we need to talk to Pastor about counseling." Jeff felt like he was throwing a dagger through his wife's heart when her face fell.

Nikki's voice cracked when she spoke. "I wish we could fix what's wrong together, but I have to respect your choice. I messed up big time. I'll stay here with Mom until you decide what you want to do."

"Technically, it's your house. I wouldn't feel right staying there under these circumstances," Jeff said.

"Jeff, it's okay. No matter how much you may have thought of the house as mine, I've always believed it was ours."

"Then why didn't you add my name to the deed, like you said you would?" he asked, standing up to leave.

"I don't know why I didn't . . ." She looked ashamed. She could tell from Jeff's tone of voice that he was hurt by her not adding him to the deed, although he'd never said anything to that effect.

Jeff tried to smile, but a scowl crossed his face. He waved his hand. "Like I said, I think we still have a lot of work to do on our marriage. Let's just give ourselves a little time apart and see what happens. I'll call you in a couple of days. Maybe by then we would have figured this out, and then we'll talk to Pastor. I just need time to get myself together and see what we can do about saving the house."

Though Nikki nodded, she felt like Jeff had delivered a death blow to their marriage. Her mind screamed for him not to leave. *This can't be happening to me.* She tried to stand up to see Jeff to the door, but her legs refused to obey the feeble signal her brain transmitted. Nikki watched sadly with blurred vision as Jeff walked to the foyer. She howled aloud when the door shut behind him.

Chapter 26

Upon hearing the wailing from the living room, Eveline and Reverend Dudley sped from the kitchen.

"Where's Jeff?" Eveline asked as she sat on the couch and gathered Nikki into her arms.

"He said," Nikki screeched, "that we need time alone. And that he'd call me in a couple of days. I lost my husband. Lord, please help me," Nikki murmured. "I didn't mean it."

Reverend Dudley looked at Nikki solemnly and shook his head from side to side. "Maybe he does need some time alone."

Eveline glared at the reverend as if to say, *I told you so.* "I'm going to help Nikki to bed. If you want to leave, Pastor, feel free to go." She looked all of her fifty plus years.

Instead of leaving, Reverend Dudley assisted her in getting Nikki off of the sofa and into the bedroom where she collapsed onto the bed.

"I'm going to the bathroom to get her one of my sedatives," Eveline said.

Reverend Dudley stood stoically next to the bed, as if

he were a sentry on duty. The minister/godfather felt miserable, like he'd fallen short regarding his ministerial and paternal duties. He started to speak, but changed his mind. The preacher sensed whatever he said to her at that moment probably wouldn't bring his goddaughter much comfort.

Eveline returned with a plastic cup of water and a pill. Nikki ingested both, then turned her back to her mother and Reverend Dudley and pulled the cover over her head.

"I guess I'll be on my way," the pastor remarked.

"That's fine. I'll take it from here." Eveline walked out of the room with the minister.

"I'm sorry I wasn't able to help more, Evie. I feel like I let you and Nikki down," Reverend Dudley said as they walked down the hall.

She shook her head. "Please don't feel that way, Pastor. You did the best you could. Now Jeff, on the other hand, I could shake him until he comes to his senses."

They walked to the foyer. Eveline took Reverend Dudley's coat out of the closet and handed it to him.

"Give him time. I haven't given up on him. He'll come around," he said.

"I hope you're right," Eveline conceded. "I know the situation is difficult for him. He must feel like I did when Lincoln lost the college fund. But we still had a roof over our heads."

"Also, you didn't grow up in poverty. That makes a difference. You know I'm going to be praying for your family. You've weathered the storm, now we just have to deal with the aftermath." He squeezed Eveline's arm. "If you need me or Laura to do anything, just call."

Eveline watched him from the window, until he started his car and pulled away. She turned off the outdoor light and walked back to the living room. Sitting on the couch, she rested her head across the back of it and closed her eyes. *Lord, I beg you to take care of my child. I don't understand why this is happening to my family again. Maybe you put this burden on me because I've gone through it before. Give me strength to face the task that lies ahead. Amen.*

Gathering herself, Eveline turned off all the lights in the house and went into her bedroom. She changed into a pair of pajamas, then went to the bathroom, washed her face, and brushed her teeth. When she finished her nightly ritual, Eveline went into her closet and removed a gown from her dresser drawer for Nikki to wear. She then walked down the hallway to her daughter's old bedroom, laid the gown on the chair next to the bed, and walked around the bed to check on Nikki. She was asleep.

Eveline removed Nikki's clothing from her body and hung them in the closet. Then she got into the bed and lay on her back. Nikki stirred, and then opened her eyes wide, sat up, and turned to face her mother. Nikki laid her head on her mother's breast and cried.

Eveline gently stroked Nikki's hair until her daughter's tears subsided. Eveline whispered, "I know it hurts, baby. But you've got to be strong. Try to get all the hurt and pain out of your system . . . let it all out."

"I don't understand why you don't hate me. The same thing has happened to you twice. First your husband, and now your daughter," Nikki moaned. Her head was congested from crying, and her voice sounded croaky.

"Now don't you go worrying about me because I'll be fine. I'm your mother, and I'll always be there for you. Why don't you go to sleep, and we'll work on your life tomorrow," Eveline said.

Nikki yawned and turned over in the fresh smelling sheets. "I love you, Mommy," she said dolefully.

Eveline began humming the tune to "Jesus Loves Me" until Nikki fell asleep.

* * *

Jeff arrived home and tossed his keys on the table in the foyer. He stubbed his toe as he walked into the living room. He knew Eveline and Reverend Dudley were probably disappointed with his decision not to bring Nikki home with him.

When Jeff flopped down on the couch, his nose twitched. He was almost certain that Nikki's perfume wafted in the air. He could almost hear his wife's voice admonishing him to hang up his coat. So he took it off the couch and hung it in the closet.

Jeff exhaled loudly. He had experienced a tough day both from a mental and physical standpoint. He felt beat. Walking into the kitchen, he scavenged the refrigerator for something to eat, finding a two-day old carton of Chinese noodles. He put the container in the microwave and, while the food warmed, he walked back to the refrigerator and took a bottle of water from it. He drank it down like he was liquid deprived. Before he closed the door, he removed another bottle.

When the timer on the microwave beeped, Jeff opened the door and pulled out the carton. The noodles were hardened because he had overheated them. He poked them with a fork, and then tossed the carton in the trashcan.

Jeff decided to forego a meal and just eat in the morning. Greasy food tended to give him indigestion anyway. He turned and grabbed the bottle of water from the table, turned off the light, and went into the bedroom where he shucked off his clothing, put on his robe, and hung his pants and shirt in the closet. After he closed the door, he noticed one of Nikki's shoes peeping from under the bed. He glanced at the side of the bed his wife slept on and swallowed hard.

Jeff walked into the bathroom and turned the faucets

on inside the shower stall. He stepped into the shower and dipped his head, letting the invigorating water pour over his body. After he got out and towel dried himself, Jeff looked in the mirror. Hurt lines prickled his face, and a shadow of a beard covered the lower part of his visage.

He opened the medicine chest and removed his razor and shaving cream. Jeff decided to stay busy. If he didn't, thoughts of Nikki would overtake his mind, and he wasn't ready for that just yet. When Jeff returned to the bedroom, he lay on top of the bed with his hands clasped behind his head. Thoughts of his wife intruded his thoughts. He fidgeted and turned over on his side. Then he sat up and opened his nightstand drawer.

An envelope with his name written on it in Nikki's loping handwriting lay on top of a batch of papers. Jeff picked it up. He was haunted by her favorite vanilla oil scent.

He held the envelope in his hand and stared at it, curious as to what Nikki had written, but at the same time, wary of what may be on the inside.

Jeff set the letter to the side. He tried to go to sleep, but thoughts of what was written inside the envelope toyed with his head and kept him awake most of the night as he tossed and turned.

Chapter 27

When Nikki awakened the next morning, the aroma of turkey bacon, eggs, and homemade biscuits teased her stomach muscles, causing them to rumble like a Mack truck. She rubbed her eyes and sat upright in the bed with memories of the previous day overflowing from her memory bank. She wished ruefully that yesterday had been a bad dream. Nikki wasn't quite ready to face reality.

She could hear her mother's footsteps shuffling down the hallway. Eveline peeped inside the door. "I was hoping you were up. I've fixed breakfast for us. Wash your face and come on in the kitchen."

"I don't feel like it," Nikki pouted. She lay back in the bed and covered her head.

"Nichole Michelle Baldwin-Singleton, front and center . . . now. I've prepared all your favorite dishes. The least you can do is indulge me and eat it. Otherwise, it'll go to waste, and you know how much I hate to waste food," Eveline commanded.

"Okay, already." Nikki sat up. Forgotten memories of her parents urging her and Linc to clean their plates at mealtime came to her mind. Eveline always reminded them there were starving Third World children who would love to be in their shoes. "You didn't have to go to any trouble. I'm not hungry anyway. A cup of coffee would've been fine." Her stomach rumbled loudly as if to verbally object.

"Tell that to somebody else. I don't believe you." She looked pointedly at her daughter. " 'Cause your body is saying something else. I can hear it rumbling from here."

Nikki ran her fingers through her hair. "Well, maybe I am a little hungry," she confessed.

"I'll see you in the kitchen in a minute. Coffee should be ready by then." Eveline closed the door behind her.

Nikki couldn't figure out why Eveline always woke her up so early when she knew Nikki wasn't an early bird like she was. Nikki stole a glimpse at the clock on her white enameled nightstand. A smiling picture of her and Jeff sat inside a gold five-by-seven wooden frame. She sat up and quickly turned the picture face down. Then she went into the bathroom.

Twenty minutes later, Nikki walked into the kitchen wearing an old pair of jeans and a denim shirt with fluffy house shoes on her feet.

Eveline was bent over the stove removing a pan of golden brown biscuits from the oven. She laid them on top of the stove. "I thought I'd wait until you came out before I finished preparing breakfast," she said. Grits bubbled under a low jet. A bowl of raw eggs sat on the counter. She put butter inside a skillet and skillfully scrambled the eggs.

Nikki walked over to the counter and took a biscuit out of the pan. Then she sat down at the kitchen table and slathered butter on it. "Mmmm, this is good." The butter seeped between her fingers.

Eveline spooned eggs, grits, and then she put three strips of bacon on the plate and handed it to her daughter.

The aroma of fresh brewed coffee filled the roomy kitchen.

Nikki took a napkin from the holder and wiped her hands. She stood and poured cups of coffee for Eveline and herself.

Eveline prepared her plate and sat at the table. She closed her eyes. "Heavenly Father, thank you for the food provided for the nourishment of our bodies. Lord, I just want to thank you for waking us up this morning. Father, keep your light on us, and your arms around us this morning as we go through the day's journey. Amen."

"Amen," Nikki added.

Mother and daughter picked up their forks and began to eat. Eveline picked up a remote from the table and turned on the CD player. Yolanda Adams serenaded them during the meal.

Twenty minutes later, they had finished breakfast, except for their coffee. Nikki took the dishes from the table and loaded them in the dishwasher. She wiped the table clean and sat back in her seat. She tucked her chin on top of her open palm and moodily stirred her cooling coffee.

Nikki looked up at her mother and said, "I'm waiting for you to beat me down. I deserve it. There're no ifs, ands, or buts about it."

"I think you're beating up yourself enough." Eveline took a sip of coffee. "But now it's time to tuck the hurt into a corner of your heart, leave it there for the moment, and deal with it another time."

"I can't believe you're saying that." Nikki's mouth dropped agape. "You don't think I need to keep what I did in the forefront of my mind as a warning not to do it again?" She nibbled her lower lip. "You have no idea how badly I want to go to the boat right now."

"I understand what you're saying, but more urgent matters demand your attention right now. Do you want to keep the apartment building? Is keeping it a priority to you?"

Nikki looked down at the table. "Yes, it is. I'd feel more of a failure if I didn't at least try to save it. But I . . . we don't have all the money. Can you loan it to us?" She held her breath, willing her mother to come to her rescue.

Eveline sighed. "I have enough money for me to live on, in addition to your father's pension, which I save. Because I took an early retirement, I don't get my pension until I become sixty-five. I have some money in savings, but it's just enough to cover an emergency. How much do you owe the casino? Have you made an effort to raise the money on your own?"

"Yes, I did; kind of." Nikki looked away, ashamed. "I took money out of my 401K plan at work, and some other accounts Jeff and I share, but I . . ." She suddenly clammed up.

"You what?" Eveline paused, as she set her cup of coffee on the table.

"I spent some of it."

"What did you spend it on?" Eveline asked Nikki ominously, as she stared at her.

"I was too ashamed to tell you the truth last night. Before I came to your house, I did a little gambling." Nikki held up two fingers barely spread apart from each other. "I planned to pay off most of the debt, but I was so upset with Jeff walking out on me, that I decided to hit the tables to take my mind off what had happened."

Eveline unclenched her jaws, and her expression softened a tad. "It sounds like you're using gambling as a crutch to avoid your problems, so you won't have to deal with them," she mused. "Your daddy definitely had a fierce addiction. He thought he could win all the time by calculating the odds. I don't know what made him think he could beat the house."

"I guess I could be using gambling as a means not to face my problems," Nikki admitted.

"What's missing from your life that you feel you have to gamble?"

"I don't think it's so much about what's missing," Nikki admitted, tracing circles on the top of the table.

"Then what it is?"

"My life is so structured, I can't explain it." Nikki waved her hand imploringly. "I really want a baby now, and Jeff says we can't until after we complete our five-year plan. I'd also like to visit Europe, but that too would interfere with his plan. The spontaneity is gone from my marriage. Sometimes I don't know that it was really there. We have a timeline for everything. And sometimes Jeff drinks too much and that drives me crazy."

"Well, you could've stopped taking your birth control. I think that would've been less of an upheaval in your life and it might be cheaper than what you're spending now. I wasn't aware that Jeff has a tendency to over drink. That's serious. I still think you should have talked to him before the situation spiraled out of control like it has now." Eveline gave Nikki her full attention, hoping a breakthrough with her daughter was about to occur.

"I guess I should have said something sooner, and we might not be in this predicament. But during our premarital counseling sessions, Pastor emphasized how the Bible says the man is the head of the household and how wives should submit to their direction. I gave Jeff a lot of leeway because of his upbringing. But I don't agree with everything he wants to do. It's not like we were in the poor house or anything, although we may be now. He took charge of our lives from day one, and I went along for the ride."

"When did you begin to change or want things to change?"

"I understand the reasons we have to save money, but the whole thing was too much for me after a while. When we'd go over finances on Saturday mornings, my stomach would always be in knots, especially if I had used my credit card to buy an outfit. I felt like I was on the witness stand, trying to explain my actions. Then my book club had a meeting, and the girls were talking about finances, and Lindsay taunted me as usual. She implied I let Jeff walk all over me. I went home and seduced my husband, and asked him to let me take over the finances. He agreed, and I handled the bills fine. I was on top of things. Then Maya took me to the casino, and I felt the pull and couldn't resist," Nikki answered candidly.

"Why didn't you just talk to Jeff about how you felt?" Eveline probed her daughter relentlessly with the intensity of a homicide detective.

"Because he was so proud of our accomplishments. Half of his conversation to his boys was about how well we were doing financially. Then as my gambling debt grew, I didn't have the heart to tell him what was really going on." Nikki looked miserable.

The doorbell sounded. Both women looked toward the living room.

"Maybe that's Jeff," Nikki said hopefully.

"I'll get it," Eveline announced. "I still have a few choice words for him." She rose from her seat and walked toward the front door.

Nikki sat motionlessly in her seat, massaging her temples. When she heard Eveline cry out, she toppled over the chair and ran into the other room. She found Eveline sitting on the couch with her head in her hands, sobbing wildly. Two policemen flanked the sides of the furniture, looking helpless.

"What's wrong? Why are you here?" Nikki asked, dreading the words that may come from their mouths.

"Who are you?" the shorter, light skinned policeman asked.

"I'm Nikki Singleton. She's my mother," Nikki answered as she sat on the couch next to Eveline.

"Ma'am, I'm sorry to inform you, but as we just told your mother, there's been an accident," the Hispanic officer sporting a thick moustache replied.

"What kind of accident?" Nikki heart pulsated rapidly like someone was running a marathon inside her chest.

"I'm so sorry, ladies. My name is Officer Johnson," the African-American policeman said. "This is my partner, Officer Perez. We're sorry to say, Mrs. Baldwin, that your son and daughter-in-law were in an accident."

Eveline's voice sounded tiny as she asked, "What kind of accident? Are they okay?" She looked up at the policemen hopefully, but she knew if they were at her home, the news couldn't be good.

"There was a gas leak at their home and the house exploded." Officer Johnson's eyes dropped to the floor. He shook his head. "I'm sorry, Mrs. Baldwin. They're both gone."

Eveline reeled back in her seat and moaned, "No, there must be a mistake. My son was here just last night. I talked to him myself." Her hair flipped as she shook her head violently from side to side.

"Are you sure they're my brother and sister-in-law? Was there a child with them?" Nikki asked woodenly. "My brother and wife had a child, and they would never leave him alone."

"There was a little boy in a bedroom in the second story of the house, but he's okay, he just suffered bruises and cuts. The explosion was contained to the main floor of the house in the kitchen. That's where the deceased were found. That's why we came here . . . the child is traumatized. We'd like to take the both of you to the hospital to identify the couple, and take custody of the child." Office Perez informed the women in a concise tone of voice.

"No!" Eveline shouted. "Linc and Shonell couldn't be at the hospital. I'm going to call him now. You'll see, he'll answer the phone." She snatched the cordless phone from the base. With shaking fingers, she punched in Linc's home number. After several rings, the call was routed to voicemail. She threw the phone across the room, and it bounced off the wingback chair. Eveline seemed to crumble with grief. She grabbed her midsection and cried aloud.

Nikki was in shock. She tried to stand, but her legs wouldn't support her body. "I need to call my brother's cell phone. I know he'll answer," she said.

Officer Johnson walked over to the chair and picked the telephone up off the floor. Then he walked back to the couch and handed it to Nikki.It took her three tries before she was finally able to dial her brother's number. She dropped the phone in her lap when she heard Linc's outgoing voicemail message.

"Oh, God." Nikki moaned and grabbed her mother. The women held on to each other and sobbed.

"If you don't feel up to going to the hospital, perhaps there's someone else you can call?" Office Johnson suggested. "Although I think the little guy needs you."

"Give us a minute. What you just told us is a shock," Eveline sobbed. She and Nikki continued to hold each other tightly.

Fifteen minutes later, with as much dignity as they could muster under the circumstances, Nikki and Eveline stood and walked to their bedrooms to get their purses. After donning their coats, they somberly followed the policemen to the squad car parked in front of the house.

Chapter 28

Thirty minutes later, Officer Perez pulled up in front of the emergency entrance of Little Company of Mary Hospital. Officer Johnson exited the car and opened Eveline's door. Officer Perez put the car in park and turned off the vehicle. He hopped out of the car and opened Nikki's door.

The color was drained from the women's faces. Eveline's mouth was turned down and her eyes were red. She could barely get out of the car. Nikki wearily climbed out of the backseat. She shivered when she looked at the flashing emergency sign over the entrance to the hospital.

The officers walked the women inside the hospital and led them to the emergency room waiting area. "Are you sure I can't call someone to be with you?" Officer Johnson asked. "I know this is a very trying time. Both Officer Perez and I would like to offer our sympathy to you and your family."

"Thank you," Nikki replied, sitting in a chair and dropping her wet face. "Would you please call our pastor and my husband?" She swallowed back tears. It took Nikki a few minutes to rattle off the numbers.

Officer Johnson wrote the phone numbers on a pad of paper. "I'll go make the calls." He walked over to the nurse's station.

Eveline looked broken, sitting beside Nikki with her arms wrapped around her upper body. "Where is the child? We'll know if it's Linc and Shonell when I see him."

"Um, ma'am, we still need someone in the family to identify the bodies," Officer Perez said solicitously.

"I can't believe it," Nikki said dazed. "This can't be happening. Not to my big brother."

"Hush," Eveline held her hand out warningly toward her daughter, "we don't know anything yet. Until I see my son with my own eyes, I won't believe my boy is gone." Her voice broke.

Officer Johnson returned and joined the trio. "Your Pastor is on the way," he informed the women. "Your husband," he looked at Nikki, "said he'll be here as soon as he can. Are you ready, Mrs. Baldwin?"

Eveline sagged backward in her seat. "I can't do it," she moaned. "I just can't go in that room."

"Mom, I'll do it." Nikki stood up, her knees shaking violently. "There's no need to put yourself through the viewing, especially if it's not Linc and Shonell."

"Are you sure, Mrs. Singleton?" Officer Johnson asked, cocking his head to the side. "I know this situation is difficult for you and your mother. We can wait for your pastor, if you'd like."

"No," Nikki said, trying her best to muster up courage for what lay ahead. "If the child is my nephew, he must be hurting and scared. We need to get this part over with so we can take care of him."

"Follow me," Officer Johnson instructed.

She looked down at her mother and patted her shoulder. "I'll be right back, Mom. Maybe Pastor will be here by the time I get back."

"This way." Officer Johnson took Nikki's arm and steered her toward the white and green double doors of the emergency room.

Nikki looked down at the floor as the policeman guided her. *Father in heaven, please don't let Linc and Shonell be in there. Mother, the baby, and I couldn't take it.*

Officer Johnson stopped in front of an isolated area, near the rear of the room. The green and white curtains were pulled shut around it. He said to Nikki, "Are you ready? It won't take long."

Nikki's heart screamed otherwise, but she nodded yes.

The policeman pulled the curtains open. He and Nikki walked inside the cubicle. He walked to one of the gurneys, and pulled a sheet away from the top, and then did the same to the other one.

Nikki slumped forward. She held out her hands, took a tiny step, and cried aloud, "Oh, my God . . . it *is* Linc!"

Officer Johnson caught her body before she dropped to the floor. He said softly, "Mrs. Singleton, is this man your brother, Lincoln Baldwin II, and the woman his wife, Shonell Baldwin?"

"Yes," she shrieked, "that's my brother and his wife!" Nikki covered her face with her hands and bawled. "God, why did you take my brother?"

The nursing staff had cleaned up the couple as best as they could, but their bodies still bore aftereffects from the horrific accident that claimed their lives. Officer Johnson took Nikki's arm and led her out of the room to a seat against the wall. He had to bear the brunt of her weight.

"I'm sorry, Mrs. Singleton. I know seeing your brother and sister-in-law like that was hard, but you did good. All we needed was a positive ID from a family member. When you're ready, I'll take you to your nephew."

"Can I see my brother one more time, please?" Nikki begged the policeman.

"Are you sure that you're up to it?" he asked.

"Yes, I need to just touch him. May I?" Nikki tried to stand up, but fell back on the chair.

"I'll talk to the nurse and see if they can leave the bodies . . . I mean leave them here a little longer. In the meantime, I think you need to check on your nephew," he said.

"You're right." Nikki stood up again and sniffled. "I know he's frightened."

They walked out of the emergency room and back to the waiting room. Officer Perez was sitting beside Eveline. Her head was bowed. She looked up as Officer Johnson and Nikki walked back into the waiting room. She had a hopeful look on her face until she saw the expression on her daughter's. She knew from Nikki's swollen eyes and blotchy complexion that her son and daughter-in-law were gone. She whipped her head from side to side, and whispered, "No, not my boy."

Nikki sat down in the chair Officer Perez had vacated and took her mother in her arms. "Mom, Linc and Shonell are in there. I saw them with my own eyes. The Lord took them home," she cried.

Eveline's eyes rolled up to the back of her eye sockets, and she fainted. Nikki patted her mother's cheek. "I'm so sorry."

"Can we get a nurse over here!" Officer Johnson shouted, sprinting to the nurse's station.

Reverend and Mrs. Dudley walked into the waiting room. They quickly strode over to Nikki and Eveline. A dusting of snowflakes covered their black coats like polka dots.

"Nikki, I'm so sorry. Are you sure that it's Linc and Shonell?" Reverend Dudley asked.

Officer Johnson returned with a nurse in tow. She administered smelling salt to Eveline.

Nikki stood, all the while, keeping her eyes on her mother. "Yes, I'm sure. I need to see my nephew. Officer Johnson, will you take me to him?"

"Sure, Mrs. Singleton. Since your pastor is here, we're assuming he will see to you and your mother getting home."

Reverend Dudley nodded.

"Officer Perez and I will be leaving after we fill out some legal forms with the hospital, and we will stop by the Department of Children and Family Services to notify them that you have taken custody of the child. Once again, I'd like to extend our condolences to your family," Officer Johnson said, extending his hand to Nikki.

"Would you like me to go with you?" Laura asked Nikki. She wrung her black leather gloved hands.

"Why don't you stay here with Eveline?" Reverend Dudley suggested. "I'll go with Nikki."

"That's fine," Laura said as she sat in the chair next to Eveline, and took the bereft woman in her arms.

"Where's my nephew?" Nikki asked Officer Johnson.

"He's in the pediatric ward. It's on the eighth floor," the policeman responded.

The trio walked to the elevator. Five minutes later, they stood in front of another nurse's station. The nurse on duty directed them to Room 806.

"We're still investigating what happened this morning," Officer Johnson informed Nikki and Reverend Dudley. "We'll be in touch with our findings over the next few days."

"Thank you," Reverend Dudley said. "Nikki, let's go get your nephew."

The two entered the room. A nurse sat in a rocking chair holding Lincoln. He sat in her lap sucking his thumb.

Nikki tried to compose herself. She wiped her face with

the backs of her hands as she and Reverend Dudley walked across the room.

Lincoln looked up and jumped out of the nurse's lap. "Tee-Tee." His body quivered. Nikki bent down and he leapt into her arms. His arms snaked around her neck, and he buried his head against her chest. His little body seemed to heave from fright. Nikki held him in her arms for what seemed like forever.

"Where are Mommy and Daddy?" Lincoln looked up at Nikki's tear stained face. He touched a wet teardrop on her face. His eyes darted to the door.

Nikki, feeling panicky, looked up at Reverend Dudley. He shook his head, indicating that she shouldn't tell the child just yet.

"They've gone away. But you're going to come home with me and Nana. We'll tell you what happened when we get home," Nikki said.

"But I want Mommy and Daddy. Why can't they come and get me?" His solemn face broke Nikki's heart. She had to will herself not to break down in front of him.

"Let's get your coat and go to Nana's house. We'll get you something to eat and we'll talk," she said.

Lincoln curled up against Nikki's body and said, "Okay." Then he put his thumb back inside his mouth.

"Can we take him with us?" Reverend Dudley asked the nurse. She looked sadly at Nikki and Lincoln. The nurse was clad in dark pants and a white top under a flowered jacket. The ID tag identified her as MRS. DUGAN.

"I believe so. The doctors have checked him out thoroughly more than once. We were just waiting for a relative to appear to claim him, and the boy has identified you as his aunt. We need someone to sign some papers for his release. I swear it was a miracle he wasn't hurt badly," the nurse observed.

"That's true." Reverend Dudley agreed. "God's steady hand was in the midst of all this grief, and He spared the child. Nikki why don't you go with Mrs. Dugan and sign the papers? I'll get Lincoln bundled in his coat, and then we'll be ready to leave when you return."

"Sure." Nikki stood up and handed Lincoln to the minister. The little boy held on to his aunt for dear life. Reverend Dudley forcibly took him from Nikki and nodded his head toward the door. "We'll be fine. Go take care of your business."

Nikki and the nurse walked out of the room to the nurse's station where Nikki signed papers transferring Lincoln into her custody.

"Mrs. Singleton, how old is Lincoln?" the nurse asked.

"He's six years old. Why do you ask?"

"He's small for his age. We thought he might be younger. His behavior seemed to be that of a younger child. The doctor says he was traumatized by the accident, and Lincoln has reverted back to a happier time as a defense mechanism to cope with his grief. The doctor says his actions are normal and suggests you get counseling for him if his behavior doesn't improve in the near future."

"Thank you for telling me. I thought he seemed a little clingy, and I assumed it was due to the accident." Nikki's voice choked up.

Mrs. Dugan gave Nikki an envelope. "Inside the envelope is a list physical and mental signs to monitor as far as your nephew is concerned. If you have any questions, feel free to call myself or Dr. Grant. Our numbers are in the envelope."

Nikki walked back to Lincoln's room, and found him waiting at the entrance of the door. She picked him up and hugged him.

"Are we going to go get Mommy and Daddy?" The little boy looked expectantly at his aunt.

"No. Nana is downstairs. We're going to get her, and then we're going to her house," Nikki informed her nephew.

"Why can't we go to my house, TeeTee?" The little boy asked insistently.

"We will, but not just yet." She pulled Lincoln closer and kissed the top of his head. He looked so much like her brother that Nikki's breath tangled up in her throat. He had his mother's nose and complexion, but the rest of his facial features were his father's.

Reverend Dudley suggested they leave, and they walked to the elevator and rode it back down to the ground floor. When they departed the elevator, they walked over to where Eveline and Laura had been sitting, but the seats were vacant.

Nikki sat down and pulled Lincoln on her lap. The boy tightened his grip around her neck. "She must have gone in there." Nikki craned her neck toward the emergency room.

"I'll go see." Reverend Dudley left her and walked through the double doors.

Nikki sat patiently and held her nephew tightly in her arms. She rocked him and sang softly.

Lincoln's eyes became heavy and he fell asleep. Even in his unconscious state, the boy whimpered, "Mommy," and a tear trickled out of the side of his left eye.

Jeff and Maya ran into the waiting room at the same time. He came from one direction and Maya from the other. When Nikki looked up, both of them were standing in front of her.

Jeff dropped to his knees in front of his wife. "Baby, I got here as quickly as I could. I called Maya. Nikki, I'm so sorry." He caressed Nikki's arm.

Maya sat in the seat next to Nikki and put her arm around the back of her friend's chair.

Nikki rocked back and forward. Putting her finger to her lips and looking down at Lincoln, she whispered, "We haven't told him what happened yet."

Eveline, Reverend Dudley, and his wife returned from the emergency room. They walked over to where Nikki was sitting, and Jeff relinquished his seat to his mother-in-law. When Eveline saw her grandchild, she wanted to scream and rail against the injustice of his being parentless. Instead, she reached her arms out to Nikki, who relinquished Lincoln to his grandmother.

"He's all we have left," Eveline murmured quietly, holding him close to her.

Nikki stood up. "I want to go back and see them one more time. Then I think we should go, Mom."

Eveline nodded her head up and down. "I had to go see them with my own eyes. God, I can't believe my child is gone." She began crying softly.

"Nikki, do you want Maya and me to go with you?" Jeff asked tenderly.

"Yes," she said shakily.

Maya walked on one side of her friend and Jeff on the other. Nikki's body wobbled a bit as they walked down the hallway. Jeff pulled her body toward him and enclosed his arms around her. He hugged her for a long time, all the while murmuring he loved her.

"We need to go so we can get the baby home." Nikki pulled slightly away from Jeff.

The three of them walked into the cubicle where Officer Johnson had taken her. Nikki walked over to the gurney her brother lay on. She noticed, for the first time, that his head lay at an abnormal angle. She caressed his face and bent down to kiss him.

"I'm going to miss you more than you'll ever know. Linc, I love you so much." Jeff stood behind his wife, ready to catch her if she faltered. Nikki walked over to Shonell. Her face was bruised and reddened. Nikki could see traces of blood on the white sheet underneath her head. She brushed back Shonell's hair, and kissed her forehead.

"Rest in peace, Sister. I'm going to see you again in the sweet by and by," she said.

Nikki sagged and Jeff caught her. "Let's go, baby,"

Maya walked up and hugged Nikki. "Girl, you know I'm sorry. Linc was like a brother to me. I can't believe this has happened."

They walked back to the waiting room and joined Eveline, Reverend and Mrs. Dudley.

"God, it seems like you're here one day, then gone the next," Nikki observed sadly. "I know what happened was God's will, but it doesn't seem fair. Shonell was pregnant. We thought we were awaiting a new member into the family, and instead, God has taken them home. I don't understand it." She looked wide-eyed and confused.

Reverend Dudley said candidly, "Sometimes people that transition from this life so suddenly are the chosen ones. Isaiah, chapter sixty, verse one reads: *Arise, shine; for your light has come, and the glory of the Lord has risen in you*. Lincoln and Shonell are in a better place. That place where the rest of God's children are aspiring to go. I know life isn't fair sometimes, but whatever befalls us is His will. The hurt will pass one day."

Lincoln woke up and began screaming for his parents. Eveline was too distraught to do anything with him.

"I think it's time for us to get this little fellow home. It's been a long morning for all of us." Reverend Dudley said.

Nikki took Lincoln from her mother's arms and vowed, "I'll do whatever I can for my nephew. I owe my brother and Shonell that much."

Everyone put on their coats and prepared to leave. Each one tried to find comfort in Pastor's words, but the hurt was still too raw. The Baldwin family realized dark days lay ahead for them as they would try to come to terms with their double loss.

Chapter 29

An hour later, the group arrived at Eveline's house. The adults tried to comport themselves as best they could for Lincoln's sake. Maya sat in the kitchen, making calls for Eveline and Nikki.

Lincoln sat on Nikki's lap in the living room, looking fearfully at the adults gathered around him. His brown eyes flagged from exhaustion. Eveline couldn't seem to take her eyes off Lincoln. She longed to hold the child in her arms. He was a reminder of all the family lost and the future of the Baldwin family rolled into one.

"But TeeTee," Lincoln protested one more time, "Can't we call them on the phone? Daddy will come and get me." He looked longingly at the telephone on the end table.

Nikki sniffed and took his cheeks inside her hands. "I need to talk to you, Lincoln, and I need you to be a big boy."

"Why?" He crinkled his face.

"I want you to listen to me. Nana and I love you very much, and we're going to take care of you. You're going to stay with us. Your mommy and daddy went to live with our Father in the sky." Nikki's voice crackled.

Lincoln looked at her, confused. "You mean with our God-Father who lives in heaven? Mommy and Daddy told me about Him."

Eveline couldn't suppress a groan from escaping through her lips. She stood and walked to her bedroom. Laura trailed behind her friend.

"Yes." Nikki's voice teetered. She squeezed Lincoln's hand as Jeff sat next to her and patted her shoulder comfortingly. "That's who I mean . . . *that* Father."

"When are they coming back?" he asked in innocence. He sensed the sorrow that infused the room, and uneasily thrust his thumb inside his mouth.

"They went there to be with their Heavenly Father, like you hear about in Sunday School."

Eveline screamed from the bedroom, and Lincoln's body shuddered spasmodically. His mouth dropped open as tears sprung into his eyes. The boy used his knuckle to wipe them away.

In a baby voice, he asked Nikki, "Aren't they coming back to get me and take me with them?"

Nikki's lips trembled, and she cleared her throat, clogged with grief. She looked at Jeff. He nodded his head in encouragement. "Well, they have to stay with our Father. And they didn't want you to be alone, and they didn't want me and Nana to be alone either. So that's why you're here with us. Daddy and Mommy loved you, but when our Father calls us home, we have to go." Nikki tried to explain it in a way the child could understand.

"That's a mean thing to say, TeeTee. I want Mommy and Daddy to stay here with me." His eyes widened like clear marbles. "That means they aren't coming back if I'm staying with you and Nana, doesn't it?"

"Yes, Lincoln. That's what it means. But we love you,

and your daddy and mommy would want you here with us because they knew we would take good care of you."

Lincoln shook his head no. He pummeled Nikki with his tiny fists. "I want Mommy and Daddy!" he screeched.

She took his hands and held them inside her own until the fight went out of him. She held him in her arms until he stopped crying. He lay limply in her arms.

"I'm going to put him in the bed and sit with him until he falls asleep," she informed Jeff and Maya.

"That's a good idea. I'll go with you," Jeff said, taking Lincoln out of Nikki's arms. They walked to her old bedroom.

Jeff laid Lincoln on top of the bedspread, and Nikki got into the bed beside him. Jeff lay on the other side and rubbed Lincoln's back until he fell asleep.

Jeff noticed that Nikki had fallen asleep also. Her arm was tucked securely around Lincoln's back. He rose from the bed and returned to the kitchen where the Dudleys and Maya were sitting at the table.

"Lincoln and Nikki are asleep," Jeff announced as he sat in a chair.

"Good. I know the whole family is devastated," Maya remarked.

Jeff asked, "How is Mother Baldwin holding up?"

"She's not doing so well," Laura answered. "I gave her a pill to help her sleep. My poor friend." Her eyes filled with tears.

"Jeff, are you going to be here awhile?" Maya asked.

"You don't even have to ask me something like that. Of course I'm going to stay here," Jeff scoffed at Maya. "That's my wife in there hurting."

"I want to go to my mother's house and get TJ. I also want to pick up some things at my house, then come back here and spend the night with Nikki and Mrs. Baldwin," Maya said, as she rose from her seat.

"I was going to volunteer to do the same thing," Laura said. "But if you're coming back, then I'll call the Mother Board and see if they can get a meal together for Eveline and Nikki. A dose of prayer wouldn't hurt either."

"That's a good suggestion, dear," Reverend Dudley said. "We'll go home since they're sleeping, make some calls, and then come back later."

"Like I said, that's my wife, mother-in-law, and nephew in there. I'll be here as long as they need me." Jeff looked grim.

Reverend Dudley, his wife, and Maya departed, promising to return within a few hours. Jeff walked them to the foyer and locked the door behind their exit. When he walked to Nikki's bedroom, she and Lincoln were still asleep. Then he peeped in Eveline's bedroom. Her mouth sagged open as she snored softly.

He walked into the kitchen and sat at the kitchen table, feeling ravaged with sorrow. He knew that, but for the grace of God, the bodies in the hospital could be his and Nikki's. Jeff felt crushed by guilt at his treatment of Nikki, deserting her in her time of trouble. He knew that he should have been forgiving of her dilemma.

If Nikki had died, he wouldn't have had a chance to tell her just how much he loved her. Jeff asked the Lord to guide his thoughts and deeds. He felt a heavy dose of shame after he opened Nikki's letter and read how she admitted to and apologized for her gambling problem. Jeff couldn't believe he had missed seeing it before he went to work. He begged God to bring him and Nikki back together and vowed to do anything in his power to right his wrongs.

The telephone rang, and Jeff picked it up. "Hello."

A male voice identified himself. "Hello. This is Donald Layton, Lincoln and Shonell's attorney. I saw what happened on the local news earlier today. My condolences go out to your family. I know losing them is tough," he said.

"Thank you. I'm Jeffrey Singleton, Lincoln's brother-in-law. What can I do for you, Mr. Layton?"

"I have copies of Lincoln's and Shonell's will in my office. Whenever your mother-in-law, wife, and you are up to it, I'd like to schedule a short meeting with the three of you."

"Are you saying all of us are in their wills?"

"Let's just say you all play a role. I'm sure your family is trying to cope with its grief now. If it's convenient, I'd like to meet with the family Monday morning around nine o'clock."

"I'll talk to my wife and mother-in-law and get back with you tomorrow, if you're available."

"That will be fine." Mr. Layton rattled off the numbers and Jeff jotted them down. The lawyer continued. "We'll talk tomorrow morning. If there's anything I can do to help, please don't hesitate to call me. I considered Lincoln a friend of mine as well as a client. I, too, feel his loss keenly. He and Shonell were good people."

Jeff muttered hoarsely, "I'll talk to you in the morning, Mr. Layton." He assumed Nikki and Eveline would awaken shortly, so after ending the call, Jeff located the tea in the pantry and the pot in the lower section of a cabinet. Filling the teapot, he set it atop the stove and turned the burner on low.

Moments later, Eveline walked into the kitchen dragging her feet. Her face was ashen, seemingly burdened with anguish. Jeff turned toward his mother-in-law.

"How are you doing, Mother Baldwin?" he asked, and then hugged her.

"Fair to middling, I'd say."

Jeff pulled out a kitchen chair for her. "Can I get you a cup of tea?"

"Sure, that would be fine. I just woke up, and it dawned on me that we hadn't called Shonell's parents. Her father isn't doing well. I hope the news doesn't cause him to have a setback. But one of us needs to call them."

"I can do that for you. Whatever you need me to do, just ask."

Eveline peered at him. "Are you in it for the long haul, son?" Her voice choked. "Because my daughter needs you, Jeff. And not just when times are good, but when the going gets rough. As we found out today, life is too short to get caught up in squabbles. Life is a gift, and we must live it wisely everyday."

"You're right, Mother Baldwin. I was wrong; I see that now. But you know I love your daughter more than life itself. We would have eventually reconciled."

"I hope so," Eveline nodded. "Now get me a cup from that cabinet over there." She pointed. "We need you, and we need you to be strong. Nikki and I are going to have to lean heavily on you for a while. Is your back strong enough?"

"You bet." Jeff smiled at Eveline.

Nikki, who had been standing around the corner from the kitchen, had been listening to her mother and husband talk. She whispered, "Thank you, Jesus, for sending my husband home to me," then walked into the kitchen and over to her mother.

Eveline reached up and hugged her daughter. "Lord, I still don't want to believe it. Is the baby still sleep?"

"Yes. But I know he's going to be waking up any moment. I feel so bad for him." Nikki moved one of the chairs next to where her mother was sitting.

Jeff prepared two cups of tea and brought them to the table. He sat in the chair across from his wife and mother-in-law. "A Mr. Layton called. He's Linc's lawyer. He said he wants to talk to all of us on Monday, if we're up to it."

"What did he say he wanted?" Eveline asked as she stirred a teaspoon of sugar into the cup.

"He hinted it was about Linc and Shonell's wills," Jeff answered, staring at Nikki.

"I didn't know they had wills. Did you, Mom?" Nikki asked.

"I did. They had them drawn up when the baby was born. They didn't tell me the contents of them, however," Eveline added.

The doorbell rang. "I'll get it," Jeff said as he jumped up from his seat.

Nikki laid her head on Eveline's shoulder. A few minutes later, Maya and TJ Jr. walked into the kitchen. Maya walked over to her friend. "How you doing, girl?" she asked, probing Nikki's face with a concerned look in her eyes.

"Not great. But I know we have to keep it together for Lincoln. He's still sleep." Nikki reached for TJ. He walked into her arms, and she kissed her godson's cheek.

"I talked to Mrs. Dudley. She and the Mother Board," Maya glanced at her watch, "will be here in about half an hour with food. Is there anything you need me to do, Mrs. Baldwin?"

"No, dear." Eveline rose from her seat, and Nikki motioned as if to join her. "No, stay there. I'm going to check on Lincoln. I'll be fine. Maya, would you make sure fresh towels are in the powder room." She looked over at Jeff. "I need you to make that call for me, if you feel up to it," she said.

"Sure, I'll do it now," he replied.

Maya rose also. "I'll make sure the powder room is in order."

"Who does Mom want you to call?" Nikki asked her husband.

"Shonell's parents," he answered.

"Maybe I should do it, since I'm part of the immediate family," Nikki suggested.

Jeff looked hurt. "I can do it for you," he insisted.

"I love you for trying to make my load easier, but I want to do it." Getting up, she opened a drawer and pulled out her mother's telephone book and dialed the number. "Hello, Mrs. Watson. This is Nikki Singleton." She paused. "Yes, that's right; Lincoln's sister."

Jeff watched his wife's eyes brim with tears. Though her voice wavered at times, she bravely broke the news to Shonell's mother. He walked over to Nikki, bent down, and wrapped his arms around her shoulders.

"Yes, Mrs. Watson, I can understand you wanting to come to Chicago as soon as possible. Why don't you call me back at my mother's telephone number when you've made your flight plans? I'll have my husband pick you up at the airport." Nikki glanced at Jeff. He nodded. "It's not a problem, Mrs. Watson. Yes, we told Lincoln, Jr., and he's bewildered. He knows that his parents aren't here. Yes, we're praying for all of us who've suffered this untimely loss, including you and your family. Take care of yourself, Mrs. Watson." Nikki clicked off the phone and sniffled. "Mrs. Watson is going to try to get a flight tomorrow. Mr. Watson is too sick to come with her. She was distraught, of course."

"I know she's hurting as we all are today." Jeff picked up Nikki's hand and held it in his own. "I'm here for the long haul. I'll do whatever I can to make this time easier for you and your mother."

Nikki stood up and threw herself into his arms. "Thank you, Jeff. I love you. I needed to hear that. I don't know how I'm going to make it without Linc in my life. He was my second knight in shining armor, right after my daddy."

"That's what I'm here for, and I promise to take care of you as best as I can. I'm proud of you, Nikki. Even though I know your heart is breaking, you comforted Lincoln and broke the news to Shonell's mother." He kissed her cheek.

The doorbell rang, and at the same time, Lincoln started calling for his aunt from the bedroom.

Jeff squeezed Nikki's hand. "You go ahead and see about him, and I'll get the door. That's probably the church mothers."

Nikki kissed her husband's cheek and then walked down the hallway to comfort her mother and nephew.

Chapter 30

Monday morning, Nikki awakened to find Lincoln nestled between her and Jeff in her old full-sized bed. She gently removed the child's arm from around her waist and edged her body out of the bed. When she walked into the living room, Nikki found TJ curled up asleep on the sleeper sofa. Maya had taken a few days off work to assist the Baldwins. Carole Watson, Shonell's mother, had arrived alone late Friday evening. She was staying with relatives on the south side of the city. Nikki walked over to TJ and tousled his wiry curls. Then she followed the aroma of coffee into the kitchen.

"Oh, you're up," Maya said, turning off the coffeemaker. "I thought I'd make coffee for everyone. Are you hungry? I can fix you something to eat."

"No, I'm good for now." Nikki yawned. "It's already eight o'clock; I guess I should get Jeff and Mom up. The lawyer is coming by to see us this morning."

"I called your job and talked to Fatima and Victor. I told them you wouldn't be at work the rest of the week," Maya said. "And Jeff called your brother and sister-in-law's jobs.

They asked him to call them when the arrangements have been made." Maya took cups and saucers out of the cabinet.

"The coroner is supposed to release the bodies to Taylor Funeral Home today. When that's done, we can work on the arrangements," Nikki said sadly.

"Why don't I design the obituary?" Maya suggested. "That's with your and your mother's input, of course." She poured Nikki a cup of coffee and set the pot back on the stove.

"I don't see why you couldn't." Nikki rubbed her hands on the mug, picked it up, then sipped the coffee. She added, "I'll check with Mom when she gets up. You'll also need to talk to Shonell's mom too."

"Check with me about what?" Eveline asked, walking into the kitchen. A silk black scarf covered her head as if she were in permanent mourning. She sat down on one of the chairs. "Maya dear, would you pour me a cup of coffee, please?"

"I volunteered to work on the obituaries." Maya sprang from her seat and quickly filled two cups of coffee . . . one for Eveline and the other for herself. "Are you hungry? I can whip up an omelet."

"An omelet sounds good," Nikki said. "What about you, Mom?"

Eveline looked away. "I don't want anything to eat. I'm not really hungry."

"Mom, you have to eat to keep up your strength. Would you please eat a little for me?" Nikki pleaded.

"I guess so," Eveline conceded, knowing Nikki would continue to fuss over her if she didn't. "Just give me a little bit, Maya."

"Okay. Two Denver omelets coming right up," Maya said, walking to the refrigerator to get the ingredients.

Jeff walked into the room. The blue jeans he wore had a firm crease, and the top buttons on the white shirt were left undone. "Good morning," he said, walking over to Nikki and Eveline and kissing their cheeks.

"Good morning," they replied lackadaisically.

Maya cracked eight eggs and poured them into a white plastic bowl. "Do you want an omelet?" she asked Jeff.

"Sure, why not," he said, sitting at the table with the others while Maya served as chef.

When they had completed their meals, Lincoln walked into the kitchen, rubbing his eyes. He walked over to his aunt.

"I couldn't find you, TeeTee," he complained. "I was scared." He looked adorable in the blue Power Ranger pajamas that Nikki and Jeff had bought, along with other new clothes to replace the ones destroyed in the accident.

Nikki held out her arms and Lincoln scooted onto her lap. "Are you ready to eat?" she asked.

TJ walked out of the living room, walked over to Maya and stood shyly by her side.

"Why don't you and your mother go get dressed? Attorney Layton will be here shortly," Jeff said to Nikki. "Maya and I will get the boys fed and dressed."

Eveline nodded, then she stood and walked to her bedroom. Jeff strolled around the table to Nikki and removed Lincoln from her lap.

Nikki stood and said, "That's a good idea. Call me if you need anything."

"I think me and Maya can handle the boys while you and Eveline get dressed. Hurry up," he urged her.

Half an hour later, Maya knocked on Nikki's door and walked inside. "I'm going to take the boys to my mother's house while you guys talk to the attorney. It wouldn't hurt to get Lincoln out of the house for a little while," she said.

"That's fine. We should be done in a couple of hours." She stopped brushing her hair. "Do you think Lincoln will be okay getting inside a car?"

"I think so, because TJ will be with him," Maya answered. "If not, I'll keep them occupied in the basement while you all talk to the attorney."

"That sounds like a plan. Thank you, girl, for everything." Nikki tried to smile, but couldn't.

"You know you're my sister. I'd do anything for you, just like I know you would for me," Maya said sincerely.

"You're right about that. I'll be out in a minute to see Lincoln off," Nikki said.

"Okay. I would say take your time, but you only have fifteen minutes before the attorney is due here."

"I'll be ready in a minute." The doorbell sounded. "That must be him now. Maya, would you let him in? I'll be out in five minutes."

By the time Maya walked down the hallway and around the corner, Jeff had already let the attorney inside the house, and the two men were sitting at the dining room table. She was surprised to see that the attorney was African American. He was attractive, slightly portly in build, with a chocolate brown complexion, and a freshly trimmed thin mustache. He wore his hair closely cropped to his head. He stood up when Maya entered the room.

Jeff introduced the two. "Donald, this is Maya Nelson, Nikki's best friend. Maya, this is Donald Layton."

"Pleased to meet you, Mr. Layton," Maya said as she held out her hand.

"The pleasure is all mine. And please call me Donald." He held Maya's hand a few seconds before releasing it.

Maya nervously twisted one of her braids in her fingers. "Well, I've got to go. I'm taking the boys to my mother's house," she informed Jeff, willing herself not to stare at Donald.

"They're with Mother Baldwin in her room. I'll go get them," Jeff said, leaving the room.

"Did you know Linc and Shonell well?" Donald asked

Maya as he sat back down. He opened his briefcase and removed two manila folders and set them on the table.

"I'd known Linc for most of my life. He was like a brother to me," Maya confessed. She stood next to the table.

"He was a good man, a client as well as a friend. I was so sorry to hear about the accident," Donald replied.

"Me too," Maya said, seeing Jeff walk into the room holding each boy by the hand.

Nikki, Eveline, and Lincoln walked into the room behind them

"TeeTee, Uncle Jeff says I'm going for a ride with Miss Maya. Is it okay?" Lincoln looked up at his aunt.

"That's fine, if you feel like going." Nikki looked down at her nephew.

"I think so," Lincoln pronounced, after reflecting on the matter for a short time.

"Why don't you and TJ come with me, and I'll get your jackets." Maya looked at Nikki and Eveline. "I'll have them back in a couple of hours. Mr. Layton, I mean Donald, it was nice meeting you."

"Same here." He followed her progress out of the room.

"This is my wife, Nichole, and my mother-in-law, Eveline Baldwin," Jeff said, introducing them to Donald.

"It's a pleasure to meet you. I'm just sorry it had to be under these circumstances. And please call me Donald," he said, shaking their hands.

"Please call me Nikki," she said, as they sat around the table.

"Where are my manners?" Eveline apologized. "Can I get you anything to eat or drink, Donald? There's a fresh pot of coffee on the stove. It wouldn't be any trouble if you'd like some."

"No, I'm fine, Mrs. Baldwin. If you're ready to get started, then we can begin," he said.

Nikki felt a dreamlike quality invade her body, as if the

events over the past few days couldn't have happened to
her. She shook her head to bring herself back to the present.

The attorney reached inside his designer briefcase and
removed two letters. He handed one to Eveline, and the
other to Nikki.

"Linc gave me these letters after he and Shonell drew
up their wills when their son was born. Shonell also left a
letter for her parents."

"Her mother is in the city staying with relatives. Shonell's father is too ill to travel. If you'd like to leave her letter with us, we can give it to her later today," Nikki offered.

"I should have invited her to join us too. Please excuse
my oversight," Donald apologized. "Do you think it would
be possible for me to see her later today? I can come back."

"I'll call her when we're done here, and see what her
availability is. I'm sure she won't have a problem meeting
with you," Jeff said.

"Normally I'd handle this part after the services have
concluded. But in this case, I felt it was best to do it now,
in case other family members have other ideas." Nikki,
Jeff and Eveline nodded in agreement. "Why don't I go
over the will now?" Donald passed out copies and Nikki,
Jeff, and Eveline scanned the documents.

"Oh my," Nikki said, dropping the paper on the table.
"He wants Jeff and me to have custody of Lincoln."

Eveline bit back tears, wondering why they didn't ap-
pointed her.

Donald noticed the brief flicker of dismay that crossed
Eveline's face. He quickly added, "The letters explain Linc
and Shonell's decision for asking Mr. and Mrs. Singleton
to assume guardianship of the minor child. My firm will be
probating both wills. Linc and Shonell designated Jeff as
the executor of their estates. I talked to the Cook County
Coroner's Office this morning, and the bodies have been

released to the funeral home. So you can go ahead and start making arrangements."

He advised the family of the amount of the life insurance policies and further explained that the couple had bequeathed stipends to their parents. The bulk of their estate was to be held in trust for their son, with a portion set aside for his upkeep.

"I've already contacted the life insurance companies, and as soon as death certificates are issued by the county, they can begin processing the monies owed. You can expect a payment from Metropolitan Life Insurance Company in about a month or so. Linc and Shonell have prepared a quitclaim, bequeathing their property to Mr. and Mrs. Singleton. This is done with the understanding that said property will be turned over to their son when he turns twenty-five years old. I'll start the paperwork on that. If you need money in the meantime for the funeral arrangements, I can approve the expenditure and release the money from the estate."

"I'm sure we'll need it. Thank you, Donald," Jeff said.

"I also wanted to mention, from the preliminary reports the police have made, the oven appeared to be faulty. And because Lincoln and Shonell had policies with accident clauses, we're talking about a substantial amount of money to be paid out. My office is in contact with the oven's manufacturer regarding this matter."

"I actually thought about that." Eveline choked up.

After a few moments of silence, Donald asked, "Does anyone have any questions?" The trio shook their heads and he put the files back inside his briefcase and snapped it shut.

"But I'm sure we will once everything you've said sinks in," Jeff said.

Donald reached into his jacket pocket and pulled out several business cards. "You can reach me from either of these numbers. Once again, I offer my condolences." He stood up.

Nikki stared at the envelope with her and Jeff's names neatly printed on it, while Eveline turned her envelope around in her hand. Jeff walked the attorney to the door and returned to the dining room a few minutes later.

Nikki looked at her mother. "Mom, do you want to read the letters together?"

"No, I'm going to my room. I need to lie down. I'd rather read mine alone, if you two don't mind."

"Sure, we'll be in the living room," Nikki said. Jeff stood while Eveline left the room. Then he sat back down and looked at Nikki as she said, "Wow, I'm stunned. I didn't expect Linc and Shonell to appoint us as guardians for Lincoln."

Jeff disagreed. "Actually, now that I think about it, their doing so makes perfect sense. Lincoln hasn't been around anyone else in the family except us and your mother."

"Maybe," Nikki mused. "I wonder why they named us, and not Mom."

"Perhaps the letter will explain it. Are you up to reading it now?"

"We might as well get it over with," Nikki answered wretchedly.

"Let's go in the living room. I want to hold you in my arms while we read the letter." Jeff stood up, walked over to Nikki, and pulled her chair back from the table. Goosebumps rose on Nikki's arms and her body shivered as she and Jeff walked toward the sofa.

Chapter 31

After Jeff gathered Nikki in his arms, he read aloud the letter Linc and Shonell had written for them.

Dear Sis and Brother-in-Law,

If you're reading this letter, then that means something unforeseen has occurred; like Shoney and I have gone home to be with our Maker. Don't grieve too long and hard for us. Know that we're in a better place. When we drew up our wills, Shoney and I thought long and hard about who we wanted to raise our children in the event something like this occurred. And though Mom may seem like the obvious choice, we'd like the two of you to do the honors. Nikki, you're my sister, and we've always shared a close bond, and I can't think of anyone else more fitting to raise our children.

Mom and Mama Watson are going to wonder why we didn't select them. There's nothing wrong with their doing so, except we think our children need younger people to serve as their parents.

We know that you and Jeff will raise our children in the church like we've been. And Nikki, no one can tell them and instill in them our family values like you'll be able to. I know what a difficult time this must be for all of you. But hold on to God's unchanging hand. And have faith in Him. Lean on Him.

Mom and Shoney's mother have raised their children, and they deserve their rest. What we'd like is for our children to split the summers between both sets of grandparents.

Shoney and I have watched you two grow and mature in your faith and marriage, so we know you're up to the task.

Nikki, I loved you from the day Mom and Dad brought you home from the hospital. Know that I love you unconditionally, little sis. Take care of me and Shoney's children and raise them right. That's all I ask of you.

Take care of Mom. Make sure she plays an active role, along with Ma Watson, in our children's lives.

Me, Dad, and Shoney will be waiting for you guys when you make your transitions to eternal life.

Love both of you,
Lincoln Baldwin II and Shonell Watson Baldwin

Jeff folded the letter through misty eyes and put it back in the envelope. He and Nikki held onto each other and cried for their losses.

Eveline lay across her bed with her hand thrown over her eyes. Tears trickled from the corners of her eyes. "Lord, why did you have to take my husband and son away from me? I don't think I can bear it." She sat up and swung her legs over the edge of the bed and covered her face, sobbing.

Her eyes stole over to the letter that lay unopened on the pillow. Eveline felt a prickle of resentment that Linc and Shonell hadn't selected her to raise Lincoln, especially in light of Jeff and Nikki's marital woes. Eveline knew that had her son and daughter-in-law named her as Lincoln's guardian, their doing so would have given hope for the future and a reason to feel needed. Instead she viewed herself an older woman without a husband and son.

Eveline reached for a tissue from the box on her nightstand. She blew her nose and wiped her eyes. Drawing on wisdom that comes with age, Eveline decided it was time for her to stop feeling sorry for herself. She remembered how she'd raised two children and the myriad challenges of parenthood. Eveline admitted that she was tired, and she had only begun to get her life together after her husband's death. Eveline knew in the long run that she had to respect her son and daughter-in-law's decision. She then asked the Lord for forgiveness for being selfish.

She dropped the soiled tissue in the wastebasket next to her bed and picked up the letter from her son. She held it to her chest, and then kissed Linc's handwriting, which was so much like her husband's. Using her fingernail, Eveline opened the envelope, took out the letter and read.

Hey, Momma.

I haven't called you Momma in a long time. Hmmm, let's see, since I began high school. If you're reading this letter, then that means me and Shoney have gone to our heavenly home. It can't be all bad; we know we'll see Dad and our grandparents there. What a reunion it will be.

I know you're hurting, Mom. But try not to grieve

too long. Our children need you, Ma Watson, and most of all, Nikki and Jeff.

Me and Shoney agree we've been lucky. God gave us great sets of parents. You all nurtured us and taught us to be the best adults possible. We love all of you.

Mom, we figure you and the Watsons are probably wondering why we didn't select you as guardians for our children. It was a tough choice, but since Shoney doesn't have any siblings, and I only have Nikki, she and Jeff seemed like the obvious choice. At this point, we know how much Lincoln really loves his TeeTee, and we know Nikki and Jeff will do a fantastic job raising our children.

Shoney and I have instructed Nikki and Jeff to allow our children to spend half the summer with you and the other half with the Watsons. We realize it takes a village to raise a child, and the five of you will be that village, to love and raise our children to be the best they can be.

So don't mourn for me and Shoney. We've fulfilled the purpose God put us on this earth for. We can't wait to see all of you in the sweet by and by.

Your son,
Lincoln Baldwin II and Shonell Watson-Baldwin

Eveline's vision blurred as she read the letter. When she was done, she folded her hands together, closed her eyes, and prayed. When she was done, Eveline picked up the letter and clutched it in her hand as she fell asleep. Her face became more relaxed than it had been over the past few days.

Jeff held Nikki in his arms as she sobbed uncontrollably. "God, I messed up so bad. Linc had all the confidence in the world in us to raise his child, and we aren't sure we're going to even be together," Nikki cried.

"Hush." Jeff put a finger to his wife's lips. "We're going to be together, and we're going to raise your nephew like he was our own."

"I think you're just saying that because you're caught up in this horrible tragedy. But the fact still remains that we're separated, Jeff. You're living at home alone, and I'm staying here with my mother."

Jeff took Nikki's hand in his. "It's true we're living apart. But we both know we're going to reconcile at some point in time. This isn't the time to bring up our issues. We can do that after we take care of Linc and Shonell."

"I disagree," Nikki stated heatedly. "Before we can proceed or even think about raising Lincoln, we have to sort out our lives and decide what we're going to do about our marriage. Though you've been here by my side like a bodyguard, we still have issues to work out. I talked to Mom a little about them Friday and she suggested we get counseling." Nikki raised her chin. "And I agree. I'm going to talk to Reverend Dudley about counseling us." She peered at her husband and whispered, "I don't know that we're fit to be anyone's parents right now."

"Let's just stay focused on what's at hand, Nikki. If you have issues, then your issues are mine too. I was too hasty, and I realize that now. Maybe we do need counseling, but I know that Linc entrusted us with a big responsibility, and I don't want to let him down."

"Linc didn't know about my gambling," Nikki said solemnly. "Nor how we're on the verge of being homeless."

"I know you didn't think I was going to stand by and let us lose a family heirloom; something we can one day pass down to our own children. I've already asked Ron to liquidate what's left of our investment portfolio, and I'm sure we can borrow the money if we need to."

"My credit is shot," Nikki informed Jeff. "But I really don't want to get into all of this right now. It's not a good time. We need to make sure Linc and Shonell have a proper burial and decide what to do about Lincoln."

"We can work this out, Nikki. Sometimes in the midst of our pain, are solutions to what seems like the worst problems."

Nikki eyes widened in incredulity as she stared at Jeff like he'd lost his mind. She pulled away from him. "I know you aren't suggesting there's anything remotely positive about my brother and sister-in-law's death."

"No, of course not," Jeff said. "But there could be joy for us in rearing Lincoln and molding him into the person Linc and Shonell would have wanted him to be. The future of your family lies with your nephew at this moment, Nikki. Together we can do something good. With God, all things are possible."

"Maybe," Nikki stated dubiously. "Let's just try to stick with the business at hand for now. We can revisit this topic again after we're done seeing to Linc and Shonell."

"Sure, I don't have a problem with that." Jeff dipped his head. "But we're going to have to hash out the issue when you're ready. I love you, Nikki. I was a fool for letting you go. Please forgive me." He kissed the palm of his wife's hand and tucked it inside his own.

"I love you forever and a day, Jeff. But we still need to work on some things. Lately, I hadn't been really happy in the marriage, and I think gambling was a symptom of my unhappiness with some aspects of our marriage. If getting back together is God's will, and I know that it is, then we'll patch our lives back together again," Nikki nodded.

Jeff leaned over and brushed Nikki's lips tentatively. She wound her hands around his neck and responded to his kiss. They sat on the couch quietly together until the doorbell rang.

"I'll get it," Jeff said. He rose from the couch, reluctant to leave Nikki, and opened the door to admit Maya and the children.

TJ and Lincoln carried boxes of Happy Meals from Mc-Donald's.

"Look, TeeTee, Miss Maya bought us lunch." Lincoln set the box on the table and unzipped his jacket. Jeff reached out his hand for the boys' jackets and hung them in the closet.

"Let's go in the kitchen and eat," Jeff suggested to them. "We don't want to get Nana's floor dirty."

"How did he do?" Nikki asked her friend after they were alone.

"He got a little weepy at my mother's house, but it didn't last too long. TJ hugged him. It was so cute to see one child trying to comfort another." Maya smiled.

"I bet it was." Nikki smiled at the image of TJ and Lincoln in her head. Then the smile vanished from her face. "I guess I should let you know that Linc and Shonell left Jeff and me guardianship of Lincoln."

"Well, I'm not surprised," Maya said nodding her head. "You two are the obvious choice."

"Mom became very quiet when the attorney told us. I hope us keeping Lincoln doesn't cause any problems in my family," she said wistfully.

"Give your mother time, she'll come around. What else is happening?"

"The bodies have been released to the funeral home. So we can call Reverend Dudley and set up a time for their homegoing service."

"I think he planned to stop by this afternoon. I can call him if you need to see him sooner," Maya volunteered.

"I'll speak to Mom first and see what she wants to do," Nikki said.

Maya rubbed Nikki's arm. "How are you holding up?"

"Girl, none of this seems real. I keep going into Linc's old room and just sitting on the side of the bed and crying. I miss him so much." Tears escaped both her eyes.

"I know you do, and I miss him too. But Nikki, weeping does endure for a night and joy will come in the morning. Thank God nothing happened to Lincoln. In the midst of pain, God still had your family's back," Maya said.

"I guess you're right, but it doesn't feel like it today."

"That's the operative word . . . *today*. It's going to get better. I promise you that."

"The attorney is coming back this afternoon," Nikki said, drying her face. "He's going to give Mrs. Watson her letter from Shonell."

Maya couldn't keep a hint of a grin off her face. "He seemed like a nice person." She peeked down at her fingernails.

"Yeah, I noticed you checking him out. Though the brother was trying to act professional, he was still up in your grill," Nikki teased her friend.

"You think?" Maya asked, batting her eyes. "It's been a long time since the Lord sent a man my way."

"I have eyes, don't I? And I don't miss a thing." The friends laughed together.

Eveline came out of her bedroom and went into the kitchen. Jeff had turned on the television that sat on the kitchen counter, and the boys were laughing at the antics of the Muppets on *Sesame Street*.

"Look, Nana," Lincoln exclaimed. "Miss Maya bought me and TJ Happy Meals. I got a prize too." He held up a toy figurine.

She walked over to her grandson and kissed the top of his head. "That was nice of Miss Maya. I hope you thanked her."

Lincoln's eyes expanded. "Oops, I forgot, Nana." He covered his mouth with his hand.

"Well, make sure you do. Now give Nana one of your French fries," she said, holding out her hand. Eveline released an exaggerated moan as she ate it. "That was good. Make sure you wash your hands when you're done eating." She stooped down and kissed TJ's cheek, then she walked into the living room where Nikki and Maya sat talking.

"How are you girls doing?" Eveline asked, as she smoothed her lime green caftan over her legs after she sat down in a chair.

"Mom, we haven't been girls in years," Nikki corrected her mother with a hint of a smile on her face.

"You'll always be girls to me," Eveline proclaimed. She ran her hand through her tousled hair.

"Do you want to talk to Nikki alone?" Maya asked. "I can go and sit with the boys if you want privacy, Mrs. Baldwin."

"No, you're my daughter too. It's not like we've had many secrets among us. Nikki would just tell you whatever was said at a later time anyway."

"Mom, I was telling Maya I thought you were upset by Linc and Shonell's decision for us to keep Lincoln," Nikki remarked tautly.

"I wouldn't say I was upset. I just didn't understand why they didn't appoint me. But after I read their letter and did some praying, I understand and respect their decision. Just because you have custody of him, doesn't mean he won't be staying with me some weekends, like he has been," Eveline said.

"Of course, Mom." Relief spread through Nikki's body. "We have to make an effort not to change Lincoln's life any more than it has already been."

"So does this mean that you and Jeff are getting back together? Did she tell you what happened the other day, Maya?" Eveline asked as she slid forward in her seat.

"I've gotten bits and pieces about what happened from both her and Jeff," Maya admitted.

"I know Jeff and I have major problems we need to work out. He wants me to come home, but I may stay here with you a few weeks, to decide what I want to do," Nikki said to her mother.

"What do you mean?" Maya looked at Nikki, puzzled.

"I botched things big time, Maya. I need time to examine everything I've done and what led me to where I am," Nikki said.

"And you can't do that and live with Jeff at the same time?" Maya asked her friend. She obviously disapproved.

"I don't know." Nikki took the scrunchie off her ponytail. She finger combed the sides of her head and put the band back on. "We'll see," she said.

The doorbell rang. "I guess it's the church members or neighbors with more food," Eveline remarked and stood up. "I'll get it."

Chapter 32

For the next week, the doorbell seemed to chime continuously at Eveline's house. Streams of friends and relatives of the Baldwin family poured in and out of the house, bringing cards, flowers, and nourishing food with them. Eveline drolly told Nikki and Maya, after the crowd departed, that she probably wouldn't have to cook for another month.

A week following the gas explosion, Linc and Shonell's homecoming services were held at the family church on Saturday morning at ten o'clock. The good sisters of Friendship Church and the Cregier Street Block Club had laid out a bountiful spread in Eveline's kitchen. No one had ever seen anything like it in the church's twenty-five-year history. The windows were opened inside the house, and the most appetizing aromas emanated throughout the rooms. The house was packed with people. Eveline's strength and resolve failed after Linc and Shonell's burial, and she escaped to her bed. Erma sat on a chair by Eveline's bedside, after giving her sister a light sedative.

Carole Watson wasn't faring much better than Eveline.

She lay in Nikki's old bedroom with her relatives by her side, prostrate with grief.

Nikki and Jeff represented the family presence in the living room. Lincoln seemed glued to Nikki's side, where he remained for the evening when he wasn't with TJ in the den.

Maya stood in the dining room monitoring the food. She wore an apron over her black dress and had kicked off her three-inch-heeled shoes. She blew a strand of hair out of her face and looked up to see Donald Layton shaking Jeff's hand. After he finished talking to Jeff, Donald walked over to Nikki and talked to her and Lincoln for a while.

Then to Maya's surprise, he walked toward her. She nervously ran her tongue over her dry lips and unconsciously pushed her braids off her brow, then fixed a pleasant smile on her face.

"Ms. Nelson, I'm Donald." The man held out his hand to Maya. A silver class ring shone on one of his fingers and he sported a Rolex watch on his wrist. He wore a tan suit with a brown striped shirt. A brown fedora rested on his head, which he tipped, then removed from his head. One of the sisters from the church walked over to Donald and took the hat to another room for safekeeping.

"I remember you," Maya said, wiping her hands on the side of her apron and accepting his handshake. "Please call me Maya. How are you doing, Donald?"

"Not too bad. And you?" he asked, staring into her eyes.

"I've seen better days," she confessed. "I hope the worst is over. Now we all have to adjust to life without two of the nicest people I've ever known."

"I know how you feel," he said.

One of Nikki's young cousins was running through the house and bumped into Donald.

"No running in the house," Maya said automatically.

"I'm sorry," the little boy who was missing his two front teeth said. His tie hung loose around his neck.

"He'll be running again in another minute," Maya observed.

"You're probably right. I don't have any children myself; just a niece and nephew," Donald said.

"You probably remember meeting my son, TJ, last week. His father and I are divorced." Maya wondered if she had given him too much information.

"Children are a blessing. I'd like to have some myself one day."

"They're certainly blessings sometimes and little imps other times," Maya said, trying to make a joke. "Can I get you something to eat?"

"I have a sweet tooth," Donald admitted. "I think I saw a coconut cake in the kitchen. I wouldn't mind a slice of it."

"One piece of cake coming right up." Maya smiled at him. He watched her shapely hips as she walked from the dining room to the kitchen.

Lincoln began whining. Jeff walked over to his wife's side. "You look like you need a break. I know you haven't eaten. Why don't you give him to me for a while?" he said.

"Honey, can you stay with Uncle Jeff for a moment while TeeTee gets something to eat?" Nikki asked Lincoln.

Lincoln's lip trembled. "You're not going to leave me, are you?" He blinked rapidly, and a look of fear filled his eyes.

"Of course not," Nikki reassured him. "I'm going to get us something to eat. Then we'll go in your dad's bedroom to eat."

Lincoln looked back and forth between Nikki and Jeff and reached his hand toward his uncle.

"I'll be right back as soon as I fix our plates," Nikki said.

"'Kay." Lincoln gulped. His eyes stayed on Nikki.

"Let's go in the bedroom," Jeff told him. "TeeTee will bring our plates in there."

With their plates and desserts in hand, Nikki and Maya, along with Donald, walked into Linc's old bedroom. The television was on and Jeff sat between Lincoln and TJ on the edge of the bed as the boys watched cartoons.

Nikki removed a television tray from the closet and set it up at the foot of the bed. Once Jeff blessed the food, Nikki and Lincoln listlessly picked at their meals. After announcing he'd had enough, Lincoln lay on the bed, rubbed his eyes, yawned and eventually fell asleep. Five minutes later, TJ stretched out beside Lincoln and dozed as well.

"I guess it was a long day for the little fellows too," Maya observed.

Nikki pulled the cover over both boys and kissed their foreheads.

"Why don't you two get some air? I'll stay here with Lincoln and TJ," Maya offered.

"That's a good idea," Jeff said, reaching for Nikki's arm. They walked out of the room and peeped in on Eveline, who was still asleep. Then they put on their coats and walked out the back door and stood talking in the backyard.

"Thank God Mom has a large house. Otherwise, we would've had to have the repast at the church," Nikki remarked.

"You held up really well today, babe. I know how difficult this day must have been for you," Jeff said.

"I tried," she said. "Are you going back to work on Monday?"

"I planned to, but I can take off as long as you need me. When are you going back?"

"I think I'm going to resign from my job. It'll be a full

time job taking care of Lincoln. I think he's going to need counseling in order to cope with everything."

"Are you sure you want to outright leave and not take a leave of absence first?" Jeff suggested.

"I have a feeling my job won't miss me as much as you think. There's a rookie waiting in the wings for her fifteen minutes of fame. If I decide to resume working, then I may freelance for a while," she said.

"It sounds like you've given this a lot of thought," Jeff responded. He put his arm around Nikki's shoulders.

"I admit that I have a little. Our lives have changed so drastically since the accident. I don't know if I'm going to be a good guardian for Lincoln; I just hope I will." Nikki took a deep breath and peeked quickly at her husband, "I really wanted a baby now and not when you decided we could."

Jeff's mouth dropped open. "I didn't know you felt like that. You should've said something."

"I just didn't want to disappoint you. We have a lot of talking to do, and I plan to talk to Pastor about counseling. I also need to find a group that I can meet with; people who have a gambling problem like I do," Nikki said.

"You know I can do that with you, don't you?" Jeff said.

"Let's just see what happens. I think it's best I stay with mother for a week or so. She's put on a brave front as long as she could today, but I know she's hurting."

"And so are you, babe. You don't have to go through this alone."

"I hope not, Jeff. I hope we can work through our issues and come to a meeting of the minds. But I need you to give me some space for a little while."

Though Jeff was stung by Nikki's decision, he knew he had no choice but to graciously concede to her request. It was the right thing to do under the circumstances. It was Jeff's idea that the couple separate, and he regretted doing so. He'd been trying to talk Nikki into returning home with him ever since Linc and Shonell passed. Many a day Jeff wished he had bitten off his tongue rather then suggest he and Nikki live apart. There was no doubt in his mind that God would allow his wife to return to him. He just needed to give her time to figure out when that time would be.

"You know I don't want us to be apart, but I will respect and honor your feelings. I'll come over every morning before work," Jeff said.

Nikki snuggled in his arms. "You'd better," she chided him. "I guess we should get back inside."

Jeff tightened his grip. "Our guests can wait another few minutes. It seems like it's been a long time since I've had a chance to hold my wife in my arms. Can we stay out here a few more minutes?"

Nikki relaxed against her husband's side. "Sure we can. Maya can hold down the fort for a few more minutes." Nikki had just snuggled into Jeff's side and laid her head briefly on his shoulder when they heard voices coming from the side of the house.

Chapter 33

Lindsay had come outside with Arial so Arial could smoke. The women were huddled beneath the spare bedroom window. Lindsay rubbed her hands together and shivered in her sable mink coat. Arial puffed on a Virginia Slims cigarette and exhaled plumes of smoke.

"It's a mite chilly out here," Lindsay remarked, punching her friend's arm.

"You're right about that. But it's a beautiful night." Dusk had just fallen over Chicago. "The sky is so clear. Look at the stars and the moon." Arial looked upward. She glanced at Lindsay. "I feel so sorry for Nik. First her dad passed and now her brother and sister-in-law. Thank God all of my family is still alive," she said.

"Yes, it's a sad thing," Lindsay remarked in her island singsong cadence, "but despite that girl's sorrow, she's like a cat. I swear she's got nine lives."

Arial sprinkled ashes from her cigarette and brought it to her lips. She said, "What do you mean Nikki is like a cat? You've lost me, girl. I don't see nothing lucky about half your family being dead."

Jeff and Nikki stood frozen in place at the gate of the fence, eavesdropping on the women's conversation.

"Ari, are you dense or something? I'm talking about the money. Do you know how much that family stands to gain from that accident?" Lindsay took her leather gloves out of her pockets and slipped them on her hands.

"I hadn't really thought about." Arial blew a smoke ring out of her mouth.

"There's insurance money, which will probably double due to the accident. And Linc and Shonell's lawyer is smart. If he can find negligence on the part of the stove manufacturer, then that company will have to pay through the nose." Lindsay nodded her head.

"Call me old fashioned, but I think I'd rather have my family alive instead of money," Arial remarked. "I imagine Nikki feels the same way."

"It doesn't matter how she feels, she's rich. I bet her family stands to gain millions of dollars. Someone will have to take care of the little boy, and he'll inherit pension and social security payments. I swear she comes up smelling like roses, despite everything that happens to her."

As soon as she got the last word out, Lindsay looked up to see Nikki charging from the backyard toward her. Jeff reached out, trying to restrain his wife.

Nikki looked like she was spoiling for a fight. Her face was pale and tears poured down her face. Her body vibrated with anger. "Don't you dare presume to know how I feel, or remark on any part of my life." She pointed a finger in Lindsay's face.

"I didn't mean anything," Lindsay responded, somewhat taken aback by Nikki's aggressive manner.

"How in God's name can you say I'm lucky? I'd give everything I have, all the money in the world, to bring back my father, brother and sister-in-law. I thought you were a friend, Lindsay. We may not always agree on some matters, but I can't believe you have the nerve to talk about me on the day I buried my family," Nikki shrieked with a murderous glint in her eyes.

Lindsay stepped away from Nikki with a bemused expression on her face. She held out her hands. "Whoa, now. I understand you're upset, and rightfully so, but that doesn't give you a right to take it out on me. Back off, Nikki," she said.

Nikki stepped up to Lindsay and stood toe to toe with her friend. "Or what? What you gonna do, Lindsay?"

Jeff reached out and grabbed Nikki's shoulder. "Honey, I don't think this is the right time to get into all of that."

Nikki shrugged away from Jeff's grasp and turned back to Lindsay. "No. Now is the right time. I'm sick of you criticizing me. I don't know what your beef is with me."

Arial looked uneasy. She pulled at her friend's arm. Lindsay glared at her. Arial said, "Perhaps we should go now, Lindsay. Jeff is right, now isn't the right time. Nikki and her family are still grieving their loss."

"I think anytime Miss Thing feels she wants to go a round with me is the right time." She circled around Nikki and sneered contemptuously. "Everything she's ever got in her life has come from someone else. She hasn't done anything on her own," Lindsay spat.

Her words were mean and spiteful, and Nikki felt like she'd been shot in the chest by a bullet. She shook her head dolefully. "Maya always said you were jealous of me, and maybe she was right. How dare you come to my mother's home, pretending to be my friend and tearing me down like this?" Nikki's voice rose hysterically.

"Jealous of what?" Lindsay's lips curled, and her eyebrows peaked upward. "I ain't got no reason to be jealous of you. I'm somebody. And I made it on my own, not from the spoils of someone else's labor."

Maya was exiting the front door with Donald, who was leaving, when they heard the uproar. She streaked to the side of the house with Donald in tow.

"I always thought you were a little off, but I see that you're crazy, Lindsay," Maya said hotly, when she reached the side of the house. "You should leave before I do something I may regret."

Lindsay put her finger on the side of her face and shook her head. "What else is new . . . Maya to the rescue as usual? You're still fighting Nikki's battles like you did when we were children."

"And you're still being a witch like you were when we were children. You need to grow up, Lindsay," Maya spit out.

Nikki pushed Maya aside and glanced at Jeff. "I got this," she said, and turned to Lindsay coldly. "I won't dignify your remarks with an answer. My mother and I buried my brother and my sister-in-law today, and excuse me if I'm a little bit emotional. I don't know what your problem is, Lin. I've tried to be a friend to you since we've been in grammar school. My parents were good providers, and there's nothing wrong with that. Parents want to do well by their children.

"What I have or haven't accomplished is truly none of your business. What goes on in my life behind closed doors is privy only to whom I decide needs to know. You know what, Lindsay?" Nikki barked, "I've had enough of you."

Lindsay looked shocked. She couldn't believe Nikki was standing up to her. She reared back and said, "I've had enough of you too. You always thought you were better than me because your people have money. You and Maya acted so superior sometimes, like I wasn't good enough to be in your company."

"That's not true. We've treated you with nothing but

courtesy, kindness, and love over the years; even when you didn't deserve it. If anyone has treated anyone shabbily, it's been you, and it stops tonight." Nikki held up her hand.

"Fine with me," Lindsay huffed. She turned to Arial and said, "Let's go, I've had enough of this. I won't stay where I'm not wanted."

Arial looked at Lindsay, then at Nikki, who looked miserable. "I'm going to stay here, Lindsay. You were wrong, and I don't want any part of this. Nikki has been a good friend to me, and I came here to show my respects to her and her family. You go ahead," she said forcefully.

Lindsay looked at Arial in disbelief. "So it's like that. Well, fine!" Swearing, she turned and stomped from the side of the house. She slipped on a patch of ice, regained her balance and continued to her car. A few minutes later, they heard Lindsay's car tires screech down the street.

Jeff pulled Nikki's trembling body into his arms. He murmured, "You did good, babe. It's about time you told her to step off."

"I'm sorry," Arial said. Her face was suffused with color. "I didn't expect that."

"What happened isn't your fault, Ari," Nikki replied. "Jeff and I need to get back inside. Lincoln has probably awakened."

Nikki and Arial hugged, and then all three women went inside the house. Donald and Jeff watched them.

"Wow! That was something," Donald said.

"Actually, it was long overdue. Lindsay has picked on Nikki for years, and I guess it came to a head today. I'm just glad Nikki got her off her tail. Lindsay has made my life hell on earth, and I'm very seldom around her," Jeff stated, shaking his head.

"You know they say funerals bring out the worst in people," Donald said. "This is the first time I've seen it up close and personal."

"Me too, man. It's cold out here, let's go back inside." Jeff rubbed his hands together.

"I was on my way home. Maya was walking me to my car. Tell Nikki I'll be in touch with you all next week."

"Okay, thanks for everything. We'll talk to you then," Jeff said, and then he went inside the house.

Jeff thought as he returned to the house, that his wife was on a tear. He was shocked that she'd stood up to Lindsay and turned down his thousandth request for reconciliation. This new Nikki had the ferocity of a lioness. Gone was the pliable woman/girl that Jeff had met in college. He wasn't sure how the new changes in Nikki's personality would affect the future of their marriage. Time would tell sooner than he knew.

Chapter 34

Over the next two weeks, each day after his workday ended, Jeff went home and then to bed. He rose at eight o'clock each morning and traveled to the south side of the city to visit his wife, nephew and mother-in-law. Nikki was pleased by her husband's gesture. Seeing Jeff every morning until noon made her day.

One night after getting off work, instead of waiting to see his wife in the morning, Jeff drove to his mother-in-law's house. Nikki was curled up on the couch, lying under an afghan watching a rerun of *CSI Miami*. She was sipping a mug of hot cocoa when the doorbell rang.

Nikki hopped off the couch, rushed to the window and peeped out the curtains. She finger combed her hair before she answered the door and couldn't stop a smile from filling her face when she saw Jeff standing on the steps, brushing snow off his jacket.

She opened the door wider and Jeff walked inside. "Hey, you. How are you doing?" He brushed her cheek with a kiss. She watched as he hung his coat in the closet.

"I'm okay, and you?" Nikki said, returning to the couch. He closed the closet door, walked into the room, and sat in a chair. "I don't bite, you can sit here if you'd like." She patted the top of the gold and brown brocade sofa.

Jeff stood up and walked over to the sofa where Nikki reclined. She sat up and Jeff planted his body next to hers.

"I'm fine; just missing you," he replied, leaning against the back of the couch.

"I miss you too, hon." She leaned over and smoothed down the collar of his shirt. "But Mom and Lincoln need me right now, and strangely, I need them too. It's been good staying here with them. It helps keep my mind off other things." Nikki's voice trailed off uncomfortably.

"That's good. So do you still have urges to throw away money?" Jeff asked semi-jokingly.

Nikki nodded and looked away from his face. "Without a doubt. I wish I could say I've learned my lesson, but I wouldn't be telling the entire truth. What I can say is that for the last two weeks, I haven't thought about gambling."

"Have you decided what you're going to do about work yet?" he asked. His eyes darted from the television to his wife.

"Yes, I have. I'm going to my job next week to talk to Victor about my future. I thought about taking a leave of absence from work, at least until Lincoln adjusts better to losing his parents. But I am really leaning toward resigning."

"Your decision is the right one, given the circumstances." Jeff nodded his approval. He squeezed Nikki's hand. "How is the little fella sleeping at night? Any better?"

"Not really. He often wakes up crying, asking for Linc and Shonell," Nikki admitted. "I still let him sleep with me."

"You know we should probably talk to a counselor, to get some professional advice. Doing so wouldn't hurt," he said.

"I already talked to Reverend Dudley and made an appointment for us for next week. In the meantime, I plan to get things settled with my job," Nikki proclaimed.

"I was going to ask if you'd like to go out for a cup of coffee or something tonight." Jeff ran his hand over the top of his head. "I thought maybe you'd want to get out for a little while."

Nikki glanced at her wristwatch, it was eleven-thirty. "It's a little too late for that, don't you think? And what if Lincoln wakes up and I'm not there?"

"I know your mom would be more than happy to take care of her grandson."

"I appreciate your coming all the way out here, Jeff. But I wouldn't feel right leaving Lincoln just yet. Mom fixed a tasty pot of gumbo for dinner. Can I fix you a bowl? It wouldn't be any trouble." Nikki wasn't quite ready for him to leave.

Jeff felt the same way. He missed his wife and her absence left a gap in his life. As much as he complained about Nikki not putting her clothes in the hamper or hanging them up in the closet when she took them off, he missed her presence and doing little things for her.

"You know I love Eveline's gumbo. A bowl of it would be great," Jeff answered, sitting up and rubbing his hands together in anticipation of good food.

He watched his wife as she walked to the kitchen, then he turned his attention back to the television. Nikki returned several minutes later carrying a wooden tray, with a steaming bowl of gumbo atop it and a tall glass of iced tea.

She handed the tray to Jeff, then sat back on the couch and watched her husband wolf down the tasty meal.

Nikki smiled when he was done. "Do you want more?" she asked.

"No, I'm fine for now," Jeff answered, after he greedily drank more iced tea. He put the tray on the cocktail table and edged closer to Nikki. He inhaled the scent of her hair and ruffled the ends of it.

"I've really missed you, baby. I hope you've been missing me a little?" he said.

"Of course I have," Nikki replied moodily, as if her feelings were hurt. "Being apart from you hasn't been easy on me either. I tell you, when we get back together, sparks are going to fly." Her eyes gleamed with happiness at the thought of being with him.

"So when is that going to happen? I mean, when are you coming back home?" Jeff held his breath, waiting on her answer.

"It won't be long, I promise. We just need to get some marital sessions with Pastor out of the way." She smoothed her hair down on her head.

"We knew this separation was going to take time. If there's anything I can do, just ask," Jeff said. He leaned over and picked up his glass off the tray and sipped more tea.

"The fact that you come over every morning helps more than you can imagine. Lincoln asks me everyday are you coming back tomorrow."

"Poor kid," Jeff mused while massaging Nikki's neck. "He probably thinks I'm not coming back like his parents."

"That would be my guess too." Nikki sighed audibly.

"Give him time. Lincoln will be fine."

"Oh . . . I talked to Donald today. He said he was going to call you. Did he?" Nikki scooted her body to the end of the couch and planted her feet in Jeff's lap.

"Yes, we talked," Jeff replied. "He told me that he plans

to come here Tuesday morning to discuss some new developments. He asked if I would be available."

"That's what he told me too," Nikki said. She rested her head on the arm of the sofa.

"Have you had any luck with finding a support group for gambling?" Jeff abruptly changed the subject. He lifted one of her feet and began massaging it.

"I'm still making calls." She moaned. "That feels good." Jeff's hands were wreaking havoc as he gently flexed her toes. Finding a support group was on the bottom of her list of things to do. Although she still felt the urge to gamble, the longings had taken second place behind dealing with the family's tragedy.

"I can help you, if you'd like," Jeff volunteered. He caressed the sole of Nikki's foot, causing it to arch.

"This is something I have to do for myself. Pastor and I have begun meeting, and he's been counseling me. He thinks I need to go through this process alone." Nikki crinkled her nose prettily.

Jeff replied somewhat salty as he held his hands up. "Okay then, I won't help you. I'll defer to the man with a higher calling. Is there anything else I can do though?"

"Lincoln needs a haircut. Can you take him to the barbershop tomorrow? I don't have a clue as to how a man gets his hair cut." Nikki's body melted from her husband's loving touch.

"That's no problem." Jeff nodded. "I've liquidated my . . . *our* portfolio. Ron will have a check for us on Monday. Maybe one day next week we can go out to Harrah's."

"I'm supposed to meet with the credit manager on Wednesday to set up a payment plan for the rest of the money I owe. Would you like to go with me?" Nikki asked Jeff shyly.

"Only if it's early before I go to work. I have a meeting this coming Wednesday at four o'clock. Since I've already taken days off, I don't want to have to take any more time off unless it's directly related to Lincoln. Donald explained we'll have to go to court to sign papers to make the guardianship legal, and I'll have to miss work to do that," he said.

"My meeting with Harrah's is in the afternoon, so I'll go by myself. Maybe if Mom doesn't have any plans, I can meet you for dinner or something later that night." Nikki's hands fluttered helplessly.

"That sounds good. And I guess me not being available may work out for the best. Maybe it's one of those tasks Pastor talked about. What else is pending?" Jeff asked, stifling a yawn.

"Here I am, being selfish," Nikki remarked. "I know you're probably tired. Why don't you spend the night here?"

The couple's heads pivoted to the left, they could hear Lincoln crying out from the bedroom. As they rushed to the bedroom, Nikki and Jeff met Eveline at the doorway.

"I heard him crying," Eveline said. Her face looked tired and haggard.

Lincoln lay in the middle of the queen-sized bed. His face was crumpled and tears poured from his eyes. He blubbered between hiccups, "I want my mommy and daddy." He held a stuffed rabbit in his arms and reached up and wiped his eyes.

Eveline sat on one side of the bed and Nikki on the other. Jeff reclined at the bottom of the bed.

"Come on, honey." Eveline held her grandson tightly in her arms. "What did Nana and TeeTee tell you about Mommy and Daddy?"

"I want them, and I want them now," he stuttered. "Nana, I don't understand why they left me."

"Child, God wanted your parents home with Him. They're with Grandfather Lincoln, who you were named after. We don't understand why things happen the way they do. But God left you here so me, TeeTee, and Uncle Jeff wouldn't be alone." She rocked him in her arms.

"But I want them to come back. I want to see them again, Nana," Lincoln cried. His nose was running.

"Shhh. I know, baby. But they can't come back. They're in heaven watching over you now."

Nikki walked to the washroom and returned with a warm towel. She wiped her nephew's face as he twisted his head from side to side. Lincoln continued to wail. Eveline looked at Nikki powerlessly and shook her head.

"Just let him cry and get it out of his system," Nikki whispered.

Five minutes later, he stuck his thumb in his mouth as his body shuddered. "Do you want to sleep with Nana tonight?" Eveline asked, as she stroked his brow.

Lincoln's red eyes drooped. He was obviously sleepy. He bobbed his head up and down.

Jeff rose from the bed. "I'll carry him in your room for you, Mother Baldwin," he offered.

Eveline relinquished her grandbaby to her son-in-law's outstretched arms. They walked from the room into her bedroom.

Jeff returned to find Nikki wiping her eyes with a tissue. "How often does that happen?" he asked, as he sat on the bed beside her. It tore his heart to shreds to see his wife looking so sad and Lincoln so distraught.

"Maybe every other night," Nikki admitted. She blew her nose, and then she leaned over and dropped the tissue in the wastebasket next to the bed.

"I know it's been tough for you and your mother. Just continue what you're doing. In time Lincoln will be better," Jeff promised.

"I know what you're saying is true. It's just that when I see him looking so vulnerable, asking for his mother and father, I just wonder if he'll be able to get over the tragedy."

"Sure he will. You and Eveline are strong women. Give him time." He pulled Nikki into his arms.

"Thanks for being here for me and Mom." Nikki sobbed against Jeff's chest. "I don't know what I would've done if you hadn't been around."

Jeff stroked her hair. "Where else would I be except here? You're my wife; I'm supposed to be by your side." His heart rate soared as he remembered how that wasn't his attitude a couple of weeks ago. How their lives had changed.

He continued to hold his wife in his arms until she finally fell asleep. Jeff gently laid Nikki's body on the bed and left the room. He peeped into Eveline's opened door. Her back was to the door, and she snored lightly while Lincoln slept peacefully at her side.

Jeff strolled into the living room. He turned off the television, made sure the front door was locked, and set the alarm system. Then he picked up the tray from the cocktail table and took it into the kitchen.

Warm water streamed from the faucet, as he rinsed the bowl he'd eaten from. He put the tray into the pantry and turned off the lights. Returning to Nikki's old bedroom, he undressed, and got into the bed in his rightful place . . . beside his wife.

Chapter 35

Tuesday morning at nine o'clock, the skies had opened up, and a downpour drenched the Chicago area. Two inches of rain had fallen already. Nikki stood inside an elevator of the building where she was employed. Four other equally soaked people rode up in the car with her. When the elevator reached the agency's floor, she stepped off, opened the glass doors, took a deep breath and walked inside.

Shannon, the temporary receptionist Victor hired when Fatima moved over to the designing side, was disconnecting a call. She looked up and spied Nikki. "Hello, Mrs. Singleton. I'd like to say how sorry I am about the loss of your family members."

"Thank you, Shannon," Nikki managed to say. Her eyes glistened with tears. She thought the loss would get easier with time, but so far that hadn't been the case. "I'm here to see Victor, if he's available," she said, dropping her umbrella on the floor beside her. She unzipped her leather coat and took the matching cap off her head.

"Give me a minute to check. Will you be in your office?" Shannon picked up the phone and dialed Victor's extension.

"No, I'm just here to see Victor; not to work," Nikki said. She sat in one of the plush chairs in the reception area, tapping her foot impatiently. She and Jeff were scheduled to meet with Reverend Dudley that evening for the first of their marital counseling sessions.

When Shannon hung up the phone and looked at Nikki, she said, "He said for you to come on back."

"Thanks, Shannon." Nikki picked up her coat and belongings, and walked to her boss's office.

As she walked down the hallway, co-workers expressed their condolences. Fatima asked Nikki if she would stop by her office before she left, and Nikki agreed.

She knocked on Victor's office. His booming voice told her to come in, and Nikki walked in and made herself comfortable in a chair in front of his desk.

Peering over his glasses, he asked, "Can I have Shannon bring you something . . . coffee or tea?"

"No, I'm fine," Nikki said primly, smoothing down her black skirt. She laid her coat across her lap and put her bag and umbrella on the floor next to her seat.

"How are you doing?" Victor asked. He leaned back in his chair.

"Making it the best I can. Some days are better than others," Nikki replied. "We're still adjusting."

"I know how close you and your brother were," Victor said.

"Yeah, we were. I only had one sibling, so it hasn't been easy."

Victor sat erect in his seat. "When do you plan on coming back to work? Have you figured out a timetable yet?"

"Well, that's what I wanted to talk to you about," Nikki

started. "My brother and his wife left me custody of their son, and I don't think he's quite ready for me to come back to work yet."

"Hmmm." Victor's eyes narrowed. "What are you planning to do then?" He could tell from Nikki's uncomfortable expression what was coming next. She couldn't quite meet his eyes.

Nikki picked up her purse from off the floor. She unclasped it and removed a folded letter. Nikki handed the paper to Victor. "I originally intended to take a leave of absence from work, but thinking about that idea more, I realized that wasn't going to work. This is my letter of resignation. I don't have a choice except to stop working now. My nephew needs me," she said simply.

"I can't say I'm surprised," Victor answered, opening the letter and scanning it briefly. He looked up at Nikki and said, "Are you sure you want to do this?"

"I don't see where I have any other alternative," Nikki answered. Tension had her stomach somersaulting.

"You've been with me since when?" Victor asked. He leaned back in his leather chair.

"Since I finished college," Nikki replied.

"I'd hate for you to leave the company. We have so many wonderful opportunities in the works. And they're going to put the agency on the map."

"I understand, Victor. I really do," Nikki said earnestly, "but family comes first. I couldn't live with myself if I weren't there for my nephew and my mother when they need me."

"I can understand that. But resigning seems so final. Are you sure you don't want to give your decision more thought?" he asked.

"I've done nothing but think about it for the past two weeks, along with everything else," Nikki said ruefully. "I really don't see another alternative. Lincoln has taken his parents' deaths hard and rightfully so. I haven't had a good night's sleep since the accident. I'm not complaining or anything. I'm just saying that to say how drastically my life has changed."

"Your mother is retired, isn't she?" Victor asked. He straightened a pile of papers on his desk. "Couldn't she take care of the boy?"

Nikki shook her head. "My mother isn't one to complain, but she's struggling with the deaths just as badly as my nephew. Sometimes I go into her room and find her staring at Linc's picture. I can tell just how hard all of this has hit her. There's no one else we can turn to. We take care of our own."

"Would you consider taking a three-month leave of absence?" Victor offered. He knew from the way Nikki's chin was set that she wouldn't take him up on his offer.

"Vic, I'm flattered that you're making an effort. But I don't know how long all of this is going to take. The thought of working and trying to take care of a child boggles my mind," she confided.

"I expected you were going to say that. I'm sure you'll do fine." Victor smiled. "But if you change your mind, my offer is open."

Nikki stood up. "Thank you. I appreciate all you've done for me, and if I change my mind, I'll get in touch with you." She put her purse on her arm.

"That's fine." Victor held up his hand. "No rush, but can you give Fatima a turnover of your projects?"

Nikki sighed. "Sure, I can do that. I'll stop by her office on my way out and try to set up something for early next week, if that's soon enough."

"That'll be fine." Victor walked around his desk, and he and Nikki shook hands. "I wish you only the best," he said.

"I know, and thank you for making this easier for me. I

dreaded coming here today," Nikki admitted, now that the worst was over.

"I know all too well how lives can change abruptly," Victor said, walking Nikki to the door. "Stay in touch, young lady."

"I will," Nikki promised. She turned and waved to Victor and exhaled a sigh of relief. She stopped and talked to Trey for a few minutes, before going to Fatima's cubicle.

When Nikki got to her cubicle, Fatima, who was on the telephone, waved her in. Nikki studied her co-worker. Fatima was impeccably dressed as usual. She wore a kelly green pantsuit with a black collar, complemented by a gold tailored shirt. Emerald earrings hung from her ears, and she wore the matching bracelet on her slim wrist. Fatima hung up the telephone.

"How are you doing, Nikki?" she asked in a serious tone of voice.

"I'm making it day by day. How are things going for you?" she asked.

"Busy, but I miss my mentor. When are you coming back to work? I need all the help I can get," she said.

"Well, actually, I'm not."

Fatima's eyes bucked and her mouth dropped. "Tell me you're joking. What do you mean you're not coming back?"

Nikki explained her new responsibilities to Fatima.

"I guess you don't have a choice then," Fatima said. Her telephone rang. "Give me a minute," she said to Nikki. When she completed the call, she called Shannon. "Would you hold my calls for a few minutes? I'll call you back when I'm available."

"It sounds like you're really busy," Nikki said. Her hand tightened on the strap of her purse.

"I am. I've been doing your work and mine. But I'm not

complaining. I just hate that you aren't coming back." There was a plaintive whine in her voice.

"What can I say? Life changes. You think you have everything figured out, and then your world turns upside down multiple times," Nikki said.

The women chatted for a bit. Nikki planned to return to the office the following week so she could turnover her projects to Fatima, and then have lunch.

Nikki looked at the clock on Fatima's credenza. "I've got to get out of here." She stood up. "We'll definitely meet next week."

Fatima nodded. She stood and walked around her desk and gave Nikki a hug. "I'll walk you to the elevator.

While they waited for the car to arrive, Nikki turned to Fatima and asked, "Do you like to read?"

"Why?" she asked, looking at Nikki puzzled.

"I belong to a book club, and we need another member," Nikki answered.

"Sure. I mean, I'd love to come and check you guys out. Give me the details next week at lunch."

When the elevator arrived, Nikki called out, "I will." She waved to Fatima as the elevator doors closed. Exiting in the parking garage, Nikki waited patiently while the parking attendant retrieved her car, and then headed south. Her third session with Reverend Dudley was scheduled for the next day.

During her drive on the Dan Ryan Expressway, Nikki mentally crossed items off her checklist. Eveline would home school Lincoln for the remainder of the school year, so that took care of his education. Nikki and Jeff were due in court next month and would become Lincoln's permanent guardians, and Jeff would accompany her to Harrah's next week to pay off her gambling debt.

Nikki and Jeff had retrieved some of Linc and Shonell's

possessions that were salvageable from the explosion and moved them to their house. They had setup a room for Lincoln at the Singleton residence which the couple had begun decorating. Nikki had also scheduled appointments with several child therapists for the upcoming week. Life was finally settling down to something resembling normal. Because she was left with so much of the day-to-day care of Lincoln, Nikki had little time to gamble even if she wanted to, and the urge to gamble was slowly subsiding. Nikki felt she'd made great strides as days passed with the thought of gambling never entering her mind.

At the conclusion of her first session with Reverend Dudley, the minister instructed Nikki to recite the Serenity Prayer when the urge to gamble became powerful, and while she sat at a stop light, the words slipped from her mouth. "God grant me the serenity to accept the things I cannot change; courage to change the things I can; and wisdom to know the difference."

Most people were familiar with the first verses of the prayer. It was the subsequent words that strengthened Nikki when her will to remain strong ebbed. *Living life one day at a time, Enjoying one moment in time; Accepting hardships as the pathway to peace; Taking, as He did, this sinful world as it is; not as I would have it; Trusting that He will make all things right if I surrender to His Will; That I may be reasonably happy in this life and supremely happy with Him Forever in the next. Amen.*

Traffic was light, and Nikki arrived at the church in no time. Her stomach felt like it was knotted with burning coils of apprehension as she got out of the car to begin session number three with Reverend Dudley.

Chapter 36

Nikki fidgeted in her seat as she waited for Roslyn to give her the okay to go to Reverend Dudley's office. The church secretary was talking on the telephone offering her sympathy to a church member who'd had a death in the family. Nikki crossed and uncrossed her legs; she didn't know why her spirit was so ill at ease. After all, she had managed to survive the previous sessions and had come through relatively intact.

She suspected Reverend Dudley was going to want to delve deeper into the issues that led to her gambling addiction, and Nikki wasn't quite sure she was ready to share that information. She knew how painful exposing innermost thoughts could be. Still, in the back of her mind, Nikki knew the deed had to be done if she wanted to preserve her future and marriage.

Roslyn hung up the telephone and glanced across her desk at Nikki. "That was Sister Betty Woods. Her mother-in-law passed. We'll have to keep her in our prayers."

"I will say one for her tonight," Nikki promised as she clasped her shaking hands together.

The door to Reverend Dudley's office flew open. Brothers Davis and Edwards, members of the Big Brother Committee, walked into Roslyn's office and exchanged greetings with Nikki.

Roslyn nodded and smiled receptively at Nikki, telling her that the pastor was ready to see her. When Nikki walked into Reverend Dudley's office, the minister stood up and hugged her. She immediately broke into tears. A few minutes elapsed before Nikki managed to compose herself.

Reverend Dudley took a green tissue out of the box on his desk and handed one to the young woman. "I'm going to get a cup of coffee," he informed her. "Would you like something to drink?"

Nikki nodded her head.

"I'll be back in a moment." The minister left the room and closed the door behind him.

It didn't escape Nikki's attention that Reverend Dudley could have easily called Roslyn and asked her to bring refreshments to his office. She thanked God that her pastor had given her an opportunity to try to calm her nerves.

Reverend Dudley returned shortly with a cup of coffee for himself and tea for Nikki. He set his cup on the desk and handed Nikki hers.

Nikki eased the cup to her mouth with quivering hands, sipped the warm liquid, and then put the cup on the desk.

"Have you been reciting the Serenity Prayer?" Reverend Dudley asked. "Has it been helping you any?"

"I have," Nikki admitted. "And yes, reciting it does help."

They sat in comfortable silence for a short time. Then the minister kindly asked Nikki, "What ails your soul?"

"I feel like there are so many things going wrong for me . . ." Her voice trailed off and then she continued speaking. "I struggle with a strong sense of inadequacy and a heavy dose of guilt." She wrapped the tissue around her fingers.

"Tell me why you feel that way?" Reverend Dudley queried his goddaughter soothingly.

"I feel inadequate on so many levels." A wave of sadness traversed her face. Nikki held up a finger, "I've let my family down." Then she held up another finger. "And most of all, I am so ashamed of putting me and Jeff in this financial predicament." Nikki's eyes traveled to the window behind Reverend Dudley. She was too mortified to meet his eyes.

"Remember that no matter what you do that you're a child of God, and our Heavenly Father forgives our sins. I think sometimes that we mortals have a hard time forgiving ourselves. I know you feel persecuted with all that has transpired; the debt, Linc and Shonell's passing, and now you've been entrusted to raise your nephew. Keep in mind, Nikki, that God doesn't put more on us than we can bear. Think of how Christ died for us on the cross and all that He had to endure. If He hadn't sacrificed His life, where would we be now?"

"I hear you Pastor, but I just can't get beyond the feeling that I let everyone down." Nikki's voice rose then fell into a whisper.

"When all is said and done, no one can judge you but God, and He is merciful. He never said our path in life would be easy. But know that He is there with you every step of the way, and He's there to help you overcome every misstep you make. Second Timothy, the first chapter, verses seven and eight reads: *God did not give us a Spirit of fear but of power and love and self-control. So do not be ashamed of the testimony about our Lord or of me, a prisoner for his sake, but by God's power accept your share of suffering for the gospel.* Nikki, let go and let God and give Him your burdens."

"That's easier said than done." Nikki moistened her dry lips.

"Trust me when I tell you that it's not impossible. Give me your hands," Reverend Dudley urged Nikki.

She stretched them across the desk and bowed her head.

"Father above, help your child to see the light. Reassure Nikki that she's not alone. Help her to realize the battle is not hers but the Lord's. Father, guide Eveline, Jeff, and me, as we show Nikki that we're by her side as she struggles through her tribulations. Give your child strength and peace of mind. Amen." Reverend Dudley firmly held Nikki's hands a moment later.

Nikki asked the minister in a timid voice, "How do I get over my feelings of inadequacy, Pastor?"

"You keep reciting the Serenity Prayer, take each day one at a time, and most of all, remember that you are a child of the Most High King. He will not desert you or leave you alone," Reverend Dudley said solemnly. "Read the Bible, pray, and don't be afraid to ask Him for help. What else is bothering you?"

Nikki felt a stirring in her heart. Maybe it was time to let go of the burden and discuss it with someone. "Pastor," she said hesitantly, "I feel so guilty about Linc and Shonell's deaths and getting money from their estate."

"Humph," Reverend Dudley snorted. He leaned forward in his leather chair. "The last time I checked, it cost money to survive. Housing, utilities, clothing, food . . . you need all of that to raise Lincoln."

"But why them and not me? It just doesn't seem fair." Nikki moaned as tears trickled down her cheeks.

"Because life is hard sometimes, and it isn't fair. Just remember to keep your eyes on the prize; attaining a state of grace so we can see God one day. We may never understand why things happen to us in life. Still, everything that happens is a part of God's master plan. We face challenges in life that make our faith stronger."

"What if I'm weak and can't stop gambling? I am so scared I may backslide." Nikki's face dropped to the floor. Tears dotted her skirt.

"Then you pick yourself up, and you pray for forgiveness and try again. Rome wasn't built in a day. And eventually, you will attain the life God intended for you." Reverend Dudley paused to allow his words to sink in.

Nikki nodded and crossed her legs. "My friend, Lindsay— we've been friends since we were in elementary school— says I was born privileged, and she complains how I never had to work for anything, how everything I have was handed to me. She makes me feel so low. She made some pretty harsh statements to me the night of the funerals, and I was never more wounded in my life."

"You can't allow anyone control over your life or emotions but the Lord. Lindsay probably has issues with aspects of her life, and that's why she's critical of you. Still, you have to forgive her. Think of Jesus when He carried His cross back on Mount Calvary, how heavy His burden must have been. If He could endure death for all of us, then you can surely withstand your pain, knowing that the Lord is always there to dry the tears from your eyes. Make a pact with yourself to this day forward dedicate your soul to pleasing the Lord. And Nikki, when you feel low or like giving up, go look at Lincoln and remember how Linc and Shonell entrusted you with their most precious gift from God, their son. And take comfort in that knowledge regardless of what someone else says."

"I had never thought of it that way." Nikki nodded as she took in everything Reverend Dudley had said.

"Embrace life and live it to the fullest because tomorrow is not promised. Take comfort from knowing God knows what's in our hearts." Reverend Dudley wrote down scriptures he wanted Nikki to read, then handed the paper to Nikki, and she placed it inside her purse. The minister glanced at his watch and said, "We have another ten minutes or so to go. How are things going with Jeff?"

"That's one area of my life that's going fairly well. Jeff comes over daily. He spends time with Lincoln, and we're communicating very well. I look at him sometimes and though he doesn't say a word, I feel him wondering how we came to be in this situation. He liquidated our portfolio so I'll be able to pay off my entire debt to Harrah's. Jeff insists he wants to go to Joliet with me when I pay off the bill."

Reverend Dudley's eyebrow lifted. "Well, that might not be a bad idea under the circumstances."

"He doesn't trust me anymore," Nikki said sadly.

"He will again in time, and patience is the key. Second Peter, first chapter, sixth verse reads: *And to knowledge temperance; and to temperance patience; and to patience godliness.* Hold fast like Job."

"I know you're right, and I will," Nikki vowed. "This too shall pass." She smiled and stood up. "I guess it's time for me to go. You've given me a lot to think about, Pastor, and I promise that I will follow your instructions. After God, comes family, and my family is so important to me. I love them."

Reverend Dudley rose from his seat. He walked to Nikki, picked up her coat from the chair, and held it so she could put it on.

After she zipped her coat, Nikki put her cap on her head. "I feel hopeful that I will beat this thing. I mean my addiction." She snapped her finger. "Oh . . . Pastor, I meant to ask you what you thought about Gamblers Anonymous."

"I think it serves its purpose in society. Why do you ask?"

"I was thinking about attending a meeting just to see what it's like."

"Our blessings can come from many sources. If you

think it would be beneficial to your continuing recovery to attend the meetings, then by all means do so."

Nikki walked over and kissed the older man on the cheek. "Thank you for being my minister and godfather and for being so open-minded."

"You're welcome, Nikki. That's what we do. I couldn't do any less for my best friend's daughter. Now go see to your mother and that wonderful nephew of mine. Tell Eveline I said hello. I'll see you next week at the same time." Reverend Dudley walked Nikki to the door.

As Nikki walked to her car, her mind processed, like a computer, the information she had discussed with Reverend Dudley. Nikki held her head higher. There was pep in her step, and her soul was lighter than it had been in months. She couldn't wait to talk to Maya and tell her about her session with Reverend Dudley and the progress she felt she was making.

And Nikki also wanted the 411 on what she perceived to be a budding relationship between her best friend and Attorney Layton.

Chapter 37

Later that evening, Eveline had gone to church for a finance committee meeting and Lincoln had gone to bed early. He and Eveline had a field trip planned for the following day. As the boy slept, Nikki thought to give Maya a call.

"Hey, girl," Maya said after Nikki greeted her. "What's happening with you?"

After Nikki gave her the details of her meeting with the pastor, she finished with, "I think the question should be what's going on with you? I have a feeling there's a new man in your life."

Maya laughed out loud. "I don't want to jinx myself as far as Donald is concerned, but I can say so far so good. We went out for dinner last week and have a date for dinner and the movies this weekend."

"That's good, Maya," Nikki gushed enthusiastically. "I'm happy for you. You deserve nothing but the best."

"You know I have been out of the dating game for so long that I don't have a thing to wear," Maya remarked casually. "It would be nice if a sista's best friend could go shopping with her before her date. I took the day off work. Donald is taking me to a fancy restaurant out in Orland Park."

"I wish I could go with you. You know how much I love shopping." Nikki sighed. "But I can't. Jeff and I have errands to run tomorrow. Our first marital counseling session with Pastor is tomorrow morning, so I'll have to pass."

"I can't complain then. It's time you and Jeff got it together. He's been as cross as a hungry bear since you two have been living apart," Maya remarked. "I think I'll treat myself to the works at a spa."

"Okay, I guess that means you really like this guy," Nikki replied.

"I do, but I don't know, Nik." Maya groaned. "His family has money. They all seem like overachievers, and I barely scrapped through college. I doubt if I fit the Layton family mold." Maya sounded worried.

"I think all you need to concentrate on is what Donald wants. If he didn't like what he saw, then he wouldn't be with you. Don't borrow trouble, and at this point, don't worry about his family," Nikki advised her friend.

"I guess you're right," Maya agreed dubiously. She changed the subject, "So are you nervous about your and Jeff's meeting with Pastor tomorrow?"

"A little bit, but not too much," Nikki answered.

"Good. Everything will come together and work for the good of God. I know both you and Jeff have had more than enough time to figure out what went wrong in your relationship and correct it. And best of all, you're communicating."

Nikki raked fingers through her hair. "You're right on all counts. Sometimes I feel funny talking to Pastor about my personal problems, but he manages to get information out of me anyway."

"I'd look at it as another leg of spiritual journey. Don't get caught up in semantics," Maya advised her friend. Her line clicked and she checked the caller ID unit. "Nikki, I've got to go, I'm on call this week at work. That's probably someone from Jeff's department. I'll talk to you later."

When Nikki hung up, she left her bedroom and went into the kitchen to put on a kettle to boil water for tea. She walked into the room that used to be Eveline's office that had become Lincoln's room. He was fast asleep.

Nikki's mood was pensive as she sipped from the cup of hot tea. She returned to her bedroom after she rinsed the cup and put it in the drain. Nikki called Jeff. She had an urge to hear his voice before she went to sleep. After she talked to her husband for a few minutes, Nikki hung up the telephone and dropped to her knees. She prayed fervently that all would go well for her and Jeff during their session with Reverend Dudley.

After she awakened Friday morning, Nikki rose from the bed, showered, and then dressed. She walked to the kitchen where Eveline had prepared breakfast and did little more than pick at her food. She was too preoccupied by thoughts of her impending appointment to enjoy the meal.

Usually on Fridays, if the weather permitted, Eveline took Lincoln outside the house on a field trip to a Chicago point-of-interest. Today they were traveling to The Museum of Science and Industry, where they would view a film at the IMAX Theater.

"I wish you were coming with us, Tee-Tee," Lincoln told Nikki as she pulled his navy blue skull cap on his head. Nikki made sure his mittens were firmly fastened to his snowsuit. "The movie me and Nana are going to see is in 3D, so I'm going to get glasses."

"I wish I could come with you and Nana too. Maybe next time," Nikki promised the boy. She kissed his cheek.

Eveline waddled into the kitchen wearing a brown, bulky, down coat and waterproof boots on her feet. She looked down at her grandson and asked, "Are you ready, young man?"

"Yeah. I can hardly wait to see the movie, Nana." There was a twinkle in his eyes that had missing for a long time, and it warmed the women's souls.

Eveline looked at Nikki and rubbed her arm comfortingly, "Don't worry. You're going to be fine."

Nikki tried to smile at her mother reassuringly as she nodded. "I know. You guys have a fun day. Jeff will be by soon to pick me up." Her eyes strayed to the clock on the wall.

"I'm praying for you," Eveline said just before she and the boy left.

Nikki went into her bedroom and hurriedly made up the bed. She grabbed her purse, took out a tube of fuchsia-colored lipstick, and lined her lips. Then she unwrapped and combed her hair. The doorbell rang and Nikki grabbed her purse and went to the foyer. Jeff stood at the door, and she let him in.

"Good morning." Jeff had a tranquil expression on his face, and his dark eyes were filled with determination. He pecked Nikki's cheek.

She moved away from him. "You're cold." She opened the closet door, removed her coat and put it on.

"It's windy outside. The hawk is soaring over Chicago today. Are you ready?"

"As I'm ever going to be," Nikki quickly retorted with a wry expression on her face.

"Let's go then. I left the car running."

During the ride, the couple chitchatted about Jeff's job, Lincoln, and their upcoming activities. Before long Jeff had pulled into the church parking lot. As Jeff cut off the car, Nikki dipped her head and whispered a prayer.

When she finished, Jeff smiled at her and said, "Asking for a little divine intervention, are we?"

"Well, it won't hurt, that's for sure." Nikki grinned back. She opened the car door.

"Just a minute," Jeff interjected. "I thought it wouldn't hurt if I said my own prayer."

"Sure, by all means." Nikki closed the car door and bowed her head.

"Lord, we come to you humbly as we know how," Jeff began. "We ask that you open our minds and hearts to understand and use the words of wisdom that Pastor is about to impart to us, Father. Give us strength and courage to do your will and, in the process, bring us closer as a couple. Amen."

"Amen," Nikki intoned.

"Let's do this." Jeff said.

Chapter 38

"Good morning, Mr. and Mrs. Singleton," Roslyn greeted. "Pastor has been waiting for you. Go on in."

Nikki's legs trembled slightly as she walked toward the Pastor's door. She wore a gold cross on a chain around her neck, and she rubbed it. She and Jeff walked inside the masculine, decorated, paneled office.

"Would you close the door, Jeff?" Reverend Dudley asked.

Jeff obeyed, then he and Nikki sat down in the two brown and beige striped chairs placed in front of the minister's desk.

Reverend Dudley greeted the couple and made small talk to put them at ease. Then he stared at Nikki and Jeff and said, "I'm glad you two decided to proceed with counseling. Personally I don't think we'll need many sessions. In the long run, how well our talks go depends on the two of you and how hard you choose to work at your marriage. Before we begin, I'd like to pray."

Nikki and Jeff bowed their heads, and Jeff took his wife's hand.

"Father, how blessed we are this morning, grateful you woke us up and allowed us to see another day. And for that we say thank you, Lord. Father above, I ask that you bless this couple as they go about the business of strengthening the bonds of matrimony. You said in the Word that those whom God has joined together, let no man put asunder. I know that when we are done in this place, Jeff and Nikki will have the victory. They will be wiser, stronger, and more tolerant of each other just as your Son, Jesus is of us. Amen."

"Amen," Nikki and Jeff said. Nikki's stomach began to settle down.

"You know what's ironic," Reverend Dudley began saying, "Sister Meesha Morrison has been trying to get me to start a couple's therapy group here in the church. The premise would be for couples to discuss their issues in a group forum. Right about now that sounds like a good idea."

Reverend Dudley continued. "We are not here this morning to point fingers or place blame on one another. Instead, we want to figure out how you two can do things differently in your marriage and handle crises in a smoother manner. I plan to counsel from the spiritual side where applicable and also from a practical side."

Nikki and Jeff nodded.

"The way I see it—and correct me if I'm wrong—is that we have several factors affecting the marriage. Is that accurate?" Reverend Dudley looked at Jeff, and then Nikki.

Jeff piped in. "Yes, Pastor. We have Nikki's addiction and our separation."

Nikki leaned forward in her chair. "We also have Jeff's controlling tendencies."

Reverend Dudley nodded thoughtfully. "That doesn't sound too bad. Some people come to see me with laundry lists of issues. Your issues, in comparison to ones I hear from others, are a piece of cake. Not that I'm trying to downplay your problems or anything. Let me ask you this, do you love each other, and are you committed to strengthening your marriage?"

"Most definitely," Nikki answered without hesitation.

"And you, Jeff?" Reverend Dudley asked.

"For sure, Pastor" Jeff's voice was firm. "Nikki means more to me than life."

"Praise God," Reverend Dudley said. "As long as that potent ingredient is in the marriage, then you're in good shape. Now let's go back in time. Jeff and Nikki, do you remember what attracted you to each other?"

"I do," Jeff lifted his hand. He glanced at his wife. "I'm sorry. Would you like to go first?"

"No, the floor is all yours." Nikki made a sweeping gesture with her hand.

"I love how optimistic she is about life. Most of all, I love the goodness inside her heart. Nikki is a kind, beautiful person." Jeff said.

"And how about you, Nichole. What attracted you to Jeff?" Reverend Dudley asked.

She sighed and a smile filled her lips. "I was attracted to his take charge attitude about life. There didn't seem to be a problem under the sun that Jeff couldn't solve. I always felt safe with Him and I still do . . ."

When her voice trailed, Jeff looked thoughtful and stroked his chin as he waited for Nikki to continue speaking.

"I was drawn to his openness, and at the same time, his vulnerability. Most men put on a macho act, but Jeff could admit his failures. Most of the time I felt like a true helpmate, except for when it came to the budget." Nikki shifted her body in the chair.

Reverend Dudley laid his clasped hands together as he placed his elbows on his desk. He swiveled his chair toward Jeff. "How about you, son. Do you have anything you want to add?"

Jeff opened his mouth, but then shook his head.

"How did working on the budget make you feel, Nikki?" Reverend Dudley probed.

"Like I was in the line of fire every day. I prayed I hadn't made any mistakes, and I think because I couldn't talk to Jeff about how I really felt, I felt the urge to gamble. I knew going to the boat was wrong. Somehow things just got out of hand."

Reverend Dudley's eyes touched on Nikki then Jeff. "If you had to list an ingredient that is integral to marriage, what would it be?" he asked the couple.

Jeff looked up at the ceiling, and then at Reverend Dudley. "That's easy because we kind of lost our way. Communication comes to mind for me."

The minister nodded. "What about you Nichole?"

"Forgiveness," she said in a firm tone of voice as she nodded her head.

"You're right," Reverend Dudley nodded approvingly. "Colossians, third chapter, thirteenth verse, states: *Be gentle and forbearing with one another and, if one has a difference against another, readily pardoning each other; even as the Lord has forgiven you, so must you also forgive.* You've heard that before, I'm sure."

"Yes," Nikki interjected. "The Bible even says we must forgive seventy times seven times." She touched her husband's hand. "Jeff, have I maxed out on forgiveness from you?"

"Of course not," Jeff said intensely. "I hope I haven't either."

"You haven't," Nikki reassured him.

"I agree those traits go hand in hand," Reverend Dudley said. "If your spouse understands where you're coming from and mistakes are made, then it makes it that much easier for one to forgive. We mere mortals aren't perfect. In a marriage, it's important for those lines of communication to stay open and work overtime."

"I see the point you're making." Jeff's eyes widened, and he nodded his head as if the words Reverend Dudley spoke took root and blossomed in his mind. "Perhaps if Nikki and I had talked about our issues, we would not have ended up being separated."

"I believe you're seeing the light," Reverend Dudley teased. He held up his Bible. "Remember anything you want to know about life is found in this book." Reverend Dudley laid the Bible back on his desk. "Let's switch topics. Jeff, is there anything about Nikki's behavior that tests your patience? Don't hold back. I'd like to keep the negatives at a constructive level. Look at them like a leaky faucet that needs repairing."

Jeff turned to Nikki and said apologetically, "Honestly, I didn't know you felt the way you did about handling the finances and that you felt pressured. I wish you had come to me and talked about it." He turned to the pastor. "Outside of the gambling, I have no major complaints about my wife. She can be a little lax about cleaning the house sometimes. That's about it."

Nikki spoke up. "Another reason why I didn't want to confide in Jeff about the gambling and mounting debts is he drinks a little too much sometimes. Maybe that's his escape." Nikki stole a quick peep at her husband.

"I, I, I don't . . ." Jeff stammered. Then he ceased speaking as if the air had gone out of his sails. "Nikki's right. Sometimes I do drink too much when life seems to overwhelm me. I've noticed that habit and I've been making an effort to cut back on the drinking."

The couple continued the open dialog with Reverend Dudley's direction. They managed to keep their emotions on a tight rein and were attentive when Reverend Dudley counseled them and forthright in their answers to his questions. Before Jeff and Nikki knew it, the hour had elapsed. Nikki exaggeratedly mopped her brow as if she had been doing taxing physical labor.

"I think this has been a good start," Reverend Dudley observed. "And of course, I have a little homework for you to do before next week's session."

Nikki removed a small pad of paper from her purse. She tore off a sheet and gave it to Jeff. Then she took two ink pens from her purse.

"Nikki, I'd like you to find scripture in the Bible that talks about wives and their roles in a marriage," Reverend Dudley instructed. He looked at Jeff and said, "I'd like you to find a scripture describing a husband's role."

Jeff and Nikki jotted down notes. Then they looked anxiously at the minister.

"Is that it?" Nikki asked.

"For this week, yes. Nikki, I'll see you on Tuesday." Reverend Dudley stood and walked around the desk. He shook Jeff's hand and hugged Nikki.

The couple thanked the minister for his time and headed out the door. During the drive to Eveline's house, Jeff and Nikki began making plans to redecorate the spare bedroom at their house for Lincoln.

Chapter 39

A month later, on a Friday afternoon, Jeff took a vacation day from work. He, Nikki, and Eveline were standing in the third bedroom, Nikki's office. That was the room that would be converted to Lincoln's bedroom. They had one more couples' session with Reverend Dudley on Wednesday, and Nikki had finished her individual sessions with the pastor. She and Lincoln planned to move with Jeff the following weekend.

When Nikki arrived at the apartment, she swallowed a lump in her throat. She missed being home and noticed the apartment was immaculate, as she'd known it would be.

"I think you should've brought Lincoln's bedroom set from his house instead of buying new furniture," Eveline uttered. She stood with her arms folded across her chest, while Jeff measured the walls.

"Mom, when I talked to his pediatrician this week, she suggested getting everything new. She said it would help his adjustment. If we brought his old furniture, it would be a constant reminder of his life with his parents," Nikki patiently explained to her mother.

"Well, doctors don't know everything. Sometimes you have to use a little common sense. We don't want him to forget his parents, right?" Eveline interjected. She walked to the closet and opened the door. She peered around the space. "At least there's plenty of room for his things. And how are you and Jeff going to pay for a new bedroom set anyway?" she asked nosily, turning back toward them.

Jeff answered, "Donald has petitioned the court to release some of the money from Linc and Shonell's estate for the expense. All he needed was the doctor's recommendation."

Suddenly they heard a crash come from the kitchen and rushed out of the bedroom.

"He did it," TJ said, pointing to Lincoln after the adults entered the kitchen.

"I didn't mean it, TeeTee," Lincoln said, cowering away from his aunt. Tears sprung into his eyes.

Nikki bent down and picked up a knick knack that had been sitting on the edge of the counter and put it back in place.

"It's not broken, Lincoln. Everything is all right. But I want you boys to stop running." She patted Lincoln on his head. "Why don't you go into the den and watch television? You two need a time out. I think we have some juice in the refrigerator and some snacks."

" 'Kay," Lincoln said as he and TJ ran out of the kitchen.

"I'll fix their snacks," Eveline volunteered. "You and Jeff go and finish the measurements for the room."

"Thanks, Mom." Nikki squeezed her mother's arm, as she and Jeff walked back to the bedroom.

Jeff picked up the measuring tape and wrote the dimensions on a pad of paper. "I guess we're going to go through an adjustment ourselves. Our first order of business will be childproofing the apartment," he said.

"You're right about that. I'll have to move the breakables that I have in the living room so Lincoln won't accidentally damage them," Nikki said.

"That sounds like a good idea," Jeff agreed.

"Maya warned me that our lives are going to change drastically."

"She's probably right," Jeff said. He began putting some of the objects in the room into boxes he had picked up from the grocery store. "Speaking of Maya, it sounds like things are heating up with her and Donald." Jeff arched an eyebrow.

"I'm sure she's having a good time. Donald seems like a good man," Nikki said.

"Yeah. I checked the brother out myself. Come on over here, gal, and give me a hand," Jeff said to Nikki. "Where do you want to put your computer?"

"The furniture store had a one-piece, compact computer desk. I'd like to go back there and pick one up tomorrow." Nikki massaged the area between her eyes. She walked over to her desk and began helping Jeff put items inside the boxes. "Maybe we should paint the room before the furniture is delivered."

"We can do it tomorrow tonight," Jeff suggested.

Nikki placed her hand on the side of her face. "Let's see, tomorrow we're taking the boys to Chuck-E-Cheese. Why don't we go there around noon, stay for a couple of hours, and see if Maya could keep Lincoln while we paint? That way, the room will be good and dry before the furniture is delivered," she suggested.

"Good idea. I know Maya will call later, and we can run that plan by her then," Jeff said.

"Okay."

As they continued packing up the boxes, they could hear the sounds of the boys' laughter coming from the den. Eveline returned to the bedroom. "It looks like you're making progress in here. How do you feel about giving up your private space, Nikki?" Eveline bent over and picked up a few papers that had fallen on the floor.

"Jeff and I were just talking about making adjustments. I guess this will be one of them. Honestly, I don't mind." Nikki shrugged her shoulders.

"Good. Now what color did you plan on painting the room?" she asked.

"I was thinking maybe an azure blue. I know Linc planned on Lincoln playing Pee Wee baseball, so I was thinking about painting a baseball themed mural on this wall." Nikki pointed at the wall to the left of the window. "I also took a picture of Linc and Shonell to Osco and had it blown up. I thought I'd frame the picture and hang it over his bed," she said.

Eveline nodded her head approvingly. "That's a great idea. We must never let him forget his parents."

"Speaking of his parents, Donald asked Jeff and me if we'd given any thought to adopting Lincoln in the future." Nikki cut her eyes at her mother.

Eveline's hand fluttered to her throat. "Goodness gracious, I hope not. Lincoln is our legacy. Why, he's the only surviving male Baldwin. Wouldn't you have to change his name to Singleton?" she asked, clearly perturbed by the idea.

"Not really. Donald says we can hyphenate it to Singleton-Baldwin. It's more a formality than anything else. If you're not comfortable with our doing so, then we certainly don't have to do it," Nikki reassured her mother.

"Let me think about it. Things are just happening so fast," Eveline said sorrowfully. "I just don't want Lincoln to forget where he came from."

Nikki walked over to her mother and hugged her. "That will never happen, Mom. I promise you that. That's why Donald suggested hyphenating the names. He thought it might be an issue for Lincoln, particularly at school."

"Okay, I'm going to hold you to your word. Please don't make any hasty decisions." Eveline tried to smile through her tears. "I'd better go back and check on the boys. That TJ is a handful."

An hour later, they had completed their task. Before heading to Eveline's house, they decided to stop at Home Depot and pick up some paint. While Nikki and Jeff went inside the store, Eveline waited in the car with the boys.

Twenty minutes later, the couple returned to the car, and Jeff was driving to the south side. As he was exiting onto 87th Street, he asked, "Is anyone hungry?"

"I am," both boys piped up.

"Uncle Jeff, could we have McDonald's? I'd like a Happy Meal," Lincoln said.

"Is this okay with you?" Jeff asked Nikki.

"I know it's not the healthiest meal in the world, but we'll do it this one time," she said.

"Get them chicken nuggets instead of a burger," Eveline suggested from the backseat where she sat between the boys.

"Okay, McDonald's it is," Jeff said.

He stopped by the chain establishment closest to Eveline's house and purchased a Big Mac for himself, salads for Nikki and Eveline, and chicken nugget Happy Meals for the boys.

Fifteen minutes later, they were at Eveline's, and everyone sat at the kitchen table eating their meals.

"TeeTee, I like your house." Lincoln stuffed his mouth with a French fry.

"Well, I'm glad you do since you'll be living there with me and Uncle Jeff," she said.

"Do you have a Play Station like my daddy?" Lincoln asked his uncle.

"I sure do, and I have your favorite games for you to play," he answered, patting Lincoln's head.

"Can we play them tomorrow? Can TJ come over?" Lincoln glanced over at his friend.

"I don't think TJ can come over tomorrow. We'll see what his mommy says about next weekend. Maybe he can come over after church Sunday," Nikki said.

"'Kay." Lincoln smeared his nugget with barbeque sauce and took a bite.

When they finished eating, Eveline cleared the table. Jeff took the boys into the bathroom to wash up and change into their pajamas. Nikki had rented movies, and she let out the sofa bed in the living room.

"What a day," Eveline yawned. "I'm a little tired. I think I'll go to bed. Oh, don't forget to call Carol tomorrow. We promised to call her on the weekends so she can talk to Lincoln."

Nikki walked over to her mother and hugged her. "I know this is hard, Mom. Sometimes I feel like all of this is a dream that I wish I could wake up from. I know Jeff and I are going to do things you might not approve of, like taking the boys to McDonald's tonight. We're learning too, so just be patient with us."

"Oh, I hope you didn't think I was being critical or anything. And if you did, I apologize. That wasn't my intention. I'm fumbling my way around too. It just hurts sometimes."

"I know. I feel the same way."

The boys, clad in Spiderman pajamas, burst into the room. "TeeTee, we're ready to watch movies," Lincoln proclaimed.

Nikki grabbed their hands and said, "Well, come on . . . right this way."

*   *   *

Wednesday rolled around, and it was Nikki and Jeff's last session with Reverend Dudley. Roslyn waved them inside the room when they walked into her space. She smiled at the sight of the couple holding hands.

Reverend Dudley sat at his desk writing on a pad of paper. He laid the pen down and put the pad aside. His smile radiated approval and love for the couple. "I don't have to ask how you two are doing because it's written all over your faces. I'd say we've made progress, praise God."

"I think we've learned during our sessions not to take each other for granted and respect one another's feelings. We can truthfully say that the sessions have strengthened our marriage." Nikki smiled brightly.

"I thought I'd keep this last meeting informal, and instead of me leading the meeting, maybe you can tell me what you've learned about each other and what you've gotten out of our meeting. Nikki I'd like you to talk about your addiction progress," Reverend Dudley announced as he leaned back comfortably in his chair.

"I liked the way you made us study the Bible. We learned about relationships and how God teaches us how spouses should be treated. We even made notes of some of the scriptures and keep them in our wallets and framed on the kitchen wall at home," Jeff proclaimed proudly. "Mine references husbands and Nikki's wives."

"Well, why don't you share some of them with me?" Reverend Dudley asked as he dipped his head appreciatively.

Jeff made a production of taking a folded sheet of paper from his wallet. "My favorite is from Proverbs, eighteenth chapter, twenty-second verse. *He who finds a wife finds what is good and receives favor from the Lord.* Ephesians, fifth chapter, twenty-fifth and twenty-sixth verses says: *Husbands love your wives, just as Christ loved the church and gave himself up for her to make her holy.* And the last one is from Colossians, third chapter, nineteenth verse, which says: *Husbands love your wives and do not be harsh to them.*

"Excellent," Reverend Dudley extolled. He looked at Nichole. "Let me hear your list."

Nikki removed her list from her purse. "Okay, this one goes back in time, and it's from Genesis, second chapter, twenty-fourth verse and says: *Therefore shall a man leave his father and mother, and shall cleave unto his wife; and they shall be one flesh.* The next one is from Psalm, one hundred twenty-eighth chapter, third verse, and it states: *Thy wife shall be a fruitful vine by the sides of thin house; thy children like olive plants round thy table.*" She looked up at her husband and said, "I thought of Lincoln and our future children." With her eyes back on the paper, Nikki continued. "My last verse is from Proverbs, thirty-first chapter, verses ten through twelve which says: *Who can find a virtuous woman? For her price is far above rubies. The heart of her husband doth safely trust in her, so that he shall have no need of spoil. She will do him good and not evil all the days of her life.* The last one is my favorite verse," Nikki said.

"Well done. I can see that our sessions have not been in vain," Reverend Dudley commented. "I think it's a wonderful idea that you put the verses in a prominent spot in your house so you can always see them."

"That's what we thought, so if we have a disagreement, we can think about God's teachings and resolve the issue from a spiritual standpoint. I realize I hadn't been treating Nikki like a helpmate. Instead, I'd been acting like a dictator, and all of these teachings involve a lifestyle change, and we're committed to making the adjustment," Jeff spoke.

"I made the mistake of using gambling as a crutch for

my issues instead of talking to Jeff about how I felt about his making all our decisions. I was afraid to disagree with him, and that won't happen again. I kind of lost sight of the person I am. I forgot I am a child of God, and that omission caused me to make a lot of bad choices. I'm working on myself and I think I'm making good growth. Some days I feel the urge to gamble so strongly I can taste it, but go to a quiet place and recite the Serenity Prayer and a few others." Nikki glanced at Reverend Dudley. "So far I haven't done any backsliding, and that is only by God's grace. Outside of the Serenity Prayer, there is another one I recite, and I'd like to share that one with you." Nikki closed her eyes and moistened her lips. "It's from First Corinthians, tenth chapter, tenth through thirteenth verses. It says: *No temptation has seized you except what is common to man. And God is faithful; he will not let you be tempted beyond what you can bear. But when you are tempted, he will also provide a way out so that you can stand up under it.* That scripture translates to what you've been telling me about God not putting more on me that I can bear.

"Once our communications skills with each other improved, I didn't feel such a strong need to gamble. We usually pray during dinner, but with Lincoln in the house, we've make praying a priority, so he and I pray every night before we go to bed. Jeff and I read a scripture and pray after he comes home from work. I think that helps us stay on course."

Jeff nodded in agreement. "Another realization that I came away with from the sessions is how controlling I had become and how it hurt our marriage. I realize my behavior played a major role leading to Nikki's gambling addiction. I wish I could go back in time and undo all the wrongs I've done. We have forgiven each other and we realize that it takes two to make a marriage work. So moving forward we'll treat our marriage like the covenant with God it's supposed to be."

Nikki looked at Jeff proudly and rubbed his arm. She looked at Reverend Dudley. "Pastor, I have an idea I'd like you to listen to. Since Mom has been homeschooling Lincoln and will continue to do so for the next three months, I have free time on my hands. I've been attending Gamblers Anonymous meetings, and they really seem to help me and the other people attending. I'd like to suggest— and I know this idea has to go through the board—that we establish a GA group here at the church."

"Why do you think we need the group here?" the reverend asked.

"Actually my sessions with you planted a seed in my mind," Nikki said confidently. "They helped me from a spiritual point of view and the GA sessions from the addiction standpoint. I think it would benefit me and others if the two were combined. I would be willing to spearhead the effort providing the Board approves it."

"I don't know, Nikki," Reverend Dudley replied. "I would have to give this more thought. I promise you I will do that."

"That's all I ask, Pastor." She reached into her purse and pulled out a thin stack of papers. "I brought back literature from my meetings and even talked to some people on the national level. Why don't I leave these with you?" Nikki handed them to the minister.

Reverend Dudley scanned the sheets then stapled them and placed them in his top tray. He looked at his watch. "I guess we're officially done with your sessions." He looked at Jeff and Nikki. "I am available to both of you if you want to talk. We can always do more sessions, if needed. But I have a feeling you two are going to be all right. We have time for one more prayer."

Nikki and Jeff rose from the chairs, and they joined hands with each other and Reverend Dudley.

"Gracious Father, we give thanks to you this morning and every morning you allow us to see another day. Praises to you, Father, because the devil has not won, and we are claiming the victory. Thank you, Father, for Jeff and Nikki using the resources you provided to them and putting their marriage back on track."

"Yes, Lord," Nikki said fervently. She swung her arm and the bracelets on her wrists clanged like a miniature tambourine.

"Father, I come to you today asking that you bless Nikki and Jeff and strengthen them as they go about honoring one of your holiest covenants . . . marriage. Lord, let them be respectful of one another's feelings and keep the lines of communication open with one another. In your Son's name I pray. Amen."

"Amen," Nikki and Jeff echoed.

Nikki turned to her godfather and hugged him. Then she said, "Pastor, thank you for everything you've done for me and Jeff. Your guidance has been a blessing."

"It was my pleasure," Reverend Dudley replied. He shook Jeff's hand. I will be in touch with you in a couple of weeks and let you know my decision at hosting a Gamblers Anonymous group at the church."

Chapter 40

By the time spring made its debut, Nikki and Jeff had gone to court and had been officially designated Lincoln's legal guardians. Lincoln was still adjusting to the loss of his parents, but Nikki was heartened as she noted his progress each day.

Nikki continued attending Gamblers Anonymous meetings and she made great strides in fighting her addiction. She knew Eveline and Jeff always wondered if she'd slide back into her old habits; between the meetings and prayer, she didn't. Linc and Shonell's deaths helped her realize the importance of family and the folly of her ways. Nikki seldom felt the urge to gamble.

The Singletons' finances were slowly improving. Jeff still had moments of angst because they lived on his paycheck. The power of prayer helped allay those feelings, and he knew firsthand how the Lord always provided.

Donald had set up a trust fund for Lincoln from Linc and Shonell's insurance policies, in addition to their social security and pension funds. The estate also paid Nikki and Jeff a stipend for Lincoln's upkeep.

Although their finances weren't as healthy as they had been a year ago, Jeff and Nikki were doing just fine with less income.

Two weeks after the guardianship meeting, Nikki, Jeff, and Maya, along with Donald and Fatima, both of whom had joined the church, set up the meeting room for the church's first GA meeting. Nikki and Maya placed leaflets from the organization on the metal folding chairs alongside tiny wallet-sized copies of the Serenity Prayer.

The meeting was scheduled to begin in twenty minutes in the church's Rose of Sharon meeting room. Fatima prepared an urn full of coffee and placed cookies and other finger foods on paper plates.

"Girl, I'm so nervous," Nikki said to Maya while they lay the information in chairs. "What if no one comes?"

"You need to chill out, girlfriend. There will be someone here, don't worry," Maya assured.

Maya looked at Donald, who was placing pamphlets on a table in the rear of the room with Jeff. Donald winked at her and she smiled back at him. The couple's relationship had developed nicely. Donald told Jeff he planned to propose to Maya soon. He'd been looking at rings. Jeff knew that was one secret he couldn't share with his wife. If he did, he knew Nikki would go running to Maya and spoil Donald's surprise.

Two counselors from Gamblers Anonymous walked inside the room and everyone exchanged greetings. The group held a short prayer meeting before the meeting commenced.

Twenty minutes later, over thirty people had arrived for the meeting. Nikki stood at a dais in the front of the room. She tilted the microphone toward her mouth and said in a clear, forceful tone of voice, "My name is Nichole Singleton and I suffer from a gambling addiction that by the grace of God, I've been able to overcome. I'd like to welcome everyone here to the meeting this evening. But before we get started," she held up her black leather bound Bible and smiled. "I'd like to read a couple of verses that give me strength. The first one is taken from the book of Mark, fourteenth chapter, thirty-eighth verse. *Watch and pray so that you will not fall into temptation. The spirit is willing, but the body is weak.* This second one is my own personal mantra, and it brings me such comfort. It's from Philippians, fourth chapter, thirteenth verse, and it reads like this: *I do all things through Christ, who strengths me.*"

When the clapping died, Nikki looked out at her audience and said, "I'd like to call the first meeting of The Christian Friendship Baptist Church, Gamblers Anonymous Meeting to order."

Jeff looked at his wife from the back of the room. Pride and love shone in his eyes as she continued to speak.

"Remember that no matter what storms you're experiencing in your life, God will be by our side to help and heal us. Be it an addiction, the loss of a loved one, and even self-esteem issues, we can weather the storm by God's unfailing hand. Then we can sing along with Marvin Sapp, "Never Would Have Made It." The scripture from Isaiah, fortieth chapter, verses twenty-eight through thirty-one, hammers the point home even more. *Have you not known? Have you not heard? The Lord is the everlasting God, the creator of all the ends of the earth. He does not faint nor grow weary; his understanding is unsearchable. He gives power to the faint and strengthens the powerless. Even youths will faint, and be weary, and the young will fall exhausted, but those who wait for the Lord shall renew their strength, they shall mount up with wings of eagles, they shall run and not be weary, they shall walk and not faint.*"

Discussion Questions for 'Til Debt Do Us Part

1. Do you feel people like Nikki who seem to have everything are exempt from heartache because they are Christians?

2. What single incident can you pinpoint to the breakdown in Nikki and Jeff's marriage?

3. Was Lindsay a true friend to Nikki?

4. Do you think that sometimes it takes misfortune or a tragedy for people to get their act together? If so, what helped Nikki fight her demons?

5. Was Jeff wrong for opening the e-Trade account without telling Nikki, or were his intentions pure?

6. Should Nikki have been more vocal to Jeff about her wishes for a child?

7. Was Jeff a controlling husband? Did you feel Nikki let him walk all over her? Alternatively, was she too understanding by giving Jeff a pass because of his upbringing?

8. Do you feel husbands are the head of the household, or are marriages a partnership?

9. Who was your favorite character and why?

10. Who was your least favorite character and why?

11. Should the church play a bigger role in helping their members overcome addictions, or should that be left to social agencies?

12. Do you think addictive tendencies can be inherited?

13. Do events that happen in our past affect decisions we make today?

14. What are some ingredients that make a good marriage?

15. What spousal traits can tear a marriage apart?

Urban Christian His Glory Book Club!

Established January 2007, **UC His Glory Book Club** is another way by which to introduce to the literary world, Urban Book's much-anticipated new imprint, **Urban Christian** and its authors. We are an online book club supporting Urban Christian authors by purchasing, reading and providing written reviews of the authors' books that are read. *UC His Glory* welcomes both men and women of the literary world who have a passion for reading Christian based fiction.

UC His Glory is the brainchild of Joylynn Jossel, Author and Executive Editor of Urban Christian and Kendra Norman-Bellamy, Copy Editor for Urban Christian. The book club will provide support, positive feedback, encouragement and a forum whereby members can openly discuss and review the literary works of Urban Christian authors. In the future, we anticipate broadening our spectrum of services to include: online author chats, author spotlights, interviews with your favorite Urban Christian author(s), special online groups for *UC His Glory Book Club* members, ability to post reviews on the website and amazon.com, membership ID cards, *UC His Glory* Yahoo Group and much more.

Even though there will be no membership fees attached to becoming a member of *UC His Glory Book Club*, we do expect our members to be active, committed and to follow the guidelines of the Book Club.

UC His Glory members pledge to:

- Follow the guidelines of *UC His Glory Book Club*.
- Provide input, opinions, and reviews that build up, rather than tear down.

- Commit to purchasing, reading and discussing featured book(s) of the month.
- Agree not to miss more than three consecutive online monthly meetings.
- Respect the Christian beliefs of *UC His Glory Book Club*.
- Believe that Jesus is the Christ, Son of the Living God

We look forward to the online fellowship.

Many Blessings to You!

Shelia E Lipsey
President
UC His Glory Book Club

**Visit the official Urban Christian Book Club website at *www.uchisglorybookclub.net*